O9-AIC-304

PRAISE FOR THE WESTERNS OF ERIC RED

"Keeps the reader turning pages . . . brilliant. *Hanging Fire* is indeed a classic Western."
—*True West Magazine*

"This teeth-grinding, bare-knuckling, swash-buckling adventure keeps readers turning pages. A terrific read. Allow plenty of time to read this. It's hard to put down."
—*Roundup Magazine* on *Hanging Fire*

"Exceptionally fast-paced and blood-spattered. Full of action, overflowing with defiant characters and deadly gunplay."
—*Lansing State Journal* on *Noose*

THE JOE NOOSE WESTERNS
by Eric Red

NOOSE

HANGING FIRE

BRANDED

THE CRIMSON TRAIL

THE CRIMSON TRAIL

TRAIL

A JOE NOOSE WESTERN

ERIC RED

PINNACLE BOOKS
Kensington Publishing Corp.
www.kensingtonbooks.com

To John Durdaller, my cousin and my brother

PINNACLE BOOKS are published by

Kensington Publishing Corp.
119 West 40th Street
New York, NY 10018

Copyright © 2021 by Smash Cut Productions Ltd.

This book is a work of fiction. Names, characters, businesses, organizations, places, events, and incidents either are the product of the author's imagination or are used fictitiously. Any resemblance to actual persons, living or dead, events, or locales is entirely coincidental.

All rights reserved. No part of this book may be reproduced in any form or by any means without the prior written consent of the Publisher, excepting brief quotes used in reviews.

To the extent that the image or images on the cover of this book depict a person or persons, such person or persons are merely models, and are not intended to portray any character or characters featured in the book.

If you purchased this book without a cover you should be aware that this book is stolen property. It was reported as "unsold and destroyed" to the Publisher and neither the Author nor the Publisher has received any payment for this "stripped book."

All Kensington titles, imprints, and distributed lines are available at special quantity discounts for bulk purchases for sales promotion, premiums, fund-raising, educational, or institutional use.

Special book excerpts or customized printings can also be created to fit specific needs. For details, write or phone the office of the Kensington Sales Manager: Attn.: Sales Department. Kensington Publishing Corp., 119 West 40th Street, New York, NY 10018. Phone: 1-800-221-2647.

PINNACLE BOOKS and the Pinnacle logo are Reg. U.S. Pat. & TM Off.

First Printing: July 2021
ISBN-13: 978-0-7860-4683-6
ISBN-10: 0-7860-4683-X

ISBN-13: 978-0-7860-4684-3 (eBook)
ISBN-10: 0-7860-4684-8 (eBook)

10 9 8 7 6 5 4 3 2 1

Printed in the United States of America

CHAPTER 1

The cattle drive set forth after the thaw in 1887 with five hundred steers, sixty horses, and twelve wranglers, but after a hundred miles the number of hands had dwindled to nine because the rest had been murdered.

That's what ramrod Luke McGraw believed.

Even if the rest of the outfit thought the deaths were an unlucky string of unfortunate accidents.

McGraw didn't believe in accidents and damn sure didn't believe in coincidences. Three men dead in two weeks was no coincidence.

He rode beside the herd of cattle moving across the plain still covered with the last snows of winter. He shivered. It was getting warmer, but not by much. Unlucky, like everything else on this doomed trail so far. As he sat in the saddle on Jenny, his big chestnut-brown mare, the rugged cowboy reflected on the troubling sequence of unfortunate accidents that had plagued the cursed cattle drive from the moment they had departed the Bar H Ranch in Consequence, Wyoming, west of Wind River, driving the steers four hundred miles southeast to Cheyenne, on the other side of the state. The herd had to be delivered to the big Cattlemen's Association auction in just over a month, and the long winter had delayed their departure. Still, they had enough time by the trail boss's reckoning; covering ten miles a day, it should have been a five-week journey, but the deaths had put them behind schedule.

First there was rover Ox Johnson, who fell off his horse and broke his neck. They blamed it on the whiskey, for the man was a rounder known to drink on the job.

Then a week later, driver Jed Wade was gone; healthy as a horse, then one day complains his stomach hurts and next thing anyone knows he's frothing at the mouth like a rabid dog and five minutes later, boom, stone-cold dead. They couldn't blame that on the whiskey because Wade was a teetotaler who didn't drink. And it sure wasn't the chow from Fred Kettlebone's chuck wagon that killed him, because the whole crew ate that, and Fred was the best cook anybody had ever ridden with. Snakebite was what some of the outfit were blaming for the cause of Jed Wade's untimely demise, but McGraw had never seen or heard of anybody dying that way from getting bit by a snake. However, he'd heard tell of some poisons that would do it to you, and Luke's suspicions were raised.

Both wranglers got a Christian burial on the trail because the trail boss insisted, even though she wasn't a religious woman; the great outdoors was the cattlewoman's church and McGraw figured she wanted to bury her men in the earth under the open sky where she herself felt close to God. The wrangler put no stock in men who refused to work for a woman because Luke McGraw had nothing but respect for Mrs. Laura Holdridge, his boss at the Bar H Ranch. All of the men in the outfit did. Or did they?

As Luke McGraw sat on his horse, guiding the long march of longhorn steers across the rolling hills, listening to shouts and yips of the eight other ramrods driving the cows, McGraw looked around for Mrs. Holdridge, but she was nowhere to be seen. He spurred his horse and sat tall in the stirrups, seeing two of the longhorns were getting into an altercation and locking horns in the middle of the herd. The combative animals needed to be separated before the outfit lost a steer, because while that would have meant steaks every night for the crew and lots of good eating on the trail, Luke knew Mrs. Holdridge couldn't afford to lose a single cow, and it was his job to make sure she didn't.

A week ago, McGraw took his trail boss aside and shared with her his suspicions that the deaths in their outfit were not accidental but deliberate. She listened attentively and then simply asked, "Why?" And he had no answer, just a gnawing conviction these were not accidents.

The Sharps rifle exploding in cowpuncher Clay Fullerton's hands two days later and blowing his face off was no damn accident, no misfire like everybody assumed. Fullerton was zealous about his guns, oiling and cleaning his rifle and revolvers every night. He could take a firearm apart and put it back together. Clay's death made three, and nobody in the outfit really thought anymore that the experienced wranglers' deaths were accidental. Now everybody was watching their back and looking over their shoulder, sleeping with one eye open, if they slept at all. A few were sleeping in the saddle, catching some shuteye on the trail. A palpable sense of dread had settled over the crew, and suspicion and tension between the men was tightening like a noose. All of the wranglers hated to camp, now fearing getting murdered in their slumber. Everyone felt safer out on the trail, saddled on their horses driving the herd, with nothing but wide-open spaces around in every direction where you could see what was coming at you.

The two argumentative longhorns needed to be separated directly; an expert horseman and seasoned cattle wrangler, Luke McGraw skillfully eased his horse into the herd, staying calm though surrounded by thousands of tons of fast-moving steers, their hooves thundering across the tundra. When he reached the middle of the moving mountain of cows, he felt his mare miss her step, so he tapped his boots in his stirrups against her flanks to speed her canter to keep pace with the herd. Then he reached out from his saddle and separated the two moving steers that were snorting and going at one another with their four-foot-long horns. One of the angry steers tried to gore the horse, but it wasn't McGraw's first rodeo; he grabbed one horn in each glove and wrestled the head of the cow in the other direction, diverting its attention and using his horse to force the steer away from the one bothering it. Soon, the whole herd was moving smoothly again, torrents of cattle stinking like a river of cow shit rushing past on both sides of his horse. Luke took off his hat, wiped sweat from his brow, and looked at the distant open eastern horizon, the direction they headed.

It was a long way to go to Cheyenne, their destination where the steers would go to auction at the big cattle show, three hundred miles across hard, frozen tundra.

With the outfit dropping like flies, the ramrod was thinking they were never going to make it, when a lasso looped over his head and shoulders and jerked taut, catapulting him clean out of the saddle. Luke McGraw hit the ground hard and the last thing he saw was hundreds of hooves coming at his face before he got trampled to death.

CHAPTER 2

"Luke was our friend and our brother, part of our Bar H family. We're going to miss him . . ." As Laura Holdridge said a few words over her late wrangler Luke McGraw's grave, the cattlewoman was wondering who to send his back pay to, only to grasp she had no idea if the man had a wife or children. Despite her heartfelt conviction her crew were her family, Laura realized she knew almost nothing at all about the wrangler she had employed all these years, or perhaps any of the wranglers who worked for her, for that matter.

The eight somber faces of her other drivers stood in a sad circle around the grave, as she spoke softly. "He loved the outdoors. He loved animals. Loved animals more than people, we all figured. We hope wherever you are, Luke, that dog of yours, Blackie, is up there with you, because everybody knew how you loved him and how much you missed him . . ." Laura eyed the faces of her rovers, wondering how she really knew any of them now.

All the lady trail boss knew was four had died on the cattle drive the last couple weeks, and at this rate, all her crew would be dead before they got the herd to Cheyenne.

Laura had to get her livestock to market at the cattlemen's auction. Every cent she had was in these prime steers, and if she did not get a good price for her cattle she was going to lose the ranch she had been struggling to run since her cattleman husband passed away and left her a widow.

That had been a year ago. She had been on her own ever since, independent minded and self-sufficient, getting by on pure grit and stubborn determination, running a working ranch of twelve men and making a go of it. Laura Holdridge was a Wyoming woman born and bred, hardy and fit, damn beautiful with long blond hair and a well-built statuesque figure that turned heads when she went to town; at thirty-one years of age, the cattlewoman knew how desirable she still was, but there had been no time for romance because running the cattle ranch took up every waking moment. And that's how Laura Holdridge needed things to be, because she missed her husband, Sam Holdridge, so much she couldn't bear it sometimes, and running the ranch kept her mind off his loss that had left a hole in her. And her outfit kept her from being alone.

"Goodbye, Luke." Finishing her speech at the shallow grave, Laura looked up into the faces of her wranglers circling the plot, hats in hand, forming an oval of mourners. Wearing a poker face, her eyes traveled from one face to the next, then swung to the next face, and the next, observing each of the eight cowboys' expressions very closely.

One of her wranglers was a killer.

The murderer stood five feet from her.

Who he was, she did not know.

How could she not know, Laura wondered, how could she not have some clue who the killer was when she knew these hands who worked for her and lived at her ranch, who she saw every day? But she obviously didn't know them at all, and now she better be careful.

It was one of the eight, but which one?

Curly Brubaker, Wylie Jeffries, Joe Idaho, Charley Sykes, Frank Leadbetter, Rowdy Maddox, Billy "B.J." Barlow, and lastly, Fred Kettlebone; friendly faces she knew as well as her own, or so she had thought.

Most of the wranglers' eyes were downcast, grieving, in an ill-tempered, dismal mood. They would be taking the foreman's death very hard. McGraw was well liked among the cowboys and she wondered who would want to kill him. Two of her ramrods, Brubaker and Sykes, met her gaze, then looked away, not like they were guilty, just subservient to her like all the cowboys in her outfit were; she made sure of that, had her crew well trained. As a woman in the West, and a cattlewoman to boot, respect was everything and she had to work twice as hard as a man to get it. But all that said, Laura knew her men loved her, and she loved them right back, because she was loyal to her outfit, they were like a family to her. She paid them well and fed them well and they would do anything for her, she knew. Now she had lost four of them.

The woman's heart was breaking, losing Luke McGraw. She wanted to cry but she couldn't in front of the men. She always had to be strong. Her heart might break, but Laura Holdridge never would.

They had buried the foreman in a shady copse of white birch trees at the edge of an airy open plain. She had helped dig the grave herself. The crew had voted on the selection of the spot, but the whole outfit knew it was a place of peace and quiet their fallen friend would have appreciated, and in life would have enjoyed spending time in. He would be spending a lot of it here.

"You boys go on and say a few words now, say your goodbyes." Taking off her sweat-stained Stetson, Laura heaved a huge sigh, turning away from the grave to face the open plain. The gigantic herd of cattle was standing as far as the eye could see, it seemed, grazing on the tall grass near the parked wagons. The sight of the herd daunted her now. Behind, she heard the soft, quiet words of the wranglers each in turn saying their piece over their departed saddle mate. A few wept. The lady trail boss thought the sadness in their voices couldn't be the voices of men who murdered McGraw, or Johnson, or Fullerton, or Wade. But one of them did.

When Laura recovered the trampled corpse of Luke McGraw, what was left of it, off the hoof-trodden muddy plain, she knew he didn't fall out of the saddle and his death was no accident. The cowpoke was born in the saddle and the best rider her ranch had, and the cattle-woman was no fool. *Why didn't she listen to McGraw when he warned her a week ago?* Sometimes she was too damn stubborn for her own good and his warning didn't make sense to her then, but it sure did now.

McGraw's clothes were bloody, muddy rags, so the cattlewoman respectfully removed them from his person for burial. She washed the body and cleaned up his remains, doing the best she could because his condition would have meant a closed-casket burial back in civilization, but this wasn't civilization, it was the open trail. And it was danger-ous, with no law for hundreds of miles.

She saw the raw rope burn across what was left of his upper body and knew he had been lassoed off his horse.

It had taken skill to throw that rope in a moving herd of cattle. Her ramrod Brubaker was a stud with a lasso, but that didn't mean anything because the other wranglers could also throw a rope, and any one of them could have pulled Luke McGraw off his horse with a good toss.

That the killer would strike again was a dead certainty, the only question was who was next. For some odd reason Laura Holdridge did not fear for her own life, having an intuition she herself was not the killer's target, her men were. Why? She trusted her instincts, but that didn't stop her from strapping the massive Colt Dragoon revolver under her coat and lately keeping it under her pillow.

The five hundred head of prime Wyoming beef stood before her scattered out across the plain, giving her bovine looks that seemed to say, *Let's get a move on.* It was time for the outfit to get back on the trail. They had to make time. It was over three hundred miles to Cheyenne and the outfit had a schedule to keep if they were going to cross that considerable distance, the whole of the state of Wyoming, and get there in time for the two-day cattlemen's auction three weeks from now. The murders of her wranglers had slowed down the cattle drive, already costing several days dealing with the burials. Getting the herd to Cheyenne presented an impossible task now there was a killer in the outfit picking off her wranglers, and there seemed nothing she could do about it.

What the hell was she going to do?

She knew what she *should* do. Go to the law. Report the killings. Ride back to the local sheriff in Wind River or ride ahead to the U.S. Marshal, report the deaths, and let the authorities investigate. And the minute she did that, her outfit and the cattle would be detained for an investigation.

Guaranteed then she would not make the auction and by this time next year, would have lost the ranch, everything she and her husband worked for, and her men would be unemployed. Going to the law was the right thing to do. But it was suicide for her ranch and those in her employ. She had discussed it with the wranglers earlier in the day before the burial, and they were all agreed to report the deaths once they made it to Cheyenne; it is what McGraw, Johnson, Fullerton, and Wade would have wanted, too.

There was one other thing she could do.

Quit.

Turn the herd and abandon the cattle drive, put them back in her corral. Pay her wranglers what she could. Sell the cows at a huge loss after the auction. Her outfit would lose money but keep their lives. Perhaps then the killings would stop.

Laura didn't know what to do at this moment, had never felt so helpless and overwhelmed in her natural life. The entire combined weight of the massive herd of steers filling her field of vision suddenly felt like it was sitting on her bosom—a crushing weight of those tons of cows bore down on her, and Laura couldn't catch her breath; her heart was pounding, her pulse racing. *Pull yourself together, woman!* she excoriated herself. *You will not fall apart in front of your men! Be strong!* Through sheer force of will, Laura Holdridge settled down, regaining her composure. Inhaling deep refreshing breaths of the clean Wyoming air into her lungs, Laura willed herself to stand straight and be calm, and her panic attack was carried off in the wind.

The cattlewoman was not a quitter. She never quit once in her whole entire life. But she had the lives of eight souls she was responsible for as trail boss. She had to ask them whether they wanted to turn back or push on.

She walked back to the men at the grave. "Listen up."

Eight pairs of eyes immediately locked on her, she had the full attention of the hardy cowpokes standing before her. She was the boss.

Laura Holdridge addressed the rovers as the first among equals, looking each man directly in the eye as her gaze swung across their attentive faces while she spoke. "Boys, we all know we have a killer in the outfit. He's murdered four of us. That pisses me the hell off, as I'm sure it does eight out of the nine of you. What burns my ass the most? That's he's one of you. I trust all you boys with my life, each and every one of you, but unless one of you fesses up now, I got no idea in hell which one of you has our outfit's blood on his hands."

As she stood before them by the oak tree, Laura witnessed paranoid, distrustful glances traded by men who had always been friends. It broke her heart to see. But she remembered what her mother always said: *Nothing wrong with a broken heart so long as it don't break you.* The cattlewoman looked perspicaciously into the eyes of each and every cowhand—not one had the eyes of a killer.

For the first time Laura doubted her faculties.

"How do we know it's one of us?" Leadbetter asked, looking at his fellows. There were a few nods.

"We don't," she replied evenly. "But who else could it be?"

"Not us."

Laura hadn't thought about that, but now she did. "You mean a killer who's not part of the outfit, not riding with us but shadowing us, watching our every move, and when our guard is down and this individual sees an opening, that's when he strikes."

"Could be."

"Smells like Injun to me," Kettlebone, the cook, offered. "Them Injuns is so quick when they attack they don't make a sound and you never see 'em. One minute you're reaching up to scratch your hair, the next minute you've been scalped, your hair and skin is gone on the top of your head and all you is scratching is skull bone." A few of the men groaned in disgust. "I have seen Apaches do this with my own eyes, boys."

"Ain't no Apache in Wyoming, Fred," Brubaker argued. "Just Shoshone. And that tribe ain't warlike and they don't scalp. I count a bunch of 'em as friends."

Laura shook her head. "Brubaker's right. The Apaches are three states away, our cold doesn't agree with them. Like the man says, the only Indians we have around these parts are the Shoshone and they're a peaceful tribe. Nope, this isn't Indian trouble. It's something else, or someone else."

The wranglers all muttered agreement.

"Boys, maybe it is a killer stalking our herd murdering us, or maybe the killer is one of you boys, though I hope it ain't because I'd hate to have to hang one of you boys. Except for *you,* Leadbetter." She pointed at the youngest wrangler, Frank Leadbetter, a hulking kid probably just out of his teens whose beard was just growing in. She teased him to lighten the grim mood and shake off as best she could some of the dread they all were experiencing.

"It don't make no sense," Sykes mumbled.

"Why is this happening?" Idaho moaned.

"Ain't it obvious?" Laura faced her men soberly.

"Somebody doesn't want us to get our cattle to market. They'll do anything to stop this cattle drive. That's what's happening. What do you boys think?"

Every head nodded in agreement.

"Who you think is behind it?" asked Kettlebone.

"We all know who's probably behind it," Laura spat. "Calhoun, who else? But I can't be sure. Don't make no difference, it doesn't matter who it is. Somebody's got it out for us. That's the situation. Way I see it we got two choices: turn back or push on. We can go home. That's one choice. The other choice is we get the herd to Cheyenne or die trying. I'm putting it to a vote."

"It's your herd, Mrs. Holdridge. You're the boss," Curly Brubaker, the new foreman, insisted. "It's your choice."

The cattlewoman shook her head, fairness in her gaze. "It's your lives. It's your choice, too. The Bar H Ranch isn't just me, boys, it's all of us. We ride or die."

"Ride or die!" several rovers repeated. Moved by her words, the wranglers' spirits were lifted, the outfit's morale boosted by fellowship and cowboy orneriness.

"Let's vote," the cattlewoman said.

"Wait." Billy Joe Barlow put up his hand, looking at the others. "Sorry, ma'am, didn't mean to interrupt, but if I may, before we vote, if it was just up to you, Mrs. Holdridge, if it was, what would you do?"

Laura Holdridge was on the spot. All eyes were on her. She searched her soul before she spoke, and when she did it was what she truly believed with all her heart.

"If it was just up to me, I'd think to myself: This is my herd, am I going to let any man stop me from getting my herd to market like I got a right as a free American to do? And I'd answer: Nobody is going to take away my freedom. I'm moving my herd, and if they want to stop me they'll have to shoot me, and let them try, because I'll shoot right back because I'll fight to the death for what's mine. You asked me what I'd do if it was up to me, Barlow? I'd drive these longhorns to Cheyenne. Ride or die."

The outfit's faces had not a dry eye.

"OK. Let's have us that vote." The cattlewoman took a deep breath. "Anybody wants to turn back, raise your hand."

No hands went up. Not one.

"Votes are counted." Laura grinned. "We're going to Cheyenne."

The entire outfit let out a huge cheer, throwing their hats in the air, and Laura Holdridge never loved her boys more than she did right then.

The mood grew somber once more as they gathered again around Luke McGraw's shallow grave, because Billy Joe Barlow and Rowdy Maddox hadn't had the chance yet to say their piece, and Rowdy was going on and on.

It was then Laura saw something that caught her attention. Stepping away from her men, the cattlewoman looked out across the valley, raising her hand to her brow to block the sun so she didn't have to squint.

Far in the distance, two horses had crested the rise above the sprawling valley across the five hundred head of steers standing stationary on the plain. She swore she recognized the two riders.

Could it be them?

What were the chances of running into them again, out here of all places?

The cattlewoman had eyes like an eagle, and sure enough, she recognized the two riders as Joe Noose and Bess Sugarland, a bounty hunter and lady U.S. Marshal, who had stopped by her ranch a few weeks ago. She had liked them very much. They'd stayed the night in her house and left the following day on U.S. Marshals business, tracking a killer. Joe Noose had left quite an impression on Laura. A third man had been their companion, another marshal Laura recollected, but she disremembered his name or anything else about him. Whoever that man was, he wasn't with them now. Laura could see Noose and Bess up on the rise looking in her direction but figured they couldn't recognize her from this distance so she better catch their attention before they rode off.

Laura Holdridge smiled, her face brightening like the sun, as she whipped off her Stetson and flagged it over her head at Joe Noose and Bess Sugarland, and they waved back and rode down the ridge toward her.

Feeling a weight lift off her bosom, the cattlewoman heaved a sigh of relief. It was the perfect time for a talk with a friendly U.S. Marshal, given everything that was going on with the murders in her outfit. Plus Bess was a woman, the only lady marshal Laura had ever met, and the two of them had gotten along famously at the Bar H Ranch. Maybe the law could help. Laura kept her gaze fixed on the small figures of the riders and horses as they approached at a comfortable stride, growing larger in her field of view as they skirted the sprawling herd and rode her way. Friendly faces.

The bounty hunter Joe Noose was a very big man; she had almost forgotten how big. The mountain of a cowboy rode tall in the saddle toward her, a formidable figure who would physically intimidate lesser mortals. Nobody would mess with this man, Laura thought admiringly. Today the bounty hunter wore a heavy leather coat over a bright blue denim shirt and a yellow kerchief. He was close enough now that when his broad brown Stetson hat lifted, his pale blue eyes flashed in hers and Laura remembered the kindness and goodness she saw in that gaze when they had last met, because beneath his tough, dangerous exterior, the biggest thing about the man was his heart. Laura was very glad to see Joe Noose.

His riding by was the first stroke of good luck the cattle drive had enjoyed since departing on their unlucky journey. Joe Noose was exactly the man she needed in her most desperate hour.

If she could only convince him to stay.

That gave her an idea.

Slipping into her big cowgirl personality as easily as a pair of blue jeans, Laura became her loud and gregarious extroverted self as the two rode up to her. "Joe Noose and Marshal Bess Sugarland. I'll be damned," the cattlewoman hollered out. "What are the odds of running into you way out here?"

"Good to see you, Laura." Bess leaned down to shake hands. The cattlewoman exchanged a warm grin with her. "I see you're getting your cattle to market."

"Yeah, well, hoping to, anyhow. It's a long way from here to Cheyenne." Laura's gaze darkened as she slid a sidelong glance at her wranglers. "We ain't exactly off to an auspicious start. Did you catch that man you were after?"

"We did. Up in Destiny."

"But . . ." Laura had noticed Bess's shuttered expression. *The third man who wasn't here now.*

"It was complicated."

"Weren't there three of you before?"

"I'm afraid now there's just two."

"I'm sorry."

"We are too."

Laura saw Joe Noose observing the rovers standing around the freshly dug grave beside the shovel stuck in the ground. She saw him glance at the Bible in her hand. His somber expression made it clear he understood the outfit had been holding a service interrupted by his arrival. "Looks like you lost one of yours, too." Noose said.

"Four. So far," Laura replied sadly. "One a day out of my ranch near Consequence. One back in Sweetwater Station. One by Muddy Gap. Ox Johnson, Jed Wade, and Clyde Fullerton were their names. Luke McGraw here today makes four."

Bess traded *what the hell* glances with Noose.

As they swung their gazes down to her, Laura stood planted on both boots, fists on her hips, looking boldly up at both of them on their horses, taking their measure. The cattlewoman's mind was working behind her eyes. "Take a ride with me." She made it less a request than a friendly order and her tone broached no refusal. Noose and Bess shrugged and nodded, and Laura mounted her horse in one swift, strong motion. She tossed the Bible down to her foreman, Brubaker, who caught it. "Curly. Finish reading over Luke. Rest of you men, pay your respects and be back in the saddle in fifteen minutes. We're moving out in twenty."

Spurring her horse, she rode in the lead back toward the herd. The marshal and bounty hunter rode after her. Laura slowed her mare so Noose and Bess could catch up on either side of her saddle. She didn't speak until they were well out of earshot of her crew.

"Those deaths were no accident. My four rovers were

murdered. Somebody on my crew is killing my wranglers. I can't prove it. I don't know who the killer is. Somebody doesn't want me to get my cattle to market. I believe this individual or individuals will murder every one of my outfit, including me, to be sure these steers don't make it to Cheyenne. So I'm asking for your help."

Bess looked at Noose.

Noose looked at Laura—who was looking at Joe.

"You're a bounty hunter, Mr. Noose. A damn good one, I understand. I will pay you five thousand dollars cash reward for you to discover the killer on my crew and stop these terrible murders. A dead-or-alive bounty."

The marshal raised her eyebrows.

The bounty hunter tightened his jaw, swinging his glance back at the receding figures of the cowboys standing around the grave. "You positive your rovers were murdered, and it wasn't just accidents?"

"Five thousand dollars positive."

"Saying your suspicions are true, it ain't as easy as just asking them which one of them is the killer, Mrs. Holdridge. I'd have to ride along with you a spell, sniff around for starters. *You* know I'm a bounty hunter. Do any of them?"

Remembering Joe's stay at her ranch, Laura thought back about any encounters the bounty hunter had with her ranch hands, and didn't remember any offhand. "No. Don't think so. They'll recognize the marshal here as the law because she was wearing her badge, but they don't know who you are."

"What are you thinking, Joe?" Bess asked.

"I'm thinking I sign on with Mrs. Holdridge's cattle

drive as a replacement wrangler, go undercover, and find me a killer."

Laura's heart leapt in her chest with hope and beat faster with excitement, but the cattlewoman didn't want to say the wrong thing and screw this up, so she kept her mouth shut and let the two friends talk amongst themselves.

"You don't know the first thing about cow punching." Bess laughed.

"I've done a little," Noose replied.

"When?"

"Ten, maybe twelve years ago."

"Joe."

"Nothing to it."

"You will be kicked in the skull or trampled or gored by a bull the first day out, *if* whoever the killer is on this drive doesn't put a bullet in your back first."

Noose gave Bess a knowing look and she rolled her eyes. He swung his gaze to Laura, his pale eyes steady as he extended his hand. "I like you, Laura. Think you got guts running these cattle and crew to Cheyenne, a woman in your situation, and I don't want to see you fail. I'll take the job."

Laura Holdridge shook his hand with a firm grip, brushing her windblown blond hair out of her eyes. "Thank you."

"Thank me later."

"We move out in ten minutes," the cattlewoman said, outwardly all business but inside so excited she could bust. She wanted to throw her arms around Noose and Bess and kiss them, so happy and relieved was she. But habit and prudence told her to keep her feelings hidden behind her boss-lady demeanor. And with that, Laura brusquely yanked her reins and swept her horse around, riding hard back to the livestock and wagons, as her men returned from the grave, back to their horses, and mounted up, ready to move the herd.

Behind her back as she rode off out of earshot, the last words Laura overheard the marshal say to the bounty hunter were, "Joe Noose, what the hell are you getting yourself into?"

Plenty, the cattlewoman thought as she and her wranglers rejoined the herd, yelling, "Move 'em out!"

"Guess this is farewell for now."

The time had come for them to split up. Joe Noose and Bess Sugarland sat in their saddles saying their goodbyes.

"Come with me on the cattle drive, Bess. It'll be an adventure and I sure can use your help."

"I can't, Joe. I'm a U.S. Marshal and I got a sworn duty to uphold. I've been away from Jackson for three months. If my daddy were alive he'd have had my badge for taking that long a leave of absence. But it had to be done and we got our man. It's OK, my deputy Nate Sweet is a good man and he's covering the office, but it ain't fair to him, neither, his taking care of all my responsibilities. It's a two-week ride back to Jackson, so I need to get a move on and get home. Got a town to protect. Gotta earn my salary." She trailed off.

"I know." He nodded. Her sense of duty was one of the things he most admired about her.

"Buck up." The marshal took the bounty hunter's hand and held it in hers. "You don't need my help anyway. After

The Brander, how bad can this killer be? You'll flush out this villain in that outfit in two days and be back in Jackson a couple days after me. You'll see."

"I hope so." Joe noticed Bess's expression change when he added, "I'm doing this for Laura Holdridge. She deserves my help." He saw she had let go of his hand.

Bess looked off at the mountains, gathering her thoughts. Breaking his gaze was unlike her, since she was so direct. When Bess turned her face back to him, Joe noticed it was flushed and not from the weather.

"You like her, don't you?"

Joe saw the flash of jealousy in Bess's face, a pain in her guileless expression she didn't understand or know how to hide. Realizing he'd hurt his best friend's feelings pained Noose inside more than a bullet in the gut.

"I like her, Joe. She's a good woman."

The worst part was Bess had it all wrong, but Joe didn't know how to tell her. The two companions sat on their horses on the rise, looking at each other with so much they couldn't say, but now it was time for their farewells.

"See you in Jackson," Joe said, tipping his Stetson.

Bess searched his eyes. "You got something on your mind, tell me, partner."

Joe wanted to tell Bess how he felt about her, but somehow the thought of that scared him spitless. "I hate goodbyes, Bess."

"This ain't goodbye," Bess said softy with a smile, her eyes wet, a hitch in her voice. With those parting words, the lady marshal snapped the reins and turned her horse away from him to begin her long ride.

And Joe almost said it.

He wanted to. The words were on his lips.

Bess, you have nothing to be jealous about.

But Joe knew if he said that, he'd have to say the next part.

You're the only woman I want to be with.

And then he'd have to say the rest.

I love you.

So Joe Noose said nothing.

As Bess Sugarland rode away, a piece of Joe Noose rode with her. His heart.

In its place, on his chest above his heart, the bounty hunter felt the old scar of the cattle brand burned into his flesh start to tingle and sting like a phantom pain, the way it always did when there were wrongs to right, justice to be done, and he had to act. The white-hot fury of the brand filled the empty hole where his heart felt missing, adrenaline pumped through his body and he was ready for action, his purpose clear for today: help the Holdridge woman track down the killer in her outfit and stop him from murdering her wranglers so she could get her cattle to Cheyenne.

It's going to be a hell of an adventure, Joe Noose thought, tearing his eyes away from the distant speck of Marshal Bess Sugarland on the plain, swinging his gaze over to the valley where the procession of longhorn steers on the march moved out with the covered wagons, the rovers and their horses driving the herd with whoops and hollers and cracks of bullwhips. Laura Holdridge rode gloriously out front of the herd on her wagon, her golden hair blowing in the wind. The valley rang with the voices of the men as the ground shook with the thunder of hooves, sounds of jubilation and life. It was quite a sight.

Joe was going to miss the woman he loved.

But he'd see Bess in Jackson soon enough. Sure, it wasn't going to be the same without her. For now, he had a job to do, and for a while at least, that was enough.

The cattle drive was on the move.

He better get on after them.

CHAPTER 3

Joe Noose remembered how to do it.

Riding his horse beside the herd of longhorn steers, a raging river of hundreds of tons of cow flesh surging across the prairie, the deafening thunder of hooves pummeling his eardrums, his nostrils clogged with the smell of manure, the job of cow punching was all coming back to him now from years ago when he did that work; the main thing the bounty hunter recalled was that a cattle drive was hard redneck work.

It was back in '67, when only fourteen, after drifting around the West working a lot of jobs, when he'd worked as a wrangler for a brief spell. Joe learned the trade on the Calhoun Bar T Ranch in Texas. A hardworking quick learner, Noose hired on as a ramrod on the famous Calhoun cattle drive from Texas to Kansas. It was back in the good old days when the legendary cattle baron old man Thomas Calhoun ran things before his crook of a son took control of the Bar T Ranch and it became an infamous cattle empire built on the blood of Texans. That Texas-to-Kansas cattle drive had two thousand head of prime longhorn beef fed on the grassland plains. Joe and fifteen other wranglers drove the gigantic herd across harsh badlands in grueling conditions under dangerous circumstances. Progress was laborious; they covered ten miles a day on average, on a good day fifteen, and it was a thousand miles to Abilene. During the period, Joe felt he had friends and wasn't alone anymore, that he belonged. The work was tough but the whiskey and laughter and fellowship young Joe enjoyed were golden days.

The journey was not without incident. Two months into the cattle drive a gang of armed outlaws tried to steal the herd, and gun work was required. On that hot day in Oklahoma, young Noose and the fifteen rovers got ambushed and found themselves cornered in a box canyon surrounded by six deadly sharpshooters. The rovers outnumbered the rustlers three to one, but the outlaws held the high ground and occupied choice shooting positions. Ambushed at dawn while they slept, the wranglers were undressed and unarmed, having left their gun belts behind in their panic to flee the flying lead. That is, everyone but Joe Noose, who slept with his gun belt on, out of habit. But his Colt Peacemaker had only six rounds. In a desperate shootout, young Joe shot all six of the outlaws dead in a blazing fifteen-second gunfight, never once needing to reload—each of his rounds fired from his six-cylinder revolver was a kill shot. His unharmed saddle mates looked at Noose in a whole different way after witnessing his fearsome display of violent firepower; from then on they treated him like a god, but he was no longer one of them. Gods and mortals don't mix, so Joe collected his wages and left the cattle drive before it crossed into Kansas.

He was a loner by nature who went his own way and didn't fit with a group for very long, even a group of wranglers his age who were his friends. He never saw those rovers again, but it was for the best: Joe Noose had a feeling he was a lot better with a gun than he was at punching cows anyway.

In the fullness of time, determined to do what he was good at and born to do, Joe Noose found a job that suited him; as a bounty hunter, he could use the fearsome trade-craft of the gunfighter for good, if he chose to do right. It was always up to him. And Joe was free to practice his personal brand of law enforcement and deliver his own idea of rough justice. He could never be a normal lawman bound by the laws that constantly change. Instead, he was outside the law, but still enforcing the letter of it guided by his own wits and conscience. Noose only took bounties and went after rewards where he could use his pistol to make things right. All across the West, folks knew his rep-utation: if the reward was dead-or-alive, Joe brought the man in alive, if he could.

That's who he was now, years after he recovered from a savage branding at age thirteen that brutally ended his days as a violent juvenile delinquent and left a permanent scar on his chest that had set him on the correct path. From that day forward, young Joe had pulled his life together and tried to make an honest living. The branding had haunted him his entire adult life every step that he took; the red-hot iron had driven his actions, defined his char-acter, made him who he was. It was only a month ago when Noose finally had his face-to-face reckoning with that very same branding iron and the man who wielded it for evil, where Joe Noose finally made his peace with being branded himself. Or so he hoped. The branding scar in his chest he would take to his grave, but the branding scars in his soul were healing.

He was feeling pretty damn good at this moment, running the herd, the sun in his face and the fresh air in his lungs. Joe savvied the horse between his legs felt the same way he did, knowing they usually thought alike.

Noose looked down at his other best friend, the one he rode on, his magnificent bronze stallion, Copper. The horse had been with him on all his recent adventures and braved incredible danger with fearless fortitude; courageous like his master, though Joe sometimes wondered if you could rightly be called courageous if you were truly fearless, because while he himself wasn't fearless, he swore Copper was. Noose had given the horse his name. A year ago, Joe had confiscated the stallion from a vicious bounty hunter he'd gunned down who had maltreated and physically abused the stallion. Joe only intended to use the horse to get away from the gang of bad men who were chasing him, but once he got on the steed he never got off, and man and horse became inseparable. It didn't take long for the kindness and good treatment the good-hearted man gave to the badly abused stallion for the animal's indestructible spirit to emerge. And so he became Copper, dubbed by Joe because in the sunlight his tawny golden-blond coat shone like a suit of metal armor.

Right now, Copper was happy to be alive, charging along beside the countless longhorn steers at a prancing canter with a swagger in his bold four-legged step. Joe rode comfortably in his saddle. Copper's head was held high on his enormous neck, golden withers wafting in the wind. The bounty hunter cracked a huge grin when he patted his steed and it looked back at him, smiling as horses some- times do, and damned if that amazing horse didn't wink.

The string of longhorns went as far as the eye could see in both directions, a sea of jagged horns. Above, the sun shone in a bright blue sky filled with clouds, as below them the oceans of frost-patched grass and snowcapped mountains stretched far and wide. The shadow of a bald eagle falling across the herd made the rovers look up in wonder to see the bird extend its amazing seven-foot wingspan and swoop up and down the length of the herd, not once but twice.

Joe laughed, turning in his saddle, craning his neck to watch the bald eagle's magnificent avian display, hoping every day would be just like this one. Easiest job he ever had so far. The bounty hunter was enjoying it while he could.

It was three hundred miles to Cheyenne and spring was in the air. On a day like this, it was perfectly natural to think nothing stood in their way.

But Joe Noose knew better.

It was time to talk to the boss lady.

CHAPTER 4

Spurring his horse to a gallop, Noose was gaining on Laura Holdridge's covered wagon, the cattlewoman cracking the whip in the driver's seat at the reins of her team of four horses pulling her rig alongside the longhorns, and as Joe rode up alongside the wagon, he could see the look of determination on her face like nothing was going to stop her.

Leaning out of the saddle, the bounty hunter grabbed his horse's tether and tied it off the rear transom of the wagon. Standing up in the saddle he reached for the rail of the wagon, jumping off his stallion onto the sideboard of the covered wagon. Winking at Copper, Joe said, "Be right back." Then, buffeted by the wind, dust, and dirt, he made his way to the front of the moving wagon.

Joe Noose swung into the driver's seat beside Laura Holdridge, who sat forward, holding the reins and using the whip. She turned her face to him.

Joe extended his hand, introducing himself although they had already been introduced. "My name's John Smith."

"You said your name's Joe Noose," came her confused reply.

"Not with these men. A few may have heard of me. I have a reputation." It was noisy outside the wagon with pounding hooves of the cattle and horses and the racket of the wagon itself. Noose and Laura had to speak up to be heard, but Joe sat close to Laura so they could shout in each other's ear; amid the cacophony of the cattle drive, none of the wranglers riding beside the steers could hear a word of what was said on the wagon. "They can't know who I am or this is not going to work."

"What if they've seen you somewhere before?" She shouted in his ear, keeping face front and eyes on her team.

"They won't recognize me. I didn't recognize them at the grave when Bess and I rode up today and I'm fairly certain I've never met any of them. The false name should do the trick to conceal my identity. "

"OK."

"It's understood until we get to Cheyenne, call me John. Or Smith. Or anything you want to call me. Anything but Noose."

"I call all my crew by their last names."

"Smith then."

"OK, Smith." The dusty wind was in their faces, blowing their hair and clothes, carrying the leathery smells of the hundreds of steers, an endless succession of horns stretching far ahead into the big country. "We better give you a cover story my boys will believe about why you joined the outfit. I'm gonna say my husband, Sam Holdridge, had you on his crew when he went to Canada and bought three hundred head two years ago. The outfit didn't go with him on the trip because we needed them on our ranch, so he brought the cattle home with hired hands he picked up in Calgary. So you're from Canada if anybody asks. Where are you from, anyway?"

"A lot of places." Noose shrugged.

"Well, now you're from Canada."

"Always wanted to go there. That about covers it then."

She turned her face to him, behind her windblown golden hair, fixing him in her steady blue-eyed gaze. "Anything y'all need from me, just name it, hear?"

"There is one thing mebbe."

"Name it." She cracked the whip with a vigorous *"Yee-ah!"*

"A notebook and a pen to write with."

"Take the reins." Laura handed Noose the reins and climbed out of the driver's seat, ducking through the flap of the covered wagon. Joe snapped the reins and kept the horses moving. He leaned over and looked around the transom to check on his stallion he tied off on the speeding wagon. Copper kept up at a comfortable canter, giving its owner a look that said it was wondering what's going on. Joe cracked a grin and sat back straight in the creaking driver's seat bouncing on the wooden axles of the wooden wheels.

The mounted wranglers herding the cattle were looking at him, giving him looks, wondering who the hell he was and what he was doing on their boss lady's wagon. Noose knew he better get back on his horse before the time he was spending with Laura started looking suspicious.

The canvas flap parted. The cattlewoman came out of her covered wagon, swung a leg over the driver's seat and dropped beside him. In her hand was a small leather-bound notebook with a pen attached. "It's an old diary I keep meaning to use but never do." She handed it to him.

The notebook fit snugly in the palm of his hand. "Is this what you need?"

He gave her back the reins and flipped through the blank pages. "It'll do. Need one of these on a murder investigation."

"A diary." Laura was confused.

"A murder book."

"How can anybody murder anyone with a book?"

"That's exactly what I said when Marshal Bess first told me what they call one of these." Joe laughed, shaking his head. "During the investigation, I'm s'posed to make notes in this notebook of what I see and hear, make a list of suspects, write down clues and keep track of all the details and so forth, which'll help us get the killer. At least so I'm told." Laura looked over as she cracked the whip on her team of horses hauling her wagon. "I've never actually used one of these notebooks, mind," Joe admitted with a shrug. "But Bess tells me every marshal uses a murder book because it helps them think. Use deduction, she calls it. This job seems as good a time as any to school myself in using one."

He opened the murder book, took the pen, and on the first page he wrote his first entry: *SUSPECTS.*

Gesturing with his arm, the bounty hunter indicated the men on horses around her wagon, shepherding the herd. He counted nine, including the cook. Any one of them could be the killer. "Why don't we start by you pointing out each of your men and giving me their names? That'll help me put names to faces."

Setting down the whip, the cattlewoman pointed out each man in her outfit. "On the left of the herd, that's Charley Sykes, Curly Brubaker, and Rowdy Maddox is the one with the red kerchief. Right of the herd, you got Joe Idaho, Frank Leadbetter, and the real skinny one is Wylie Jeffries." Joe scribbled it all down in the book. "Behind us, Fred Kettlebone, our cook, driving the chuck wagon. Yonder on the other side of the cows, that's Billy Joe Barlow. Started out with four more when I left the ranch in Consequence. These are who I have left. With five hundred steers, can't afford to lose any more."

As one by one, Laura told him the names of her wranglers, Joe Noose wrote all those names down in his murder book, and now he had his list of suspects.

SUSPECTS

Charley Sykes.

Curly Brubaker.

Rowdy Maddox.

Billy Joe Barlow. "B.J."

Wylie Jeffries.

Frank Leadbetter.

Joe Idaho.

Fred Kettlebone.

Eight men. One of them was a killer.

Joe closed the murder book and put it in his jacket. "Don't lose that book," Laura warned. "One of my boys gets their hands on it, we got trouble."

Noose patted his pocket. "Stays with me all the time." Both Laura and Joe noticed that they were getting more and more suspicious looks from her outfit the longer they sat together on the wagon in conversation. "I better get back and join the outfit before your drivers start asking questions," Joe said as he rose.

"Good idea." Laura nodded, snapping the reins.

Joe swung out of the driver's seat onto the transom. Noose looked back at her as he climbed onto the sideboard on the side of the wagon. "Remember, Mrs. Holdridge. It's John Smith, don't forget. Make one slip and call me Noose, my cover's blown."

"Good luck, John Smith. What's the next step?"

"I meet the men."

Joe Noose leaped off the wagon and landed in the saddle of his horse. Mounted, he untethered Copper and off they rode. The next thing Laura Holdridge saw was the bounty hunter on his gorgeous golden steed galloping on ahead of her wagon to join the rovers, waving his hat with a holler.

CHAPTER 5

The cattle drive made fifteen miles by nightfall.

The outfit set up camp along a tributary of the Snake River beside miles of grazing land where they stopped the herd. The outfit assembled the three wagons behind a grove of towering pines whose branches kept the hot sun out of their eyes until it set; once the sun went down the temperature dropped twenty degrees, and the night became black as pitch. The vagaries of Wyoming weather were something the outfit was used to. The cattle were calm, some asleep on their feet, the stock as tired as the drivers were after pushing the herd dawn to dusk with only one short break to rest and graze. It was quitting time for the rovers, but the newest member of the outfit's day was just getting started.

Joe Noose did not get off his horse when the rest of the wranglers dismounted after the long, hard ride. Not right away. The saddle gave him a high vantage point: twelve feet up—the combined height of his stallion then himself ground to eyeball; his vantage overlooked the entire camp. Noose closely observed the outfit's activities. First thing the bounty hunter noticed was the outfit was not one big happy family; the drivers had split off into factions. Three, by his count.

The first faction of wranglers called it a day and hung up their spurs, trudging to the chow line, whispering to one other.

The second group of wranglers had pounded stakes into the ground near the supply wagon and strung a lariat between them to fix a rope hitch for the horses, then took off the saddles, hanging them on the wagon. This tight-knit outfit, the biggest group, ignored the new hired hand, Joe; they looked through him like he was invisible, but Noose up on his horse was actively listening to every word he could make out, which wasn't much because everybody was whispering.

There was a lot of hushed talk going on, Joe noticed, and he wondered why; obviously these men had something they didn't want not just him, but each other, to hear.

The bounty hunter remained in the saddle, pretending to be occupied as the other rovers dismounted, heading straight for the chuck wagon. Raucous and raunchy laughter now ensued. The wonderful smell of grilled beef and roast corn filled the air; if it tasted as good as it smelled, Joe thought, that meant the chow would be good on the trip.

The cook's name was Fred Kettlebone, one of the names so far Joe had put a face to. He was fat and jolly, had a moon face, thirty or thereabouts, with a big mouth on him, always busting his saddle mates' britches. On the trail today while the herd had stopped to graze, Noose had seen Kettlebone wrestling a wayward steer back into the fold with just his bare hands, and Noose figured the cook's fat was probably mostly muscle. It smelled like he was a great cook.

It was deep country dark out here under the stars. From up in the saddle, Joe had an unobstructed view of the men gathered around the chuck wagon but knew they couldn't see him; fifteen feet from the flames of the huge campfire everything fell off into pitch-black, and Noose and Copper were over a hundred feet away. The outfit sat around the chuck wagon, grabbing their plates of grub and digging in with appreciative noises. His stomach was growling. The longer Noose watched from on top of Copper, the more the good smell of the food was making him hungry, so Joe dismounted. He took a few minutes to rub down his horse, then put the feed bag on him, making sure his friend was fed first, and ambled toward the chuck wagon.

It was time to find out who he was riding with.

"What took you so long, pardner?"

Joe Noose had just helped himself to a heaping plate of food—steak and mashed potatoes and plenty of it—and joined the rest of the outfit seated around the campfire, returning nods of greeting from a few of the eight cowboys, and sat on the ground when the grizzled wrangler named Wylie Jeffries asked him the question.

"Had to take care of some stuff," Noose replied. "I'm the new guy. Hope I didn't hold you boys up none." Joe cut into his steak and dug in.

"Hold *us* up?" Jeffries chortled. "Son, at chow time, this outfit waits on each other like one hog to another."

"Pretty good chow, eh?" Frank Leadbetter said with a mouth full of food.

"That's a fact." Joe smiled, keeping one eye on his food, one eye on the men.

"Hey, Kettlebone, the new man likes your grub!" Leadbetter yelled toward the chuck wagon.

There was crashing of metal pots followed by a string of expletives over at the chuck wagon. A twangy, high-pitched voice hollered back. "Well why the hell wouldn't he? My food's best in the West. Tell the new hand he lucked out, him hooking up with this outfit."

The rovers all stopped smiling at that last comment, eating a few bites in thoughtful silence.

A big, rugged, gregarious wrangler, still chewing, looked Joe straight in the eye, leaning forward to extend his hand. "Curly Brubaker."

Noose forcefully returned the manly shake. "John Smith."

Brubaker didn't let go of his hand. The wrangler's grip tightened and so did his stare. "What's your real name?"

"Just told you."

A ripple of laughter went through all of the wranglers.

"We'll get it out of him, won't we, boys?" Brubaker winked at the others.

Joe looked up and saw eight sets of eyes looking at him.

Charley Sykes, a lanky good-times cowboy type, patted Joe on the arm. "Relax, we're just funning with you, Smith. So where did Mrs. Holdridge find you?"

"She didn't. Her husband did. I hired on with Mr. Holdridge in Calgary two years ago when he needed those three hundred head brought to Bar H. That's how Mrs. Holdridge and I met."

Curly was watching Joe carefully, sizing him up. Noose returned the favor. Took a few mental notes about Curly based on his quick first impressions. Noose believed first impressions were the most important; if you listen to your instincts, you know just about everything you ever need to know about a man in the first five minutes you say hello. Brubaker was clearly the oldest cowpuncher in the outfit, pushing fifty or thereabouts. Ten years older than the next oldest man, judging by the faces in the firelight of the campfire. He looked to have seniority over these men. Noose guessed Curly was now the outfit's master sergeant, its present leader, which came as no surprise with his experience. He'd have to add that to his notes in the murder book.

"You must be hard up for cash to sign onto this jinxed drive." The rangy, pockmarked rover Idaho smirked, throwing a joking glance at his buddies.

"Eh?" Joe acted innocent, chewing a tender piece of juicy steak, charred black on the outside and red within. "Why do you say that?

A pall fell on the outfit.

"You saying you don't know?" Rowdy Maddox asked incredulously.

"Know what?" Joe looked at the faces. "Let me in on the big secret, boys."

As Noose studied the eight wranglers he saw a lot of head-scratching and shifting on the ground as the men exchanged glances, unsure of what they should tell the new hand, or who should be the one to tell him. It was uncomfortable.

Curly had not once taken his eyes off Joe, his finger under his nose in a gesture of contemplation.

A big meaty hand fell on Joe's shoulder, smelling of spices. Noose looked to see Fred Kettlebone looming over him in his blood-smeared butcher's apron, clutching a gore-covered cleaver. The heavyset cook wore tiny spectacles on his broad face, reflecting bonfire flames. "Hi, new fellow, I'm the cook, Fred Kettlebone. What's your name?"

"Smith. John Smith"

"What's your real name?"

"Why does everybody ask me that?"

"I'll call you Smith if that's your pleasure. Four of our wranglers have died on this cattle drive, Smith. That's what nobody's telling you."

Joe made an expression of mock horror. "Four men have died on this drive?"

"And counting. More to come."

A few of the wranglers got agitated and raised their voices at the cook. Leadbetter, who looked little more than a young teenager, got furious. "Goddammit, Kettlebone, you shouldn't even be saying crud like that, it's bad luck is what it is."

The cook threw his head back and laughed with a sound like a braying donkey. "Bad luck was the day we all signed on to this drive of the damned in the first place. Come on, Frank, you can't be so stupid as to think this is anything like over. You know the killer is gonna strike again. Just a question of who and when."

"Did you just call me stupid?" Leadbetter leapt to his feet and got in Kettlebone's face, clenching his fists.

Behind his tiny spectacles, Kettlebone didn't break the stare-down but lowered his voice. "Thinking this killer won't kill again isn't just stupid, greenhorn, it's suicidal.

Whoever the killer is, he's not going to stop until he kills each and every one of us. To think otherwise is—yes, kid—*stupid*."

Leadbetter spat on Kettlebone's boot.

Joe Noose just sat calmly on the ground, munching his grub, looking up at the two men standing over him about to fight, studying the other rovers jumping to their feet to cheer them on. He figured he was going to have a lot of entries in the murder book tonight.

The atmosphere was charged with cowboy testosterone as the rawboned teenage rover cricked his neck, readying for a fistfight, and leaned even closer to the cook. "What I want to know is why you know so much about this killer, always telling us what the killer's thinking, what the killer is about to do, and such and such. What I want to know is why you know so much about him."

"Consider your next words very carefully, my friend," Kettlebone whispered.

"I think you know so much about this killer because *the killer is you, Kettlebone*."

"Take that back." The cook's porcine eyes, magnified behind his spectacles, glittered with hate.

"Or what? You gonna hit me with your meat cleaver?"

"No." Kettlebone dropped the cleaver on the ground. "I'm going to hit you with this." The cook punched the young rover in the face, hard.

Staggering back, Leadbetter's hands flew to his nose, cupping it to stop the gushing blood. "You broke my damn nose, you son of a bitch!"

"Take it back." The cook advanced with a crazed look in his eyes, so angry he was about to cry.

"It's broke!"

"I ain't no killer. You take it back."

The men went for each other other's throats and began grappling.

Joe Noose set down his plate, shot to his feet, and wedged his huge frame between the two fighting men— grabbing each by the throat in one huge cow-hoof-sized mitt, he pulled them apart effortlessly, tossing them with each arm in opposite directions, where both wranglers landed hard on the ground. "Break it up!" the bounty hunter growled, rearing to his full height, towering over the other men, who stared in astonishment at his sudden ferocious display of force. Everyone fell silent as Joe's pale blue gaze traveled like rifle crosshairs across the faces of the rovers.

Joe Noose's squinting eyes turned deadly, and what he said next he said to each and every man in the outfit, look- ing from face to face, making eye contact with each and every one. "Well, one thing I'll tell you boys. Somebody tries to kill *me* on this cattle drive, he can consider himself warned. He'll find I ain't so easy to kill. And if a man tries to shoot me, I shoot him and the man standing next to him. Understood?" The bounty hunter didn't raise his voice because he didn't need to.

Noose was a truly dangerous man, a killer by nature, and when he showed that side of himself, everybody rec- ognized it. Now, he showed that side. He lifted the lid and gave the outfit a quick glimpse of the brutal side of him- self, capable of savage violence. He didn't have to pull a gun; it was all in his eyes.

And as Noose looked back and forth among the faces of the wranglers, it was the eyes he was studying, and the ones that had fear in them were the men he would rule out first as suspects. Cowards were not capable of the killings that plagued this cattle drive; the cold, brutal murders that showed premeditation. Two men had fear in their faces after Noose got tough with them a moment ago. Tonight, Joe would be crossing them off his list of suspects.

"Tough guy," Curly Brubaker replied. His eyes showed amusement but no fear.

"Tough enough," Joe replied.

"We'll see how tough you are, Smith, or whatever your name is. It's three hundred hard miles to Cheyenne. And from what I saw today, your cowpunching skills are a little rusty."

The outfit disbanded, and headed for their sleeping rolls. Fred Kettlebone grabbed the plates and washed them in the water barrel, avoiding Joe's gaze as Noose lingered, watching the wranglers depart into the darkness before heading off back to his horse and his own sleeping roll.

"Smith."

Joe turned. Curly walked out of the shadows and walked up to Noose. They were almost eye level with each other as the other man spoke first. "I'm telling you straight to your face that I believe you are not who you say you are. I don't know what your story is, but I know what it *ain't*. See, I was on the Bar H Ranch the day Sam Holdridge brought in the herd from Canada and I remember the face of every man on that crew. Not one of 'em was you."

"I—" Joe was about to claim he left the cattle drive in Wind River.

Curly put up his hand. "Save your breath. It's enough for you to know I got my eye on you. You bring any trouble to this outfit, I'll end you, and if you think Mrs. Holdridge can protect you, think again."

"You got bigger problems than me on this trail, Curly."

"Think I don't know that?" Brubaker said tragically, raw pain in his eyes. For a moment the tough ramrod fumbled, like he didn't know what to do or say.

Noose saw an opening and he took it. "I'm not your problem, Brubaker, you have my word on that. But maybe I can help."

Like a switch had been thrown, Curly's eyes went cold. "You're not part of this outfit, Smith. Stay out of our business."

Before Joe Noose could say anything more, the ramrod had turned and stormed off back to the wagons. The bounty hunter was alone in the big outdoors by the chuck wagon, so for a few moments he gathered his thoughts, listening to the nearby lowing of the cattle. The cloud cover making the night so dark had passed and now the moon was bright enough to read by.

Reaching into his jacket, Joe Noose took out his murder book and pen, and on the page marked "Suspects," he scratched out the names Wiley Jeffries and B.J. Barlow. Then, by the name Curly Brubaker, he scribbled a question mark.

CHAPTER 6

Nearby, while the others slept, another man in the outfit was writing. His fingers scribbled with a pencil on a piece of notebook paper in the moonlight . . .

A new guy joined the outfit today. He should have chose himself another outfit, any outfit. Bet the boss lady didn't tell him the rovers on this crew are getting murdered. The new guy calls himself Smith but the talk among the boys is that ain't his real name. He looks like he can take care of himself. He's going to be harder to kill than the others. But I'll bury him deep just like I did McGraw and Johnson and Fullerton and Wade. Nobody on this cattle drive makes it to the end of this trail alive. He may be big but he'll never see me coming. None of them saw me coming. Mister, whoever you are, you're in the wrong place at the wrong time. Because now I'm going to have to kill you."

The hand tore the paper out of the notebook and struck a match. Holding the paper over the flame, he watched as the fire consumed it to ash.

CHAPTER 7

Joe Noose slept with one eye open that night.

The big cowboy hardly needed to be concerned, because his loyal horse Copper was a very light sleeper, especially when it sensed danger abroad, as it did in this outfit; whenever the stallion sensed mortal threat, it kept watch over his master while he slumbered. The bounty hunter was stretched out on his bedroll with his head on his leather saddle less than three feet away from Copper's hooves while the horse half-dozed on its feet with its its eyes open, hooves that would have launched at the head of any man who attempted to interfere with its owner. The first night, no one did.

It was cold, and Copper appreciated the blanket that Noose had tied over his back and belly. The horse wondered if its owner needed it more, seeing the smaller blanket wrapped over the man at his hooves with his head on the saddle. Copper sensed Joe wasn't asleep and was feeling the same danger the stallion did. Copper had full confidence that Joe would deal with any threat the way he always did.

Cold though the clean night air was, it was much warmer than the long ride over the last few months had been, through the dead of winter, a chill that remained in the stallion's bones. The bullet wound in its shoulder from last summer still ached, and its leg was stiff tonight. Copper knew it had almost died when it had been shot, and only the love and care of its master kept it alive. Then when winter came, they had gone off on another adventure. The horse had worried much about his master during that time over their eventful journey, but now the business was done, its owner was back to his old self.

Wherever Joe Noose was, Copper belonged, happy with his master riding in the saddle on his back.

Over its long night of semi-wakefulness, the horse remained alert to its surroundings; many other new, strange horses slumbered nearby, tethered to the rope hitch. Copper enjoyed the company of many mares, and the stallion felt a tingle by the female horses' proximity, like a pleasant itch it wanted to scratch. Copper heard the sleep-breathing of the other animals, and knew it was the only one awake. Farther off, out of sight, the horse felt the presence of the vast amount of cattle, also slumbering. Night birds and coyotes and other creatures made sounds out there where the horse could not see. The hours passed slowly and agreeably for Copper, who with the whole world asleep, felt close to his master by his hooves, knowing they were the only ones who were, on and off, awake, keeping one another company. It was all the companionship the bronze stallion ever wanted and would ever need.

Then the sky began to brighten and Joe woke and fed

Copper a carrot as all around the strange horses and cattle and men began to stir.

After a quick breakfast and pots of coffee served at the chuck wagon, the cattle drive moved out before the sun broke over the big mountains. While Noose saddled Copper, he observed his surroundings closely and saw Laura Holdridge exit her covered wagon—the trail boss being the only member of the outfit who had her own private quarters, since the rest slept in the outdoors, or in tents when it rained. The woman was up first with Fred Kettlebone, the cook, a few minutes before the eight other wranglers had risen. Soon the smells of eggs and beans and coffee floated over the clearing and Joe saw the half-asleep rovers stagger their way toward the chuck wagon. With a pat to Copper's head, Joe sauntered off to join the others.

A half hour later, his stomach full of the good strong coffee and tasty hot food, the bounty hunter rode with the others moving out the herd.

The nine men and horses, their string of sixty horses, three wagons, and five hundred head of cattle crossed seven miles that morning, following the trail along the winding Snake River that their cattlewoman boss had mapped out. The weather was clear and the big sky overhead cloudless. The Snake took them due north in a near unbroken straight line, but as the map showed, on the eighth mile, the river curved sharply to their left and doubled back northwest for fifty miles. The body of water was too far to circumvent on land; to continue east they would have to ride the herd a full week north and then south again to continue to their destination. It was here at this junction where the water was widest and deepest that they would have to cross the livestock in order to continue their southeast passage toward the town of Cheyenne over two hundred and ninety miles away.

In his saddle, on his game and vigorous golden horse Copper, Joe Noose rode toward the front of the long procession of longhorns and saw the bend of the Snake River approaching a half mile ahead. The river looked wide, and the swell of the rapids indicated certain depth. He remembered enough from his cowpunching days to know that a river-crossing with a full herd was one of the most dangerous parts of a cattle drive if the river was deep and the current fast and strong; you had to move the steers into the river fast, with as much momentum to their charge as it was possible to muster, to keep the cattle in a straight line—if the cows broke formation, it was easy for the rovers and their horses struggling in the water to be trampled and drowned. The worst possible thing that could happen was a stampede: if the longhorns panicked crossing the river, the deadly chaos of that many rampaging tons of livestock could spell catastrophe. Then the necessity of firing pistols into the air to try to scare the beasts back into formation only contributed to the danger with the risk of stray bullets falling out of the sky hitting the men.

The short version was there was only one way to do a river crossing with a large herd of cattle . . . carefully.

Looking over his shoulder, Noose saw Laura Holdridge climb off her covered wagon where she had been driving the team, swing over the side into the saddle of her Appaloosa mare, and gallop on ahead of the herd, whistling

with her fingers in her mouth and waving her Stetson for
the men to stop the steers.

"Hi-yaaaah!" came the cries of the wranglers down the
line. Joe heard his own voice joining them, louder than
most. The eight wranglers all rode toward the front of the
cattle drive and there the men congregated to slowly, de-
liberately, control the front of the herd, slowing and bringing the lead longhorns to a halt, with the rear of the herd
coming to gradually stand still behind them. It was akin
to stopping an avalanche, Joe thought, and avalanches
were something Noose had some recent experience with.

When it was done, the wranglers reined their horses
and stood by the stationary cattle. Joe Noose was surprised to discover he had a big old grin on his face when
he looked around and met the gazes of the other eight
rovers, who were all grinning, too, eyes full of warm camaraderie and cowboy satisfaction, and in that moment,
the bounty hunter knew how good they were at their jobs;
better, he shared the sense of accomplishment and felt like
he was part of a team, and that he made a contribution. It
was a good feeling.

But the good feeling was fleeting because now all the
outfit's gazes had swiveled to the distant figure of Laura
Holdridge a half mile ahead of the front of the herd, sitting
on her horse at the bank of the mighty Snake River. Noose
tipped the brim of his Stetson down over his eyes to block
out the direct sunlight so he could study her lone figure.
The cattlewoman sat in the saddle, studying the breadth
of the river before her, with an occasional glance west to
one side and east to the other along its expanse. Joe knew
what she was thinking, as sure as if he could hear her
thoughts. It suddenly became very quiet, almost silent,

with the cattle and wranglers motionless, just a creak of saddle and clink of bridle, all sound subsumed by the omnipresent roar of the great river.

Laura Holdridge, Noose realized, had a decision that was hers and hers alone to make: to cross the river with the herd or not. Her other choice was to detour fifty miles, which would cost critical days. With the delays caused by the deaths of her now shorthanded crew, the cattlewoman could not afford to lose that time if she were to get her livestock to Cheyenne by auction; on the other hand, if she crossed the river and lost any of her outfit, their blood would be on her hands.

The bounty hunter watched her small figure sitting tall on her horse, back straight in the saddle, and the slight tip in her profile told him she had come to her decision and Joe felt certain, knowing her a little and yet a lot, that he knew what that decision was.

Noose was wrong. It wouldn't be the last time he would misjudge this tough Wyoming woman.

Spurring her Appaloosa, Laura swung her mare around and rode straight into the river. Horse and rider disappeared in an explosive splash of fresh clear water. The men watched as her tiny figure resurfaced, clinging to the saddle as her horse crossed the Snake River, walking part of the way and paddling the rest, until, after five minutes they finally reached the opposite shore. The drenched Laura and her Appaloosa emerged on the distant river bank, then turned around and rode right back into the river, walking and swimming the five minutes through the heavy currents until they broke onto the near shore at a staggered stride..

Decisively, the trail boss galloped back to the front of

the herd. There, soaked head to boots, she faced all the wranglers and her piercing blue-eyed gaze met theirs one by one, including Joe's. Taking off her hat and shaking out the water, her wet golden hair fell loose around her hearty, ruddy, beautiful face. Then she spoke.

"River's deep, boys. Hundred yards across if it's a foot. Half of that the horses can walk, the rest is too deep and they'll have to swim. Saw for myself. It's dangerous to cross the cattle, can't tell you otherwise. Each one of us will be taking our lives in our hands. Our other options set us back days and we won't make Cheyenne, so we got two choices—cross or turn back. Yesterday I gave this outfit the choice to turn back and I'm giving it to you again. Your lives are your own, so I'm putting it to a vote. Anyone for turning back, raise your hand."

Noose looked around at the other wranglers. Not one hand raised. But one by one, the rovers grinned.

Laura Holdridge grinned right back at them, and the moisture in her eyes wasn't from the river. "Let's get wet."

"Hi-yaaaaah!" came the cry of the outfit, filling the air, as they drew their pistols and fired into the air, startling the five hundred head of cattle into sudden movement, and within seconds, two thousand hooves were pounding the earth, driving five hundred longhorn steers straight for the river, unstoppable, and building up a huge head of steam as the cattle's speed increased with the gathering momentum of a dozen locomotives. One after the other, the three wagons pulled by their teams of horses rolled down the banks into the river with huge splashes, raining the outfit with frigid spray. Noose spurred Copper, firing his pistol with one hand and gripping his stallion's reins with the other, riding alongside the livestock with the rest of the rovers as the wide Snake River rushed up to greet them.

At that moment, Joe Noose understood why Laura Holdridge commanded the total respect and loyalty of an outfit of big tough men, and the bounty hunter admired her leadership right down to the ground.

This outfit rode as one and they rode one way.

Ride or die.

Five hundred cattle poured like cement into the big river under the bright hot sun, and the ten riders and their horses were soon submerged up to their saddles. The shock of the icy glacier waters made for a lot of bellowing steers, snorting steeds and cursing cowpokes, but that didn't stop them pushing on. They were committed, and the brutal cold of the Snake River made man and beast want to get to the other side damn quick.

The three wagons lumbered and lurched across the river, the rapids flowing over the top of the wheels trailing churning cavitations in their wake. Laura drove her rig in the lead.

Wylie Jeffries kept one hand on his saddle pommel, watching the mountainous undulating backs of the steers and their rows of horns in a long wet procession through the rapids. They were staying afloat. The water was icy cold, which froze the veteran wrangler to the bone but kept him clearheaded, and he knew it was damn good motivation for the cows to get to the other side. The wrangler looked up and down the herd crossing the river and saw the other rovers staying on their horses, taking it careful and slow, staying calm with cool heads shepherding the immense march of livestock. *So far, so good.* All Jeffries knew was what his friends did: they were earning their pay this day.

His horse's hooves found solid ground in a shallow section of the river, and Jeffries was able to adjust his seat in the saddle for better balance. Beside him, the gigantic soaked shoulders and skulls of several steers bumped against the side of his horse, hammering his leg painfully. *Stay away from the horns!* Using his reins, he eased his dun mare to his right a few feet, giving the cattle some breathing room.

Wylie Jeffries spotted the new man, Smith or whatever his name was, giving him a watchful glance, but Smith's gaze traveled on and the wrangler noticed that the new replacement was giving all of the rovers watchful glances, paying more attention to them than those hundreds of steers that his job was supposed to be paying attention to.

Thing was, Curly Brubaker wasn't paying enough attention to the herd either, because he was too busy watching Smith.

Because he was temporarily distracted, Jeffries didn't see who fired the shot that blew one of the horns and half the head off a nearby steer, so close it got him splattered with blood. But before any of the rovers could react, the already river-spooked herd were seized with a blind panic and many began to stampede in the water, the long single-file procession quickly breaking off into sections, the cattle dangerously heading in three directions, slowed by the currents but moving with terrifying force. The wranglers were all pulling on their reins, steering the horses out of the path of the steers. The awful look on his boss lady's face as she witnessed what was happening put the rover's heart in his throat.

Thunk!

A bowie knife buried deep in Wylie Jeffries's back, the razor-sharp heavy blade cutting through layers of leather duster, cotton shirt, flesh, muscle and bone and lung. The wrangler stiffened, blood exploding from his mouth, his scream a wet gurgle through gritted teeth, his torso rotating as he slumped out of his saddle, bulging eyes seeing nobody around him and realizing the knife had been thrown.

By then he was unhorsed and his whole body was submerged in the surging, splashing, spraying water and he tried to scream but all he got was a lungful of water that made him expectorate, gag, and suffocate. Grabbing helplessly for the knife in his back, his fingers couldn't reach the haft covered by his wet clothing layers. Jeffries could swim, unlike most of the other drivers; with all his will to live he kicked and paddled and struggled as he kept his head above water. Through his river-blinded vision, all he saw was a chaotic blur of rampaging cattle and men on horses firing their guns and trying to control the herd, some of them now on the other side, while all he heard was the deafening lowing and bellowing of the steers, shouts of the men, and cracks of pistol shots over the roar of the Snake River, but somehow he got the damn knife out of his back. Wylie Jeffries was hurt bad, he knew, the blade had cut deep, but his arms and legs worked and he could swim, dammit, and he struck out for shore. Somebody was trying to kill him, and if he just could reach solid land—

That's when two big gloved hands grabbed him by the

throat and crushed his windpipe like a vise, powerful arms too strong to fight, pushing his head under water, as in the second before his eyes sank below the surface he looked up into the face of his killer and was shocked by who he was, and his last thought before he drowned was he had to warn the outfit.

CHAPTER 8

When, an hour later, Wylie Jeffries's dead body was recovered and dragged ashore by Frank Leadbetter and Curly Brubaker, Laura Holdridge broke down and cried. None of the outfit held his death against her, Joe Noose saw in their faces—this was what they signed up for—but the cattlewoman held it against herself.

There was no knife in Wylie's back because it had been lost in the river, so none of the outfit knew at first that he had been stabbed.

The full herd, having been successfully rounded up, stood on the bank fifty yards away, drying off. The three wagons were parked nearby, draining water still pouring out of them.

The wranglers, the bounty hunter, and the trail boss stood over the dead rover's pale lifeless corpse, his face frozen in a rictus of terror. Noose thought that the expression was peculiar, like he'd seen something that scared him to death.

"I'm sorry, men." Laura sniffled. "Wylie's death is on me."

"I don't think so," said Noose. She looked at Joe. They all looked at Joe.

"What the hell are you taking about, Smith?" Curly growled.

Noose knelt and opened Jeffries's duster, revealing his shirt completely soaked with blood, then unbuttoned the shirt from the collar to the chest, exposing his bare torso, and seeing no wound there, roughly peeled the shirt from the corpse's shoulders and exposed the naked back.

Joe had a pretty good idea what he would find.

The deep, ugly open knife wound in his upper back, along with flower-shaped bruising on the blue skin of his neck—the mark of lethal pressure made by human hands.

"This man didn't drown. He was stabbed, then when that failed, a pair of strong hands finished the job. Look at the marks." Joe rose and faced Laura with a grim nod. "This man was murdered, Mrs. Holdridge. That's a fact. And last night the boys told me he ain't the first." Noose turned to face the other wranglers. *One of you did it.* "One of you boys must have seen something."

One by one, gazes averted or downcast, the men shook their heads. Joe spat in the dirt in disgust. "What kind of chickenshit outfit is this? One of your men, your friends, was murdered and you expect anybody to believe not one of you saw jack shit?"

"I believe my men." Laura shook her head. "None of them saw anything. That was why the killer shot the steer and stampeded the herd. He knew it would keep us distracted."

"Well, Mrs. Holdridge, let me put it this way." Noose looked at Laura. "You can believe your men, that's up to you. You can believe all of your men . . ." He held up a finger and pointed it like a pistol barrel across the faces of the seven rovers. "All but one."

The bounty hunter stormed off toward the wagons, the cattlewoman watching him go with wounded eyes.

"Hey, Smith, where the hell you think you're going?" yelled Curly Brubaker to Joe's back.

Noose grabbed something off the hooligan wagon, two things, then walked back to Curly, shoving one shovel into his hand and keeping the other for himself.

"Gotta bury him, don't we?"

It took three hours to dig a decent grave for Wylie Jeffries, lay him to rest, cover him up, read scripture over him, and for the men who wanted to say a few words over him to get them said, and by then they had lost another half a day.

To make matters worse, it had started to rain. By the time the cattle drive had moved out at three o'clock, the ground had turned to mud and steers' and horses' hooves were fetlock deep in sludge. It was slow going, but the outfit pushed stubbornly forward through the sheets of rain, the men now in raincoats with dripping Stetson hat brims pulled down over their faces.

In Copper's saddle, Noose closely observed the wranglers up and down the procession of cattle, saw that although every man had his hat low on his face, everybody was eyeballing everybody and watching his own back. The gray, cold, overcast light and hard-stinging drops relentlessly pelting the wranglers made the mood miserable,

grim, and paranoid, the atmosphere of distrust growing
with each sidelong glance among the rovers.

The wagon train and marching cattle crossed a plain,
then a hill, then a field and another plain after the Snake
River crossing. Nobody said a word to anybody else, and
the only voices were calls to the cattle.

Keeping his bronze horse at a dogged trot, Noose had
time to think; he wasn't certain why these murders were
taking place. Somebody was trying to stop the cattlewoman from getting her livestock to auction was the most
likely reason. But there were a lot of ways to do that without killing five men, a hanging offense. This was personal.
It was deliberate. Somebody in this outfit had a score to
settle with others in the outfit, a graveyard grudge. *Why
now?* These men lived and worked together, ate together,
slept together every day for years at the Bar H. Noose realized he knew absolutely nothing about this outfit, had
no idea at all who these men were, but he intended to get
to know them fast, before there weren't any left to know.

Then it came back to him suddenly: Joe remembered
the night a month ago at Laura Holdridge's ranch house
at the Bar H with his traveling companions, Marshal Bess
Sugarland and the marshal he knew as Emmett. The three
of them had accepted the cattlewoman's hospitality to stay
the night. Joe had been asleep alone in his bedroom when
he felt like he was being watched. Pretending to be asleep,
Noose had opened one eye and seen the silhouette of a
head and face pressed against the window, backlit by stark
moonlight. By the time Joe had grabbed his pistol, rushed
to the window and thrown it open, the man had fled,
and Noose just caught a glimpse of his fleeing figure in

the moonlight. He had thought that it was The Brander, the deranged killer he and the marshals were hunting at the time, but Joe now believed it wasn't.

Now he reckoned whoever was spying on him was one of the crew of the Bar H Ranch, one of the same rovers in this outfit. That man was riding with him now.

Racking his memory, the bounty hunter tried to retrieve a mental picture of the figure he saw run off that night a month ago—*a sheepskin coat, chaps, a hat*—but what he remembered mostly were just shadows; it had been too dark outside for Joe to see the face of the man at the window, but that man had seen Noose because there was a lamp inside the bedroom.

Every wrangler in the outfit was acting like they had never seen Noose before, even if a few believed he wasn't who he said he was. But one of the rovers was lying and *had* seen him before. That meant there was every probability that the man on this cattle drive who knew who the bounty hunter was, what he did for a living, and why he was here, was the killer himself.

That put Joe Noose at a disadvantage.

Three and a half miles on, the chuck wagon's wheels got stuck in the mud and the team couldn't pull it free. It was the heaviest rig on the drive, so if any of them would get stuck, it would be the cook's. Kettlebone was cursing and whipping the horses when Noose swung a look over his shoulder and saw the stalled chuck wagon. Looking ahead, Joe saw the filthy, sodden train of livestock begin to slow as the wranglers prepared to halt, so he raised his arm and waved the rovers on, gesturing for the outfit to go on without him.

"I'll help Cook get the chuck wagon loose!" he yelled. "Keep moving the herd, we'll catch up!"

Far ahead, past the sea of horns, Joe saw the flash of gold of Laura's hair as she removed her hat and waved back from her wagon, leading her drivers and livestock on.

The bounty hunter rode back toward the mired chuck wagon, grabbing his opportunity to have a few words alone with Cook, who if he was like most trail cooks in Joe's experience, knew everything that went on in his outfit and all the gossip among the crew.

The heavyset cowboy with the spectacles wasn't in the mood for any conversation or any verbiage other than a string of profanity as purple as his enraged face. He kept uselessly lashing his helpless team.

"Stop whipping the horses, mister. Ain't gonna help you or them." Noose pulled Copper right alongside the chuck wagon and swung the horse around, looking the rig over. "We got to lever the wheel outta the mud. You got a four-foot two-by-four and a log on that wagon?"

His glasses fogged with condensation, Kettlebone cracked the whip against the horses' backs even harder until Noose jumped out the saddle onto the transom and fiercely grabbed the whip from him, snarling, "I'm gonna whip you with this if you hit those horses one more time."

The bounty hunter glared and the cook backed down, throwing a glance ahead to see the men, horses, and steers were far in the distance and he was alone with the tough, dangerous stranger who had just joined the outfit, who nobody knew anything about and who was ready to use

Kettlebone's own whip on him. "We need a heavy board and something to lever it with, get down under that wheel with the board and use it to lift the wheel out."

"I got nothing like that on the chuck wagon, god-dammit!"

Jumping off the chuck wagon, Joe was already ankle-deep in mud, giving the stalled rig the once-over. "Sure you do." Noose pointed at the heavy barrels on the rear of the carriage. "Gimmie that barrel. Push it down."

"It's full of sugar, friend!"

"Good, means it's heavy. Give it here." When Kettle-bone equivocated, Noose reached up and tipped the keg off the wagon, dropping it into the mud as the cook screamed curses at him. The barrel was heavy and wrapped with iron, seventy-five solid pounds, and Joe used his boot to wedge it behind the stuck rear wagon wheel, deep in the muck.

"The board."

"I got no boards," the cook mocked, "less you wanna pull a piece off the wagon."

"That'll work."

"Wait!"

Unsheathing his gleaming bowie knife, the bounty hunter drove the blade into the edge of one of the four-inch-thick planks on the side of the chuck wagon, prying out the nails with a few jerks of his wrist and tearing a heavy six-foot board, suitable for his purposes, off the side of the rig.

Opening his mouth to say something unwise, Kettle-bone was silenced by a mean glance from Noose, who bared his teeth. "Get your fat ass down here and give me a hand now!" Leaping off the platform, the cook grabbed the other end of the board and helped the bounty hunter wedge it under the rear axle, balancing it on the overturned barrel, cramming the end of the plank beneath the wheel. "Push!" Noose barked. "Cram it in there!"

It took a combined effort of the two strong men to get the board under the wheel, and step-by-step, working side by side, wedge it in there. Noose looked over at Kettle-bone and flashed a crooked grin. "Now we got this time to spend together, how 'bout you tell me why the drivers in the outfit are getting murdered and who is doing the killing?"

"You get right to the point, doncha, mister?"

"Saves time. By the body count, I'd say time is something you boys and that lady are running out of right quick."

"I don't know who the killer is."

"Is it you?" Noose asked quietly. The cook met the bounty hunter's piercing pale gaze and returned his un-blinking stare, both men nose to nose. Suddenly it got very quiet, just the fall of the rain. "You the killer, boy?" Joe's eyes looked right through Fred.

"No," the cook replied, his eyes never wavering.

"Prove it."

"Because none of them was poisoned. I'm the cook. How else you think I'd do it if it had been me? It'd be easy enough to poison the food and nobody would even know they'd been murdered."

The bounty hunter cocked an eyebrow. "One of the murdered men said he did have stomach complaint. Push!"

Both men leaned their full weight onto the board,

levering on the barrel, and the back of the wagon lifted. "Yee-ahh!" Kettlebone yelled to the horses in front of the wagon, and they leaned into their bridles and harnesses to pull the rig, but the wagon wheel, stuck deep, barely moved.

"It's gonna work," insisted Noose. "Help me wedge the board in tighter. Get it in there!" Breathing hard, Noose gasped, "So saying it ain't you, who do you think it is?"

"I have ideas."

"I'm all ears."

The cook stubbornly shook his head slowly back and forth. "I ain't no snitch."

"Fair enough." Joe put his back into hoisting the plank cantilevered on the barrel, Kettlebone beside him straining and grimacing, using all his considerable weight, and to-gether, the two men lifted the wheel out of the mud.

"Yee-ahh!" Kettlebone screamed at the team of horses, and the four quarter horses pulled the rig with all their might, the chuck wagon getting unstuck and starting to roll. The cook scrambled onto the rear transom as it began to move, gesturing to the bounty hunter falling behind the departing rig.

"Gimme that damn sugar barrel before we lose it!" Joe picked up the seventy-five-pound sugar barrel and tossed it to Kettlebone, who got knocked on his ass when he caught it, and then the wagon chassis plank Noose launched at him. The cook dropped the loose board on the rain-slick transom as he scrambled into the driver's seat and picked up the reins.

In the wake of the departing chuck wagon, the bounty hunter raced on foot to his horse and swung up into the saddle, taking off at a gallop until he rode alongside the cook on the rig. To be heard above the noisy racket of the splattering hooves and clanking wagon suspension, Joe Noose had to shout. *"You don't want to give me the who, how about the why?"*

Fred Kettlebone yelled back, *"You want answers, mister, the hooligan wagon where the drivers keep their belongings, that's where you'll find answers! Look in the hooligan wagon! Every man has a war sack with his name on it, with all their belongings inside! Even the dead men have their war sacks with all their stuff . . . their stuff and . . . !"*

"And what?"

"I've said all I'm gonna say!" Kettlebone's lips tightened as he stared straight ahead at the team pulling the rig as he shouted to Noose, *"Figure it out for yourself. Nose around those war sacks! See what turns up!"* The cook swung his head to look the bounty hunter on the galloping horse beside the wagon straight in the eye. *"But a word of advice. You go through another man's property in this outfit, best be sure nobody catches you. Messing with a man's personal belongings is justification for a lynching."*

"Obliged." The bounty hunter tipped his hat.

"You're on your own, Smith!" Fred Kettlebone shook his head. *"I don't know you, and you 'n' me, we ain't never had this conversation! Yee-ahh!"* Cracking the whip, the cook brought his horses to a full gallop as the chuck wagon rattled and shook as it accelerated over the muddy trail of cattle hooves.

The stranger who called himself Smith on the great bronze stallion quickly overtook the wagon, charging ahead like a bolt of lightning to catch up with the herd off in the distance.

Fred Kettlebone was glad John Smith, or whoever he was, was here, it was just too bad he wasn't going to live very long.

CHAPTER 9

The outfit and their herd made only five miles that day, what with the death and burial and weather delay. When they lost the light, they called it quits. A sense of defeat and dread disproportionate to their circumstances hung over the crew as they harbored the cattle, circled the wagons, and hitched the horses under an unbroken black cloud filling the vast sky. Even when the smell of cooked beef and baked beans wafted over the camp from the direction of the chuck wagon, nobody had much of an appetite.

It was chowtime. Noose leaned against the hooligan wagon across the camp, arms crossed over his massive chest, and watched some of the wranglers huddling around the campfire a few hundred yards across the camp. He closely observed several cowpunchers having a knife-throwing competition on a painted bullseye target set up on a nearby tree. A blade-tossing contest seemed in bad taste to the scowling bounty hunter, tonight of all nights, given today's deadly events. The licking flames of the roaring logs glimmered on the swift sudden flashes of polished steel from the hurled blades as one rover after another took turns throwing his knife into the tree—*thunk, thunk, thunk*—closest to the target. The faces of the cowboys looked sinister in the dancing shadows of the campfire, their eyes black as bats.

The gleam of another kind of metal caught Joe's eyes: silver coins changing hands. The rovers were gambling and betting on who was the most accurate at tossing a blade.

Charley Sykes was the hands-down winner; he threw a dead-center bullseye with his bowie knife, burying it to the hilt in the tree during each of his three turns, standing twice as far back as his nearest cowpuncher competition. The surly, hulking, long-haired redneck had a cocky self-confident swagger collecting his money that made it obvious to Noose that when it came to throwing knives, Sykes was the best blade in the outfit, and knew how good he was.

Good enough to throw a knife into Wylie Jeffries's back in a raging river of stampeding steers?

Perhaps.

As if he suddenly felt Noose's gaze drilling into the back of his head from across the camp, Sykes turned his face to lock eyes with Joe. In the firelight, the rover's eyes reflected the dancing flames as his mouth broke into a savage grin; then, incredibly fast, the flash of glinting steel and Sykes's bowie knife quivered in the tree, thrown so fast Joe didn't see the toss, hitting dead center in the bullseye. The fun over for now, Sykes turned his back on Noose, retrieved and sheathed his big blade, then rejoined the rest of the drivers sitting around the circle of the campfire, eating chow and swapping jokes.

Noose took a head count.

Seven.

All of the rovers present and accounted for.

Uncrossing his arms, Joe slipped into the hooligan wagon he had been leaning against. Nobody saw him sneak into the rig. He moved as quiet as a cat. Careful not to make the boards creak, he slowly pulled himself up on the transom and once aboard the rig, flattened himself by the sideboard, listening for any sounds of footsteps or someone moving nearby. The only sound was the hoot of an owl. Peering over the rail, he still counted seven rovers by the campfire. Satisfied he was not being observed, Noose swiftly ducked through the canvas flap into the darkened interior of the covered wagon.

Inside the air was close, smelling of leather, dirt, soiled clothes, and dust. Closing the canvas flap behind him, Noose crouched down and looked around. The darkened shapes of the war sacks, large feed bags the cowboys kept their belongings in, were set side by side on shelves on opposite sides of the wagon. It was too dark to see, so Joe carefully struck a match, cupping his hands around the flame to provide him just enough light to see by, but shielding the dim illumination from view of anyone outside. Or so he hoped.

The flame flickered on the cloth sacks, some more filled than others, made of sack material that was worn and ratty, tattered in places with stitched-up holes. Tags were attached to each one bearing the initials of the men that owned the war sacks: *C.B., F.L.* and the others. Joe sorted through them expeditiously, finding clothes, photographs, dime novels, a few wallets or change purses with little cash.

As he crawled on his hands and knees, the boards of the wagon creaked noisily. He froze, listening for footsteps, and heard none. The distant drone of muffled conversation broken by occasional laughter continued uninterrupted from the direction of the chuck wagon. The bounty hunter tried to be as quiet as possible as he continued his search.

His stick match went out. He lit another.

The five dead wranglers' war sacks were purposely separated on the back shelf of the rig. Out of respect, he imagined. When Noose searched the belongings in those bags, to his surprise Joe discovered a great deal of valuables: cash, and expensive items that clearly belonged to other drivers—wallets, cigar cases with cigars, silver belt buckles, whiskey flasks, and more; certain of these articles had their names or initials carved or engraved on them, and those initials were clearly not *L.M., C.F., J.W.,* or *O.J.,* the initials of the dead men on the war sacks.

Why did dead members of the outfit have the property of the living ones? Noose wondered, remembering Fred Kettlebone's cryptic tip that Joe would find answers to his questions in the hooligan wagon.

Somebody was coming.

Snuffing the match, Noose rolled on his back and hid under the bench of the wagon.

The rig quavered and the sideboard creaked as someone clambered aboard. A silhouette of a rover appeared by the canvas flaps of the opening of the covered wagon, shrouded with darkness. He wasn't here to discover Noose, Joe realized. Whoever it was had some other agenda, and was being very careful not to be seen or heard. A pair of boots the bounty hunter didn't recognize trod quietly past his face with a jingle of spurs inches from his nose. One of the wranglers had snuck in and started going through several of the dead men's war sacks.

Noose grabbed the man by his arm, surprising him in the act of his theft, enough to sweep his legs out from under him, drag him to the floor, and straddle him without much fuss. Joe clapped his hand over the mouth of Joe Idaho, who stared up at him wide-eyed, shaking his head *no* as his huge captor pulled back his fist threateningly. Noose confronted him in a forceful hushed whisper. "You're Idaho. Thief, eh? I'm turning you over to Laura Holdridge directly."

The captured rover's desperate words were muffled by the bounty hunter's large hand covering the lower half of his face, and he kept shaking his head, breaking a sweat.

"OK, you want me not to tell your boss you're a thief?" Joe inquired. Idaho nodded quickly. "Then, mister, you're going to tell me what you're hiding, what all the men in this outfit are hiding. Tell me why you all are getting killed. That's the arrangement. I take my hand off your mouth, you use that tongue of yours for talking; one shout I'll knock you out, friend." Noose clenched his poised, pulled-back fist tight enough for his knuckles to crackle.

Another nod.

Joe removed his hand.

"I ain't no thief," Idaho gasped in a furtive whisper. "I w-was just getting back my property from men don't need it no more."

"The dead men."

Nod.

"How did they come to have your property?"

"I lost it to 'em at poker. Clay Fullerton and Luke McGraw were card sharks and they ran a crooked game, and me and a lot of the other men been losing everything we had to 'em. It's been going on for months, since back at the ranch, before we ever went out on this drive."

"I don't buy it. Those men have been dead a while, what took you so long to reclaim your property? Sounds like bullshit to me," Noose growled, rolling Idaho on his stomach and twisting his arm painfully behind his back. "Next words out of your mouth better damn well be the truth, or you're gonna be roping with one arm."

"It's t-true, I swear it! I don't know why I waited so long," Idaho moaned in agony. "McGraw and Fullerton joined forces and teamed up to fleece the other men in the outfit. I think Johnson was in on it, too. Wade was cheating. The outfit had us a regular card game where they took everybody's wages—except Leadbetter, who don't play cards—or made them loans with ever-increasing interest. They had them a sweet little scam. The rest of us, we didn't know they was card sharks at first, and when the men found out, they were steamed, all of us was. It's the truth, I s-swear. *Ow!* Please, Smith, let me go."

"You telling me a lot of the rovers had it out for the dead men?"

"One or two of us especially, yes."

"Which ones?"

"Can't say."

"Yes, you can."

"I ain't no snitch!"

"Who are they?" Noose bent back Idaho's arm until he heard cartilage pop, the shoulder joint close to breaking. The man slapped the floorboards in anguish.

"You can bust my arm, mister," Idaho spat between gritted teeth. "But I'd die before I rat out my friends."

With a grunt, Joe Noose released Idaho and climbed off him, satisfied what he heard was the truth, and pretty sure this rover was no killer. The cowpuncher sat up and rubbed his arm, looking fearfully at Noose. "Go on, get your property." Joe cocked his thumb at the war sacks. "You're right, dead men don't need it. I got what I needed to know. From what you've told me, some of you wranglers are very bad gamblers, heavily in debt to those dead cowboys, and that's a good motivation for murder."

"You gonna squeal to the boss lady on me?"

The bounty hunter squinted. "Not as long as you don't tell the outfit I was in here going through their personal effects. Wasn't here to steal."

"Why *was* you going through their stuff then?"

"Curiosity."

"Deal." Joe Idaho scrabbled a fistful of his cash and belongings from Luke McGraw's war sack and hurried out of the hooligan wagon.

The bounty hunter was right behind him.

Before he blew out his lamp by his bedroll, Joe Noose made a few brief entries in the murder book with his pen.

First he scratched out the name of *Wylie Jeffries* under *Suspects* and wrote it under *Victims*.

Under *Suspects*, beside the name *Charley Sykes,* the bounty hunter wrote: *Best with knife in outfit*, a dash, then *Jeffries stabbed in back with a knife, probably thrown*.

Under *Victims*, Noose made a notation beside the names

Luke McGraw, *Ox Johnson*, *Clay Fullerton*, *Wylie Jeffries*, and *Jed Wade* that the murdered men, at least some, were card sharks who cheated the unluckier gamblers in the outfit of their wages and valuables, and took further advantage of the other rovers, making them loans and charging unfair interest. Joe wrote *Motive* in large letters.

He put a question mark beside all of the surviving wranglers on the list.

The bounty hunter rubbed his eyes, trying to remember the initials and monograms on the watches, belts, and pistols he had seen in the war sacks of McGraw, Fullerton, Johnson, Jeffries and Wade in the hooligan wagon—property the dead men confiscated from other drivers for gambling debts incurred during their crooked card games, leaving one of the cheated men in the outfit broke and insolvent, desperate enough to be driven to murder to get his money back . . . and if he knew the victims had cheated him, plenty of motivation to kill for revenge. *But then why would the valuables still be in the dead men's war sacks? It wasn't adding up.* It was so dark in the hooligan wagon all Noose had made out in the war sacks were the wads of cash, and on the jewelry and watches Joe's fingertips had only felt different initials from the names of the dead men on the war sacks.

He would have to go back in daylight, bringing Laura Holdridge with him. Noose decided to go to the cattle-woman's wagon and speak with her about his findings directly.

Joe closed the murder book and was just about to blow out the candle when he heard a rough, inebriated voice. "What you wr-r-writing in th-thash book?" Charley Sykes slurred, rearing behind him as Noose rose to his feet and spun, slipping the murder book into his coat deftly, his hands dropping to the holstered Colt Peacemakers hanging on his belt, flexing and unflexing his big hands, cracking the cartilage of his knuckles.

Charley Sykes swayed on his boots like a drunken bull—but a soused bull, if it charges, can still kill you with its horns, and Sykes had his bowie knife palmed in his right hand. *Why didn't I see him there?* Joe grimly realized he had no idea how long the wrangler had been standing there, reading over his shoulder, able to put a blade in his back at any time, just like Jeffries. *How could my reflexes be that slow? Damn, that was close.* The riled, paranoid rover's face flushed beet red as he pointed with the hand holding his knife. "Thash-thash my name you write, I shaw you write my damn name, what you write in b-book?"

"None of your damn business." One moment Joe Noose's right hand was empty and the next his unsheathed bowie knife was clenched in his raised fist so fast the intoxicated Charley Sykes's eyelids kept fluttering, blinking as if in astonishment at some astounding magic trick the bounty hunter had performed.

Noose was watching Sykes's eyes and knew when the wrangler stopped blinking, the first stab would come, so Joe was ready—Sykes lunged faster than he thought he would, the tip of the knife driving straight at Noose's nose. Stepping aside easily and pivoting on his boots, Joe heard the *whoosh* of the blade *hiss* by his head as Noose swung his knife hand and slashed a deep wound in Sykes's bicep, spraying blood across the tent; the rover screamed in agony, already off balance from putting his full weight into his missed thrust, and Joe let gravity take over—Noose raised his boot and gave Sykes a taste of spur as he kicked him in the ass as hard as he could. The huge wrangler went headfirst through the wall of the tent and went sprawling to the ground, face-planting in the dirt. Dust settled. The bounty hunter stepped out of the tent.

Joe Noose didn't think he would get up that fast.

Back up on his boots in the blink of an eye, as drunk as he was, Charley Sykes took the duel seriously now, ducking and weaving like a snake, taking quick, deadly jabs and slashes at Noose's face with his bowie knife. Joe felt the serrated edge nick his nose and dodged back again and again. His pale eyes were riveted on Sykes's face, not the blade, and when he saw the savage gleam in his opponent's gaze, anticipated the next thrust of the knife; when it came, Noose spun and ducked with fearsome speed, feeling the fist with the blade go past his head, throwing his shoulder hard into Sykes's thrusting underarm and using his whole body mass to drive the violent rover against an oak tree, where the knife slammed home harmlessly. Surprised and off balance, Charley Sykes tried to yank his weapon out of the tree, but it was stuck deep in the trunk—as he looked anxiously around at Noose. Expecting the wrong end of a knife, he got Joe's fist instead, three times in the face, knocking two of his teeth out. The stunned wrangler slumped to the ground.

Yanking the bowie knife out of the trunk of the tree, the bounty hunter heaved it far into the dark woods. "Trying to cut the new man ain't no way to welcome him to your outfit, or didn't your mama teach you no manners? Why'd you pull a blade on me, Sykes?" Joe Noose picked Charley Sykes up by the throat with one hand and slammed him against the tree at the edge of camp, pulling back his other fist to smash the man's face in. "Wylie Jeffries in the river was killed with a knife, and I seen how good you were with one tonight. Before you met me, that is." Joe grinned coldly. "It's you killin' these rovers, aincha?"

"It wasn't me!"

"Liar!"

Squirming under the bounty hunter's strangulating grip on his throat, the wrangler gagged out the words, "I didn't kill them drivers . . . but I know who did."

"Who?" Noose loosened the pressure on Sykes's neck slightly, using his hand and the muscle in his arm to keep him pinned against the tree trunk. "If it ain't you, then which man done it?"

"If I tell you, my life ain't worth spit. He'll kill me too."

"Don't worry about him, worry about *me.* Your life ain't gonna be worth spit anyway unless you spill your guts now."

"I ain't telling you shit." Joe pulled back his fist to plow it into the fallen wrangler's jaw, and the man's gaze wavered. "B-but I'll tell the boss. I'll t-tell Mrs. Holdridge. It's her outfit and she gots a right to know. This has to end."

With a grunt, the bounty hunter released the wrangler, who dropped onto his tailbone and slumped against the tree.

"I'll get her. Then bring her back here directly." Joe pointed down at Sykes. "And, mister, when I do, you better tell her every last thing you know or the last words coming out of your mouth better be your prayers."

Sykes nodded, beaten, blood seeping from his jaw.

Taking two long strides to the nearest horse, Noose took a lasso from the saddle, uncoiled it, and quickly wrapped the rope around the felled rover and the tree three times, binding Sykes's arms to his torso, then pulled it taut and knotted it. He grabbed the yellow handkerchief from around the man's neck and stuffed it in his mouth to silence him. "Stay put," Noose growled, stalking off in the direction of Laura's wagon.

When he got to her quarters, Joe rapped on the wood with his thick knuckles. Her silhouette moved in shadow behind the canvas in the warm light of a coal lamp. In a moment, she poked her head out, brushed-out hair down around her shoulders and brush in her hand, but still fully dressed.

"What is it, Joe?" the cattlewoman asked wonderingly, searching his grim face.

"Your man Sykes and I got into an altercation. I've got him tied up nearby. Says he knows who the killer is been murdering your men, Laura, but he'll only talk to you. You better come with me."

With a gasp, Laura urgently grabbed the coal lamp and ducked out of the canopy, dropping off the wagon in her boots. Hastily, she followed Noose's swift paces toward the tree.

In the moonlight ahead, Charley Sykes's large figure sat on the ground against the tree, his bulk shadowed in the lee of the branches.

He didn't look at them as they approached.

When he got within a few feet, Joe's boot squished in wet mud on the dry grass.

Laura lifted her lantern, casting a glow of firelight on her wrangler tied to the tree.

She jumped back with such a start she nearly dropped the lamp.

Charley Sykes's throat was brutally slashed from ear to ear, his head gruesomely thrown back, eyes rolled up in a pale bloodless face, because most of his blood he sat in, the grass wet black with it.

CHAPTER 10

Cocking the lever of her Winchester, Laura Holdridge aimed the barrel of her rifle at her six surviving wranglers sitting on the ground.

She swapped glances with Joe Noose, who was on the other side of the men keeping his Henry rifle leveled at the rovers. "Charley Sykes was murdered tonight," she said. "But one of you boys already knows that."

Joe had seen raw fear on the faces of the six sitting men when he and Laura had roused them at gunpoint from their sleeping rolls and force-marched them to the chuck wagon five minutes ago. That look of fear grew when their trail boss made them take off their gun belts and they were disarmed. Now, in the lamplight, Noose watched the drivers' expressions upon hearing the news of Sykes's murder change from fear to shock to remorse to fear again, yet none of their reactions gave him a clear indication as to who the killer might be.

Murmurs and whispers traveled through the outfit.

Their boss walked slowly around them with her gun. "One of you boys murdered Charley Sykes," Laura said, her voice breaking. "Just like you murdered Luke McGraw

and Ox Johnson and Clay Fullerton and Jed Wade and
Wylie Jeffries. Now Charley Sykes. How could you? Why?
These men were your friends. We ride as an outfit. We ride
as a family. But now the devil rides with us. Never thought
I'd live to see that day I'd be pointing a gun at my own
crew. I hate that it's come to this, boys, but the way I'm
feeling right now, whichever one of you is the killer better
confess, or I'm just gonna start shooting and maybe get
lucky. So I ask you again, which one of you did it?"

"I know I didn't kill nobody," Curly Brubaker said.

"Me neither," said Fred Kettlebone.

One by one, four others all claimed they were innocent.
Frank Leadbetter said nothing, Noose noticed.

"Then one of you is a *liar*." Laura scowled. "Your soul's
going straight to hell and I promise to send it there." She
clenched her Winchester, moving the muzzle back and
forth across the faces of her crew. "I swear on my dead
husband's grave." She traded looks with Joe, who nudged
his jaw at Leadbetter.

"How come just now you didn't deny doing the murders?" Joe asked.

Frank looked up at Noose without blinking. "If I was
the killer, what good would it do saying I wasn't? Every
man here says they're innocent when one of us ain't, so
what do you expect?"

"How do we know the killer *is* one of us?" Brubaker
snapped at Laura.

"Of course he's one of us, who else could it be?" she
retorted.

"How can you be so sure, ma'am? You even considered
that the killer might be an assassin out there tracking

us, keeping up with the herd but staying out of sight? Murdering us when we ain't looking? For all we know, this individual could be some kind of professional killer. It ain't out of line that maybe instead of right away suspecting the men who have worked for you for ten years, you'd give us the benefit of the doubt and give a little thought to it could be someone else, Mrs. Holdridge."

The cattlewoman considered that possibility again. Her gaze wavered when she looked to the bounty hunter. *What do you think?*

Noose shrugged. *Possible.*

The rovers all exchanged troubled, uncertain glances filled with fresh suspicion and doubt.

"It's got Injun written all over it," Kettlebone grumbled. "Like I told you boys. Mebbe an Injun assassin paid by the white man."

"Stop making excuses." Noose cradled his rifle, walking around the seated wranglers. "I find it tough to swallow that one of you men don't know something or has any clue about which one of you is the murderer. I respect your outfit sticks together and nobody wants to be a snitch, as long as you get it through your thick skulls that one of you means to kill the rest." Most of the men avoided his eyes, and the ones who didn't had resentful gazes, being interrogated by a stranger. He stared them down. "It's plain to see how pissed off you are that the new hired hand, somebody you hardly know, is questioning you, and you're probably doubly pissed off that your trail boss, who you worked for so long, is trusting me to hold a gun on you, but the reason she turned to me is that I'm the one man in this outfit Mrs. Holdridge knows positively ain't the killer.

You boys ought to realize the same. I ain't your enemy and I ain't your friend. I'm just a cowpoke like you trying to earn a living and help this outfit get the cattle to market without getting killed, so I get paid. How about a little cooperation?"

Looking over at Laura Holdridge, Joe Noose saw the hopeless look on her face knowing none of her men were going to talk. She met his perspicacious gaze with a tight shake of her head. *This is useless.* "OK, boys, collect your weapons and get your asses out of my sight," she muttered. "First thing tomorrow we bury Charley. Then we got fifteen miles of territory to get these steers across by sunset, so get some rest and try not to get murdered in your sleep. I can't afford to lose any more hands."

The drivers all rose grumpily to their feet, swearing under their breath. Curly Brubaker, Frank Leadbetter, Rowdy Maddox, Billy Barlow, Joe Idaho, and Fred Kettlebone retrieved their gun belts and slunk off into the darkness toward their bedrolls. "Not you," Noose said, touching Frank's arm with the muzzle of his Henry rifle. "You stay. I want a word with you."

The teenage Leadbetter stopped and threw uncomfortable glances between Joe and Laura, who both braced him. "What do you want to talk to me for?"

Noose spoke forcefully. "Tell us your whereabouts tonight around the time Charley Sykes had his throat cut."

"Near as I can remember, I was answering nature's call."

"Anybody see you do that?"

He shrugged. "Why would they?"

"Notice you keep to yourself, don't fraternize with your saddle mates much."

"What is that supposed to mean?"

"Do I need to spell it out for you?"

"You'll have to. I can't read or write."

"Why don't you pal around with the other drivers?"

"I'm a greenhorn. The other rovers is all older than me, they all got more experience and they're always picking on me because I'm the kid. Well, sir, I may be only twenty-one, but I been around cattle my whole life and I'm just as good a driver as any one of them."

Joe traded glances with Laura. She nodded in agreement.

Leadbetter went on. "But I can see what's going on here."

Curious, Noose asked the teenager what he meant.

Lowering his voice to a whisper, sneaking a furtive glance in the direction the drivers went, Frank said, "I can't read or write but any fool can count. With every man we lose on the cattle drive, fewer men are left to stop the others from doing something bad, like stealing the whole herd or having their way with their sexy lady boss—no offense, Mrs. Holdridge—or both."

"None taken, Frank," Laura replied "You heard any talk in this outfit about any of this?"

Leadbetter shook his head. "Just loose talk."

Joe nodded at Laura to let the young rover go, and Frank walked off to join the others at the bedrolls.

As they stood alone together in the lee of the chuck wagon and quietly conversed, the bounty hunter told the cattlewoman he believed the young cowpuncher was not their killer, and she agreed. "Frank Leadbetter worked for my husband and me for ten years and I trust his loyalty."

"Is he good with a gun?"

Laura nodded decisively. "A dead shot."

"Good," Noose replied. "Because if there is a treacherous plot among the wranglers to steal your herd by force, we can use that kid's pistol on our side."

Joe Noose was a light sleeper.

He awoke to the sound of hooves.

Someone was riding toward the camp. Riding very quietly, at a slow trot, so as not to attract attention or awaken any of the outfit.

Lifting his head from his saddle, which he used as a pillow, and sitting up in his bedroll, the bounty hunter slid his Colt Peacemaker smoothly from his holster and listened, his senses alert.

The lanterns were all extinguished and the camp was cloaked in darkness. A low-hanging mist covered the ground. The moonless night made it impossible to see more than twenty feet in any direction, and until his eyes adjusted to the dark, Noose had only his keen ears and sharp hearing to track the horse and rider with as they made their approach.

When Joe heard the sound of more hooves fifty yards away, it sounded like the horses tethered to the hitching rope stepping aside to make way for another horse entering their midst. Rolling silently to his feet, Noose did not waste time putting on his boots, and walked barefoot in a low, quiet diagonal to the horses, his raised pistol barrel going where his nose went. Ahead, he heard the clinking of stirrups and squeak of leather as someone swiftly dismounted, then the metallic sound of a saddle cinch, and bridle, being undone. Finally, a muffled *thump* as the saddle was dropped in the dirt close to where the other saddles were stowed.

By the time he reached the area where the outfits' horses were tied, the rider, whoever he was, was gone. By now Noose's eyes had adjusted sufficiently to the darkness where he could see the remuda standing in the stillness. He counted them. Sixty-one including Copper; there were no new animals, so the rider was not an outsider, he had been riding one of the outfit's horses.

One of the rovers had ridden out of camp in the middle of the night, so his departure from the outfit would not be detected, and now he had returned. Where had he gone, wondered Joe, and why the secrecy?

Figuring he could tell which of the wranglers had been out for a midnight ride if he could find the horse and place it to its owner, Joe wasn't sure where to begin, until he felt a warm snout nuzzle him on the shoulder and looked over to see the bronze shape of his best friend Copper, whose warm brown eyes were locked to his master in the gloom. The stallion tossed his head to the right several times, trying to tell him something.

Noose followed Copper's gaze.

Three horses stood a few feet away.

Copper exhaled and nudged his snout at the horses, and Joe immediately understood. With a grin, he patted his steed's head and made his way over to the three horses tied to the wagon.

Touching his hand to the flanks of the first, it was cool as the night air.

He touched the second mare, whose haunches were also cool.

When Noose placed his palm on the third horse, a black stallion, the flesh was warm to the touch and lathered with sweat, freshly ridden and reeking of exertion.

Near the hooves lay several saddles, stowed on the ground. Crouching down, it didn't take long using the touch test to determine which saddle had just been ridden by the warmth of the leather.

Joe struck a match. Cupping his hand to hide the flash of flame, he lifted the saddle and looked beneath it.

Saw what was stamped in the leather on the underside.

Noose glared at the Bar T insignia under the saddle and felt his blood boil. It was the Calhoun brand. Joe hated the Bar T and everything it represented; the Calhoun Cattle Company had been founded in Texas with a thousand longhorns and now claimed over a million head, monopolizing the cattle business in several Western states and recently setting their sights on Wyoming. Bar T was a criminal syndicate, nothing less.

But it didn't used to be until the old man, Thomas Calhoun, retired and his evil son, Crispin Calhoun, took control of the Bar T and started doing things his way. The younger Calhoun's ruthless depredations disgraced the family name and drove his father into an early grave. Now, many years later, Crispin Calhoun still sat on the throne of the Bar T. His mighty cattle dynasty was richer and more powerful than ever as he expanded his empire into Wyoming. Bar T was advancing like the Roman army, forcing local ranchers off their property and acquiring their land and cattle by any means necessary, including extortion, intimidation, rustling, and, so it was rumored, cold-blooded murder. Crispin Calhoun intended to control the cattle business in the United States and took even the smallest independent ranch holding out against him as a personal affront, a threat he had to crush. And he did, again and again.

In the past, when Noose heard the stories about the villainous cattle baron, he felt his branding scar getting hotter against his flesh as his blood boiled in fury at the injustice of this wealthy and dangerous villain's crimes against defenseless hardworking folks, which continued to go unchecked. Bribing his way out of countless criminal convictions and jail time by paying off judges and lawmen, Crispin Calhoun threw money at law enforcement to look the other way because the cattle baron figured he had enough money to buy anything, but he figured wrong: Noose wasn't for sale. Calhoun needed to be stopped and Joe Noose was just the man to do it. Someday soon, Joe had a hunch their paths would cross.

Just then Noose noticed that the Bar T brand looked different—the *T* that used to be shaped like an upright cross was upside down, like an inverted crucifix; Crispin Calhoun had changed the brand, but why?

Joe Noose reckoned the satanic implications of an upside-down cross was fitting, because Crispin Calhoun was as close to the Antichrist as a soul could get.

Dawn broke.

Wylie Jeffries's lonely grave lay undisturbed on the wide-open plain beneath a gunpowder sky. The wind blew across the plain, wafting granules of dirt from the plot onto the muddy imprints of the long-departed cattle and horses.

Then came the sound of hooves.

Fifteen horses passed along on the same route, following the trail of the cattle drive. Sixty dirty hooves pounded over the dead wrangler's grave, punching deep grooves in the dirt, heading southeast in the direction of those they followed, until soon the horses were gone.

Jeffries stayed dead.

CHAPTER 11

Far away, U.S. Marshal Bess Sugarland arrived home to Jackson Hole, Wyoming. She stopped first at the grave of her father, the late U.S. Marshal Nate Sugarland who was killed in the line of duty two years before. His plot and headstone lay in a small local cemetery in a nearby valley called Solitude, a place as empty and peaceful as the name implied, which looked out on the Teton mountain range towering up against limitless sky. It was a humble graveyard surrounded by a small black corrugated fence below an unmarked metal archway, where inside a several-hundred-foot-square area were thirty-five gravestones and head markers laid out in uneven rows. Bess came to this peaceful place often for she felt close to her father here, and here she could talk to him, or at least his spirit.

Walking up to the gravestone, the marshal took off her hat, happy to be back.

"Hi, Pop. Been a few months since my last visit. Sorry it's been so long. Was on a job. Marshal business. Knew you'd understand the badge comes first. You always told me that. Duty first to public safety was always your motto. Anyways, we got our man and I just got back to Jackson today, so the first thing I wanted to do was come see you, because it's been a while and I've missed our talks, Pop. Where do I start?"

When Bess spoke to her late father she was carrying on a regular conversation with him; not that she didn't accept her dad had passed, simply that she chose to keep him alive in her heart. Her way of doing that was talking to him like she always had. Resting her head on her father's gravestone, the marshal smiled as she felt the fragrant spring breeze waft her hair, and it seemed she caught a whiff of her old man's leathery scent.

"Since I put on this badge I've learned how lucky I was, Pop. My father was Nate Sugarland, the best U.S. Marshal in the country, and you taught me everything I know. Most men who take this job have to learn how to be a marshal through hard firsthand experience, where a mistake can kill you, out there all alone. But not me. I was never alone because I had you. I always felt safe. Learned how to do this job by watching you ever since I was a kid, then learned hands-on when I became your deputy. You taught me the ropes, Pop. Nobody gets training like that. It's our family business. Always had confidence, and it all came from you believing in me. You made me the best U.S. Marshal I can be, and every day I try to do you proud."

Bess wrapped her coat tighter around her shoulders as a sweeping wind tore down the plain and blew away the flowers somebody had set on a nearby grave. The metal C-E-M-E-T-A-R-Y letters rattled above on the wrought-iron gate. She held on to her hat as she stood amidst the headstones and basked in the atmosphere of the lovely little graveyard in the shadow of the gargantuan Teton mountain range rearing in the west, snowcapped granite peaks so high they vanished into the clouds. The valley was alive with carpets of yellow flowers. The air smelled clean and fresh. Solitude was the place on earth her outdoorsman father loved best; it was where he came to hunt and fish, sometimes with his daughter, often alone, and in this sprawling valley Nate Sugarland was the happiest. It was why she buried him here. When she visited his grave, Bess Sugarland always felt close to her father, here in this beautiful place.

A radiance of sunlight created by the colossal clouds parting overhead had lit up her father's tombstone, as if by providence, the very moment Bess Sugarland walked beneath the cemetery gate, like the finger of God had touched her old man's grave in a ray of divine evanescence. Now, a few minutes later, a bank of darker clouds passed over the sun and the pretty light faded, and with it the marshal's joyous mood, shadows descending on the cemetery and doubts descending on Bess's soul, like a dark veil inside and outside her.

She came here to talk to her father, but he was dead.

It was just her.

And Bess suddenly felt very alone.

The young woman mostly never got lonely.

Not when Joe Noose was around.

But he was far, far away now, clear across Wyoming.

So to chase away the doubts, Bess did what she always did, and talked to her father. Settling on her posterior, the marshal leaned back against the headstone, tilting her face to the wind. She winced, squeezing her eyes tightly closed. "I'm jealous." She opened her eyes and exhaled. "There, I said it, Pop, OK?"

Head laid against the gravestone, Bess plucked a dandelion and stuck the flower stem between her lips, closed her eyes, and was silent, breathing in the fresh air and listening to the winds on the plain; in them or inside herself she listened to the voice of her father only she could hear.

"You know very well who I'm jealous of. That beautiful blond cattle lady with that sexy way about her that makes Joe look at her the way he does. Joe chose going with Laura Holdridge on her cattle drive instead of coming back here to Jackson with me, where he belongs. And I'm sore about it, Pop. That woman got her hooks in him. I hate it."

Breathing in the fresh air, Bess shut her eyes again and communed with spirits of the dead. Now and again she spoke to herself. "Why are you asking me why it bothers me, Joe being with Laura, Pop? You know damn well why I don't want Joe Noose with her."

She spat out the flower.

"Because I want Joe with me." Bess grabbed her hair in both hands and scrunched it up in her fists. She reflected and expelled a wistful, relieved sigh. "No, I'm not really jealous, Pop. Yes, I know Joe doesn't love Laura. He's not going to fall in love with her. Joe's in love with me. I'm the one for him. Like he's the one for me. We both know it. But Joe won't kiss me, Pop, he won't touch me no matter how much I want him to. And I know he wants to. It's because of you, Pop, though it ain't your fault. Joe feels it's his fault you got killed, because if he hadn't gone after Frank Butler and those villainous bounty killers, Butler wouldn't have shot you. Joe blames himself. He feels it's on him I lost my father. Of course it wasn't his fault. It wasn't nobody's fault but the man who pulled the trigger, Frank Butler. But Joe's gonna spend the rest of his life trying to make it up to me and have my back. Whenever he gets romantic feelings, he feels he's taking advantage of me, which I know is the last thing he'd ever do, Pop. What would you say to Joe if you were here? I wish Joe was here. I miss him something fierce. Joe Noose is the man for me. You'd have really liked him, Pop. He's a good man who fights for what he believes, who knows the difference between right and wrong, and there's no lying in him. He's fearless like you. Lord knows you don't have to worry about Joe treating me good, because all he ever thinks about is being good to me. I love Joe, Pop. With all my heart. And I think Joe loves me, too. Loving each other ain't the problem. The problem is us ever doing anything about it."

She leaned her head back against the stone. "Got any advice for me, Pop?" She cracked a grin and chuckled. "Go to work, huh? Hell, I knew you'd say that."

Getting up off the ground, Bess kissed Nate's headstone, brushed the dirt off the seat of her jeans, pulled back her hair, and strode confidently out the gate to her horse. Swinging into the saddle, the marshal shined her badge with her sleeve, tugged the reins to swing her chestnut mare around, and took off at a determined gallop to the town of Jackson a few miles away.

The town hadn't changed when Marshal Bess rode in. When she walked back into the U.S. Marshal's office the place looked the same as when she left it. Nobody was there but Deputy Nate Sweet, sitting at his desk writing reports. He looked up as she sat down at her desk and all he said was, "It's been quiet, Marshal."

That was all the welcome back Marshal Bess Sugarland needed.

It was not quiet for long.

The three men who barged into Marshal Bess's office an hour later were mad as hell, saying they had business that needed to be taken care of right away. She turned from her desk to the men, all of whom she knew, ready to be town marshal again. "Zachary, Moses, and Levi, what can I do for you boys?"

"I want my wife, Marshal," Zachary Laidlaw boomed in the minister's oratory delivery he used from the pulpit of the Lutheran church on Sundays. His voice projected, and so did the booze Bess could smell clear across her desk. His eyes were muddy and bloodshot.

Not liking the look, Bess rose and walked around the table to face them, up close and personal. Leaning her butt back against her desk, she crossed her arms and eyed the three surly men. "Haven't seen her, but I'll look around my office and see if she turns up."

Laidlaw didn't laugh, and the minister gave her a look she didn't appreciate.

"Well, my humor, I suppose, is pretty rusty, because as you probably noticed I have been away for several months on U.S. Marshals business—a manhunt, in case any of you were wondering—and my able deputy, Nate Sweet, has been handling my duties. That ends today and I hereby resume my full powers and authorities as U.S. Marshal of the town of Jackson. I'm here now, so you boys can just relax while I get everything straight. Minister Laidlaw here is looking for his wife. What are you two here for?"

"Our wives, they gone, too."

"We want 'em back."

The look of incredulity Bess Sugarland gave Nate Sweet made her fellow lawman struggle to keep a straight face. "There been a run on spouses while I been gone, Deputy?"

"So it appears." Nate chuckled.

Rearing to his feet, the bristling Minister Laidlaw smashed his clenched fist down on the marshal's desk in a violent rage. The papers jumped but Bess didn't. *"The point is, Marshal, our wives have run away and we want to know what the hell the U.S. Marshal's office intends to do about it!"*

The female lawman didn't blink. "The first thing I'm going to do is break that hand next time you punch my desk, so you won't be able to read scripture or wipe your ass."

He stood, fuming, locking eyes with her, radiating ugly anger.

"Do I make myself clear?" she snapped.

Zachary Laidlaw broke the stare-down, standing unsteadily with his fists clenched at his sides in his frugal black ministry cloak, a red net of broken capillaries in his florid face.

"Sit down and shut up." The minister sat. "I don't care if you are a minister, you watch your manners while you're in the U.S. Marshal's office, *my office*, or I'll teach you some."

Looking the three men in the eye each in turn, the marshal elicited cooperative nods from each before continuing. Uncrossing her arms, she leaned back against her desk.

"So let's start over with the part where you three men came in here because your wives ran away." She took her pad out and scribbled a note with her pencil. "What are your wives' names?"

"My wife's name is Vera."

"Vera Laidlaw."

"Correct."

"Beulah. Beulah Best. I'm Levi Best."

"Which is why I'm guessing you both share the same last name," Bess quipped, shifting her gaze to Moses Farmer. "Your wife is Millicent, everybody calls her Millie. Just so happens I know Millie pretty good. Where's she gone off to, Mose?"

"Puzzleface."

"Puzzle-what?" the marshal asked.

"Puzzleface."

"What's that?" Confused, Bess glanced over to Sweet for clarification, and her deputy made a placating gesture with his hands, a worried expression on his face.

"A lot's gone on since you been gone, Marshal. I'll fill you in on the details directly." The marshal was still watching him. "Puzzleface is a gambler who's new in town."

"They're shacking up with him!" Levi cried.

"Puzzleface stole our wives!" Mose choked.

"It's a good thing I'm back." The marshal sighed. "I go away for a few months and the whole town falls apart." Studying the faces of the angry husbands, Bess considered the whole situation, tapping her boot.

For a minute or two nobody said a word, then Moses spoke up. "You're the law in this town, Marshal. I knew your father, Nate, and he was a great lawman."

"I know that."

"You wear his badge now."

"Yes, I do."

"That badge means it's your job to enforce the law and get our wives back."

"That is not exactly the law, Mose."

"It's the marshal's job to enforce our rights and bring our wives home." Mose Farmer fumbled.

The men were all flustered; the meeting with the marshal clearly had not gone as they expected. The three angry husbands didn't like the circumspect expression the lady marshal had gotten on her face.

"What right do you have to force your wife to do something against her will?" Bess asked softly.

"Husband rights!" Levi sputtered.

"Property rights," Minister Laidlaw solemnly declared.

"Excuse me?" Bess blinked, taken aback.

"My wife is my property and I want her back."

Marshal Bess whistled, shaking her head in disgust. "Well, boys, all I can say is it's no surprise why your brides ran off on you. I'll see what I can do about getting them back." Rising to her feet, the marshal showed the men to the door with a shooing gesture. "Get out of my office while I look into this. Go on and git. My deputy and I will be in touch." She slammed the door in the husbands' faces before they could get another word in, muffling their protests, and the sound on the porch of the men's departing boots shortly followed.

Standing by the window, Marshal Bess thoughtfully watched the three husbands amble off down the street, wildly gesticulating in commiseration as they entered a saloon. She felt Deputy Sweet at her side. "So who the hell is Puzzleface?" she asked him.

"It's a long story. I'm getting ready to tell you, just trying to figure where to start."

"Start at the beginning and end it by telling me what the hell Puzzleface is doing with three married women who ran off on their husbands."

"It ain't what you think," Deputy Nate Sweet said as he grabbed the bottle of Idaho whiskey from his desk drawer and poured some into two shot glasses that he set down on Marshal Bess's desk.

Then he sat down across from her and told her the whole story.

Well, almost.

CHAPTER 12

"We got company."

Joe Noose walked up to Laura Holdridge as she fetched herself a cup of coffee from the steaming pot on the stove. The outfit had broken for lunch, and the rovers were gathered around the chuck wagon. The herd stood grazing a hundred yards to the east, stretching as far as the eye could see.

The bounty hunter was pointing to the northwest, the way they had come, and as his gloved finger drew the cattlewoman's gaze, she saw the horses and riders approaching a half mile away.

"Trouble?" Joe asked her, watching her narrow squint.

"I don't know."

"Want me to give the outfit the heads-up?"

"I'd be obliged."

Laura stood with her arms crossed, hair blown about her face in the wind as she squinted impassively at the men and horses growing ever larger as they came on at an unthreatening but unwavering pace.

Walking a few paces to the chow line, Noose clapped his hands to get the rovers' attention and gestured with his arm for them to follow. "Men and horses coming, men. Bring your weapons. But we don't know if it's trouble or not, so no quick trigger fingers." The wranglers all put down their plates, grabbing rifles from their saddle scabbards and checking the loads on their revolvers as they fell in behind the bounty hunter, who returned to the cattlewoman's side to see that the posse had nearly reached camp.

At fifty yards, fifteen men pulled up their horses and two wagons and the man who rode in the vanguard dismounted.

The leader of the posse was dressed like an English gentleman in a black suit, silk vest, and bowler hat beneath a weathered leather duster. A gold pocket watch on a fob glinted in his vest pocket. The tall man was in his forties, fit and very groomed, with dashing features behind a waxed blond handlebar mustache, and sideburns. He advanced with a confident, aristocratic stride on costly British riding boots that reached the knees of his fancy riding breeches, attired like a robber baron. Beside the pocket watch, a brace of Colt Dragoon revolvers came into view strapped to his gold-buckled belt. The gentleman stranger walked up to Laura Holdridge, doffed his bowler hat, and extended his gloved hand. "My name is Cole Starborough," the man said with an East Coast upper-crust American accent. "Do I have the pleasure of speaking to Mrs. Laura Holdridge of the Bar H Ranch, ma'am?"

Joe Noose instantly hated this man on sight, with every fiber of his being. *Why, he wasn't sure, not at first.*

Laura Holdridge did not shake Cole Starborough's hand, so he withdrew it. "I am she," the cattlewoman replied, crossing her arms while holding his gaze. "You know who I am but I've never seen you before in my life. State your business."

"You heard the lady," added Joe Noose, his unblinking gaze locked on Cole Starborough.

The gentleman smiled, revealing white teeth below his waxed handlebar mustache that looked sharp, like they had been filed to points. "I represent the Bar T Ranch, and these men are my operatives. Your drivers can stand at ease, Mrs. Holdridge. We mean no harm."

"Maybe, maybe not, Mrs. Holdridge," Joe Noose said, standing right behind his employer, hand poised over the butt of his holstered Colt Peacemaker. "But this ain't no chance encounter. These boys have been shadowing us the last fifty or so miles."

Starborough's gaze met the bounty hunter's and held it a few seconds too long.

"State your business or move on, mister," Laura said.

"I am here to make you a business proposition." The gentleman presented an embossed business card in his expensive black-leather-gloved fingers. The writing on it was in fancy script. She took it and her face visibly darkened as she read it. Her eyes were bullets when her gaze lifted from the card and drilled into Starborough's unblinking gaze. "You're one of Crispin Calhoun's men."

"I am Mr. Calhoun's junior partner at the Bar T Ranch, here on official business as Mr. Calhoun's representative, sent at the personal request of Mr. Calhoun himself."

"What business would that be, Mr. Starborough?"

"I'm here to buy your cattle."

Laura laughed.

"Take every last head off your hands."

She laughed harder.

"Cash on the barrelhead, Mrs. Holdridge." Cole snapped his fingers and a husky, well-dressed operative in a Stetson reached into his saddlebag.

Noose's hand dropped to the handle of his revolver, ready to draw, fire, and blow the man clean off his horse, but the only thing the man withdrew from his saddlebag was a leather satchel that he tossed to Starborough. Joe kept his hand on his gun until the unflappable leader of Calhoun's men unsnapped the gold clasps and opened the bag.

It contained piles of hundred-dollar bills wrapped in bundles. The satchel was heavy with cold, hard cash.

Behind Noose and Laura, the six wranglers had taken a few steps forward to eye the money in the open case Starborough held before their trail boss.

"How much is in there?" the cattlewoman asked with a raised eyebrow.

"Four thousand dollars, Mrs. Holdridge."

"I have five hundred head of cattle, Mr. Starborough, but you probably already know that. You're offering me eight dollars a head. Those are Texas prices and this is Wyoming. In Cheyenne, my prime steers are going to auction at thirty to forty dollars a head. In other words, the money is an insult, but you probably already know that, too."

Cole Starborough chuckled and smoothed his waxed blond mustache. "With all due respect, ma'am, you'll never make it to Cheyenne. We both know that. Not in time to deliver your herd before the cattlemen's auction ends in less than three weeks. Cheyenne is two hundred and fifty miles from here, through the bowels of Wyoming. Nobody could drive a herd that far across that kind of terrain, even if they weren't shorthanded in their crew, as you appear to be."

At the last, Laura's eyes turned steely and suspicious.

"Respectfully, Mr. Calhoun is offering you a good price for your entire herd of livestock, in cash. Right here in this satchel. Take it. Then you can turn these steers over to my operatives and myself, we'll drive them the rest of the way, and you and your outfit can take it easy, turn around, and get back to the Bar H. Because respectfully, Mrs. Holdridge, eight dollars a head is better than nothing at all, and nothing is what you're gonna have when you get to Cheyenne weeks after the auction has closed, when you will have to turn around and drive these cows all the way back, assuming you still have any rovers left to drive them."

"The lady just gave you her answer," Noose snarled, baring his teeth.

"I was asking your boss, not you." Starborough bared his own, which looked like fangs, sharp as they were.

"You asked me and my answer is no. But before you ride that cash back to Calhoun, there is one thing I want to know from you, Mr. Starborough."

"And that would be what, ma'am?"

"Are you the one who's been killing my men?"

The gentleman henchman looked like he'd been slapped, the color leeching out of his cheeks on a face that turned the color of curdled milk. "Did you just accuse me of being a murderer?" he whispered, aghast.

"You're Crispin Calhoun's man, aincha? I wouldn't put anything past Calhoun, who'll do anything to see I don't get my stock to Cheyenne, because he don't like the competition, especially when it's a woman. You work for the bastard, so I'll ask you one last time if you've been killing my crew following his orders."

Starborough stiffened and his eyes went flat as he screwed his bowler hat onto his head. "I won't dignify that with an answer." Then he smiled courteously. "So regarding Mr. Calhoun's offer to purchase your cattle, I take it I'm to tell my employer your answer is no."

"Tell your boss this." The cattlewoman leaned forward and got nose to nose with the henchman. "We're going to Cheyenne and when we get there, I'm gonna shove five hundred head of cattle all the way up Crispin Calhoun's ass, and you'll be sitting on the horns, you snake oil son of a bitch."

Joe needed all his willpower to bite back a grin.

Cole Starborough considered Laura a long moment, then smiled with sharp teeth, tipping his hat. "Safe journey, Mrs. Holdridge." Closing the satchel, he tossed it up to his other operative, who dropped it back in his saddlebag, then turned his back and walked away toward one of the wagons.

"He didn't deny killing your drivers," Noose said.

"No, but he looked mortified at the accusation, didn't you think?"

"Reckon I'm gonna have me a word with that man."

"Joe—"

But Joe Noose had already strode off after Cole Starborough.

* * *

"When a man's been in prison, he can never wash out the smell, no matter how hard he scrubs." The hard look Joe Noose gave Cole Starborough told the stranger Joe saw right through him, and all those expensive clothes and fancy grooming didn't fool Noose, who knew Cole came from dirt just like he did.

Starborough lifted his leg and put his boot on the upper spoke of a supply-wagon wheel. There was a vague insult to the gesture, a display of casual disregard, as if he owned his wagon and the herd it belonged to, but like a lot Joe sensed about this smooth customer, it was nothing he could be called out on. The English riding boot was of the finest leather Joe had ever seen before. Noticing Noose looking at the boot, Cole took a handkerchief out of his vest, spat on it, and cleaned the trail dust off the toe and heel of his boot. "Imported from London. Custom made," he said. "Fifty dollars a pair." Still slowly wiping his boot, without moving his head, the henchman swiveled his eye to meet the bounty hunter's gaze with a surprising force, demonstrating Starborough was tougher than he looked and not to be trifled with. A tincture of mocking in his voice, he asked, "How much did your boots cost?"

Noose didn't react. Both of them knew Joe's old cowboy boots had seen far too many miles, the stitching attesting to a lot of mending.

After a beat, Starborough rolled down his trousers over his boot. "Looks like you can use a new pair, sir." He stood up, faced Joe Noose, looked him square in the eye, and tipped his bowler hat. "Hope we can do business. By that I mean, your boss lady and me."

The dapper gentleman turned to walk back to his horse but halted after two steps, as if he had an itch he had forgotten to scratch, then looked back over his shoulder with a grin Joe wanted to punch off his face and said, "A snake sheds its skin four times a year, it don't need to scrub." With a tip of his bowler hat, Cole Starborough's parting words were, *"Ave tenebris Dominus."*

"Up yours," Joe replied to the henchman's back as he departed.

The bounty hunter leaned against the wagon, crossed his arms and considered the conversation he'd just had. Joe now believed Cole Starborough to be a dangerous man. He hated him the minute he laid eyes on him, and after their encounter hated his guts even more. The bastard was going to be trouble. But Noose knew how this would end.

He was not a superstitious man, but a few times in his life he'd had premonitions and gotten a glimpse of what lay ahead. Mostly what he had seen came to pass. Now, watching Calhoun's hatchet man gallop off with his men, Joe Noose had one of his premonitions, knowing for a true fact Cole Starborough was a man he was going to kill.

"Before this thing is done I'm going to have to kill that man," Cole Starborough muttered, lowering his solid gold-plated steel spyglass with a gloved hand and handing it off to his subordinate.

"Which man?" Earl Moore's brow furrowed as he hefted the heavy unwieldy telescope extended to its full three-foot length, peering through the eyepiece. Aiming the field glass at the procession of cattle stretching clear across the horizon, he saw they were on the move.

"The big stud riding point," Cole said, pointing. Moore

focused the lens on the front of the wagon train, where Joe Noose was riding lookout on the cattle drive a mile away.

"Why you gonna kill him for?"

"Because if I don't he's going to kill me."

"What did you ever do to him?"

"I was born."

"You been reading too many books, Cole. Instead of spouting philosophy to me, save those flowery words for Mrs. Holdridge, blow sunshine in her ear and sweet-talk her into selling that herd."

"She won't sell. Any fool can see it ain't about the money for that stubborn woman, Earl."

"It's always about the money. Calhoun is being penny-wise and pound-foolish. Can't we offer her a few bucks more a head and put paid on it?"

"She won't take it."

"If it ain't about the money, what does she want?"

"What I think?" Starborough chuckled. "I think that women wants to do exactly what she told me: drive her five hundred steers all the way up Crispin Calhoun's ass, horns first."

Earl Moore laughed. "Fair enough. But where does that leave us? It was our job to carry out Calhoun's orders to buy that herd, and he's a man who don't take no for an answer."

"Calhoun gave us one order," Cole sharply retorted, holding up one black-leather-gloved finger in front of Moore's nose. "The order is Laura Holdridge's herd must not reach Cheyenne. The cattle drive must be stopped by any means necessary." His black eyes fierce behind his curled waxed mustache sometimes made Starborough resemble a villain in a Victorian melodrama when his blood was up. Now that he had his subordinate's attention, he lowered his voice. "That is our order."

"And we failed."

"Don't be a fool, Earl." Starborough looked at Moore like he was an idiot. "Calhoun made me his junior partner at the Bar T Ranch and put me in charge of this operation for a reason. Tell me, why is that?"

"Because you kill people for him."

"Wrong."

"Because you do all his dirty work."

"A great man like Calhoun never gets his hands dirty. He has people for that, and I'm just one of them. That isn't why he put me in charge."

"Hellfire, Cole. I don't know what the heck you're talking about half the time."

Cole leaned in so close he was nose to nose with Moore. "Calhoun made me his right hand and put me in charge because I use *this*"—Starborough tapped his own temple with his gloved forefinger—"*before* I use *this*." Cole tapped the handle of his holstered Colt revolver.

"We all know how smart you say you think you are, Cole."

Starborough drew his revolver lightning fast and the barrel was between Moore's eyes before he had time to flinch, and by the time he did flinch, Cole was spinning the pistol around his trigger finger back into his holster in one smooth deadly move that took under a second. His face broke out in a dashing grin and he laughed contemptuously as browbeaten Moore's head seemed to shrink into his shoulders.

"Follow along, Moore. I'll walk you through it again. Listen and learn. What have I told you is the most important part of any plan?"

"Have a plan B."

"Right. Plan A was buy the lady out, but she didn't want to sell, which means plan A failed and now we go to . . ."

When Moore looked up he had the look of a beat dog. "P-plan B," he stuttered.

"Didn't hear you."

"Plan B."

"Exactly." Cole nodded condescendingly like he was speaking to a child. "We go to plan B. Subterfuge and sabotage. Buy off her crew. Disable her wagons. Whatever it takes. And I have my spy."

"What spy?"

"I have a man inside Laura Holdridge's outfit." Starborough smiled, very pleased with himself.

"You didn't tell me that."

"I don't tell you a lot of things. Now you know. One of her wranglers is on the Calhoun payroll, not hers. He's been my eyes and ears since they hit the trail, sending me reports. And he'll do more than that if I need him to."

"What if plan B fails?"

"We have plan C. Take the herd by force. It's our contingency plan. The last resort. If we have to kill the outfit and steal those cattle, we do it in the canyons before Cheyenne, where it's a hundred miles of nothing but badlands without another living soul. They call that part of Wyoming 'the Big Empty.' Nobody will ever find the bodies because the Big Empty tells no tales."

"I hope it don't come to that."

"You got a problem if it does?"

Moore threw a look to the other thirteen operatives cleaning their guns a few hundred yards away. "I knew what I signed up for. The rest of these boys Calhoun hired are triggermen and I reckoned gunwork was going to be involved. It ain't my first rodeo. I just hope it ain't my last." His gaze lingered on a formidable freighter wagon the posse had nicknamed, *the war wagon.*

"You worry too much. You need to trust me." Starborough said.

"Because you got it all figured out."

"Yes, I best believe I do."

"For all our sakes, you better hope so. If that herd gets to Cheyenne, Calhoun will murder us."

"We're stopping that cattle drive, one way or the other. Failure is not an option. The only way those steers are getting to the cattlemen's auction is with us driving them in with the Bar T brand stamped on their asses. Follow my orders and we'll all be getting a fat bonus. Just remember this: Calhoun is the boss, but he can't be here and for this operation he put me in charge, so that means out here on the trail, I'm the boss."

"You're the boss."

"Any more questions?"

"Just one." Moore shifted uncomfortably. "Those wranglers of Mrs. Holdridge's she says were murdered. Did Calhoun have anything to do with that? Did you?"

"That's the second time today somebody's asked me that question," Starborough snapped, brow furrowed in visible agitation. He turned away from Moore and stalked back to his horse, saddled up, and signaled the others with a wave of his arm. Moore and the rest of the posse mounted their horses and rode after their boss.

All day Calhoun's seasoned operatives rode with stealth, shadowing the cattle drive, riding parallel to the five hundred head of steers, never closer than a mile away, invisible to the Bar H outfit but sticking to Laura Hold-ridge's herd like glue.

CHAPTER 13

At a full gallop, Cole Starborough's posse got ahead of Laura Holdridge's herd fairly quickly because the cattle moved much slower. Calhoun's operatives had the advantage of speed and the necessity of haste—the canyon pass was on the map, and her outfit would need to get the cattle across it, so it was important Cole got there first.

An hour later the posse had ridden up a wide natural trail of rock and dirt between a mountain to one side and a towering column of granite jutting against the sky on the other. Starborough put up his hand for his operatives to stop and the posse halted. He turned his horse to face them, pointing on ahead where the trail continued through the woods and grasslands. "Ride due east half a mile and wait for me. I'll be there directly," he said, adding with a nasty grin, "and cover your ears."

As the fourteen riders galloped off, Cole dismounted and grabbed a six-stick cluster of dynamite from his saddlebag, setting the dynamite on the ground and tying on a very long fuse. Striking a match, he lit the fuse and as it burned down in sizzling sputters of sparks toward the high explosives, Starborough was away on his horse.

As the procession of longhorn steers cleared a rise, the granite pinnacle of the pass came into view. In the driver's seat of her covered wagon, Laura Holdridge pointed at the trailhead and yelled to her wranglers, "There's the pass, boys, we're a third of the way to Cheyenne, right on schedule—"

Before she could finish her sentence came a deafening explosion; the air was sledgehammered by a colossal low-register *boom* that shook the ground, making the horses rear and spooking the cattle, who felt the jarring shock wave beneath their hooves. The rovers all saw it, struggling to control their horses: far off in the distance, before their startled eyes, the granite peak of the canyon pass blew up in a massive detonation of dynamite. It was there, then it was gone. The surprised outfit looked on in disbelief as the top of the massif disintegrated in great turbulent clouds of flying rocks and dirt that shot skyward, raining down in an endless shower of stone and gravel. When the smoke began to clear as the echo of the blast faded, the pass lay in rubble.

Exchanging alarmed, grim glances with Noose and Brubaker on their horses, Laura then cracked the whip on the team pulling her wagon, her rig still in motion, yelling at the rovers to push on, and the outfit kept driving the herd, heading toward the pass to survey the damage and see if it was as bad as they all feared.

It was worse.

The ride took them fifteen minutes, and when they got there, Joe Noose knew exactly what they would find, that there was no longer any way through. Jumping out of the covered wagon after pulling her team to a standstill, Laura Holdridge walked slowly ahead past the halted horses of her dismayed wranglers, coughing in the thick hanging smoke and dust. It cleared to show that the blasted pass lay in a fifty-foot-high pile of rubble, the trail buried beneath tons of boulders and big rocks; an impassable barrier the cattle drive could not hope to penetrate.

"The damn posse did this," said Noose.

"Damn right that damn posse did this," agreed Laura. "That hatchet man of Calhoun's, Cole Starborough he said his name was, well, he probably set the dynamite and lit the fuse himself. I knew that man was the type to play dirty. Well, I got news for him! He don't know me if he thinks I'm gonna let this slow me down! If he thinks destroying this one trail means we can't go no farther he better think again, because there's lots of trails, and if we can't find one, we'll make one! It's gonna take more than a few sticks of dynamite to stop us from getting this herd to Cheyenne! Turn these cows south, boys!"

She didn't have to tell her crew twice. They had plenty of heart. With whoops and hollers, the wranglers began steering the five hundred cows down an embankment.

Joe smiled as he watched the outfit's unflappable, indefatigable spirit; in the face of any obstacle, these men just took it in stride and pushed on, and it gave him fresh admiration for both the rovers and their trail boss.

"I hope that posse sees this ain't stopping our progress,

not for one damn second," a tight-jawed defiant Laura crowed. "Especially that Starborough character."

"He's probably watching us right now," observed Joe, riding along with the herd.

"Then I hope he sees this!" She grinned as she lifted her arm high.

And held up her upraised middle finger.

At that very minute, Cole Starborough was indeed watching the outfit through his pair of field glasses half a mile up the trail, his icy grin of triumph frozen on his dashing face when he saw the cattlewoman's rude hand gesture. He lowered the spyglass with a frowning scowl.

"Think they're gonna give up and turn around?" wondered Earl Moore, sitting on the horse beside him, his tone of voice indicating he thought the question rhetorical.

"No, I do not," replied Cole, handing him the binoculars. "But neither am I."

"What's our next move?"

"We ride ten miles to the next county, same place they're going but we'll get there a lot quicker. I intend to have a few words with the local sheriff in Rawlins." His duster flapping, Cole Starborough swung his huge steed around and charged off with the posse at full gallop right behind him.

The posse reached the outskirts of the town of Rawlins after an hour of easy riding across country. Cole halted them on the field outside of town, telling them it would be easier for him to talk to the sheriff alone, and for his operatives to wait. The gentleman henchman didn't seem to think this would take long.

He rode off alone into town, making a calculated impressive entrance aboard his stallion that always struck awe in the yokels, who regarded him like a king in their midst. Starborough saw the heads of the local farmers turn as he rode off alone on his big black quarterhorse in his custom leather saddle, in his expensive duster and bowler hat that made him look like an English gentleman. Cole was a peacock by nature, and liked being a dashing and formidable blade. The act wouldn't fool anybody back in Virginia, but here in the West, folks ate it up. Starborough was so glad he had gone west. The frontier suited his nature.

"Sheriff, my name is Cole Starborough and I work for Crispin Calhoun of the Calhoun Cattle Company and Bar T Ranch. May I present my card?"

The henchman smoothly withdrew an embossed business card. The sheriff took it and slipped it in his pocket. "A little far west, aincha, son?"

"I don't understand."

"The cattle auction's in Cheyenne in a few weeks. I thought Calhoun and every other cattleman doesn't miss that every year."

"That's quite true, Sheriff." Cole sized up the lawman as one of the rural irascible peace officers he had plenty of experience handling.

"So that's why I asked what you're doing this far west of Cheyenne, when you should be on the other side of the state," Sheriff Roberts said.

"Yes, I will be going there directly. But first, I need to report a crime, Sheriff."

Sheriff Roberts looked up.

"Well, you came to the right place." The lawman pointed to the badge on his chest, and gave a big smile. "I'm the sheriff and that's my job." He turned toward the small single-story brick building and gestured Cole to follow along. "Come on in and I'll take your report."

Dumb hick, Starborough thought, every bit the gentleman as he politely followed the lawman into the sheriff's office, removing his hat as he entered.

He sat across from the sheriff's desk and nodded to the three deputies cleaning guns and washing out the empty jail cell. *Crackers*. But it helped that the sheriff had a few deputies for the task Cole came here to give him.

Truth was, Cole Starborough loved the West but hated the cowboys and regular people who lived there, people whom he considered uneducated, ignorant, and beneath him. Cole was a highly educated man but he didn't come out West to make friends, he came because it was *lawless*. The American frontier was the last savage, untamed place where a real man could indulge his true nature, in blood up to his elbows, and make his fortune. He could let the beast in himself loose and take what he wanted; his cattleman boss had given him his opportunity, and let Cole Starborough off the leash.

"'*Nature red in tooth and claw*,'" Cole muttered to himself, lost in thought.

"What did you say, son?" Sheriff Roberts looked up from getting his pencil and paper out of the drawer. "Okay now, let's see."

The lawman was staring at him, brows knitting, with a

look of fascination. Cole raised his eyebrow. "Is there a problem, Sheriff?"

"Son, anybody ever tell you that you look like General Custer?"

"I'll take that as a compliment, sir."

"You are both handsome devils."

"Funny you should mention that. George Armstrong Custer was in the class ahead of me at West Point."

"You went to West Point?"

"Indeed I did. Custer and I have blond hair and favor the same mustache and hairstyle, so both of us were mistaken for each other all the time back attending school in Virginia. Excellent fellow."

"Bet you wish you were as great a general as he was, huh?"

Cole's eyes hardened. "My grades were higher than Custer's. George was at the bottom of his class when he graduated in '61, did you know that?" Sheriff Roberts shook his head. "Myself, I was in the top third of my class when I left school."

"You didn't graduate from West Point?"

Starborough slowly shook his head.

"A prestigious school like that, why not?"

"Two reasons. First, I wanted to get in the cattle business because that's where the money is and I knew my military training would come in handy out here on the frontier, as it has proven to be. I am junior partner in the fastest-growing cattle ranch in these United States, and I expect to make my fortune before I'm fifty."

The small-town working-class Wyoming sheriff was unimpressed by a fancy man bragging about money. "And the other?"

"I beg your pardon?"

"Reason. You said there were two reasons you left West Point."

"I didn't want to end up like Custer."

"How so?"

"With a hundred arrows up my ass and a hundred dollars in my wallet."

Roberts's mouth dropped.

Cole's face broke into a brilliant dashing grin flashing pearly rows of sharpened sharklike teeth. Sheriff Roberts couldn't tell if Calhoun's foreman was making a joke or not, but figured he must be, because showing that kind of disrespect to a great general in the Indian wars and American hero in Wyoming, so near the Little Big Horn River, was begging to get punched in the mouth. On the other hand, getting his fist anywhere near those disturbing razor-sharp teeth could cost you a handful of fingers, so it all evened out. Anyway, the small talk was over.

"You came here saying you had a crime to report, Mr. Starborough. State your business."

"Yes, Sheriff. As you know, the cattle business is a highly organized profession and in my position as Crispin Calhoun's junior partner I am fully informed on every detail of legal and illegal activity among my cattlemen counterparts."

"Get to the point."

"For the ethics of the industry, Mr. Calhoun believes, as I do, it is the responsibility of the cattle business to police itself; therefore, when we learn of illegal activity among members of our profession, it is our responsibility to report it to the authorities, and that, Sheriff Roberts, sir, is why I am here today."

"Go on."

"You need to know that a cattle drive is coming through your county today with stolen cattle in the herd. The trail boss is named Laura Holdridge of the Bar H Ranch in Consequence, an outfit notorious for criminal activity, and stealing rustled cattle is just the beginning of her crimes . . ."

Now Cole had Sheriff Roberts's full attention. The lawman was writing down every damn lie that Starborough told him.

CHAPTER 14

It was a two-hour ride out to Puzzleface Ranch, and Deputy Nate Sweet rode alone, journeying west of the town of Jackson to where the spread lay on the banks of the Snake River a mile east of the Teton Pass.

It was a very secluded and private piece of property; the big ranch house and corral were cradled in the bosom of a deep verdant valley surrounded by a forest of aspen and birch trees that came into view long before the tall gate with a wooden "P" atop did. As the deputy rode up the dirt path into the ranch, he spotted six saddled horses in the corral; the women at the house enjoying Puzzleface's hospitality no doubt were the owners.

Deputy Sweet had gotten to know Puzzleface quite well a few months ago while Marshal Bess Sugarland was off hunting a serial killer with Joe Noose; he knew things about the enigmatic figure the lady marshal did not know, and the truth about Puzzleface would surprise and even astound her.

Deputy Sweet knew Puzzleface's secret, but had given his word he would never tell, and Nate was a man of his word. The whole ride over, he struggled with the rightness of this. Because he believed Bess needed to know who Puzzleface was, if she was going to be able to enforce the law, and it was his duty as a sworn Deputy U.S. Marshal for him to tell her. Everybody in Jackson Hole had the wrong idea about Puzzleface. So did Bess. Those kinds of misunderstandings meant things could go sideways in a hurry and people could get hurt. It was going to come down to his duty or his word—he couldn't honor both—and that's why he was here, because Deputy Sweet needed to talk to Puzzleface directly.

The slight figure on the big horse came into view as the lawman rode up the path toward the house . . . Puzzleface waited, ready to intercept him.

From a distance Sweet could already recognize the trademark black waxed mustache, goatee, and sideburns, but was not yet close enough to see the facial scar that gave "Puzzleface" Taylor his nom de guerre. Puzzleface wasn't short, wasn't tall, of medium build and height. The man whose horse blocked his path had the elegant air of a dandy, dressed, as usual, in a well-tailored black coat over a green silk vest, a ruffled white shirt, red suspenders, and worn-out polished cowboy boots. No gun belt was visible because Puzzleface, who was never heeled, didn't wear one, the deputy already knew. A weathered Stetson with a brim that had lost its shape sat on his small head. There was something of the riverboat gambler in his appearance and Puzzleface always took pride in his grooming. He remained in his saddle on his big Arabian that was a lot of horse for a little man, and watched Sweet approach.

The deputy rode up and they exchanged a friendly handshake.

Laying eyes on Puzzleface for the first time in weeks,

Sweet was again struck how the face staring back at him captured your attention; behind the heavy goatee and waxed mustache, Puzzleface Taylor had a fine bone structure with generous lips and surprisingly sensitive brown eyes in a delicate face marred by the jagged scar shaped like a jigsaw running from his left cheek, through the top and bottom of the left side of his lip, to the chin. The scar was the first thing you saw, but once you got past that you noticed the eyes, and those soulful eyes pulled you in. "What brings you out here, Nate?"

"Marshal's back," the deputy replied.

"I see." Puzzleface swung his gaze to meet Sweet's in the opposite saddle. "Does she know my secret?"

"No."

"She doesn't know who I am?"

"I didn't tell her. Nobody else could have told her. Only Doctor Jane and me know."

"You gave your word."

"Relax. I didn't tell the marshal anything." *Yet* he almost added.

Ever observant, the gambler picked up on the slight hesitation in the way the lawman's lips moved, so his own reply was measured and careful. "Good. She doesn't know."

"But . . ."

"What?"

"But Bess needs to know."

Fiercely Puzzleface shook his head *no*, as Nate knew that he would the whole ride down, but Sweet had to say his piece.

"Listen to me. Now Marshal Bess is back, she's the law in town, not me, I'm just her deputy, not wearing the marshal badge no more. That was just temporary while she was away on assignment. Marshal Bess is the law, she's in charge if there's trouble, and there is . . ."

Sliding a glance across the horses to the deputy who paused for emphasis, the gambler's circumspect gaze clouded with caution as the lawman continued.

"If there's trouble, it's the marshal who has to handle it. She needs to be informed about you if she's going to protect your person and your property, because right now in Jackson there's loads of misunderstanding where you're concerned, and plenty of folks in town have got the wrong idea about you. And the marshal's one of them."

Shifting uncomfortably in the saddle, the small man simply shrugged. "I'm not bothering anyone, Nate. I'm a peaceful human being. Don't even own a gun. I bought the Puzzleface Ranch from my legitimate gambling winnings, and live quietly on my spread with a few women who are staying in my house."

"That's the thing that I rode here to talk to you about. Those women staying with you have husbands. Husbands who want them back."

"They don't want to go back."

"Why not?"

"They can't."

"Why can't they?"

Puzzleface stared straight ahead, jaw tightening, stubbornly closemouthed.

"Why can't these women go back to their husbands?" the deputy pressed.

"That's their business."

Sweet adopted a tougher tone. "And it's their husbands' business, who made it the marshal's business, which makes it my business." Deputy Sweet pulled his horse alongside

Puzzleface and got close. "Listen up, Puzzleface. There hasn't been this much talk since we locked up that wildcat lady outlaw Bonny Kate Valance last summer. The talk in town is you're keeping a harem of married women in your house committing adultery and you are engaged in fornication with other men's wives. They're accusing you of committing acts of moral indecency at Puzzleface Ranch. That talk has gotten back to Marshal Bess."

Shaking his head, Puzzleface chuckled softly, twisting his waxy mustache. "They think I would be with a woman."

"Of course they think that. They don't know any better."

"You have a point."

"So you see how this looks?" Sweet sighed.

"Appearances are deceiving and people are stupid. I don't care what people think." Puzzleface shrugged. "Let the good people of Jackson think whatever they want, Nate. Adultery is not against the law."

"But prostitution is." The deputy's eyes narrowed. "And people claim you're running a brothel." Puzzleface laughed. Sweet didn't. "Running an unlicensed whorehouse is against the law and the marshal can lawfully ride out here and raid your home and lock you and those runaway brides in jail. Whoring-out married women. Whose angry husbands are getting ready to grab their guns and ride out here and take their wives back by force."

"If they come on my land that's trespassing, and if they force their wives to go with them that's kidnapping, and you and the marshal have to arrest them—"

"Which ain't gonna do you any damn good if these boys burn your house down or shoot you and their wives, because you may not carry a gun, Puzzleface, but those pissed-off husbands certainly do, and they'll use 'em.

Trust me. There's big trouble coming, very soon, unless this gets sorted out with these wives. And this is why I'm telling you, Puzzleface, you got to let Marshal Bess Sugarland in on your secret so she understands. She's the law for Chrissake. Because otherwise the marshal can't help but get the wrong idea. And she can't do her job."

"You can't tell her," came the same reply.

Deputy Sweet sighed, seeing the shadows in Puzzleface's eyes and knowing all the reasons those shadows were there.

"Nobody else can know."

Deputy Sweet nodded. Taking off his hat, he sat in the saddle and looked at the heavy-beamed two-story cabinstyle ranch house a hundred yards away. In the big windows, oval shapes of female faces were pressed to the glass. It gave him a thought. Nate swung his gaze back to Puzzleface and jerked his gloved thumb toward Puzzleface Ranch. "Let me come inside, meet these women, have a few words, see them for myself, just confirm for the U.S. Marshal's office the women are all OK and not being held against their will. Then I can ride back to Marshal Bess and give her my report and then I've done my job, she's done her job, and she can say nothing's going on out here. Fair enough?"

"Fair enough."

They rode up to the big ranch house and tethered the horses by the corral, dismounted, and entered the mudroom together into the cozy warmth of the big house.

"Time to change into something more comfortable." Puzzleface turned to Nate Sweet with a sigh of relief, pulling gloves off of slender fragile hands whose soft fingers touched the facial hair.

Peeled off the mustache.
Peeled off the goatee.
Peeled off the sideburns.
Revealing the woman's lovely young face but for the jigsaw scar that ran from her cheek to her jaw that her gambler husband had once given her.

To escape his violent clutches, the woman named Rachel had disguised herself as a man and called herself Puzzleface. Making her living at poker, traveling far, she came to Jackson masquerading as a gambling man, hoping her husband would never find her, but find her he did. Deputy Nate Sweet had seen to it the husband would never bother Rachel again, and she and the kind, tough deputy had been loyal friends ever since. He protected her secret.

"Rachel," Nate said, tipping his hat. "It's good to see you yourself again."

She mock-curtsied with a bell-like laugh. Rachel then replied in her normal voice a few octaves higher than the low husky one she adopted in her Puzzleface disguise the world knew her as. With a welcoming gesture, Rachel gracefully ushered Nate into the living room.

"Ladies, may I present my good friend Deputy Nate Sweet of the U.S. Marshals Service."

There, three women in robes and pajamas rose to greet him hesitantly and shyly, and she said, "Deputy, I'd like you to meet a few new friends of mine . . ." Rachel introduced the three women, who curtsied. "This is Vera Laidlaw, Beulah Best, and Millicent Farmer. They're staying in my house as my guests."

"Everybody calls me Millie," said Millicent.

Sweet doffed his hat politely. The women were having tea. They wore freshly laundered garments and looked

bathed and fresh, if very nervous in the presence of a
lawman. Nate observed Millie had the remains of a black
eye that was not recent, and Beulah's arm was in a sling.
Rachel saw him notice this. "As you can imagine, those
injuries did not happen here," she said flatly.

"Are you ladies all right?" Sweet asked carefully.

Nods.

"Your husbands are looking for you."

"That's why we're here," said Vera.

"So they can't find us," added Beulah.

"You won't tell them where we are, Deputy, will you?"
pleaded Millie.

"Is the reason you are hiding from your husbands because they hurt you?" the deputy asked gently.

"Oh, no, I broke my arm falling down the stairs
and—" Beulah blustered, but the sharp look from Rachel
and imploring looks from Vera and Millie silenced her.

It didn't take brains to see what was going on here.
Sweet's brow furrowed—if there was one thing that got
his blood up it was a man hitting a woman; he'd seen his
own father do it to his mother enough times. Nate knew
the look of a battered woman all too well, and knew Rachel
did, too. And the deputy knew how to speak to a woman
who had been abused: as gently as possible.

Quietly he sat on the couch across from them, his hat
in his lap, and the three wives sat, too. "Ladies, Rachel is
a friend of mine. I'm not here to take you back to your
husbands, I'm not here to arrest your husbands or get them
in any trouble, but the marshal sent me out here to be sure
you're okay and that you're here at Rachel's house of your
own free will."

"You won't make us leave?" asked Millie tremulously.

"No, Mrs. Farmer, I won't. You're a free woman, married or not, and can stay where you please under the laws of this state."

"What if Zachary, Levi, and Mose come out here and try to make us leave?" asked Vera, worried.

"You don't know what my husband is like when he gets riled or liquored up, Deputy," hastily added Beulah.

"You're on private property, and if your husbands set foot here uninvited, that's trespassing and there are laws against that. The marshal would take a dim view." The wives exchanged urgent, emotional glances, still afraid but more reassured.

In the next room, Deputy Sweet became aware of movement, someone behind the door, trying to stay hidden. He looked toward the doorway. "Whoever you are, I know you're there, so why don't you come out now?"

When she stepped into the doorway, the deputy was surprised to see it was Dr. Jane Stonehill. After Puzzleface had been shot by her husband a few months ago, Sweet had taken her to Dr. Stonehill and together they had discovered the gambler who they thought was a man was really a woman, and became the first two people in town who knew Puzzleface's secret. *Now the three wives made five, Sweet guessed, all the more reason the marshal needed to know too.*

"Hello, Jane," Sweet said, a tinge of sarcasm in his voice. "Suppose I shouldn't be surprised to see you here."

"Good afternoon, Nate." Dr. Jane smiled warmly. "I was just about to change Beulah's bandages." In her arms, she carried a tray with bandages and solvent.

"Don't let me get in the way."

The physician knelt by Beulah and professionally undid her sling and unrolled the bandages. Underneath was an ugly break spotted by livid bruises. Deputy Sweet winced and Dr. Jane looked up at him as she cleaned and redressed the arm. "It's important what Rachel's doing, giving a shelter to these women. You can't make them leave. If they go back to those animals they're married to, one of these women is going to get killed."

Deputy Sweet rose and put on his hat. "I ain't making any of them leave. Just had to come out and see for myself what was going on here, and now I can report back to the marshal. Good day, ladies." Nate tipped his hat with a warm smile.

Rachel rose and walked him to the door, taking him aside to speak privately out of earshot of the others. "What are you going to tell the marshal?"

He looked down at her squarely. "I'd like to tell her more than you want me to. It would help me help her understand what's really going on here."

"You mean tell the marshal who I really am?"

"That's what I mean. She should know."

Rachel's gaze clouded with concern. "What if she tells somebody?"

"She won't. Whether you believe me or not. But right now, the marshal can't help but think that those three women are runaway wives shacking up with a gambling man having his way with them. A lot of public sentiment would support those husbands coming out here and taking their wives home, trespassing or no. If Bess Sugarland knew you are a woman, especially one who has been thumped yourself, I guarantee she would understand about you giving these women sanctuary and providing a safe shelter for them. She'd throw the full weight of the U.S. Marshals Service behind defending you with armed force if necessary. But you won't let me give her that information."

"I can't." Rachel shook her head.

Sweet sighed. "So who are you supposed to be, you living here in Puzzleface's house anyway?"

"His housekeeper."

"You ain't making my job easy, Rachel."

She smiled warmly and kissed him on the cheek. "If it was easy, everybody'd do it," she replied, opening the door for him.

The woman who called herself Puzzleface watched the lanky lawman lope to his horse, mount up and give her a wave, if not exactly a smile, as he rode off back toward Jackson. Rachel watched her friend travel off, the sight of him making her feel warm inside.

Deputy Nate Sweet had shown her there were good men in the world who could be trusted, not just bad ones.

Chapter 15

The entire ride back to Jackson, Deputy Sweet wrestled with his conscience, burdened by the conflict between his sense of professional and moral responsibility, struggling to make up his mind whether his duty as a lawman overrode his personal sense of honor; there was the very real danger that Marshal Bess could make a wrong move dealing with the wives seeking sanctuary at Rachel's house if she were not privy to the information that Puzzleface was a woman. Dire consequences could result, which were in his power to avoid, but to do so meant breaking his word to a friend. Nate was a simple, straightforward man; this was the first time the obligations of his badge had required him to make a complex judgment call.

During the whole lonely ride back, the difficult choice weighed heavily on the young lawman. Two hours later, when he entered town and rode past the saloon, Deputy Sweet decided to go in and have a whiskey, hoping it would clear the confusion from his mind and help him make a decision, resolving by the time he got back to the U.S. Marshal's office he would make up his mind to either tell Marshal Sugarland the truth about Puzzleface or not.

Five minutes after he entered the bar, the matter took care of itself.

Evening settled on Jackson, the vast expanse of sky darkening in the gloaming. The day was coming to a close and the marshal wouldn't begrudge her deputy one drink, since it was close to quitting time, Sweet was thinking as he dismounted his palomino and tied it to the hitching post beside the bar beside several other saddled horses that looked familiar.

The Broadway Bar was a long open room still smelling of cut lumber, the pinewood-planked floor covered with sawdust. It had been recently constructed and open for business only a year. The fanciest fixture was the authentic brass footrail on a long bar running the length of the saloon, but other than a few tables and chairs randomly placed in the space, the bar was unfinished. A few customers sat at one of the tables and several more stood at the bar. Behind the bar, shelves were fully stocked with bottles of whiskey and kegs of beer.

Walking up to the bar, Nate nodded at John Robinson, the affable bartender, who walked up to him with a friendly grin, polishing a glass. "Evening, Deputy. Hear Marshal Bess is back in town."

"That she is, John."

"Give her my regards."

"I'll do that."

"You did a good job covering for her in her absence."

"Thanks, sir."

"The marshal's been gone, what, a few months?"

Sweet nodded.

"Where's she been?"

"Hunting down a killer. Got him up in Destiny."

"Is she OK?"

Another nod. "Marshal Bess is a woman who can take care of herself."

"Destiny, huh? Cold as a witch's tit up there."

"That's what I was told. Nice new mirror." Sweet indicated the full-length mirror behind the rows of bottles behind the bar, which still had tape on the glass and other signs of recent installation. "When did you put it in?"

"Two days ago. Installed it myself. Starting to look like a real saloon."

"Just need the swinging doors."

"They're coming. What can I get you?"

"Whiskey."

"Coming right up." A moment later, Deputy Sweet had a shot glass set in front of him and the barman was pouring a generous slug. As Nate raised the glass to his lips, he looked across the counter at the big mirror against the wall and caught his own reflection and those of people behind him sitting at the tables.

Three men he hadn't paid attention to when he walked in were crowded together at a table in the corner. It was the three disgruntled husbands who'd made a fuss in the marshal's office earlier that day. They'd been drinking ever since, from the looks of them. Zachary Laidlaw, Moses Farmer, and Levi Best were in animated, aggressive conversation. A half-full bottle of bourbon was on the table beside an empty whiskey bottle. And two revolvers. A rifle leaned against the wall. The deputy took a careful sip of his drink and watched their reflection steadily out of the corner of his eye. The three of them had a bad air about their congregation, and the lawman's gut told him these men were up to no good.

Sweet caught the barman's eye and quietly gestured him over. "John, how long them boys been here?"

"You mean Zachary, Levi, and Moses?"

"Yeah, them."

"Been drinking all afternoon."

"Pretty liquored up, you'd say?"

"I'd say. That's their second bottle of whiskey."

"Thanks." The barman went back up the counter to serve another customer, and Deputy Sweet edged down the bar a few stools to be nearer to the angry husbands, keeping a close watch on their reflections. The three men's attention was fixed on one another, and they hadn't noticed Nate yet as he eavesdropped and caught snippets of their conversation.

"—our wives, goddammit—"

"—screwin' our women and the marshal expects us not to do anything—"

"—she's a woman and she's on their side—"

"—hens stick together—"

"—we'll show them who the rooster is—"

"—I say if that lady marshal won't enforce the law we'll enforce it ourselves—"

"—ride on out there to that ranch and shoot that Puzzleface son of a—"

"—hear hear—"

"—Let's go. You boys ready—?"

"—finish our drinks."

Deputy Sweet tensed up as he saw the three men drain their glasses, snatch the revolvers off the table and holster their weapons, ready to get up from the table. He tore his gaze off them long enough to lean over and grab John Robinson's arm as the bartender walked past, whispering urgently.

"John, do me a favor. Run on over to the U.S. Marshal's office and get Bess Sugarland back here and tell her to bring her rifle. We got trouble. Tell her those husbands are getting ready to ride out to Puzzleface Ranch and get their wives back by force. Hurry."

The bartender saw the steel in Nate's eyes, nodded tightly, and was out the door like a shot, running up the street.

Deputy Sweet's hand was by his holstered revolver as he stepped away from the bar and turned to face the two husbands—Zachary and Levi—getting up from the table.

Mose was gone.

Sweeping his gaze quickly around the saloon, the lawman saw the third husband was not in the bar, having departed during the few moments he had been distracted sending the bartender to fetch the marshal.

As Zachary Laidlaw and Levi Best swaggered drunkenly toward the door, Deputy Nate Sweet blocked their path. "You boys ain't going anywhere."

The men looked outraged. "You can't tell us what to do, Deputy!" Laidlaw huffed.

"Fre-free country!" Best slurred.

"Keep your hands away from those guns, gentlemen."

Nate's hand rested on the stock of his own revolver; one look in the lawman's hard and alert eyes was enough for the inebriated men to go nowhere near their own weapons—they weren't that drunk.

"Where's Mose Farmer?"

Levi stuck his chest out like a stud rooster. "He's getting his wife, jus' like we's doin'." His words came out garbled by booze.

"He armed?"

"Hell yeth Winchester rifle. Pow. The law won't geth our wifes we'th geth 'em usself."

"Shut up. You're drunk and the only place you're going is jail to sleep it off."

The husbands began yelling and hollering at the deputy at the same time he heard the sound of boots running up the street. The door to the bar burst open and Marshal Bess Sugarland barged in with her Winchester repeater cocked, loaded, and leveled from the hip. "What's going on here?"

Deputy Sweet pointed. "These men were fixing to ride out to Puzzleface Ranch, bringing guns to get their wives and shoot Puzzleface. I stopped these two, but one got past me. Sorry, Marshal."

"Mose Farmer." Bess got her face close to Nate's and sniffed, and he saw her eyes flick to his when she smelled whiskey on his breath.

"He's on his way out there now."

"You men are under arrest." Bess pointed her finger in Zachary and Levi's faces. "The charges are public drunkenness."

"You can't—!"

"Get their guns, Deputy, while I get the cuffs on 'em."

Ten minutes later, after the two U.S. Marshals had the two husbands locked in jail, both lawmen were on their horses galloping for Puzzleface Ranch, praying they were not too late.

CHAPTER 16

"We got trouble." Hearing Laura Holdridge's yell from her covered wagon as she whistled for her cowpunchers to slow the herd, Joe Noose squinted into the distance and saw them.

On the horizon a quarter mile ahead, the figures of four mounted lawmen blocked the trail, pinprick metallic flashes of badges, visible at this distance, glinting in the sun. The men cradled rifles openly displayed. One of them in the vanguard had his gloved hand raised for the outfit to stop.

The wranglers hollered and shouted, steering the cows with their horses and gradually brought the five hundred marching cattle to a complete standstill, an activity that again for Joe brought the avalanche in Destiny to mind, but stop it the outfit did.

As soon as the cattle drive had halted, the lawman who'd raised his hand rode briskly in their direction. As he got closer, a sheriff's badge on his sheepskin coat came into view. He pulled up on his Appaloosa directly beside Laura's wagon. The man's lean, pinched face was as fierce as a hawk's, but his manner polite. "I'm John Roberts, sheriff of Rawlins. I take it you're Laura Holdridge?"

"What can I do for you, Sheriff?" she replied.

"We've received a report that your herd includes stolen cattle, ma'am."

"This is all my herd, Sheriff. The Bar H brand."

"It's my duty to check your livestock to confirm that. I'm afraid my deputies and I are going to have to detain you until this matter can be properly investigated."

"What possible reason could you have to accuse me of having stolen cattle in my herd?"

The bounty hunter saw the cattlewoman getting red in the face and tried to catch her eye to warn her to calm down. It was plain to see somehow this was a trick.

"Well . . ." Sheriff Roberts took off his Stetson and scratched his head. "It's been reported to me personally that some of these cattle have the Q brand. That particular brand belonged to a rancher named Abraham Quaid down in Consequence, whose cattle had been rustled and Mr. Quaid himself murdered during the theft last year."

"Reported by who, may I ask?"

"We just need to check your cows, ma'am, then if—"

"It was a man named Cole Starborough told you that, wasn't it? Earlier today, I'll wager. Had a posse with him, about fifteen guys. Let me tell you something, Sheriff. Starborough works for Crispin Calhoun, the big cattleman, one of my chief competitors. Calhoun is trying to stop me from getting my herd to Cheyenne for the Cattlemen's Association auction and he'll stop at nothing. That posse already dynamited the damn pass back there so I couldn't get my cattle through, but we did. This so-called report he gave you so you would detain us is nothing but harassment to slow me down. My late husband was Sam Holdridge and we run a reputable ranch at the Bar H, everybody knows that—"

"Mrs. Holdridge—"

"Please listen to me, Sheriff. I need to keep moving."

"Ma'am, please calm down. Just answer one question for me."

"Sure."

"Does this herd of yours contain any cattle with the Q brand on them?"

Joe saw Laura get flustered. "Yes, as it so happens, some of my cattle *do* have the Q brand. I bought them fair and square and have the bill of sale to prove it."

"Do you have it with you, Mrs. Holdridge?"

"No. It's back at my ranch in Consequence. Two hundred miles from here. I'm in a hurry, Sheriff. I have two weeks to get these cattle to Cheyenne or I'll miss the auction."

"From who did you purchase these cattle, ma'am?"

"Judge William Black. He is our district judge in Consequence. I'm sure you can ask him and he'll verify the sale."

Shifting in his saddle, Sheriff Roberts's posture tightened up. "That would pose a problem because Bill Black was brutally murdered nearly two months ago."

"What?" It was news to Laura, if not to Joe.

"He died under very suspicious circumstances and even if these cattle were legally sold to you by Judge Black, as you say, rustled cattle from a murdered rancher sold to you by a murdered judge is a matter that requires explanation. I need to hold you here for questioning."

"Who murdered the judge?" the cattlewoman gasped.

"We don't know." The lawman shrugged.

"Judge William Black was killed by a fiend they called The Brander. I know. I killed him. My name is Joe Noose." Joe had slowly ridden over to Sheriff Roberts, who looked at him with a piercing gaze.

"And exactly who might you be, mister?"

"I'm a professional bounty hunter. Last December I was enlisted by two U.S. Marshals and together we tracked down this fiend who butchered over a dozen people. They called him The Brander, and I'm sure you heard the name. As it turned out, this lunatic wanted revenge on Judge Black and the local sheriff, Bull Conrad. Both of those men were crooked and accomplices in an organized criminal operation where the sheriff used outlaws to commit crimes and the judge cut them loose, with both Black and Conrad divvying up the stolen loot and property. One of those crimes was rustling the Quaid cattle and killing the old man, Abraham Quaid. That's why The Brander burned that dirty judge to death with a red-hot branding iron." There was much more to the story but Joe Noose didn't tell the rest, doubting the lawman would believe him, even though it was true.

Not surprisingly, Sheriff Roberts wore a very dubious expression on his face, squinting at Noose. "Anybody who can verify that wild story, Mr. . . ."

"Noose. Yes, Marshal Bess Sugarland in the U.S. Marshal's office in Jackson Hole will corroborate the story. I rode with her. I saw the bill of sale Mrs. Holdridge had for the Q-brand cattle, and so did Marshal Sugarland. She'll tell you the same."

The lawman's stern gaze eased. "She by any chance be Marshal Nate Sugarland's daughter?"

"One and the same."

Joe could tell that held a lot of water for this peace officer. "Where is the marshal presently?"

"Back in Jackson, or should be near about now. We split up when I joined the cattle drive around Wind River a week ago, and it's about a week's ride to Jackson from there. Rawlins has a telegraph, right, Sheriff?"

Roberts nodded.

"Wire her. Bess'll tell you these cattle here are not stolen and were legitimately purchased by Mrs. Holdridge, who knew nothing about the deaths of the men involved with the Q-brand cattle rustling and swindle."

"I didn't know, Sheriff, I swear," agreed Laura.

"We have a telegraph in town ten miles from here," the sheriff said. "If we wire Marshal Bess Sugarland and she corroborates Mr. Noose's version of events, that's good enough for me, Mrs. Holdridge, and you and your outfit and cattle are free to go. But until then, I require that you remain in my jurisdiction until this matter is sorted out."

Joe swapped glances with Laura then looked steadily at Sheriff Roberts. "Well, what the hell are we waiting for?" he said quietly but firmly.

The lawman turned and rode back toward his men up the trail. The bounty hunter tapped his horse's flanks with his boots and rode after him.

The cattlewoman took a deep breath, watching the riders disappearing in the direction of town until their distant figures were out of sight. She hoped Joe Noose would be back soon, and told herself to settle down and be patient. It was not easy. Tying off the reins of the team of wagon horses, she sat on the driver's bench, looking for a while at her own strong clasped hands folded in her lap. Hands that looked useless to her now. When the trail boss looked up, the six faces of her wranglers were watching her sympathetically from their saddles, waiting to be told what to do next. "Fall out, boys. Grab yourself some coffee. Try not to get too used to sitting on your asses." Laura Holdridge smiled with an ironic sigh. "We may be here for a while."

CHAPTER 17

Cole Starborough's posse were resting their horses ten miles away in a deep valley near the county line. They were miles ahead of the cattle drive, and the boss gave his operatives a fifteen-minute break to water the horses and have a smoke. With a few minutes to kill, he had one himself and lit a fine cigar.

Puffing smoke, Cole walked up to the war wagon.

To the casual observer it looked like any other freighter wagon a group of cowboys might be pulling, until one took a closer look and saw the sides of the wagon painted to resemble wood were in fact steel-reinforced armor plates. The war wagon was a mobile armory. On the side was engraved the triple-C lettering of the Calhoun Cattle Company.

Exhaling clouds of cigar smoke, the stogie clamped between his sharp teeth, Starborough pulled open the metal doors and surveyed the weapons within.

Rows of rifles and pistols and boxes of ammo.

Crates of dynamite and fuses, the sticks of high explosive wrapped in cylindrical clusters.

And in the center of all the other stockpiled weaponry, the apple of his eye: a massive, custom-built five-foot-long by four-foot-high munitions case constructed of polished oak. It resembled a small coffin, which was fitting.

The gentleman henchman ran his hands over the length of the polished wood case with pride. Unbuckling the metal clasps, he lifted the lid, and the metallic reflection of what lay within danced across his eyes wide with lust as he beheld his ultimate weapon.

A massive Gatling gun lay inside a velvet-carpeted case beside its disengaged folded tripod mount. It was big as a small artillery cannon, which it partially resembled. Behind the huge twelve-barrel rotating cylinder on the firing end were draped .50 caliber cartridge belts flopping out of the breech near the rear hand trigger crank. The gleaming steel was polished to a sheen. Many crates of replacement ammo belts were stacked beside it. More ammo belts were stacked in a separate crate. This latest modern weapon was capable of bringing down a full cavalry detail of men and horses. Fully loaded, the Gatling gun was ready to fire.

The machine gun was Cole Starborough's last resort. He would deploy it to annihilate Laura Holdridge and her entire outfit if all else failed.

The Gatling gun was a dreadful, fearsome weapon. It would reduce the wranglers to piles of meat in a matter of seconds. Even if their bodies were recovered, identification of the human remains would be impossible.

While he dearly wished it would not come to that, while he hoped he would never have to use the machine gun, as he gazed on the mighty weapon, part of him did.

If all else failed.

* * *

Joe rode Copper alongside Sheriff Roberts three miles north toward the town of Rawlins. The three deputies had been ordered by the sheriff to remain with the outfit and the herd to be sure they stayed put. Noose could see that the straight-arrow, clean-cut local lawman had taken one look at the bounty hunter's scruffy, longhaired, unshaven appearance and did not believe one word of his story about being enlisted by U.S. Marshals to catch a killer, or that he had been deputized. Roberts said as much on the ride to town.

"Mister Noose, I think everything you've been telling me is a total crock of shit."

"It's all true, Sheriff. Marshal Sugarland will verify it and vouch for me when you telegraph her."

"How do you and Marshal Nate Sugarland's daughter come to know each other?"

"I killed the men who killed her father."

"That so?"

"That's so."

"The Butler Gang."

"Them. I didn't kill all of them, Bess killed some herself, but I pulled the trigger on Frank Butler, the man who pulled the trigger on her father."

"So you're a big hero."

"Not even close."

"Well, Nate's daughter must think you are."

"Then she'd be dead wrong. If it wasn't for me, her dad would still be alive."

"How so?"

"Let's just say I made an issue out of something with

the Butler Gang I probably shouldn't have and it fell into Nate Sugarland's jurisdiction and became his duty to deal with, something that if I had to do over again, I'd have left alone."

The two rode for a while in silence, crossing a creek, then riding over rolling grassy hills, with pines like green arrowheads rising up the mountains in the west. They picked up the trail two miles east.

The bounty hunter and the sheriff were riding at a brisk clip, but not fast enough for Joe, who was painfully aware that every hour Laura's herd was detained delayed them another hour on their journey to Cheyenne, and the outfit was already so far behind. "Sheriff Roberts, you think we can ride mebbe a little faster?"

"What's your big hurry?"

"The outfit back there needs to get to Cheyenne and they're already running way behind schedule."

"Those rovers and cows ain't going anywhere until I finish my investigation, and if the Jackson marshal doesn't verify your story, you'll all be facing charges."

"Marshal Bess Sugarland will verify everything."

"We'll see."

They passed a wooden sign that said RAWLINS. The trail turned through rows of shady pines and when the horses came out the other side, a small town lay ahead. It was an agricultural town and scattered farms and fields of crops stretched in all directions. Joe could see a grocery and feed store, a few other shops, a stable, a corral for horses and pigs.

"Where's the telegraph?" Joe asked, wondering.

The lawman swiveled his head and shot Noose a look of sheer dislike.

"You don't trust me, do you, Sheriff?"

Roberts stopped his horse on the outskirts of the town and swung around to face Joe dead on and looked him square in the eye. "You're a man of violence, Mister Noose, I can see that. Whichever side of the law you're on, I ain't exactly sure, but I know men like you, and where you go death comes with you. It don't matter whether your intentions are good or bad, people die around you. There's a place for men like you, but it ain't here, not in my town."

"I don't have any plans to stay. Passing through. I'm just helping Mrs. Holdridge get her cattle to Cheyenne."

Sheriff Roberts looked in Joe's eyes for a long time with a gaze like flint. He didn't know what to make of Noose, and that bothered the lawman and made him uncomfortable in Joe's presence. The bounty hunter realized there wasn't much he could do about it, just get this business over and done with as quick as possible.

The town of Rawlins was a place that Joe Noose had never been before, but he had no curiosity about it because he would never be coming back again if he could help it.

Five minutes later they reached the one-story square brick building with the bars on the window that Joe took to be the sheriff's office and jail.

The telegraph must be in the lawman's office.

Riding his horse across the street to the hitching post instead of using the one in front of his office, Sheriff Roberts dismounted and tethered his palomino. His moves were spare and economical with no wasted motion, as if he was getting ready to move fast. Keeping a close eye on the lawman, watching where the sheriff's hands were in relation to his guns, Noose patted Copper and slid out of the saddle onto his boots in a jingle of spurs. He didn't bother to tether his horse because he didn't want to occupy his hands, and Copper knew to stay put.

"Telegraph's inside my office," the lean hawk-featured lawman said, heading across the street, keeping pace side by side with the bounty hunter each step of the way, so neither man was behind the other.

The open door to the sheriff's office was twenty paces ahead, the inside dark, just the steel bars of a cell visible. The spurs of the two men tambourined on the dirt with each footfall. The open doorway drew closer, and Joe tried to see if he saw a telegraph inside but couldn't see from this distance. He didn't see any telegraph wires on this side of the building.

What if there is no telegraph inside the sheriff's office?

Noose realized that Sheriff Roberts might have other plans. Why this local lawman might have brought him out here wasn't hard to guess. There may not be a telegraph inside the sheriff's office, but there was a jail cell. Roberts's intentions might be to lock him up. Back at the herd, the lawman's tactics may have been to separate the most dangerous gunfighter from the rest of the men in the outfit under the pretense of going to town to send a wire. Just like separating an angry bull from the herd. Obviously the sheriff could see Joe was a killer and the one he had to worry about.

Joe Noose had stayed alive this long because he anticipated situations and how to react, and he did so now.

If putting him in jail was Sheriff Roberts's plan, his strategy would be to get Joe inside the sheriff's office in a controlled space where the lawman would attempt to disarm him, and one way or other get him into the cell.

As Noose walked in lockstep with Sheriff Roberts

across the quiet street toward the sheriff's office, inside of the building only darkness was visible through the open doorway and barred windows. Joe hoped this local sheriff wasn't going to try and arrest him, because Noose had already decided he was not going to let himself be arrested today. That wasn't going to happen. Whether some sheriff believed him or not, Joe Noose was a deputized marshal with the full weight of the U.S. Marshals Service behind him.

He'd try to just wound the lawman if gunplay was unavoidable.

Ever watchful, the bounty hunter saw the lawman's left hand resting on the gun in his holster as he walked on the right—realizing the sheriff was a left-handed gun was important to know in the next few seconds.

They stepped onto the porch and darkness and shadow fell across their heads and shoulders as they reached the doorway.

"After you," Roberts said with a gesture for Joe to go in first.

Noose exchanged glances with Roberts; he couldn't ask the lawman to go inside first now without raising his suspicions, knowing in the next few seconds a lot could happen. He knew how it would play out—

When Noose entered, the sheriff would be behind him, able to get the drop when his back was turned, and Noose would hear the sound of a gun quickly drawn from its holster, then the order for him to raise his hands. Noose anticipated all of this and was ready for it, prepared to drop and roll, kicking his boots out into the peace officer's shins, knocking the sheriff off balance, grabbing his left hand, twisting his gun wrist, and relieving him of his first weapon as he fell and snatching his second pistol from his holster when he hit the ground, punching him in the face once hard to knock him out, then handcuffing the unconscious sheriff inside his own cell. After that, Joe would have to figure out how to subdue the deputies back at the herd, but first things first—

Joe Noose stepped inside the sheriff's office.

Sheriff Roberts came in behind him.

The lawman's footsteps went to the left with no sound of any gun being drawn, instead the mechanical clicking that Noose recognized as a standard Western Union telegraph system. Turning around, the bounty hunter saw Rawlins's sheriff sitting behind the unit, putting on a set of headphones. Picking up a pencil, Roberts looked expectantly up at Noose. "Ready to telegraph the Jackson marshal? Walk me through your story again, Mr. Noose, and please keep it simple so I'm clear on what I need Bess Sugarland to verify." With a relieved exhale, Joe Noose recapped his story and John Roberts took it down, tapping on the telegraph, sending a wire to the Jackson U.S. Marshal's office.

They waited for a return transmission for one hour, then two, then three.

After the fourth hour, Joe began to worry; if the marshal or her deputy were on duty they would have wired back. *Had something happened to Bess?* Roberts, who also found it irregular, continued to telegraph Jackson every half hour, but as it got later and later, the result was sadly the same.

There was no response from the U.S. Marshal's office in Jackson.

CHAPTER 18

The house out at Puzzleface Ranch was quiet and still.

Rachel stood by the mirror in her bedroom and brushed her long hair so it fell naturally over the side of her face with the scar, and what her hair didn't cover, her high collar and the makeup she had just applied mostly did.

In the living room, the women were gathered. Dr. Stonehill had again just finished changing the dressing on Beulah's broken arm. Rachel came in from the kitchen with a tray of fresh tea in china cups and saucers. Millie and Vera were engaged in a lively discussion about the way the town of Jackson was growing, and how good it was that the women had formed a political force in the town council. Smiling at the safe and happy fraternity of ladies in her house, Rachel went over to the bookshelf and took down a leather-bound volume of *Pride and Prejudice* by Jane Austen; it was four in the afternoon, the light through the curtains coloring and shadows congealing, the time when while the women had been under her roof, they had read aloud to one another for two hours before dinner. Somehow, though the concerns of Elizabeth Bennet and Fitzwilliam Darcy seemed mild compared to their own, the independent Lizzie's success at romance by remaining true to herself was a tale that inspired them during these days of sanctuary and provided them all succor.

In the back of her mind, Rachel vaguely remembered not locking the front door when the deputy had left, but by the time she heard the heavy footsteps in the hall and the ugly cock of the pistol it was too late.

Millie screamed. When Rachel whirled, dropping the tray of tea and the cups in a shattering crash on the floor, she found herself face-to-face with Mose Farmer brandishing a Colt Dragoon. He had a drunken lopsided grin, and while he wasn't pointing the revolver at the ladies he might as well have been, because everything about his aggressive demeanor was armed and dangerous.

The women backed away deeper into the living room, but his hulking figure blocked the doorway, barring their escape. The only other way out was through the windows, and they'd never make it. Instantly, Rachel put herself between the man and the wives and doctor, but the husband was looking over her shoulder past her to his cringing wife.

"What are you doing here, Mose?" Millie shrieked.

"I'm here to take you home, honey," he growled, holding out his arm with a beckoning gesture. "C'mon now, come here."

Millie backed farther away and Rachel positioned herself in front of her even as Vera, Beulah, and Dr. Jane tightened around Mose's wife in a protective circle.

"This is Puzzleface's house and you're trespassing on private property, Mr. Farmer," Rachel said to Mose, holding his slippery, volatile, alcohol-fueled gaze. The Colt Dragoon was still pointed at the floor, but in his quaking hands the barrel began to inch up and rise in her general direction. "Leave now and there won't be any trouble. You are trespassing on Puzzleface's property."

"I'll deal with that son of a bitch, directly." Mose spat. "You just see if I don't. But first, I'm taking my wife home where she belongs."

"I-I ain't going with you, Mose," Millie stammered.

"Now you don't mean that, honey. Come to old Mose."

Vera took a step forward, blocking Millie, and shook her finger scoldingly at the enraged husband. "Millie ain't going with you, Mose Farmer, she's staying right here with us, so you can just turn yourself around and take you and that gun of your'n back to Jackson!"

The nasty laugh it elicited made the women tremble. "Oh, you're *all* coming home. You too, Vera. You too, Beulah. Zachary is on his way, and so is Levi, and we is all heeled, so if this Puzzleface gets in our way we'll shoot him dead. We know what he did. We know what he done to our wives. And it's him against the three of us. It's gonna be a reckoning, you women best believe that. We gonna make him pay!"

"You're talking murder!"

"We're your husbands and we're defending our rights because you're our wives!" Mose declared righteously.

"Zachary wouldn't dare."

"He'll dare plenty. He gonna take his bullwhip to you, Vera, he told me so. Same goes for you, Beulah, when Levi gets here. So the best thing for all you ladies to do is keep those big mouths of yours shut before you get in more trouble than you already is. *Sit down!*"

The man's bellow of rage was so terrifying the four

women did what he told them and sat, because he was waving his gun around now.

"You're our wives and we're you're lawfully wedded husbands, and you made the whole town laugh at us."

Rachel spoke softly and calmly. "Mose, you calm down now."

He babbled to his frightened spouse, his hulking bulk filling the refined room like a bull in the china shop. "I'm taking you home, Millie, I'm taking you home and it's all gonna be like it was. You'll see. We're going home just as soon as Levi and Zachary get here. They're coming. They said they was. So we're all just gonna sit and wait 'til they get here."

Mose Farmer brimmed with bravado, confident he had the backup of his two friends. But as the minutes passed, his glances toward the window and the empty ranch outside became more frequent and furtive. "We're leaving as soon as Zack and Levi come, Millie, because I promised I'd keep an eye on their wives for 'em. We wait."

They waited.

And waited.

The hands of the clock passed the quarter hour and they waited as the hands passed the half hour and the light in the room dimmed as the sun sank past the windows and the room was bathed in the deep red hue of twilight that made the four women shiver because it was the shade of fresh blood.

Still they waited.

Mose Farmer couldn't sit anymore. Jumping up, he clenched his pistol, pacing back and forth, his boots thumping the carpet in a restless drumbeat, the craving for another drink growing worse and worse, as before the huddled hostages' eyes their captor unraveled as it dawned on him his two friends were not coming. The large man seemed to shrink in size, shriveling as even in his inebriated state he realized the only one of the three husbands who had committed actual crimes of trespassing, breaking and entering, and kidnapping was him. He was alone. Mose couldn't understand it. "You cowards abandoned me." He cussed the two men who were not here. "Left me twisting in the wind."

Night had fallen and outside the windows it was pitch-black.

A sullen Mose Farmer came to a decision. "They ain't showing. OK, Millie, I'm taking you home, and those chickenshits can deal with their own wives. Us, we're leaving now. Just as soon as I shoot that dirty rotten son-of-a-bitch Puzzleface right between the eyes for screwing my wife."

The wives exchanged flabbergasted glances—they hadn't realized their husbands could possibly have thought they were being unfaithful until right now, and Millie started to say something, but Mose waved her silent.

"Puzzleface isn't here," Rachel said.

"Who the hell are you, anyway? Another one of his harem? Whose wife are you?"

"I'm his housekeeper."

"Then you know where Puzzleface is."

"He isn't here, I tell you."

"Where is he?"

"Puzzleface went to town."

"That's a big fat lie. Just come from Jackson. We'd have

seen him in town. He's here. You're the housekeeper, so you're gonna take me to him. You ladies stay put. That goes for you, too, Millie. Fact, I'm puttin' you in charge. I'm leaving for a few minutes with Rachel while she takes me to Puzzleface. I know you women got your lover boy stashed somewhere in this big house. Hell, can't wait to meet him. Want to see what he's got that I don't, that all the wives want. Then I'm going to shoot that thing of his clean off. Right before I blow his brains out. And when I come back, I'm taking my wife home." Mose grabbed Rachel by the hand and stepped out of the room, pulling her with him, holding the gun in her back with the other hand. He looked back inside the room at the four other women. "Any one of you tries to escape, I'll kill the maid." Shutting the door on their terrified faces, he locked it and pocketed the key. "Take me to Puzzleface." The poke of the barrel of the cap-and-ball Colt Dragoon in the small of Rachel's back made her jump, but got her moving. "Let's go."

"I already told you I don't know where he is."

"You're lying."

"I swear Puzzleface is not here. Cross my heart and hope to die."

"Don't bullshit a bullshitter. I know Puzzleface is in this house."

"Look for yourself. Check everywhere. Every room. You won't find him. I guarantee it."

"What's your name?"

"Rachel."

"Pretty name."

"Don't hurt me."

"I'm not going to hurt you, it's the man you work for I'm after. After I kill Puzzleface I'll take my wife and leave and nobody else needs to get hurt, least of all you." Rachel bit her lip, stopping a crazy urge to laugh. "Take me to Puzzleface, Miss Rachel, I ain't gonna ask you again, you're his damn maid and you know where he is, so stop trying to protect him and tell me where he is!"

Mose marched Rachel in front of him; she was grateful he couldn't see her face, only the back of her head, because as her mind raced to figure out what to do, Rachel was certain her expressions gave away a million tells. *How was she going to handle this? What was she going to do?*

Mose was looking for Puzzleface.

Who *was* her.

It was physically impossible for Rachel to make Puzzleface show up without getting into her male makeup and costume, which would mean getting away from Mose for a few minutes, and he wasn't letting her out of his sight.

She couldn't be in two places at once.

Or could she?

As she led Mose Farmer room by room through the house, opening doors and closets, stalling for time, Rachel's mind concocted a desperate scheme.

"Puzzleface better show before I lose my patience, 'cause when that happens I lose my temper, and you don't want me losing my temper. Ask Millie."

"She told me."

Behind her, Rachel heard Mose choke, coughing into his fist, as they moved through the house. It sounded like his wife telling on him unnerved him. "What did she say?"

"You beat her. Said you broke her arm, and her jaw. She

loves you even though you hate yourself. Says you argue. Blames herself for that. She says whenever you lose an argument with her you use your fists."

"It's my temper. I can't control myself."

"Millie knows. That's why she ran away, and why she's not coming back."

They kept walking down the hall, him keeping the Colt Dragoon jammed in her back, using his foot to open doors and look into the empty rooms, one after the other, but he was distracted. "She makes me hit her. She pushes me to it."

"That's what my husband used to say," Rachel said, staring straight ahead as she was force-marched. "It's the same excuse husbands who hit their wives always make after they've beaten them, right before they tell those women they love them and promise they'll never hit them again, and then hit their wives harder next time. Women who have nowhere else to go, and let themselves get beaten by men too weak and stupid to think with anything but their fists. I know how it feels to be beaten up every day in a marriage I was afraid to leave because I was alone. Millie felt she was alone. So did Vera and Beulah. We are not alone. And men like you can't hurt us."

"What has any of that got to do with Puzzleface poking my wife? We've checked the whole damn house and—!"

Mose swung around in circles, yelling into the house at the walls and ceiling and waving the huge pistol around, Rachel cowering, afraid it would accidentally go off. *"Puzzleface! Show yourself! Puzzleface! You screwed my wife so I'm gonna take your life, you no-account sonofabitch—you hear me, Puzzleface!"* Kicking the wall,

Mose whirled on Rachel, his blood way up. "I ain't leaving until I kill him."

"Why won't you believe me when I say Puzzleface is not here? He didn't screw your wife, Mose. He didn't screw any of those women. I should know."

The man got an ugly suspicious glint in his eye as he regarded her sourly. "Why you coverin' for Puzzleface, eh?" Mose approached her, his expression bitterly paranoid. "How much he pay you to cover for him, huh, Rachel? What else you do for Puzzleface, huh? You go rope other pretty ladies for him to bed? You *pimp* for him?"

"What?"

"You go out and find other men's wives and bring 'em back here for Puzzleface to fornicate with, like those wives in the other room, like my wife, my Millie?"

"He didn't screw your wife, Mose! He didn't screw any of those women! He never laid a hand on them! Puzzleface would never do that! *I should know.*"

He took a step closer, leaning in, nose to nose, tapping the gun barrel lightly against the front of her skull. "How do you know?"

"I know."

"How do you know? Tell me, Rachel, can you see into a man's soul? Can you see into Puzzleface's soul?"

"I know his soul as well as I know my own."

"You two must be mighty close then."

"Closer than you can imagine."

"I can imagine a lot. You bet I can. I can imagine you two are related, like he's maybe your brother." Mose tickled Rachel's hair with the barrel of the revolver. *"That's it*, ain't it?" Rachel's eyes darted left and right, to and fro, looking for a way out. "He's your *brother* and *you're* his *sister*, protecting him. I'd do the same for my brother. I always knew you two looked similar. I can see the family resemblance. Reckon you two could be twins."

"I am his maid, not his sis—"

"Maid?" In a sudden unexpected spasm of violence, Mose grabbed Rachel around the throat from behind in a stranglehold, as his other hand brutally jammed the muzzle of the Colt Dragoon under her chin, jerking her head back so her face pressed against his, cheek to cheek, his mouth and lips to her ear as he whispered, "I'm gonna give you 'til I count to ten to tell me where Puzzleface is or I'm going to blow your pretty brains all over these fancy walls, and with your head shot off, and no maid, who's gonna clean up the mess? Ready? Here we go. *One . . . two . . . three . . .*"

His words spitting out a mouthful of murder, Mose had every intention of pulling the trigger when he finished his countdown.

Shutting her eyes, Rachel said her prayers using her final breaths.

When she opened her eyes, the last thing she knew she would ever see was the view through the big picture window, of moonlit Puzzleface Ranch outside. It looked like a classical painting: the moon, the trees, the corral, the creek, the two horses in a perfect still life—*except the horses were moving and the riders who dismounted wore U.S. Marshal badges!*

Outside the house, Marshal Bess landed in a crouch dismounting the saddle, knees bent, staying low, eyes on the house a hundred yards away. She clenched her cocked and loaded Winchester in both gloved hands, staying still as an Indian, knowing the big oak tree the horses stood under blocked the bright moonlight, hoping it made her deputy and herself invisible to anyone inside the house.

Staring straight ahead, she saw movement through the south window, a few people, faint voices. Hearing a rustle of grass, she saw Deputy Sweet sideways crabwalk next to her out of the corner of her eye, but kept her gaze focused on the house.

"His horse is here," he whispered.

The marshal shot a quick glance to where Nate was pointing—luckily he saw what she hadn't—and recognized the butt-ugly nag from the bare patch on its posterior.

"Means Mose Farmer is in the house. I better go talk to Mose and see if I can get him to give up peaceably. Otherwise we're going in. Presume he's armed and dangerous. Shoot to kill. There are four innocent women in there. Try not to kill any of them." Feeling the weight of his gaze waiting on orders, the marshal swept her even blue gaze to her deputy. "You take the back."

Just like that Sweet was gone, and by the time the marshal blinked, her deputy was clear across the yard taking position by the barn in the rear of the house, socking his carbine to his shoulder. Gave a hand gesture. *Ready.*

Taking a deep breath, Bess drew air in her lungs, and yelled in her loudest voice in the direction of the house, *"Mose Farmer! This is the U.S. Marshal. Give up! We have you completely surrounded! Throw out your weapons and come out with your hands up!"*

Inside the study, Mose Farmer was so startled by Bess's loud voice that without thinking he instinctively released Rachel and threw himself against the wall beside the window, out of the marshal's line of fire—letting her go freed his hands so he could hold his Colt Dragoon in a two-hand grip; lucky for Rachel, because one second before, Mose had counted nine.

"That you, Bess?!" Mose shouted around the curtain.

"It's me, Mose! And Deputy Sweet! Anybody killed?"

"Not yet they ain't!"

"Keep it that way. Those women hurt?"

"Nobody's hurt, Marshal. But all that can change! In the house with me I got my wife Millie, Vera Laidlaw, and Beulah Best, and Puzzleface's maid, too, name of Rachel. Ain't harmed a hair on their pretty heads and ain't gonna s'long as the marshals give my wife and me safe passage! What do y'say, Marshal?"

"Let Vera and Beulah go, Mose!"

"I can't, Marshal!"

"Yes you can! Release the wives!"

"I'm holding Zachary and Levi's wives for 'em! Their husbands is coming to get 'em! My friends'll be here any minute and the three of us are taking our wives home!" Just saying it filled Mose with a rush of hope and some of his earlier bravado returned. "Zachary and Levi are on the way, Marshal!"

"They ain't coming!" Marshal Bess's voice yelled back. "Zachary Laidlaw and Levi Best are behind bars! Arrested them right before they rode out here!"

"Th-they said they was coming . . ."

"Those friends of yours sitting in jail right now are in a heap of trouble, Mose, but that ain't nothing compared to the trouble you're in! Kidnapping! Breaking and entering! Assault! Throw out your guns and come out peaceful, so nobody gets hurt!"

The fugitive's brain was swimming, he clawed his greasy hair, all confused, banged his own skull hard against the wall to clear his head, thinking, thinking, remembering why he came out to Puzzleface Ranch in the first place. "Millie! I'm taking my wife! That's all I want! If I let my hostages go, will you marshals give me the road, my wife and me?"

"I can't do that, Mose. You know I can't."

"OK. OK. How about a two-day head start?" Mose was pulling his hair out, his brains felt like scrambled eggs. "What do you think, Marshal?"

There was a long pause.

At last: "Let me get this straight, Mose. You're offering to release *all* of your hostages except your wife. In exchange, you want my deputy and me to stand aside and let you ride out of here with Millie and give you forty-eight hours before we come after you?" Marshal Bess's voice sounded different, she was talking not yelling, like she was getting closer.

"Yeah, that works!"

"But if I'm going to talk terms with you, Mose, you gotta throw me a bone!"

"What kinda bone?"

"Rachel! Let her go! Send her out!"

Rachel.

Mose had forgotten all about her! When the fugitive swung his frantic gaze across the room to where he had last seen her, Rachel was nowhere in sight.

Taking off like a shot, the frantic man scrambled out of the room, down the first hall, down the second hall, and kicked the locked door off its hinges.

Outside in the darkness, Marshal Sugarland heard the chorus of female screams ring out inside the house and tensed up, trading glances with Deputy Sweet. "What the hell's going on?" Nate shouted.

"I don't know!" she yelled back, edging closer to the door. At least there hadn't been any gunfire so far. Not yet.

"I'll kill 'em, Marshal, you hear me, I'll kill 'em!" Mose shouted out at Bess from the living room, grabbing Millie by the hair and shoving the cap-and-ball Colt against her skull. "And I'll start with my wife!"

Puzzleface stepped into the doorway.

"It's me you want." Rachel wore her mustache, goatee, and sideburns, unrecognizable as a woman in the colorful gambler's disguise she'd hastily donned.

"Wha—?" Mose swung his head in the direction of the voice and when he found himself staring into the face he thought was the man who was screwing his wife, he just completely unraveled. *"You horny varmint, I'll kill you!"* Mose wailed. Pushing Millie to the floor freed up his gun arm as he swung the barrel of the revolver at the hated figure in the doorway and fired—*KA-BOOM!* The explosion and smoke and flame filled the small room, but Puzzleface had run off like a jackrabbit before Mose pulled the trigger, and when the smoke cleared the gambler was halfway up the hall.

Vera, Beulah, and Millie were screaming their heads off, hugging each other in terror.

"Come back, you no-good wife-screwing little turd!" Mose yelled, taking off up the hall as he fumbled with his heavy revolver, taking aim on the fly at the quicksilver gambler who ducked around the corner.

Outside in the front of the house, Marshal Bess jumped when she heard the shot, trading taut glances with Deputy Sweet in back of the house. Inside was filled with screaming. *"No!"* she yelled, sprinting, with her rifle at the ready, to the front wall of the house. She flattened herself against it, by the door, yelling inside.

"Mose! Stop shooting! Mose, goddammit!" The shots were the same gun, coming from all around the house.

At least while he is chasing me he can't shoot them, Rachel thought, trying to outrun the man with the gun. The first thing she had anticipated was Mose would take a wild shot the instant he saw her in Puzzleface guise, so she started running the second she saw the gun come up. Mose Farmer being drunk and his reflexes slow factored into her calculations. The second thing Rachel had anticipated was after Mose missed, if he missed, he'd chase after her with the gun and forget all about Millie, Vera, and Beulah. Hearing the man's pounding footfalls at her heels, she knew Mose was out of the room with the three women—*and this was Millie, Vera, and Beulah's chance!*

"Run! Run!" Rachel screamed at the top of her lungs back into the house as she bounded up the staircase.

KA-BOOM! A bullet whistled past her ear and punched a fist-sized hole in the banister as she fled down the hallway of the second floor with Mose right behind her.

"Hurry! Run!" she screamed again.

Down in the sitting room, the three women stopped screaming long enough to catch a breath, and this time they heard Rachel screaming for them to run and they didn't need to be asked twice. Vera had a dazed expression hearing Mose's footsteps down the hall, and when she looked at Beulah, who was so shaken up from screaming her lungs out, it took them both a moment to realize Mose was upstairs and had taken his loaded revolver with him, putting them out of danger. But only when they looked at Millie screaming in their faces *"We gotta get out now!"* did they somehow get it through their skulls it was time to flee.

Those three wives started running for whatever door was nearest, so rattled the third muffled gunshot upstairs got them screaming all over again, so they ran right past the front door and because the three hysterical ladies kept bumping into one another in their disorganized flight, they made a wrong turn into the guest bathroom, and had to turn back.

Somehow they finally reached the back door.

And made it outside to safety.

Positioned behind the house, his long rifle lined up on the back door in case Mose made a run for it, Deputy Sweet wasn't expecting three women to come bursting out the door in a caterwauling knot of arms and legs and heads and hair instead. Nate was off like a shot, throwing his arms protectively around the women, using his body as a shield as he swiftly force-marched the wives to the safety of the empty barn behind the house. When Sweet had the rescued hostages safely stowed behind the hay bales, he ran to the door and called across the yard to Bess, positioned at the front of the house. "The women are safe, Marshal! Three in the barn!"

"Two still inside! The doctor and the housekeeper!"

"What's going on?"

"Hell if I know! Next gunshot, we're going in!" He

nodded acknowledgment of her curt hand gesture: *She'll take the front, he'll take the back.*

Inside on the second floor, Rachel was playing a game of hide-and-seek with Mose Farmer, where if he found her he'd kill her. She could hear him a few rooms away, kicking open doors, hunting for who he thought was Puzzleface. Taking refuge in the laundry room for the moment, she stole a glance out the window and felt a wave of relief seeing Nate getting Millie, Vera, and Beulah into the barn where they'd be safe.

Herself, she wasn't so sure about.

Mose had the gun but she knew the house, her one advantage. She heard another loud crash a few doors away as the drunken husband kicked in what sounded like her closet. "I'm gonna find you and blow your pecker off for screwing my wife!" The violent noises of Mose ransacking the house looking for Puzzleface accompanied a verbal string of death threats that paralyzed Rachel with fear.

Catching a glimpse of her reflection in the window, Rachel saw the mustached and goateed male visage and breathed it in, drawing strength from the male alter ego, Puzzleface, who could do everything she wanted to and couldn't.

Like run!

Bolting out of the room, Rachel ran straight for the staircase as a shot rang out right behind her, creasing her ear, the terror of being nicked by an actual bullet turning her legs to rubber, and she tumbled down the steps and landed in a heap at the base of the staircase, flat on her back.

The sound of a pistol cocking.

Throwing a desperate glance up at the top of the steps,

Rachel saw Mose's approaching shadow on the ceiling, and swinging her gaze to the nearest door, reached out and pulled it open, crawling through the doorway even though she knew where it led.

The basement.

And there was no way out.

Mose Farmer saw Puzzleface wiggle through the door as he came down the stairs cocking his pistol. He reached the door in a single stride and heaved it open to face a short descending row of wooden steps leading to the cellar and knew he had Puzzleface right where he wanted him. "Say goodbye to your pecker, you peckerwood," he slurred. Keeping his Colt Dragoon leveled at his waist, Mose took his time getting down there because he was drunk and had to duck his head under the low ceiling.

It surprised him to discover several mattresses laid on the basement floor that looked like they'd been slept in recently. There were pillows and blankets in disarray. It was an odd sight. In his drunken stupor, Mose assumed the worst. "Oh, you filthy animal, my wife wasn't enough for you, you need to keep extra women in your basement?"

"It's not what you think."

Turning to the sound of the voice, Mose Farmer saw the huddled figure against the wall and figured he had Puzzleface cornered. He raised his pistol. "I got you now, you horny varmint. Say goodbye to your pecker because I'm gonna shoot it off."

The figure turned their face to look at him.

It was Rachel.

Mose held his fire, confused, *because it was just the two of them in the basement, wasn't it, and he saw Puzzleface come down here, so . . . ?*

But he never completed his train of thought because hearing somebody behind him in the cellar, Mose Farmer whirled around right into the stock of Marshal Bess Sugarland's rifle as she hit him in the head and knocked him cold.

A few hours later in the U.S. Marshal's office in Jackson, the three wives were reunited with their husbands, on the other side of the bars. The men sat in jail as Bess took their wives' statements and Nate wrote down what they said in his report. Rachel, the housekeeper, had asked to give her statement first, and once it had been taken by the lawman she had left. The women were conflicted and uncomfortable having to go on the record about their domestic abuse, but Rachel encouraged them to speak freely, and the hard looks and big guns on the hips of the lawmen kept the men they were married to from acting up.

Rachel left the marshal's office saying she was going back home. Bess told her to ask Puzzleface to come in tomorrow so she could ask him a few questions, and the housekeeper promised she would.

Fifteen minutes later, while getting Millie Farmer's statement, Marshal Sugarland turned over the questioning to her deputy while she got up to stretch her legs.

Walking to the open doorway, she got a breath of fresh air, when something caught her attention. Halfway up the block outside the doctor's office, Dr. Jane Stonehill was deep in quiet conversation with a small man with a goatee, dressed like a riverboat gambler. Their heads were bowed together in a conspiratorial manner. Bess's brow furrowed and she called to Nate. "Sweet?"

"Marshal?" He looked up.

Standing by the doorway, peering out, Bess wagged her finger for him to come over. Excusing himself, Deputy Sweet walked over to the marshal, whose gaze had not left the two people in conversation outside the doctor's office, and she pointed out the one who looked like a gambler. "That this Puzzleface character I keep hearing about?"

"That's him, Marshal."

"Wonder what he's talking to Doctor Stonehill about." When Bess shifted her gaze to Nate's face beside her she could swear she saw his eyes cloud as he shrugged, and got the same feeling she'd been having: her deputy knew something about this Puzzleface business that he wasn't telling her. "That's all. Go on back and take them reports, then escort those ladies home if they want to go, or to the hotel if they don't. Their husbands stay in jail tonight until the arraignment tomorrow."

"Sure thing, Marshal." Sweet nodded obediently.

"And deputy." He looked at her. "I smelled alcohol on your breath at the bar earlier."

Here it comes, the deputy thought. "Yes, ma'am."

"Reckon if you hadn't stopped in the saloon for a drink you wouldn't have seen those men to stop them and we could've had a genuine massacre on our hands at that house tonight. So that drink's on me."

"Yes, ma'am." He smiled. She smiled back. Deputy Sweet returned to his desk. "Now where were we, Mrs. Farmer?"

When he looked up, Marshal Sugarland had left.

* * *

The moon was bright tonight in the big Wyoming sky, casting long shadows black as ink, but otherwise visibility was good. Bess stepped off the office porch and went the long way around the building to the stable so Dr. Jane and Puzzleface didn't see her. Then she quietly saddled her mare, careful to avoid a squeak of leather or clink of bridle and got on her horse slowly without a sound of stirrup or spur. Her marshal father had years ago taught her how to do that. Mounted, she trotted quietly to the edge of the corral that offered her a clean view of the street, stopping the mare in the shadows, out of the sight of the two people she was observing. For several minutes, Dr. Jane and Puzzleface's conversation continued, their figures close and conspiratorial, and the lady lawman watched them the entire time without being seen.

Presently, the two people shook hands and Puzzleface walked to his horse tethered to the post outside the doctor's office, as Doctor Stonehill went back inside. Now the gambler's horse caught her attention when he mounted it and she recognized the burgundy gelding.

It was Rachel's horse she had ridden from the ranch to come to Jackson and give her statement earlier.

What was going on here?

If Puzzleface had Rachel's horse, how had the housekeeper ridden back to the house as Bess presumed she had? Perhaps she took one of the wives' horses.

Untying the gelding, Puzzleface got situated in the saddle and rode off at a brisk canter on the road heading west of town toward the gambler's ranch.

Giving him just enough of a lead so he wouldn't notice

he was being tailed, Marshal Sugarland rode her mare out of the corral and onto the street and followed at a discreet distance.

The ride back to Puzzleface Ranch took two hours and Bess kept a loose pace several hundred yards to the rear of the other horse and rider ahead of her. The trail wound around tall hills and down into wide valleys and there wasn't another human being in sight. It was a dark night, and the marshal lost sight of Puzzleface several times before catching up again, but she felt certain he was headed home, and didn't fret.

Halting her horse in the woods outside the ranch, Marshal Sugarland arrived at the house a few minutes after Puzzleface did, in time to see him come out of the corral and enter the house. The place was dark, and there was no sign of Rachel, who Bess considered might have retired. It was very quiet outdoors on the outskirts of the spread, with just the ceaseless musical drone of crickets keeping the lady lawman company. Sitting in her saddle, Marshal Bess kept the house under close surveillance, and caught just a single glimpse of Puzzleface through the window before he disappeared into the next room, and moments later the next person she saw in the window was Rachel, moving through the rooms with a candle.

Puzzleface didn't reappear.

That struck her as odd.

In the early morning hours later that same night, it was dark as pitch at Puzzleface Ranch and there were no lights on in the main house. Out in the darkness, off in the distance, came the quick trot of horses and presently a light appeared, and as the light drew closer it was a coal oil lamp held in the gloved hand of one of three hooded, cloaked figures on horseback, to see their way in the dark. The mysterious trio towed a fourth rider covered in a blanket. Riding up to the back door of the house, two of the hooded riders remained saddled while the third, the one with the lantern, dismounted. Blowing out the lamp, total darkness once again descended. The silence was broken by an urgent knock on the back door of the house.

The light of a single candle bloomed in the upstairs window of the house and the glow of the flame floated like a fairy past each darkened window drifting ethereally downstairs to emblazon the hallway as Rachel opened the back door and quickly gestured to the riders. The door was held open just a crack so only a witchy trickle of illumination escaped.

With urgency, the two mounted cloaked and hooded riders helped the blanket-swathed figure out of the saddle into the waiting arms of the one on foot, who handed them off to Rachel, who swiftly ushered the person under the blanket inside the house, shutting and locking the door.

Immediately the three riders galloped off into the night and were gone, but before the last one got on their horse they relit the lantern and in the glow of the light the face under the hood was revealed as Doctor Jane Stonehill, the Jackson physician, looking into the night to be sure they were not being observed.

Farther off in the darkness, a lone unseen figure on horseback was watching. The glint of moonlight reflected off a metal seven-star badge. Marshal Bess Sugarland sat in the shadows on her saddle, keeping Puzzleface Ranch under surveillance as she had been all night long. From the clandestine activity she just witnessed, her suspicions had been confirmed that something very strange was going on in Jackson Hole, and Marshal Bess was sure as hell going to find out what.

CHAPTER 19

As dawn broke three hundred miles to the southeast in Rawlins, Laura Holdridge sipped her coffee, wondering if the cattle drive would be detained for yet another day. Joe had not returned all night, and she could only assume he was waiting at the telegraph office for a confirmation of the story from his lady marshal friend in Jackson. The trail boss hadn't slept a wink, feeling with every passing minute that the chance of getting her livestock to Cheyenne became an increasingly remote possibility, like the sands in an hourglass draining her future with every grain. She could ill afford to lose another day.

Over at the chuck wagon, the outfit was having breakfast. The two deputy sheriffs stationed to guard the drivers and cattle from leaving were having coffee with the wranglers, joking and swapping stories. The local lawmen were all right, just doing their job.

Presently, the cattlewoman saw two riders approaching from the direction of town, the last place she had seen the bounty hunter ride off.

It was Noose and Sheriff Roberts. Her heart lifted as she made out the grin on Joe's face. He wore it all the way up to her when he reined his horse, Copper. "We reached Bess by telegraph this morning. She confirmed the story."

The lawman rode up and nodded respectfully. "You and your herd are free to go, Mrs. Holdridge."

The cattle drive proceeded due east on a southern trajectory throughout the morning. The five hundred head and seven-man outfit pushed on across five miles of rugged hill country, the sky weighted with heavy clouds, until on the seventh mile the prairie leveled out into an open plain and the sun came out, the temperatures rising to ninety degrees. The rovers and the steers began to bake but still they pressed forward.

In the driver's perch of her covered wagon, Laura Holdridge had the map of Wyoming open behind her, her brow furrowed with worry as she occasionally consulted it when she saw a landmark, marking their progress with a pencil on the map. Now and then she looked up and scanned her surroundings. There was no sign of the posse Noose believed were tailing them, but she knew if he said so that they were out there.

When the outfit broke for lunch ten miles southeast of Rawlins, Joe Noose noticed that Billy Barlow was not among the circle of men with the plates and cups. He heard several shots ring out several hundred yards away and looked up quickly. Joe Idaho chuckled. "Relax, Mr. Smith. That's just Billy practicing his shooting. He's the worst shot in the outfit, thinks wasting ammo is gonna make him better, but we all know it's because he needs glasses because his distance vision is poor."

"Ain't nothing wrong with glasses," said Kettlebone,

polishing his bifocals with a dirty shirttail, making them more smeared than before.

Rowdy Maddox shoveled another spoonful of beans into his mouth. "Dumb kid's too proud to wear spectacles and one day that's gonna cause him to get stuck on the wrong side of a longhorn. Stubborn bastard."

Another string of evenly spaced shots rang out over the plain, followed by a string of distant profanity. Joe drained his coffee and stood. "Maybe I can give the kid a few shooting tips." The bounty hunter strode off in the direction of the gunshots, carrying his empty coffee cup.

Behind him, scowling, Curly Brubaker never took his eyes off Noose.

Just over the hill, down in a grove, Billy Barlow was facing away from Joe, holding his Remington revolver in a wavering grip, shooting a gnarled oak tree fifty yards off. The gun cracked thrice. He missed all three times, little puffs of dirt appearing far off.

"May I see your weapon?" Joe held out his hand in a friendly way.

The rover shrugged and handed it to him. The gun was in very poor condition. "When was the last time this gun was cleaned, son?"

"I don't know."

"Clean it. If you don't know how, I'll show you. Otherwise it's gonna blow up in your hand one day. Here, try mine." Joe spun his shiny, freshly oiled Colt Peacemaker out of his holster, flipped it around in the air, caught the barrel and held the butt end out to Barlow.

"You don't mind?"

"Take it."

Billy took it, testing the weight and heft of the big revolver in his left hand. "Beautiful gun, Mr. Smith."

"She and her sister serve me well. Noose tossed the empty metal coffee cup in his hand a hundred feet. It landed on the ground between a rock and broken branch. "You see the cup, Billy?"

"Sure."

"See what's on the left of it?"

"Branch."

"See how many twigs on that branch?"

"Three."

"Nothing's wrong with your eyesight. Your shooting technique's your problem. Shoot the cup."

"I can't even hit a tree."

"Try. I want to see how you shoot."

"OK." Barlow shrugged, raised his left arm with the pistol quick and sloppy and yanked the trigger of the Colt, the mule kick of the .45 knocking his arm up as the gunshot exploded and smoke filled the air. When it cleared, the cup sat on the ground untouched. "Told you I can't shoot for shit."

"You're not doing it right." Joe reached out and grabbed Billy's left arm, raising it horizontally. "Do not touch the trigger yet. First, take the time to aim, don't be in such a rush. Now look down the sight until you got the notch on the barrel lined up between the notches on the back of the gun settled on the cup. Tell me when you do." Barlow squinted, impatient, trying to point the Colt at the cup in the grass a hundred feet away. Finally, he nodded. Noose let go of his arm. "Hold that position, nice and easy. Still got the target sighted?" Billy nodded. "Don't fire." Joe pushed Billy's arm holding the gun aside. "Find the target again, line it up like you just did. Don't *point* the gun. The barrel is an extension of your arm. See the target. Reach out and *touch* it with the barrel."

More relaxed now, the rover squinted and lined up the shot, then he nodded.

"Now don't pull the trigger, squeeze it. Nice and smooth. Like stroking a lady's hair. "

Barlow fired.

The cup jumped in the air with a flash of lead striking metal.

"Good shot." Noose smiled. Barlow let out a whoop of glee. "Shoot it again."

The wrangler forgot everything Joe taught him the next time he fired and missed. He scowled, embarrassed. "This gun's aim is off."

Joe laughed. "*Your* aim is off. This gun is perfect."

"I say your pistol's aim is off, Mr. Smith."

"That so?" Joe Noose regarded Billy Barlow with a cocked eyebrow and small enigmatic smile as he flipped open the cylinder and shoved six fresh .45 caliber cartridges into the slots and spun the gun closed with a ratcheting *whirr* like the castanet of a rattlesnake. "Wanna bet?"

"Five bucks."

"Easy money." The bounty hunter slid the Colt Peacemaker into his holster and faced the fallen metal cup a hundred feet away. Blindingly fast, he quick-drew the revolver and fanned the trigger, firing from the hip. The first bullet kicked the cup in the air with a sharp *ptank*. The second shot spun it higher into the sky. Barlow's mouth dropped as Noose's second and third shots were direct hits on the cup spinning through the air at two hundred and three hundred feet as each successive bullet kicked it back. Showing off, Joe turned his back, holding the smoking gun, and when he heard the distant impact of the metal cup hitting the ground, swung around, arms extended, elbows locked, holding the Colt in a two-hand grip and without a second's hesitation plugged the tiny target of the tin cup twice more in tiny distant flashes of sparks. Billy was laughing and clapping as Joe flipped open the cylinder, dumped his empties, slapping in six fresh rounds, closed the pistol and spun it back in his holster in one smooth movement.

Then his hand came up with an open palm.

Barlow greased it with a five-dollar bill.

"Keep practicing," Joe said.

"Thanks for the lesson, Mr. Smith," Barlow said, shaking his head and whistling as he walked back up the hill toward the camp.

With a smile, Joe turned and loped off a few hundred feet across the grass to retrieve the bullet-riddled mangled hunk of tin that was all that remained of the coffee cup. "Reckon I owe you one of these bucks, Kettlebone." He chuckled.

Curly Brubaker jumped out behind Joe with a loaded shotgun. "Hands where I can see 'em!" Noose froze, his jaw clenching. "Go on, stick 'em up!"

Noose slowly raised his hands, his back to Brubaker. "What's on your mind, Curly?"

"I saw your shooting contest with Billy Barlow just now, and if that's not proof you ain't who you say you are, nothing is."

"I'm turning around, Curly." Brubaker raised the shotgun but Noose fearlessly turned fully around to face him with a steely gunfighter gaze.

Curly was in awe. "The way you shoot. Nobody shoots

like that. Never seen no man shoot the way you do. Definitely not no rover, where the pay is nothing like the money a man as good with a gun as you makes, if he's smart, and if there's one thing I know about you it's you're smart, too smart to work this cattle drive for rover wages unless you come for something else. I'm going to ask you one last time to tell me who you really are and if you don't, I'll blow your guts out and who you will be is a corpse."

Joe Noose didn't reply. His silence rattled the armed wrangler, who couldn't shut up. "I don't know *who* you are, but I know *what* you are. *A shootist.*"

Noose fixed Curly in his pale-eyed gaze. "If you actually believe I'm a shootist, you realize I could draw my gun and shoot that smoke wagon out of your hands before you had a chance to halfway pull the trigger and my next bullet would be right between your eyes."

His hand shaking on the shotgun, Curly started sweating and shaking as he faced the ice-cool bounty hunter with his hands up, deadly calm and still, the coiled spring stance, the unnerving gunfighter gaze glued on Curly.

"Put down the shotgun, Curly, you're not going to use it, I can see it in your eyes. You're no killer."

"But *you* are. What are you doing here? *Who are you?*"

"My name is Joe Noose, Curly. I'm a bounty hunter. I'm here to help."

"Help? This ain't none of your business."

"Laura Holdridge hired me, so yes, it is my business. I'm being paid to discover the killer in your outfit and that's what I intend to do, with or without your cooperation." Joe Noose screwed on his hat and started to leave. "If you want to help, I can use all the help I can get. If not, stay out of my way. Understood?" As he walked back up the hill, Noose delivered parting words. "For whatever it's worth, Curly, I know the killer ain't you."

The bounty hunter kept walking.

Joe Noose didn't get ten feet before Curly Brubaker rushed up behind him. "I want to help."

"Thanks." Noose turned and extended his hand.

Curly shook.

The only time anybody in the outfit smiled lately was when their trusty cook Fred Kettlebone served up the chow. His tasty trail foods like chili, steak, stews, and eggs reliably lifted everybody's spirits. The fat man made the best coffee any of them had ever tasted, including Joe Noose, and he made it strong enough to "float a horse-shoe," as he was given to say, which was the way the men liked it. Not surprisingly, given all the troubles of late, the irascible chef in charge of the chuck wagon had become ever more popular in recent days, despite his porcupine personality becoming even more prickly.

The cattle drive had pushed hard and covered twenty miles by sundown, picking up lost time and helped by agreeable terrain. The sun was just a glowing thread stitch-ing the horizon to the sky as the outfit heard the dinner bell clang and hurried over to the chuck wagon. Joe Idaho collected some wood from the supply wagon and quickly made a roaring campfire, creating a sense of well-being covering the rovers like a warm blanket in the chill night air.

When the cook served up a heaping helping of spicy trail chili from the steaming pot, a hungry Joe Noose was the first in line and decided to sit with the others. When he settled by the campfire a piece of paper fell out of his pocket. It was a handwritten note. As he lifted a spoonful of the steaming chili to his lips, he read the scribbled words:

> *The chow tonight will kill you.*
> *Dig in. It's your last meal.*

"Hold it, boys!" Joe dropped the spoon in his metal bowl of chili and set it on the ground, jumping back from the bowl like it was a live rattlesnake and holding up the note. The other wranglers had just sat down or were getting their bowls of food and nobody had taken a bite yet. "Somebody slipped me a note saying the chow is poisoned. Don't nobody eat it."

"What the hell you talking about, Smith?"

"That your idea of some kind of joke?"

The other wranglers—Brubaker, Barlow, Idaho, Maddox, and Leadbetter were getting seated around the campfire about to dig in to the chili. All eyes went to Noose, who picked up his chili bowl like it was a bomb that might explode. The bounty hunter tossed the chili in the fire and passed the note to the other cowboys. Suddenly terrified of being poisoned, all of the drovers put down their bowls without eating.

"What the hell's wrong with you jackasses?" When the cook, Kettlebone, saw the cowboys refusing to eat his chow, he got furious and ran over to the campfire waving his arms, screaming at the men to eat the great food he cooked, until the dirty looks from the circle of paranoid wranglers shut him up.

Joe Noose rose to his feet and showed Fred Kettlebone the note. "You better look at this, Fred."

The cook pushed his spectacles up his nose and squinted

to read the note, then he laughed. "This is bullshit. A prank. The chili ain't poisoned."

The bounty hunter picked up one of the ramrod's un-eaten bowls and shoved it in Kettlebone's fat hand. "You so sure of that, prove it. Eat it."

Kettlebone laughed too loud and broke a nervous sweat, seeing the other wranglers rising to circle him with their hands on their pistols in their holsters.

Shaking his head, Fred Kettlebone opened his mouth and tossed back the entire bowl of chili in one huge gulp. He burped, farted, and smiled, showing them it was safe to eat. "See?"

The hungry wranglers cautiously picked up their bowls of chili and were about to dig in, but Joe Noose's eyes remained fixed on the cook. Swinging his arm in a sweeping arc, the bounty hunter knocked all the chili bowls out of the other cowboys' hands before they took a bite, the men all looking at Fred Kettlebone in shock—the cook had gone into seizures, foam frothing from his mouth, eyeballs rolled up in their sockets revealing the whites as blood poured from his nose and ears, the spasms worsening until he dropped dead face first into the campfire, becoming engulfed by fire as his fat body became a human torch and his roasted corpse was incinerated by the flames before the yelling men piled on top of each other could pull him free.

In naked horror, the wranglers all backed away from the steaming corpse beside the campfire and the awful stench of burning human flesh, eyeing each other in mortal dread, retreating into the shadows and some drawing their guns. When the bounty hunter looked over his shoulder he saw the horror-stricken face of the cattlewoman framed by the flames of the campfire as she stood paralyzed in a rigor mortis of shock; Laura Holdridge saw the whole thing and couldn't tear her eyes away from the charred body.

"Don't look." Noose walked over and gently took Laura by the arm, leading her passive figure back to her covered wagon and helping her up onto the platform.

He was about to head off when she called to him.

Joe climbed up on the sideboard of Laura's covered wagon. When she pushed aside the canvas flap and entered, he followed her inside because that seemed what she wanted. Noose had to duck to stand upright inside because the quarters were small. She didn't speak at first, just adjusted the level of flame in her lantern. It cast a burnished glow on her belongings in the wagon; he was struck by their femininity, a soft safe haven for the woman to come to when she took off her cattlewoman spurs, out of sight of the tough men she' employed. Knitted quilts, pillows, and comforters on the duck-feather mattress. Books on a small shelf. An open steamer trunk containing her neatly folded wedding dress she traveled with in memory of her husband, her nightgowns, and a larger trunk filled with chaps and jeans and work shirts. Her hat and gloves and gun belt hung on a peg. A basin large enough to take a whore's bath in, with soap and a hot water bottle sat on the shelf, beside a pile of neatly stacked towels. Two vases of wildflowers she had found time to pick were placed on the floor. Her traveling quarters smelled of wood and leather and soap and lady scents.

On the ledge by her bed was a framed sepia daguerreotype photograph of Laura Holdridge with a big, rugged, handsome, formidable man maybe ten years her senior. Joe Noose recognized him as her late husband, Sam Holdridge, whose painting he had seen at her ranch house when he and Marshal Bess Sugarland had stayed the night last month. His young wife was clearly in love with him in the daguerreotype from her devoted expression as they posed for the photographer. In the photo Laura was younger and looked more innocent, but with the same bold, brash, spirited look in her gaze she still had now as a widow and trail boss. The cattlewoman saw the bounty hunter looking at the photo.

"My husband, Sam."

"You made a handsome couple."

"Please sit. Wherever."

Joe sat on the floor and crossed his big legs Indian style. Laura sat on the bed, a vibration going through her limbs like a tremor, and he recognized she was shaking from nerves. Her mouth trembled and he didn't know what to say, or why she'd asked him into her covered wagon, but he sensed she wanted to talk, so he sat and he watched her patiently, ready to listen when she was ready to speak, knowing she would get to it in her own good time.

"I wish Sam was here."

"I'm sure you do, ma'am."

"Sam would have known how to handle this. He knew how to handle everything that's going on. I always counted on him being there, you see, taking care of things." Her hands were clasped in her lap, and the tears began to roll down her cheeks as she wept. Suddenly she looked so small and lost he almost didn't recognize her. Joe had never seen Laura look vulnerable before, and it came as a shock to him. Only when seconds later she completely broke down in convulsive sobs of despair, did the bounty hunter realize how stoic the cattlewoman had been and the burden on her shoulders keeping everything inside, being strong for her men. "I can't do it by myself."

"You don't have to. You have your men. And you have me."

Joe got up from the floorboards and sat patiently on the bed by Laura's side. He put his arm gently around her shoulders, like a friend, wondering if that was enough.

"Hold me." She whispered it like a child.

Joe sat inside the covered wagon and put his big arms around Laura, whose whole body shook. He had never seen her look fragile before and it surprised him, because the cattlewoman was so formidable a personality. There was only so much a soul could take, he reckoned. There wasn't much he could say or do right now except hold her, what she needed right now, so that's what he did, and the minutes turned to hours in the cozy confines of the covered wagon as her sobs softly continued throughout the long night, and once in a while a lonely coyote howled far off in the hills.

CHAPTER 20

The outfit had made camp in a basin in the hills.

Laura Holdridge woke before everyone else and decided to take a walk to the stream over the hill to refill her canteen. Joe Noose had spent part of the night in her wagon, she curled in his arms, until before daybreak when he left so he could be back in his sleeping roll when the other men awoke so they didn't get any ideas.

Laura felt wonderful and energized this lovely morning, her senses tingling, her cares gone from her mind at least for now. She strolled past the slumbering rows of steers, some on the ground, some on their feet, stretching off into the purple predawn; the sight of the herd, *her* herd, filled her with the true pride of a cattleman.

She felt very good indeed this morning, basking in a fine sense of well-being. The sun was just rising on the Wyoming horizon and once she walked over the hill, the camp and the cattle were out of view, and she slowed her pace to enjoy the walk and solitude. It was only a short distance from the herd to the river and a few of her stray cows stood drinking at the water's edge. She joined them on the bank of the tributary looking out at the rapids dappled with sunrise.

Laura crouched and dipped her canteen in the rushing river.

As the water flowed into the pouch, she saw her tousled reflection in a rippling pool, golden with dawn. The reflection of another who appeared in the water was just a blur, but she knew who stood behind her from the smell of his cologne.

Without rising, the cattlewoman swung a hard inquisitive look up at Cole Starborough, who offered a gloved hand to help her up.

"Good morning, Mrs. Holdridge."

A figure on horseback rode slowly over the top of the hill. Her golden hair was backlit by the rising sun.

"There she is." Noose rose and turned his head, squinting to see Laura make her approach on a horse that wasn't hers, riding it slow, trotting like on eggshells. "Something's wrong," Joe muttered.

Laura Holdridge gradually came into view as the lone figure on the horse approaching with an agonizing slowness. Her head hung, hair hanging over her face, shoulders slumped in the saddle.

The men of the outfit gathered behind Noose, who put his hand up for the others not to get any closer, his eyes gravely locked on the cattlewoman. "What's the hell's that?" Joe growled.

It was hard to spot, but some kind of string or yarn trailed from Laura's saddle back over the hill.

"Mrs. Holdridge, are you OK?" Brubaker shouted.

Laura lifted her head, raising her face, tears of shame,

fury, and fear in her eyes as she shot out a shaking arm and held her hand up in warning. "Stop."

Noose put up his hand and the rovers halted.

"Stay back," the cattlewoman said, as with shaking hands she pushed her coat flaps very, very carefully aside and the men jumped back when they all saw it.

Fifteen sticks of dynamite were strapped on her midriff in a makeshift vest of field bandages wrapped tightly in a crisscross pattern that firmly bound the rods of high explosive to her torso. From the sticks the fuses were twisted together around a spool of detonation wire that trailed out of her saddle down to the ground; the string that Joe had spotted unspooling back over the hill.

With the last step of the horse's hooves, the detonation cord had completely unspooled and grew taut, and Laura halted her horse. She could go no farther.

"What the hell do we do?" Leadbetter asked.

"Don't move," Noose replied.

A piercing metal whistle drew their attention to the top of the hill.

Cole Starborough was framed in silhouette against the sunrise. Slamming the wooden box in his hands to the ground, he jerked up the plunger, locking his elbows, gripping the handle in both gloved hands, poised to push down and inject the plunger in the detonator. "You know what this is! I push down and your lady boss and each one of you gets blown sky-high! Don't even think about trying to shoot me, because I get shot, I fall right on top of the plunger. You men understand me?"

The fuming outfit nodded.

A hundred yards away up the hill, Starborough stood in

a crooked position bent over the plunger of the detonator, his face to the outfit below, keeping his seething eyes fixed on them. "Very slowly! Drop your gun belts! Watch those hands!"

"What do you want?" Noose yelled up at Cole.

"We're taking the herd!" the gentleman henchman yelled.

"Nooooo!" screamed Laura, shaking her head in a fit of tearful fury.

Joe caught her eye fiercely, made a hand gesture for her to stay calm.

"This is how it's going to work!" Starborough shouted. "You're going to just walk away! Leave the herd! Get on your horses, leave your gear, ride away! Go home! End of the trail, boys!"

"Go to hell!" Laura screamed over her shoulder, back up the hill at Cole.

With a savage snarl, Starborough pressed down, injecting the plunger a couple notches into the detonator, not far enough to blow the explosives, but down the hill the outfit all heard the metallic clicks and jumped. "You will get to hell first, Mrs. Holdridge, followed in quick succession by each and every one of your men, unless you cooperate. Now will you cooperate?"

"Yes," Laura said.

"Excuse me, I didn't hear you!"

"Yes! Yes, you son of a bitch!" she shouted.

"Good! Drop those guns, boys, c'mon, belts off, kick 'em away! That's it! Now raise your hands! Step back from those guns! My men are coming down to collect your firearms!"

Cole snapped his fingers and five of his operatives in dusters and bowler hats came over the hill and walked down to Joe and the outfit, who had backed away ten paces from their weapons. The five men had their guns holstered, but before the wranglers could get any ideas about jumping the thugs while they picked up the confiscated gun belts and pistols on the ground, Cole snapped his fingers again and another five operatives rose atop the hill with rifles shouldered and trained down the hill, covering their comrades. When the guns had all been collected, the five of Cole's men quickly and efficiently executed his orders.

First, Calhoun's posse ran off the pack horses by untethering the animals and firing their guns in the air by their heads, frightening every one of the horses into bolting off into the plains, taking the supplies strapped to their harnesses with them. All the hapless disarmed outfit could do was watch the horses disappear in clouds of dust. The only horses the wranglers had left were the ones each wrangler rode.

Noose hoped none of Starborough's men made a move on Copper because if they tried, Joe knew he'd blow Cole to smithereens with his own dynamite, even if Laura exploded in the process. Luckily the posse left his bronze stallion unmolested but they weren't finished.

Joe smelled the stench of coal oil and his guts clenched; the posse men uncapped fuel cannisters and went around to the outfit's wagons, splashing the flammable liquid accelerant over the wood and canvas of the rigs. Matches were struck.

The posse burned all the wagons.

Strapped with dynamite, Laura choked, witnessing roaring flames incinerate her wagon and the wedding dress she knew it contained—the waves of heat from the

blaze washed over her as it burned the precious gown
Laura Holdridge wore exchanging vows with Sam Holdridge; all those irreplaceable memories of her husband
reduced to ash. Overwhelmed by a sense of indescribable
loss, the bereft cattlewoman shut her eyes, unable to bear
the sight of her wagon disappearing in a fireball rolling
skyward as the hot tear rolled down her cheek.

Unarmed, Noose and the wranglers kept their eyes on
Starborough. *He wasn't going to kill them,* Joe reckoned;
he had what he wanted.

"Ride away!" Cole ordered.

"That's my herd!" Laura yelled at the top of her lungs,
as if she wasn't strapped with dynamite.

"The herd is ours!" Cole shouted. "Tell your boys to ride
away! My men are running the steers from here!"

"Let Laura Holdridge go!" Noose roared. "This is her
outfit and she comes with us!"

Brubaker cupped his hands over his mouth and hollered,
"We ain't going nowhere without our boss!" The rovers
all joined in rowdy vituperative vociferations of solidarity
directed up the hill at the posse.

Cole patiently let the men quiet before he loudly stated,
"Mrs. Holdridge stays with us as the guest of the Calhoun
Cattle Company until the day after the cattlemen's auction
in Cheyenne, at which point she shall be released unharmed!"

Joe was aghast. "You're taking her hostage!"

"My guest, sir! I'm her host! She will be rejoining you
all shortly!"

"That's kidnapping!"

"It's business! This is a warning! Don't do anything

stupid! If you try to come after your boss or take back the herd, I promise you will never see Mrs. Holdridge again!"

Laura caught Joe's eye. "It's OK, Joe," she told him stoically. "Get the men out of here before Starborough changes his mind. Hear me, Curly? Get everyone saddled up and hit the trail. We lost this round. But this ain't over." She, Noose, and Brubaker traded fearsome glances between them . . . *It's war.* She gave them a nod. "Ride or die." The cattlewoman flashed the bounty hunter and head ramrod a brave, bold grin. "Don't worry about me. I can take care of myself."

The wranglers slunk to their horses and took to the saddles like beat dogs. Joe Noose was feeling like forty miles of bad road himself as he mounted Copper, when his golden stallion looked back with the saddest look he had ever seen in his eye.

The outfit's horses were already on the move, retreating south, out of the blast radius of the explosives. Yanking his reins, the bounty hunter swung his horse around so he faced the cattlewoman. She sat up straight and strong, chest and jaw out as if she was proud of the fifteen sticks of dynamite strapped to her person, wearing it like battle armor. Just like her.

He locked eyes with the bravest woman he'd ever seen.

"I'll see you soon," Laura said in a tone as loaded as a gun. The side of her mouth was turned up in the subtlest of smiles.

Touching the brim of his hat, Noose nodded with a savage smile that wasn't subtle at all. He didn't reply, nothing needed to be said.

They understood each other perfectly.

With a fierce jerk on his reins, Joe Noose broke away

on Copper, galloping down the breadth of the herd of longhorns, charging aggressively through Starborough's mounted operatives descending on the string of cattle to take possession of the livestock; the riders and horses got out of his way, fast.

Swinging his head over his shoulder, Joe Noose saw the lone figure of Laura Holdridge strapped with dynamite sitting on her horse, shrinking smaller and smaller behind him.

I'll see you soon.

Damn soon.

CHAPTER 21

At the Calhoun Bar T Ranch in Abilene, Texas, a mixed crew of Latino rovers were bringing in the herd from Juarez.

A Mexican cowboy ramrod delivered the herd to the Calhoun stockyards. High spirits abounded. Tonight there would be *muchas cervezas*.

In the office above the big slaughterhouse on the spread, cattle baron Crispin Calhoun, master of all he surveyed, stood by the window looking down at the stockyard at the herd of longhorns pouring into the corral. The only part of Calhoun that moved were his lips as he counted each and every head.

The foreman of the rovers collected his money and jumped on his horse, but before he could leave, two of Calhoun's ramrods rode up and intercepted him.

"Mr. Calhoun wants to see you."

"What about?"

"Ask him."

The Mexican foreman shrugged, nervous and excited to be meeting for the first time the legendary cattleman who ruled the West. Perhaps it would be to thank him for bringing in the herd and offer him a promotion. He rode with the two very big cowboys toward the weathered slaughterhouse. The tallest structure on the ranch, it had been erected centrally to the layout, looming over the warrens of stockades and corrals.

To be polite, the Mexican rover doffed his dirty hat when he was led up the stairs to the top floor of the abattoir that served as the cattle baron's office. There was the famous Calhoun, a smaller man than the foreman expected for such a storied individual, standing with his back to him. For a moment, the Mexican just stood there, hat held in his hands, starting to sweat. It was hot in here. Should he cough or clear his throat to announce himself? Shifting his gaze over his shoulder to the hulking cowboy ramrods who stood like sentinels between the foreman and the staircase, he saw their eyes were locked on their boss.

Crispin Calhoun turned from his desk beside the window looking over his cattle empire. "Two thousand head of cattle left Juarez last Thursday when you moved out the herd. Today when you brought in the herd, the head count was one thousand nine hundred and ninety-nine head."

"Pretty close."

"I'm short one cow."

"Must have lost it."

"How exactly do you lose a cow?"

"Cows get lost on a drive."

"Not my cows."

"Then I don't know."

"I don't know how you lost one of my cattle either, but I do know that the average weight of a steer is a thousand pounds. Seventy-five percent of that is meat. Flesh if you

will. Does the term, 'a pound of flesh' mean anything
to you?"

"Should it?"

"You owe me fourteen hundred pounds of flesh."

"I'm sorry, Mr. Calhoun. It won't happen again. What
does beef cost a pound? Just take it out of my pay."

"Your debt is one thousand four hundred pounds of
flesh. I'm calling it in."

Two of Calhoun's hulking cowboys seized the wrangler foreman and carried the man into the bowels of the
abattoir where butchered cattle hung, a space full of sharp
implements and buzzing flies, blood everywhere floor
to ceiling, a smell of death; there the henchmen strung up
the terrified rover on heavy iron chains. He begged for
his life.

The sinister well-dressed cattle baron Crispin Calhoun
entered at his leisure, uninterested in his cowpuncher's pathetic pleas for mercy because his interests lay in the array
of butcher knives and cleavers industrial slaughterhouses
use to process mass quantities of cows and pigs. Calhoun
looked the implements over for one best suited to extract
payment for the debt, considering his options. The cowboy
henchmen stood beside the trussed foreman.

The cattleman hefted a jagged skinning knife of night-
marish proportions that took both hands to grip and would
strip the muscle and tendon like butter from the bone.
"This will do."

"I pay you anything, please don't cut me, I give you all
my money!"

"The butcher's bill is paid in flesh, pound for pound.
Next time read your Shakespeare, you ignorant uneducated wretch."

The poor Mexican foreman threw up all over himself as the cattleman brandished the skinning knife and solemnly uttered, "Ave tenebris Dominus."

Calhoun started cutting.

Throughout the night and all through the following day, the hideous, appalling screams emanated from the slaughterhouse, but out in the boonies of East Texas on rural outer reaches of the Bar T ranch, nobody was close enough to hear and if they were, they didn't listen. They knew better.

And by that time, cattle baron Crispin Calhoun had already boarded the train to Cheyenne.

"It's losing the cows he's going to be mad about, not the men he's lost," Cole Starborough said with a tone of ironic forbearance. "Mr. Calhoun couldn't care less how many of his men die—the way he looks at it now, he doesn't have to pay them—but the loss of a single steer, just one, *that* he takes personally. God help the man who works for Mr. Calhoun who loses a cow. Mr. Calhoun will take a pound of flesh from that luckless individual for every pound of flesh of that cow, exactly what it cost him. Of course, compared to a whole cow, no man has that much flesh to spare, but Mr. Calhoun will take it nonetheless, I've seen him do it."

"Good Lord." Laura Holdridge couldn't believe her ears as she sat inside a large canvas tent that had been designated her private quarters, having a conversation with Cole Starborough. He poured her a glass of wine from a bottle he brought for her comfort, then one for himself. She took small sips, not wanting to get drunk, as much as she dearly wanted to, for she had to keep her wits about her. "How?" she wanted to know.

"He flays them. A grown man has, on average, a hundred and fifty pounds of flesh on his body. An average cow, fourteen hundred pounds. Even when that man has had every last ounce of meat stripped from his bones and he's just a red skeleton, he still hasn't paid off the pounds of cow flesh he owes, and the way Calhoun sees it, the debt hasn't been paid."

"But the man who lost the cow is dead."

"Indeed. But not his dependents who inherit his debts— his wife, children, even parents."

"Do you mean to tell me? Dear God, not—"

"Take my word for it, Mr. Calhoun always has his debts paid in full, gets everything owed to him. Every dollar, every dime, every nickel, every ounce of flesh he's ever been owed, Calhoun keeps track of those accounts in his little black book up here." Cole tapped his temple with a gloved finger. "His obsession with every cent, every cow, attention to detail to the point of madness, for some would be termed a pathology, but it is his methodology, and some might call it insanity, but Mr. Calhoun calls it business. That's why he has so much money and power and is indisputably the greatest cattleman in America."

"Bullshit."

"And this is why, Mrs. Holdridge, you do not want to mess with Crispin Calhoun." The gentleman foreman got up and went to the tent opening, brushed aside the flap, turned and looked back. "You asked me why I make such a point about not losing livestock, and hopefully I have explained. This is why I refuse to lose a single cow in that herd out there, Mrs. Holdridge. I will not be the man

Mr. Calhoun extracts his pounds of flesh from. So you need not worry about the health of those steers, because rest assured I will deliver every last head to my boss without even a scratch on their horns. I'll stop by again in a few hours to check in on you."

Laura had something on her mind. "Mr. Starborough, may I ask you a question?"

"Certainly, ma'am."

"How did you know so damn much about my cattle drive? It's like you always knew our next move before we made it, one step ahead of us the whole time. You're intelligent, I grant you, but nobody's that smart."

"I had a spy in your outfit."

"That's a lie."

Laura wanted to say her wranglers were like family and none of them would ever betray her. But remembering one of the outfit was a killer, and seeing the truthful gaze of the gentleman henchman, she lowered her eyes and said simply, "Who?"

"The cook. Kettlebone."

The cattlewoman wanted to cry and it took all her willpower to keep the tears out of her eyes.

"I thought you already knew," Cole admitted. "I didn't see the cook with the rest of your outfit when we confiscated your cattle, so assumed you'd discovered him and cut him loose."

She heaved a sad sigh. "You bastard."

Calhoun's enforcer wore a sympathetic expression. "Don't take it personally, Mrs. Holdridge. Every man has his price, it's just some men's price is higher and they're better negotiators." He tipped his bowler hat and left.

Laura sat quietly on her cot reflecting on another very

civil conversation with Cole Starborough, who frequently dropped in on her to see how she was doing and to ask if there was anything he could do to make her more comfortable. "During her stay" was the phrase he preferred, even though they both knew the correct word was "kidnapped." It was how the blue bloods put things. Cole clearly had an upper-class upbringing and a well-bred background, though how he ended out West engaged in frontier criminal enterprises was anyone's guess. She was intrigued and intended to ask him. The only thing about Cole's past Laura had gotten out of him was that he'd been thrown out of West Point.

True to his word, Cole Starborough had given her first-class treatment since he'd kidnapped her, attending to her every creature comfort. He was a complete gentleman, an educated man whose air of refinement contrasted with his battlefield manner. Her tent had a bed and silk sheets, fine scented soaps, chocolates, several fine classic books, hot and cold water basins and fresh-water jugs, refilled several times a day. There were even flowers in a vase that the posse must have freshly picked on the trail. Ironically, the lifelong cowgirl couldn't remember being pampered like this. Cole Starborough treated her considerately from the moment she was in his charge; it made her not hate him as much as she probably should.

A few days ago, five minutes after she'd watched her wranglers and Joe Noose ride out of sight, Cole had immediately cut the detonation wire and removed the sticks of dynamite and entire TNT vest from her midriff. Since then, Laura had not been handcuffed or tied up or trammeled in any way. Starborough had behaved with extreme courtesy with her, as did his men. As hostages go, she was receiving special treatment, but she was still a prisoner. Night and day, the tread of boots outside her tent were a constant reminder to Laura she had the eyes of the posse on her every waking and sleeping moment, except when she had to relieve herself and was afforded privacy. Even then, the posse knew where she was and she wasn't going anywhere.

There was nowhere to go, and Laura knew it. Held captive by heavily armed professional mercenaries, she had no illusions. No matter how many gentlemanly conversations she had with Cole—who she knew was really no gentleman—she was in the bad company of dangerous men; if she wasn't hurt it was only because they hadn't hurt her yet, and all that could change. Cole Starborough and his men were killers, capable of anything.

Men on the payroll of Crispin Calhoun, the worst of the worst.

What was going to happen to her? she wondered for the countless time.

Was Calhoun going to kill her? Would his enforcer Cole Starborough be the one who pulled the trigger? She didn't know and tried not to think about it.

Her questions to Cole about what was happening were always gracefully deflected. Politely, he kept his plans to himself. After the posse took possession of the herd, Starborough drove the five hundred head for two days into northern Wyoming. The cattlewoman had no idea where the posse were taking the steers except it was the exact opposite direction of Cheyenne; each mile the herd covered in the wrong direction set Laura two miles back from her goal of getting her longhorns to Cheyenne, if by some miracle the outfit got the herd back and turned it around.

She felt her heart sink with every step of the hooves, until hope was just about lost.

Then one afternoon the posse simply parked the herd, and hadn't moved it a foot since. Cole found a place that suited him and they corralled the steers in a wide ravine, threw up some tents and made camp. Three sunrises and sunsets had come and gone, and the only thing that had changed were the flowers in Laura's vase and her sheets each day. It was just day after day of sit and wait, and Laura had no idea what Crispin Calhoun's operatives planned to do next.

Her best guess was the posse wasn't moving the live-stock anytime soon and they'd stay put. The plan seemed to be to remain here, wherever here was, and sit it out until the cattlemen's auction in Cheyenne was over. Cole Starborough had already said as much, that he intended to hold her and the cattle until then. It was overkill; in another five, maybe six days by her calculations, there would not be enough time to drive the entire herd to Cheyenne two hundred miles across Wyoming in time to make the auction, even if her outfit rode eighteen hours a day every day.

It was over. Calhoun had broken her. He'd stolen her herd, taken everything she had. Even if Laura somehow got her cows back, if she didn't sell them at the auction she would be broke; that meant having to sell the ranch she built with Sam, losing all those memories of him, and selling off the entire herd to another cattleman for a huge markdown. Laura would never sell to Calhoun and give him the satisfaction, but her outfit would lose everything; all the blood that had been spilt on this crimson trail would have been for naught.

She'd fought Calhoun and he'd won. She'd lost.

The big cattle syndicate boys had all beaten her.

This was all her fault.

They were right about her.

She was just one woman.

They were men. She had been arrogant and reckless to think she stood a chance of fighting the system, going up against the entrenched male establishment and beating them at their own game. Who did she think she was? She knew the people she was dealing with: a rich, powerful syndicate of ruthless corrupt cattlemen who would use any means at their disposal to control the beef business.

Her late husband, Sam Holdridge, had not been a man like that; knowing she had married an honest cattleman and a good, decent man gave her comfort in her dark hour. Sam had built their Bar H Ranch and grown their herd with bare-knuckled hard work and fair dealings, with Laura as his partner. They had done it together, as a team, with the muscles in their arms. On their own honorable, reputable terms, Sam and Laura had become successful cattle ranchers in the business. Perhaps not as successful as Crispin Calhoun, but Sam and Laura Holdridge could sleep at night with clear consciences because they hadn't committed criminal acts like murder, rustling, bribery, and robbery to get to the top of the cattle business the way Calhoun did.

Sam Holdridge died with no blood on his hands, but the same couldn't be said for Crispin Calhoun, whose bloody hands would never wash clean. Laura Holdridge could never live with herself if she or her husband had ever done the terrible things it was rumored corrupt big-time cattlemen did, like murdering small-time ranchers for their grazing land and rustling their cattle. Sam's soul was pure when he died; hers better be untarnished, too, if she was going to end up in the same place he was and be together again. The bold cattlewoman was not afraid to die for a lot of brave reasons, but one above all others: Laura believed with all her heart she would be reunited with her husband, Sam, in Heaven.

She would never be like Calhoun, who had sold his soul to the Devil.

Laura Holdridge's conscience was clean.

And a clean soul was something no amount of cattle and no amount of money in the world could buy.

Let Crispin Calhoun keep his filthy money.

Little good it will do him when he has to spend it in Hell . . .

CHAPTER 22

Joe Noose lifted the field glasses to his eyes, crawling on his stomach across the mesa to get a closer look at the encampment down in the arroyo a quarter mile away. The outfit had caught up with Cole Starborough and his posse, tracking them to the camp where they were holding their stolen herd and the kidnapped cattlewoman. The six men were here to get them back.

Scoping out the installation, Noose couldn't see any sign of Laura, figuring she must be in one of the tents on the ridge of the canyon where the posse had made camp. Peering through the binoculars, the installation looked like an ant hill from this distance, the posse crawling like ants around the fortifications the location provided. He counted fifteen men in the posse. A lot of guns.

The bounty hunter hated to admit the area was well chosen. The cattle were down in a basin beneath the ridge where the tents were pitched below the top of the canyon whose rock walls formed a natural keep that penned the steers in. Starborough had picked a secure place to bivouac: the camp was protected on all sides by rugged high canyon walls providing excellent cover and formidable defenses against any conventional assault; it was all high ground, with visibility for miles in all directions. The heavily armed posse lookouts patrolled the perimeter atop the ridge on all sides. Daytime penetration was not an option. The rescue mission would need to be a nighttime operation. Even then, it was going to be a challenge.

It looked like there was no way in or out of the arroyo basin other than a single goat trail. Hoof prints on the ground showed Joe the posse originally drove the steers in along this path, but that narrow trail now passed directly by the machine-gun nest the posse had since set up—to get in, Joe and the outfit had to get past a Gatling gun. No other way. How they got the herd in was the only way to get it out.

Complicating matters, rescuing Laura Holdridge made this operation a double extraction; both breakouts had to be synchronized because Joe and the rovers would only get one shot at this. Knowing the cattlewoman's exact location beforehand was crucial; they had to pull her out quick while moving the steers. The problem remained. *Where was Laura?*

Minutes passed as Joe used the field glasses to survey every square inch of the camp as thoroughly as he could from this vantage on the mesa to the south. Inside the canyon, he scoped out ten tents on the ridge below, three deep, tents in front blocking his view of the ones in back. He decided she logically had to be in one of those tents.

"What do you savvy, Joe?"

"I think it's gonna be tough getting in there. Tougher getting out. Have a look-see." Noose handed off the binoculars to Curly.

The wrangler looked through the field glasses and

checked out the camp. He whistled. "Hellfire. Getting out is the easy part, they'll carry us out in coffins. Getting in there ain't tough, it's impossible."

"Not impossible. Not easy."

"You got any ideas, Joe? Because I sure as hell don't."

Curly could see Noose was thinking, his mind working like a machine behind his eyes. "We gotta do something about the Gatling gun for starters. It fires ninety rounds of fifty cal ammo a second. Turn you to a pile of grease. That gun's gotta go."

Picking up the binoculars again, the bounty hunter studied the gun emplacement. "Mebbe have me an idea how to get rid of it."

"Just how we gonna take out the biggest gun in the world?"

"With something bigger. A lot bigger."

Joe Noose got a slow grin.

"We use the herd."

"Are you nuts?"

Fifteen minutes later at the base of the mesa, Joe Noose hunkered down with the five wranglers of the Bar H Ranch as he drew a crude map of the camp in the sand. "It could work. They won't be expecting it. If it works we just may have a chance of getting Laura and the whole herd back."

"They took our guns," Maddox pointed out.

"We're unarmed, Joe. They have weapons, we don't," Barlow added.

"On the contrary, pardner," Noose said. "We got the

biggest weapon, those five hundred head of cattle and all those horns at a full charge, an unstoppable force crushing everything in its path, and you boys know how to use the herd."

"Joe's right, we do have the biggest weapon," Idaho agreed.

"It's like any weapon, you just got to aim it properly," Joe said. "You boys know how to do that. This outfit, you're the pros. If anybody can make five hundred mean long-horns go exactly where you want 'em, it's you. We going to use those cows to knock out the machine gun nest."

Curly shook his head. "The Gatling gun has that whole trail covered, Joe, you saw it and I saw it. The gunner'll see and hear those cows coming up the trail three hundred yards away and turn 'em into hamburger."

"Right." Noose nodded. "So we got to make sure the gunner's looking the other direction so he doesn't see the steers, that what he's looking at is so loud he can't hear those cattle coming up behind him. What we need is a good old-fashioned diversion, a big one. And nothing makes a better diversion than a dynamite explosion . . ."

Now he had their attention. Using the map, Joe Noose laid out his entire action plan for the men, step by unbeliev-able step—it was crazy, it was dangerous, parts of it made no sense; they had almost no chance in hell of pulling it off, but *almost* a chance to rescue Laura Holdridge and get back the herd was better than no chance at all.

When he was finished, Noose looked at their collective hopeful, doubtful, worried faces. "Anybody got any better ideas, let's hear 'em. Speak up."

The five rovers offered no suggestions. All eyes were on

him. Joe Noose experienced a sudden profound realization like a fist in his stomach. *They all looked to him!* Five men were counting on Joe to know what to do and lead them into battle, giving orders for them to follow that meant life or death. The rovers' lives, the life of their boss and the outfit's whole livelihood depended on a string of Noose's decisions over the long night to come.

Joe realized that he and he alone was responsible for the lives of these five men—six lives, including Laura's, were in his hands. His entire life, Noose had never been responsible for anyone but himself until now. Up until this very moment, Noose had been a loner, answerable to his own moral code and responsible only for the actions he took as result; now, in the faces of the five wranglers, four of whom had become his friends, Joe saw respect and trust and a belief in Noose as a man. Knowing that they would follow him anywhere was a sobering realization. It meant he could not let them down. *So be it*, he thought.

Rescuing Laura Holdridge brought the six men together into a whole greater than the sum of its parts. Fate had brought them all to this place and intertwined their destinies and, fates sealed, there was no turning back.

Moved, Joe Noose supposed he was experiencing what leadership was; being a leader may have been a first for him, but if being responsible for others gave him this much sense of purpose, if it always made a man feel this good about himself, hell, the bounty hunter figured, he ought to try it more often.

But Joe had a big problem.

One of the five wranglers was a killer, and he still didn't know who.

Tonight would be a bad night to find out . . .

* * *

Night fell on the Calhoun camp.

Beneath the brilliant twinkling stars above in the vast canopy of black Wyoming sky, a silence lay across the immense landscape so absolute it seemed a negation of sound, as if outer space where the stars hung simply extended to earth.

In that void, the tents of the posse glowed in the canyon ridge with the light of the coal oil lamps within. Silhouettes of the posse were shadows against the backlit canvas, figures of men playing cards, men cleaning guns, men passing bottles of whiskey, and one woman brushing her hair. When she opened the flap of the tent, shadow became flesh as Laura Holdridge stepped into the opening to get a breath of fresh night air.

The three armed men in dusters and bowler hats positioned around her tent, carrying rifles at the ready in their gloved hands, each snapped a vigilant glance to Laura, who knew their attentions were benign, so she simply smiled and they smiled courteously back as she pulled her coat around her shoulders and sipped a cup of tea. The guards tipped their hats and turned their backs to her.

The cattlewoman looked out over the camp below the ridge, then over at her cattle in the ravine, the sight of them bringing a secretive private smile to her lips.

Her perspicacious gaze traveled up and down the canyon searching for the guard patrols; it was so dark beyond the glow of the oil lamps on the ridge, out past the ledge it fell off into stygian blackness. No signal lights, no fires in the basin. If Cole Starborough was making no effort to conceal the presence of his mercenaries in possession of a kidnap victim and stolen cattle, he certainly wasn't advertising it either. Where was Cole? she wondered; she hadn't seen him tonight.

Her plan was working itself out in her mind.

If she was going to make her escape, she better do it in the next few minutes. When the guard with the handlebar mustache left to relieve himself, the one with the mutton-chops sideburns would be alone on duty for those few minutes. He always had the handles of those two honking hogleg revolvers hanging out of his thigh holsters where any damn fool could snatch them. That's why as soon as Mustache left for one of his privy breaks, Laura would go back inside the tent and blow out the oil lamp. The darkness would conceal her when, after she asked Mutton-chops to come into her tent, she grabbed one of his Colt Dragoons and pistol-whipped him—in his temple, where a good hard blow, Sam Holdridge had taught her, will render the biggest man immediately unconscious. Then it had to be quick. *Get his other gun. Take his ammo. Tie him up. Use sheets. Gag him. Put him on the cot. Throw a blanket over him. Leave the tent.* When the posse next checked her tent, they would not find her; if her scheme worked, they would not immediately think she was missing because they'd assume it was Laura sleeping under the covers. And when later they looked under the covers, they'd find the unconscious guard whose guns she had taken. With luck, she would be away by then.

The cattlewoman was fuzzy on the details of what she would do after she got past her guard detail, and leaving the tent was as much of her escape as Laura had planned; to her disadvantage, Cole had intentionally kept her quarantined inside the tent the entire time except for latrine breaks, so Laura didn't know her surroundings. A partial view of the area when they set up camp a week ago was all she had to go by. The rest of her escape she was going to have to improvise: *Hide in the darkness, stick to the shadows and find a way out. Anything goes wrong, head for the cattle, hide in the herd.* Knowing her way around her cows was second nature for her, and she could play hide and seek inside the herd for days. See how long Cole and his posse wanted to search for her on foot in those steers, in constant danger of getting gored by all those horns or trampled under all those hooves . . . *Come and get me, boys, because if it's one thing five hundred ill-tempered sleeping cattle won't appreciate, it's being woke up by strangers pushing and shoving them in the middle of the night. You don't want to be around the horns of a testy steer, Mister Cole Starborough!*

The one thing Laura Holdridge was certain of was that the only way out of the camp was the same way they came in—the goat trail. But she knew nothing of the machine-gun nest the posse had installed, having been in the tent the whole time, so in her mind all she remembered was just an empty path. The cattlewoman decided to use the goat trail for her hegira, but next to her leaving the tent in the first place, unwittingly walking into the muzzle of a loaded Gatling gun was the worst possible choice she could have made tonight.

In a few minutes, the mustached thug took his privy break, just like clockwork.

And Laura went back into the tent and blew out the coal lamp.

* * *

On the outside of the canyon, on the other side of the basin where the posse was camped, vast plains stretched in all directions as far as the eye could see, which was not very far since under a fingernail moon the land was preternaturally dark.

There was movement a few yards from the base of the goat trail.

A solitary one of Starborough's men patrolled the perimeter, carrying a carbine rifle and a brace of pistols under his duster. Bored but alert, his boss told the entire posse to be extra vigilant, and since his boss's boss ran the whole damn cattle business, the sentinel kept his eyes peeled. The posse man stopped and looked around, but it was pitch-black, and fifty yards out visibility dropped to nil. He squinted into the horizon, making out the faintest black against darker black outlines of a far off mountain range. There was nothing out there.

He heard a crunch.

Looking down, the posse man saw his boots were wet with gleaming black oil, only to realize it was blood splashing over his boots, his own blood jetting from his throat slashed by a bowie knife then suddenly jammed to the hilt in his heart.

Looking up, he saw the pitiless face of Joe Noose, the last face he would ever see.

The dead man couldn't have screamed if he tried and died soundlessly.

When Noose jerked the blade free, the goon instantly collapsed because the muscle of Joe's arm gripping the knife in the dead man's chest was holding him up. No need to hide the body, it was too dark for anybody to see anything. Briskly efficient, Joe stripped off the man's duster and exchanged his Stetson for the man's bowler. He relieved the corpse of his gun belt, which he would no longer need, and buckled it around his waist. The drag of the weight of the twin revolvers in the side holsters felt good, so Joe quick-drew them, one in each hand—twin Colt Peacemakers, oiled, cleaned, and polished—his brand of sidearm. In rapid succession he checked the trigger and hammer action of each pistol with his thumb and forefinger, flipped open both cylinders confirming full fresh .45 loads in both, spun the revolvers closed with a ratcheting *whirr*, then reholstered them. He performed all this with blistering speed.

His lips parted, exposing crooked teeth in a savage grin.

His eyes told the tale.

It was good to be heeled again.

Joe reached down and took the Winchester, also fully loaded, then searched the dead man's pockets, finding two boxes of .45 cartridges. That made it easy. *Could use that same ammo for the repeater rifle and pistols both.* He shoved the boxes of shells into the deep pockets of the confiscated coat. Noose figured he better grab all the guns and bullets he could lay his hands on at every available opportunity for the battle ahead.

This was going to get bloody.

The only question was how bloody.

Noose did a last-minute check of the fit of his borrowed outfit so he'd blend in with Starborough's men. The dead man luckily had been about Joe's height and breadth but without Noose's sheer muscle mass. The clothes hung well on his frame, loose sleeves allowing freedom of movement in the arms for fist and gunwork. The duster was expensive handsome custom leather. Calhoun paid his killers well. *Nice coat. If he got out of this alive he might keep it.* The hat was not his style.

Closing the flaps of the long duster over his shirt, Noose adjusted the bowler hat on his head, tipping the brim over his face to partially conceal his features. In uniform, the bounty hunter felt confident he looked the part of one of the posse men, and would pass casual inspection as one of Starborough's operatives if they didn't get too close.

Any of them who got that close he'd shoot.

Ready as he'd ever be.

Fifty yards off to the left was the goat trail winding up the steep grade of canyon over the top of the ridge. He knew a hundred yards past the crest, out of sight, lay the machine gun nest mounted with a Gatling gun, the most fearsome bullet-firing weapon known to man. In a few minutes he would meet that gun face-to-face. One wrong move and the gunner would mow him down, reducing Joe to a pile of meat unrecognizable as a human being. Better watch his step.

Don't want to ruin the coat.

Joe looked up at the ridge of canyon he needed to scale to get into the camp on the other side. It was about two hundred feet high, and looked climbable even in the darkness. He saw no other posse men on guard duty patrolling the top of the ridge. Turning his head in the other direction, Noose looked out into the complete darkness of the plains, a solid wall of black. He snapped his fingers, the agreed-upon signal.

Presently five figures emerged as lighter silhouettes against the darkness, and as they stepped a few feet from him, the faces of Curly Brubaker, Frank Leadbetter, Joe

Idaho, Billy Barlow, and Rowdy Maddox appeared. Sweat gleamed across their features. Each man carried a knife in his fist, but were otherwise unarmed. As they stood before him, pumped with adrenaline, Joe cocked his head at the rise, then nodded to the wranglers. *You ready?*

They all nodded back.

Turning, the bounty hunter took off up the ridge, scaling it with great strides, and the five rovers were right behind him. Their leader moved with the silent power of a jungle cat up the gloomy incline, and the others put their hands and feet where they saw him put his, and kept as quiet as they could. The ground was solid rocks and dirt and easy to climb, and in a few minutes the six men had reached the roof of the ridge. There, in single-line formation, they followed Noose's lead and stayed low, peering over the edge of the canyon down into the camp. The sliver moon overhead would not reveal them to anyone more than a few feet away, so effectively were they cloaked in darkness.

The canyon basin was also very dark, but the lanterns inside the rows of tents on the ridge to their right, two hundred yards off, bathed the camp in a subdued haze of firelight. Huge exaggerated shadows of posse men with guns moved on the rock walls above their figures as they walked to and fro around the bivouac. The smell of chili and beans and fresh coffee hung in the air.

Joe pointed at the tents and whispered to the rovers, "That's where they've got Mrs. Holdridge held prisoner. Am pretty sure of it. I'm going to go free her."

A gust of breeze from the left filled their nostrils with the tang of cowhide and dung, which drew the wranglers' attention to where Noose pointed into the darkness across from the tents. There, inside a gloomy adjacent ravine, many big shapes could be discerned milling together, the oil lamps gleaming faintly off rows of longhorns. The herd.

"While I'm getting Mrs. Holdridge, you boys get to the cattle," Noose whispered to the rovers. "Get 'em ready to move out. You can't see from here, but earlier today I saw through the binoculars that the corral where the posse's stashed their horses is just to the left, a couple hundred feet toward us. When we split up, head there. Steal some horses. Get to the cattle and get ready. When Laura gets there and I fire two quick shots, get those steers moving straight up that goat trail along yonder ridge."

Pointing to the far left of the basin there was just enough moonlight to faintly make out parts of the trail leading to the top of the ridge; sections were shadow pools and somewhere out in that impenetrable darkness lay the Gatling gun in the machine-gun nest; but they could not spot the weapon—it lay hidden like a scorpion getting ready to strike.

"When you hear my two shots you get moving with the cows. I'm gonna be on this side trying to draw that Gatling gun's fire. With luck, the gunner'll be too occupied with me to see you coming up behind him with the herd and by then those longhorns will be on top of him."

The five faces of the rovers looked nervously at Noose and he saw the trepidation in their eyes, but knew they'd follow orders; it better work, Joe knew, or they were all dead—the desperate plan had a lot of moving parts, and a hundred things could go sideways when it became a fluid combat situation. The posse had them way outnumbered and outgunned, but this was their one shot at this. "You boys ready—?"

Noose fell silent suddenly, putting up his hand for the men to cease all movement. The wranglers froze.

All of them heard a crumble of gravel not far below them.

Joe looked down and saw the shape of one of Starborough's regulars on patrol with a very big Henry rifle. A *clink* of pistols on his belt, the *squeak* of leather bandoliers with rows of slugs. He wasn't more than fifteen feet from them, coming their way. There was no indication that he knew the wranglers were there, but in a few more steps he was going to trip right over them. Curly Brubaker shot an alarmed glance to Joe Noose, who had vanished.

The posse man kept coming in their direction; then, when he was five feet from the huddled rovers, he stopped. His Henry rifle nestled in the crook of his elbow, he reached into his duster and withdrew a pouch of tobacco fixings. Pinching some shag onto the rolling paper, he licked and rolled it, putting the cigarette to his lips.

Then he struck a match.

The flash of flame illuminated the five men on the ground a few paces away as the thug dropped the match and the rifle came up very quick as he aimed the barrel down at them. The huge figure of the bounty hunter rose up behind him, throwing his massive arms around the head and shoulders of the posse man, one hand on his shoulder, the other on his jaw, pulling in opposite directions as hard as he could, snapping the man's neck with a muffled *crack*, killing him instantly, and head lolling loose on his shoulders, he was dead before the match hit the ground and extinguished when the corpse crumpled on top of it.

Grabbing the dead man's Henry rifle, Noose chucked it to Brubaker, who caught it. Then Joe pulled the two Colt Navy revolvers from the man's holsters and tossed one each to Leadbetter and Barlow, leaving only Maddox and Idaho unarmed.

"Move," snapped Noose.

They split up.

The bounty hunter took off in a low sprint down the embankment in the direction of the lower ridge.

Brubaker gestured with hand signals for the other rovers to follow him, and they made off down the dark incline in the direction of the herd. Curly hoped the horse corral was where Joe said it was, and realized as he saw the bounty hunter swallowed in the darkness he would feel a hell of a lot safer had Noose been with them.

The wranglers made their way carefully along, fumbling through a hundred yards of pitch-blackness, watching where they put their feet, luckily coming upon no other posse gunmen, until soon the ground evened out and they were on the floor of the basin. Ahead in the shadows, the whinny of a horse sounded and the cowhands knew they were headed in the right direction. Fifty yards farther and they could make out the small arroyo where fifteen horses were tethered on rope hitches. But those horses were guarded. It looked like two men sat on the rocks nearby, rifles beside them.

The rovers stopped dead in their tracks, making not a sound, controlling the rapid breathing from their exertions. Getting past the posse men meant neutralizing them, but unlike the bounty hunter, the wranglers weren't killers, and knew they couldn't fire their pistols because it would alert Starborough's forces. Exchanging glances, they resolved to sneak up on the gunmen and knock them out.

Holding their revolvers by the barrels, Frank Leadbetter and Billy Barlow dropped to the ground and crawled through the dirt out of sight on either side of the posse men. The gunmen's boots were a few feet from their faces and the rovers made eye contact past the spurs, then jumped up, coldcocking both goons on the heads with the butts of their pistols hard enough to crack their skulls. With simultaneous grunts, Starborough's men collapsed in the dirt.

Barlow and Leadbetter relieved them of their revolvers and their rifles directly, and now everybody had a gun.

The posse horses watched them with equine interest as the five rovers grabbed saddles from the ground where they had been stowed and each man saddled the nearest horse. The string were formidable quarter horse mares and geldings, but the hands of the men tightening their tack and bridles were experienced and confident cowpunchers, so none of the horses gave the slightest resistance as five strangers put boots in stirrups and climbed aboard them.

In the shadows of the arroyo, Brubaker took point and rode first, Leadbetter, Idaho, Barlow, and Maddox following on their stolen horses in a single-file procession toward the entrance to the ravine a hundred yards away, where they could already see the oceans of longhorns massing in the gloom. The wranglers rode very slowly and quietly for maximum stealth. This brief ride made for their tensest moments because the short trek to the cattle stockade put them right out in the open, in plain view of the tents on the ridge; it was the period of greatest risk and should everything go south it would be now. If even one of the posse men spotted them, the bullets would start flying and the rovers would be sitting ducks.

Their hooves slowly trod across the basin floor . . . it was just a few yards farther now.

Joe Noose was surprised to see that Laura's tent appeared to be unguarded; he hoped they hadn't moved her.

The bounty hunter had made it onto the ridge without making a sound, with both Colt Peacemaker revolvers drawn, one clenched in each fist. He huddled in the shadows against the rock wall of the canyon, scoping out the distance between him and the tents. The illumination of the oil lamps inside the canvas bathed the seventy-five feet of ground between him and the first tent in plenty of light to see by. Starborough was nowhere in sight, but three posse men walked to and fro with their Winchesters in their hands, between him and what he hoped was still Laura's tent. He hoped his disguise would work.

Wrapping the stolen leather duster tightly around him, Joe pulled the bowler hat down over his face and stuck his hands gripping the revolvers under the flaps of his coat. Then he stepped out of the shadows and made a beeline for Laura's tent. Two posse men approached on either side, engaged in a dialogue, and Joe felt their eyes on him only briefly as he gave the two a small nod of acknowledgment and kept walking like he had a place to go. To his relief, there was no break in the conversation of the two rough voices now behind him as they continued on their way.

In a few more paces, Joe Noose was a stone's throw from Laura Holdridge's tent.

The outfit rode into the herd on the stolen horses under the cover of darkness and carefully dismounted. Quietly, cautiously, the wranglers gently led their horses in single file through leathery multitudes of milling cattle, trying to make no noise to spook the cattle.

Somebody suddenly jumped up in the rows of cows, someone who had been hiding in the herd.

Startled, the three rovers jumped back in alarm.

The shadowy figure drew two pistols.

The rovers retreated, throwing up their hands.

"Boys?" Laura Holdridge stepped out of the shadows of the herd into a shaft of moonlight that revealed her flushed, overjoyed face. "Oh my God, am I glad to see you!"

"Boss!" Brubaker's and the other men's faces lit up with relief. Holstering her guns, the cattlewoman threw her arms around her wranglers and they all embraced in a group hug. They all spoke in hushed whispers. "Boss, are you okay!"

"Yeah, I got away—"

Brubaker suddenly remembered, and his expression became serious. "What are you doing here, boss?"

"I was kidnapped! What do you think I'm doing here? You came to rescue me, did'ntcha? Or just the cows?" She cracked a joking grin but Curly wasn't laughing.

"You're supposed to be in the tent."

Laura didn't get it. "How did you—I'm not at the tent. I'm here with the herd. Who cares? Where's Joe?"

"See, boss, that's the thing. He came to rescue you so he went to where he thought you'd be. Joe went to the tent."

Now she understood, Laura's eyes widened as she sucked in her breath and looked up the ridge at the row of tents in the upper darkness now alive with posse movement.

"Oh shit," she said.

Noose made it to the tent.

Peering in, he saw it had to be Laura's with all the womanly trappings.

Inside on the cot, someone was moving under a pile of blankets.

"Laura, it's Noose. Wake up." Entering the tent, Joe dropped to one knee by the cot and gently caressed the shifting bedcovers. Under the blankets the figure stirred with groggy movement like someone coming out of a deep sleep. "I'm here to rescue you. Wake up."

Joe pulled the blanket away and recoiled in surprise at the ruddy, enraged face of the wild-eyed posse man with the gag in his frothing mouth. Blood dripped down his cheek from a nasty cut on his temple. Discovering one of Starborough's operatives bound and gagged in Laura's bed in the tent he expected to find her in was such an unexpected shock for Joe Noose it took him a second to grasp he was staring into the seething eyes of the trammeled thug instead.

That was all the time it took for Starborough's man to lunge forward and head butt Noose in the face with skull-cracking force. The impact of the blow catapulted Joe up off his knees then off his feet down onto the floor of the tent, where he landed on his back, wiping blood from his nose with the back of his fist.

The posse man was instantly off the cot and on his feet, recognizing Noose right away and intending to kill him without further delay. But the man forgot two important things—three things actually—as he grabbed for his trusty revolvers. First he had no revolvers, Laura took them, so his hands came up empty. Two, and also three, his wrists and ankles were tied up with sheets, seriously impairing his movements, making fisticuffs inadvisable. In other words, in his current situation, getting into a fight with a man like Joe Noose fell on the advisability chart somewhere between mortal suicide and the worst idea in the history of bad ideas.

Joe kicked him in the balls. The goon's eyes rolled up in his head so far he perhaps saw his brain, then he just collapsed like a felled tree. In a cold fury, Noose jumped on top of the groaning eye-rolling posse man and straddled him, grabbing him by the throat and shaking him. *"Where's Laura?"* Joe throttled him. *"Where is she?"* The thug's mouth was moving under the gag and he was trying to say something but the words were garbled and incoherent.

So Joe tore the gag off his mouth.

"It's Joe Noose!" the posse man screamed at the top of his lungs. *"It's Noose! He's here! Help—!"*

A brutal knuckled jab to the jaw by Noose's fist knocked the man out cold and shut him up too late, for he'd already sounded the alarm; as Joe jumped to his feet and drew the two Colt Peacemaker revolvers, he could hear the sounds of the posse's movements outside the tent coming from every direction, and as he cocked both pistols, Joe Noose knew he was going to have to shoot his way out of this one.

He stepped out of the tent.

This brought him face-to-face with Cole Starborough, whose expression was a mask of surprise, unable to believe his eyes, as he recognized Joe Noose in the duster and hat of one of his own posse. *"You!"* the gentleman henchman hissed. He stood a few feet from the tent, cradling his Winchester, flanked on either side by two of his gunmen who had their pistols drawn. *"Shoot him!"* roared Starborough.

Noose already was firing both pistols, aiming straight ahead, shooting both of the flanking posse men between the eyes, blowing the backs of their heads off before they got off a single round—he shot them first because their pistols were leveled and Cole's rifle wasn't yet, but when he turned his arm to Starborough, the enforcer had dropped and rolled as he was triggering and re-cocking and firing his Winchester from the ground, the slugs narrowly missing Joe, who dived for cover. Hitting the dirt, he saw one of the posse gunmen behind him fall, clutching his bleeding throat and gurgling blood, struck by one of Cole's rounds meant for Noose.

Figures were running past the tents and there was a lot of yelling and confusion. Cole Starborough was out of sight, changing position. A string of gunshots rang out directly behind Joe, very close. Bullets exploded against the rocks as Noose rolled out of the way onto his back, taking quick aim up at the shooter behind and putting two rounds in his chest, sending him flying back with twin fountains of blood geysering from his shirt, open duster flapping into a tent that collapsed around him like a shroud. As the canvas structure fell, it revealed three more posse men taking position with their carbines, opening fire on the bounty hunter, whose position had also been revealed by the falling tent. Trading fire with the posse men with blazing pistols in each hand, Joe jumped up on his boots and ran through the rows of tents, ducking through the maze of canvas bivouacs and kicking them down as he urgently searched for Laura Holdridge in the darkness already fogged with gun smoke.

"Laura! *Laura!*" Noose called out for the cattlewoman at the top of his lungs. He didn't care he was giving away his position. Now, some of the fallen tents had caught fire as the coal oil lamps inside shattered, igniting the sheets of canvas, and flames were billowing up across the ridge as the air reeked of burning fuel and gunpowder. Enormous exaggerated shadows of armed moving figures loomed up the canyon walls cast in the firelight like a battle of giants, only adding to the sense of chaos.

With still no sign of Laura, Joe began worrying she had been shot in the skirmish. To his right, Noose caught a quick glimpse of a posse gunman leap out, pointing a shotgun at him, so he swiveled at the hip with both his pistols, shooting the thug in the face, both guns turning his head into red soup. All around the bounty hunter, weapons flashed and bullets whizzed past his face as the close quarters combat raged on.

One of Joe's pistols was empty—no time to reload—and he holstered it.

Hearing boots directly behind him, Joe Noose spun to find himself facing Cole Starborough, dashing blond features contorted with fury behind the Winchester repeater socked to his shoulder—he shot the remaining Colt Peacemaker revolver out of Joe's hand in a flash of sparks, the impact knocking Noose to the ground and nearly breaking his wrist.

Cole advanced, cocking the rifle and aiming the muzzle between his enemy's eyes. The henchman had the bounty hunter down, under the gun, a triumphal grin of bloodsport joy on his face as his finger tightened on the trigger. "Goodbye, old man."

Three shots suddenly rang out, so deafeningly close and loud Joe thought it had to be his enemy's gun, but Noose wasn't hit.

Cole Starborough stiffened and jerked as he was shot in the back three times, his face twisted in surprise as he spun to return fire, turning his body right into three more shots that hit him in the chest, the first two rounds slamming into his duster, hammering him back, the third blowing him clean off his feet against the side of the canyon, bounced him off the rock wall and the henchman slumped in a crumpled heap. As the gun smoke cleared, Joe saw Laura Holdridge reloading her empty pistol.

Cole blinked at Laura. "How unladylike to shoot a man in the back." He collapsed flat on his face and stopped moving.

The bounty hunter was impressed as the cattlewoman helped him up, staring intensely into his eyes. "You were supposed to be in the tent," he said.

"I know," she replied.

They looked at Cole Starborough sprawled on the ground, his duster filled with ragged holes. "Normally I take a dim view of shooting a man in the back," Noose quipped. "But for that son of a bitch, I'll make an exception." The bounty hunter pried the Winchester rifle from the henchman's fingers and took it.

Holding his hand, Laura pulled Joe across the ridge toward the stockade below where the outfit waited with the cattle.

Behind them, Cole's eyes popped open and he tore open his duster to reveal the bulletproof vest!

His fingernails knocked the flattened slugs off the padded metal plate of the harness. He got up, very angry, blood smearing his face, and grabbed his Colt Dragoon pistol from his holster. Grunting in pain, Starborough staggered against the rocks and, spotting the fleeing figures of the bounty hunter and the cattlewoman, cocked his revolver and raised it to his eye, using the rocks as leverage. Cussing a string of ungentlemanly profanity, he opened fire at them.

Bullets exploded at Joe and Laura's feet as they scrambled down the ridge into the basin. Looking back, they saw Cole, somehow still alive, blasting furiously away at them, but there was no time to shoot back, only to run. Ricochets flashed on the gravel at their heels as holding hands they ran for their lives for the cattle until they reached the rock outcrop over the ravine, the slugs from Starborough's wild shots flying past their heads until they were out of range.

"Jump!" Brubaker's voice shouted from below up at Joe and Laura. The two dove down into the ravine and landed on the ground, rolling over and over and ending up on their backs, looking up at the friendly faces of the cattle and rovers looking back down at them.

Noose clambered to his feet and brushed himself off. He looked the outfit in the face. "Get this damn herd ready to move out!"

"Where you going, Joe?" Laura hollered.

"I'm going to create a diversion, don't worry about me!" he yelled over his shoulder as he ducked back into the basin and was swallowed in darkness. "When you hear my two shots, get the herd moving!"

"Get some lamps out here!" Cole Starborough roared on the ridge as the ten surviving men of his posse scrambled for their weapons. "Find those sons of bitches! I can't see anything out there, we need some light!"

Calhoun's men were looking in front of them not in back, so they didn't see Joe Noose run at a swift crouch through the inky shadows on the ridge. The bounty hunter had spotted the crate of dynamite when he'd scoped out the camp with his binoculars earlier and knew right where to find the explosives beside the tents next to the war wagon. Reaching the open crate, he seized two clusters of dynamite and stuffed them under his armpit, grabbing two belts of .45 cartridges for his Winchester and Colt Peacemakers from the armory wagon, then, sufficiently armed in his view, he scrambled up the side of the ridge to a position that would put him directly across from the

Gatling gun on the opposite side of the basin from the herd.

Joe could not see the machine gun nest because its position was cloaked in darkness on the goat trail, but he knew how to flush it out.

Up in the machine gun nest, Earl Moore hunkered behind the Gatling gun, swinging the barrel to and fro on the tripod as he scanned the basin below where all the commotion was going on. The huge machine gun with the rotating nine-barrel cylinder was fully engaged and the breech loaded with ammo belts, ready to fire. His hands gripped the handles of the triggering mechanisms. In the scattered fires of the burning tents on the ridge, Moore could barely make out the running figures of the posse, but not much else.

"You see where that outfit is from up there?" Cole's voice shouted up at him from somewhere below. Moore could just make out his boss's dark figure cupping his hands around his mouth by the light of one of the lanterns the gunmen were lighting.

"No!" Moore yelled back down.

"You see 'em, shoot 'em!" Starborough shouted back. *"Just watch where you're firing that thing so you don't hit us!"*

Just as Earl Moore raised his hand in a thumbs-up, two shots in quick succession rang out from the darkness of the sloping wall of the ravine, ricocheting off the ground a few feet from the machine gun nest. Swinging the long arm of the barrel, he rotated the Gatling gun on its axis to take aim in the direction the shot came from, and he let them have it.

On the ridge, Joe Noose was already diving for cover after taking the blind shots while simultaneously signaling the outfit to move the herd, when over a hundred heavy caliber rounds tore into his side of the canyon. *PAPAPA-PAPPAPAPAPAPAPAPAPAPOW! The huge muzzle-flashes of the Gatling gun's spinning barrels ignited the darkness on the upper goat trail, revealing the machine gun nest's position.*

Lighting the short fuse of a stick of dynamite he pulled from the cluster, Noose heaved it above him to the top of the hill. Seconds later a gigantic explosion shook the ridge, a rolling ball of fire filling the air as dirt and stones showered down on Joe Noose, who covered his head. A second barrage from the Gatling gun rained hell around the immediate area where the explosives blew up above Joe, who already had another stick of dynamite lit, he tossed with all his strength down the ridge at the posse. "Get that damn herd moving!" he growled to himself.

Down in the stockade, the rovers and their boss all heard the twin shots, then the reports of the Gatling gun, their signals to move out. Laura shot a *let's go* look to Brubaker, who waved at the men to get the livestock moving. Working their horses, the rovers got the cattle in motion, and the sea of longhorns began to flow out of the basin.

A huge explosion of dynamite shook the ravine with violent force in an immense concussion, a blizzard of debris hurling the blown-up bodies of several posse men sky-high, raining down in bits and pieces like tattered rag dolls.

High above on the ridge, the Gatling gun thundered away at the opposite side of the ravine, the lighting from its spinning muzzle punctuated by a second then a third blinding explosion of dynamite tossed from that side of the hill into the camp, the ear-splitting detonations drowning out the staccato barrages of the machine gun.

The cattle had entered onto the goat trail, surrounded by whooping and hollering cowboys on horses waving their lariats, driving the herd through a war zone. The steers needed little encouragement and they wanted out of that place as fast as their hooves could run.

Astonished by the destruction to his camp, Cole Starborough walked in a daze through the explosions of dynamite, trying to make sense of the chaos as he shouted orders to his men running this way and that in the melee.

Earl Moore was gritting his teeth, blasting away with the machine gun. He didn't see or hear the hundreds of charging cattle coming up the trail behind his back, an ocean of horns and thundering hooves of seven hundred thousand pounds of cattle, three hundred and fifty tons of steers in unstoppable forward motion with the force of ten locomotives. Moore was too busy blasting whoever was chucking that damn dynamite across the canyon; because the TNT explosions were deafeningly loud and the machine gun itself very, very noisy, Earl couldn't hear the rumble of pounding hooves growing ever louder to his rear. With the vibration of the Gatling gun trembling on the chassis as the barrel rotated, spitting heavy caliber rounds, Moore simply didn't register the ground shaking from the booming cattle hooves.

Then out of the corner of his eye, Earl saw movement in the basin below. Someone waving. Ignoring them, returning his gaze forward, he kept clenching the handles of the triggering mechanism and shooting ceaselessly into the darkness on the opposite side of the canyon, ammo belts rattling through the breech so he couldn't hear anything, the Gatling gun stitching a line of sparking ricochets in the darkness of the hill until a sudden earth-shaking *boom*, blinding flash of TNT, and eruption of rocks and geysers of dirt when another stick of dynamite detonated.

The shock wave of the blast knocked Earl Moore back and he lost his footing, landing on his ass. Cursing, he resumed blasting away, laying down fields of fire onto the hill, determined to kill the dynamite-happy son of a bitch if it was the last thing he ever did. And as he wasted another five hundred rounds of ammunition and the brass cartridge empties spewed in a glittering stream from the machine gun clattering in piles ankle-deep by his boots, Earl Moore still did not see the charging longhorns bearing down on him.

This couldn't be happening! Not to him! Unable to believe his eyes, Cole Starborough stood down in the basin and bore witness to his own ruin. It all was unfolding right in front of him. He knew exactly what was happening, how his posse was being tricked, yet was helpless to fix it. In horror, he saw the inexorable approach of the string of cattle up the goat trail closing in on Earl Moore firing the Gatling gun, crouched directly in the path of the horns. Cole screamed at the top of his lungs, waving his arms from below, trying to warn Earl to look over his shoulder, but couldn't get his attention. *"Look behind you! Behind you!"*

If the cows got past the machine gun nest, it was clear open trail and nothing stood in the way of the cattle's escape.

Finally Moore saw Cole.

Saw him pointing *behind you!*

He saw the cows.

Earl Moore had good reflexes. With seconds to spare, he swung the huge Gatling gun with all his strength around on its tripod chassis, throwing his body weight behind the breech, jamming in the fresh ammo belt and engaging the bolt as the long cylindrical rotating barrel swept a wide arc a full 180 degrees to face the horde of longhorns an instant too late, for as Earl's hands closed on the triggers, the first of those curved horns went through his head and tore his hands off the gun he never got a chance to fire.

Below, Cole's mouth gaped, witnessing the jaw-dropping carnage. Earl turned the Gatling gun around when the entire herd was on top of him and it looked like the man just exploded, hit by all those horns, and what they carried away wasn't much to speak of.

The machine gun nest was completely obliterated by the surging steers. The Gatling gun got hit by the cows and was knocked over the edge. Cole watched it fall, choked with emotion, his magnificent piece of war machinery dropping down the steep cliff with such grandeur in its descent, Starborough wanted to salute. He was relieved to see the heavy machine gun finally hit the ground in one piece. Starborough had bigger problems than repairing a Gatling gun.

The cows were free. The great herd massed in a steady streaming procession up the trail over the top of the ridge out of the basin, and from there to the open range and freedom. The wranglers of the outfit drove their steers like virtuosos, waving their hats, whooping and hollering and *laughing*! The henchman hated those men, he really did.

The last of the string of cattle escaped in a train of horns, hooves, heads, and haunches; all that beef had slipped through Cole Starborough's fingers, and he was powerless to stop them so he just sat down on the ground and put his face in his hands. When his boss heard this it was not going to end well for him.

At least he didn't have to tell Calhoun any of his steers died.

Cole didn't see any dead cows.

He hadn't lost a single cow.

He had lost all of them.

CHAPTER 23

They were free.

Dawn was just breaking as Joe Noose, Laura Holdridge, Curly Brubaker, Billy Barlow, Frank Leadbetter, Joe Idaho, and Rowdy Maddox rode the herd to freedom. They were all whooping and hollering and cheering as they drove the cattle in a thundering charge across the open plain, riding their horses and running the herd, the wind in their faces, heading straight into the glorious fireball of the sun that rose heroically across the horizon in the east.

Joe Noose had retrieved his Stetson before departing the canyon but wasn't wearing it now. Waving their hats, the jubilant cries of the wranglers could be heard over the clamor of the hooves and even the sound of Joe and Laura's own cheering voices because the cattlewoman and bounty hunter were hollering just as loud; everyone's spirits soared, pumped with adrenaline from their spectacular escape they'd be telling their grandkids about . . . *"We did it! We did it! . . . Yeeeee-aaaahhhhh! . . . We kicked their asses! . . . Got every damn cow!"* Joe was galloping Copper alongside Laura's horse, with her proud figure tall in the saddle. When he looked over and saw her brave, hardy, beautiful face framed in golden light and she looked back at him, an invincible sense of immortality passed between them, a feeling that nothing could stop them and they were going to live forever.

It sure was a great feeling, but Noose being Noose, he looked back over his shoulder at the canyon they had just escaped from, where the posse were encamped, just to be safe. *Never look back, something might be gaining on you.* The atoll of rock was miles behind them now, with no sign they were being followed. The lingering grim cloud of gun and dynamite smoke hung over the canyon basin like doom, a reminder just how badly Cole Starborough and his forces had been defeated last night.

The longhorns and horses had pushed on through darkness those first miles, trusting the cows to find their way, but as the sun lifted a vast wall of light passed over the sprawling landscape that peeled away the darkness like a wrapper so the trail became visible. Once day broke, the five hundred head of steer and the capable, indefatigable drivers who drove them had moved at a clip, skipping meals, just pushing forward through the empty badlands. They had a lot of ground to cover to make up for lost time.

The wide-open plains were so barren and desolate it was easy for Joe to see how this part of eastern Wyoming earned its nickname the Big Empty. Nothing for mile after mile as far as you could see. Sometime late in the afternoon, Noose saw far to the north a funnel of dust a few miles away; it could have been a small tornado, a dust storm, or a group of horses and riders at full gallop, like a posse. The clouds of dust were too far away to tell, but Joe didn't like that it was moving in a west to east direction, coming from behind the cattle drive and moving on ahead, overtaking the herd and dispersing into the distance in a diaspora of settling dust.

Had Cole Starborough regrouped his forces and ridden ahead to lie in wait and ambush the outfit somewhere up ahead at a time and place of his choosing for a final show-down in the Big Empty?

Joe Noose wasn't certain, but did know what kind of man Calhoun's henchman was: a man who didn't quit. The bounty hunter knew this because he understood his foe, who in some respects reminded him of himself.

In the driver's seat on the bench of her wagon, Laura tied off the reins and opened the map, studying it until she had their approximate position in relation to their destination.

Cheyenne lay ninety-eight miles ahead.

Four days' ride.

It was Friday.

The date—what was the damn date?

The tenth of February. Yes, she was sure of it.

The auction was February sixteenth.

Four days to get there.

There was a chance, the narrowest hope, that if they got lucky, the outfit could still make it to Cheyenne in time to get the cattle to auction.

If nothing went wrong.

The Union Pacific Railroad steam train crossed north-west over the Texas border into eastern Colorado on its way past Denver toward its final destination, Cheyenne, Wyoming. The grinding driving wheels of the huge locomotive drove the rolling stock down the line, towing a string of nine coaches and a brake wagon in clamoring procession throughout the night. The steam engine's exhaust belched dirty fumes into the sky, smoke and hot cinders spewing from its stack, scattering in the desert air. The tympani of the rusty wheels beat a percussive syncopation on the rail bed as the train rattled and swayed its way along the tracks. The train consisted of eight coaches. On the caboose, heavily armed Pinkerton detectives kept watch on the platform and performed regular foot patrols of the entire train; the agency had been hired for security because the passengers on this trip were the wealthiest and most powerful citizens of the Old West. The railroad was taking them all to the annual cattlemen's auction in Cheyenne, as it did every year.

The entire train was privately reserved by the six cattle barons who made up the cartel of the Cattlemen's Association. Each tycoon had an entire private car allocated to himself and his associates for his own personal use. The ninth car was the horse truck, where the cattlemen stabled their best mounts they took with them on the trip. The eighth coach was the restaurant car, its kitchen staffed with a chef imported from Paris. The seventh car was the club car, a richly appointed custom coach that inside was like a salon with opulent furnishings from plush suede leather couches and red velvet cushioned chairs to a full-length bar with a brass rail. The light fixtures holding the gas lamps were sterling silver. It was the ultimate in luxurious comfort for the men for whom price was no object and no expense ever spared.

The air was filled with cigar smoke and the smell of good aged bourbon. Five cattle barons stood it the car, being served by the bartender. They all wore expensive suits, vests, ties, and cowboy boots, and each sported well-groomed beards and mustaches. The beef tycoons all owned major herds on major spreads, coming from across the western states as far west as California and as far east as Nebraska, boarding the privately reserved steam train as it passed through their states.

The door opened and Crispin Calhoun entered the car coming from the back of the train. He was followed by a quiet armed operative, who joined the bodyguards for the other men standing against the walls. Calhoun was dressed in a black suit, black shirt with red roses, fine cowboy boots—with lifts to raise his height—and solid gold roweled Mexican spurs. He had on an elegant black leather jacket with tassels tailored from the finest new-born calfskin. Twin solid gold-plated pearl-handled Colt revolvers were slung in his holsters. The cattle baron wore a huge black Stetson, and below the brim his countenance was dark and intense. Among the rest of the cattlemen he called his peers, Calhoun was slightest of stature but carried about him a formidable sense of mortal threat, a look of violence around the eye that showed he was capable of anything. The other cattle barons all knew he was half-crazy, but his rise to the top of the cattle business in just a few years had earned the respect of his peers. For this cartel, the strong eat the weak, and the only thing a cattle-man respects is strength. It was no secret that Crispin

Calhoun killed a lot of men to steal their herds building his own empire, but the other five cattle barons in the club car didn't hold it against him; they couldn't—after all, they all had murdered rivals to steal livestock and land or to simply eliminate the competition. It was all part of being a cattleman.

The five cattlemen standing at the bar with boots on the brass rail welcomed Crispin Calhoun, who gave them a big grin and shook hands vigorously with the other members of the Cattlemen's Association.

"Gentlemen!" he said in his sibilant voice with a susurration of the vowels. "Good to see you, boys. The next round is on me. Bartender, drinks all around."

Suddenly came a shriek of steam whistle, a graunching of locking steam brakes and the train began to slow. Taking their drinks with them, the cattle barons walked out on the platform to see what the holdup was and looked toward the front of the railroad.

The locomotive was pulled up alongside a fifty-foot-high wooden water tower on a scaffolding. A member of the driving crew, a fireman in sooty overalls, stepped off the locomotive and stood on the ladder, feeding a long metal pipe from the circular water vat into the lip of the boiler on the nose of the locomotive. Water flooded down the pipe into the steam engine, refueling it for the rest of the long trip to Cheyenne. The burning coal in the locomotive firebox boiled the water that generated the huge amount of steam used to drive the giant wheels of the hundred-ton train.

Shortly, the fireman acknowledged the engineer with a wave to indicate the train was fueled. Disengaging the pipe from the nose of the engine, he cranked it on a chain back up into the tower, then swung off the scaffolding onto the footplate of the doorway to the engine.

A piercing blast of the train whistle split the air, followed by loud *hisses* of steam, *clanks* of unlocking brakes, and mechanical graunching as the engine was throttled. The steel-on-steel of wheels on rails slowly ground and the train lurched into motion. The locomotive's driving wheels slipped once, twice, three times, then they began to bite, and the train started back up the tracks, slowly at first, then picking up speed.

The cattle cartel repaired back to the bar inside the club coach, talking shop. During the discussion, as he sipped his whiskey, Crispin Calhoun gave a casual glance to the blackboard on the wall of the train car. He was familiar with it because the cattle barons, all betting men, routinely used the board to record gambling wagers on everything involving the element of chance from sports to political campaigns to cattle prices.

Calhoun's brows furrowed and jaw tightened when he recognized the word "Bar H" and the name "Laura Holdridge" written on the board in chalk. There were numbers indicating gambling odds chalked beside her name, and she had been given ten-to-one odds. His colleagues had already placed bets. The vein in his forehead began to throb as blood rushed to his face. He was very angry that his peers in the Cattlemen's Association would dare show him the disrespect to bet *on that woman* showing him up.

"Why is the widow Holdridge on our betting board?" Calhoun asked, controlling his rage.

"We're betting on the chances of Sam Holdridge's wife

getting her five hundred steers to Cheyenne," Sherman Rutledge said, puffing cigar smoke. "Right now, we give it ten-to-one odds she makes it."

"The Bar H herd will never make it to Cheyenne, mark my words." Calhoun glowered.

"What you got against Sam's wife anyway, Calhoun?" Cyrus McCullough inquired, curious about the malevolent hatred radiating off his counterpart on the subject of the woman. "Her ranch is small but it has a proud name in the cattle ranching business, and her husband was one of us."

"What do I have against the widow Holdridge? She wears a skirt." Crispin Calhoun took a long sip of whiskey, leaned on his boot on the brass tail, leveling a baleful gaze down the bar at his colleagues. "The cattle business is man's business. Who does this uppity woman think she is, thinking s*he* can be one of *us*, sit at *our* table, behave like our *equal*, join *our* Cattlemen's Association? Over my dead body, I say. The next thing she'd want is the right to vote."

There was laughter all around, but Sherman Rutledge wouldn't let it go; he didn't like Calhoun, even if the others did. "What you have against that lady is she turned down your offer to buy her ranch and livestock. Maybe that wasn't all she turned down, Calhoun." Rutledge rolled his cigar in his fingers and winked at the other tycoons. "Clearly Sam's wife wasn't impressed or intimidated by you. Maybe you're not man enough for her."

Calhoun's eyes went dead. Being made fun of made him pathological, and when he spoke his words were flat. "The widow Holdridge hasn't got a chance in hell of getting her steers to Cheyenne. I have it on excellent authority that the Bar H Ranch is already out of business."

Rutledge laughed. "They say everything is big in Texas including their mouths. Put your money where your mouth is, Calhoun. Money talks, bullshit walks. The bet is ten to one."

"Ten to one is a sucker's bet."

"Back up your big words. Put skin in the game."

"I'll show you skin." Rearing up straight, Calhoun swung his arm and slammed his little fist down on the bar, eyes glittering madly. "I will see your ten-to-one . . ." His lips drew back in a rictus grin. "And raise you *ten thousand* to one. I give you ten-thousand-to-one odds she doesn't make it." With a boozy roar of approval, the other beef tycoons clapped and applauded at the Texas cattle baron's crazed audacity, for cattlemen always enjoyed bold displays of bravado. Calhoun arrogantly eyeballed his fellow cattle barons. "There are exactly ten thousand and sixty-two steers on my ranch in Amarillo. I bet my entire Amarillo herd that Holdridge bitch doesn't get to Cheyenne."

His colleagues whistled. "In time for the auction?" Cyrus McCullough asked.

"At all."

Rutledge leaned back and puffed his cigar, did some quick math. "So let us get this straight, Calhoun. We bet *one* steer of ours, against *ten thousand* of yours? Laura Holdridge doesn't get her cows to Cheyenne, we each have to pay you one steer. She does get her cows to Cheyenne in time for the auction, you have to pay us ten thousand head of cattle, that we'd all divvy up. That is the bet you're proposing."

"Correct." Calhoun savored the doubting looks the other cattlemen now exchanged regarding Laura Holdridge's fate at this point. A few moments ago, she had been something to them, now she was nothing. *If Crispin Calhoun was that confident . . .*

Rutledge shrugged. "Well, I reckon I lost a steer because you're so damn cocky, but hell yes, it's a bet."

"We're all in." The other four agreed.

"Shall we shake on it, gentlemen, or do we toast?" Laidlaw raised his glass.

"I'll give it to you in writing." Calhoun smiled expansively. He snapped his fingers, and his operative rushed to his private car to fetch a piece of Calhoun Cattle Company stationery, with which he returned forthwith. With a flourish, Calhoun took out a gold fountain pen from his jacket and wrote in elegant script a promissory note giving his marker to his fellow cattlemen for the brazen bet.

> *Witnessed this tenth day of February 1887, I, Crispin Calhoun, do hereby wager all ten thousand cattle on my Calhoun Cattle Company Bar T cattle ranch in Amarillo, Texas against one cow each from the members of the Cattlemen's Association, that Laura Holdridge and her livestock of the Bar H Ranch will not reach Cheyenne, Wyoming in time for the American Cattlemen's Association auction on February 16th. Signed, Crispin Calhoun.*

The evil cattle baron signed his name with a flourish, and then passed the note and the pen around to each of the five cattle barons, who signed their names to the document in turn.

"I'll hold the marker." Rutledge took the promissory

note, folded it, and slid it into his jacket, patting the pocket. "Well, Calhoun, if you're wrong about this cowgirl, you're going to lose a fortune."

The evil cattleman's thin lips turned up in an icy smile as he signed for the bartender to bring another round of drinks. He took a cigar from the humidor and pulled out his cigar cutter, disturbingly fashioned from a metal tool used to castrate bulls, and snipped the end of the cigar off like it was a pair of testicles. "Safest bet of my life."

Chapter 24

Cole Starborough was thinking of the Spartans.

He was, after all, an educated man, who had enjoyed the benefits of a classical education. It wasn't history that brought the Spartans to mind—military history had been his favorite subject—but the strategy and tactics of warfare.

The narrow gorge that lay before him was a tight fit, a natural corridor walled in by hundred-foot-high canyon cliffs on two sides. The location would have done the Spartans proud at the Battle of Thermopylae where by forcing Xerxes's overwhelmingly superior forces into a tight space that pinned them, the Spartans took the high ground atop the cliffs and shot their enemies with arrows and spears like fish in a barrel. If it was good enough for Sparta, it was good enough for him. For this identical squeeze tactic was exactly what Cole intended to use on Laura Holdridge and her outfit when they came down the trail as it passed through the tight passage between the cliffs where they would die.

Cole wouldn't lose a single cow.

Calhoun's henchman walked on the high cliff looking

down a hundred feet into the narrow gorge to the dusty bottom below; the space was tight, ten to fifteen feet in width its entire length, barely enough room to squeeze a cow through. The steers were going to have to be marched in single-file formation through the passage. When the bullets from Starborough's rifles on top of the gorge started flying, and hell rained from above down on the Bar H outfit's heads, it would be over in a matter of seconds. The rovers would never know what hit them. Hell, they'd never even get a shot off. Not that it would matter if they did. There was no way out.

Cole looked down into the chasm, switching his thoughtful glance to the entrance and exit of the quarter-mile gorge, mentally determining where to position his gunmen to cut off any escape for the outfit and livestock. He'd have his guns already in position at the exit when the Bar H herd arrived. His riflemen, strategically hidden at the entrance, would have to move into position as soon as all the rovers were in the gorge, so they weren't spotted, because the element of surprise was crucial. Once the men and cows were inside the chasm, soon as the shooting began, Cole did not worry about a retreat. The corridor was too tight to turn a steer, and cows don't back up, so the only way for the cowpunchers to escape was forward, right into his artillery. Nobody in the outfit gets out alive.

Then, once the smoke cleared, Cole Starborough would simply go down with his posse, take possession of the ownerless cattle and drive them to Cheyenne.

They would leave the corpses of Laura Holdridge, her drivers, and that big son-of-a-bitch Joe Noose for the vultures; the buzzards out here in the Big Empty would strip their bones clean in a matter of days, and that would be the end of them.

In a matter of hours, the livestock would be his, to be turned over to his boss, cattleman Crispin Calhoun, each cow to be rebranded with the Bar T monogram and become the Calhoun Cattle Company's property to be sold at the auction in Cheyenne.

Five hundred head.

Cole reminded himself to tell his gunmen to place their shots carefully and watch their aim.

Don't hit the cows.

The loss of even one steer would displease Crispin Calhoun very greatly; the cost of that animal would not simply come out of Cole's salary, it would come out of his hide. Literally.

But the henchman felt confident there was nothing to worry about.

"The scout's back, Mr. Starborough."

Looking up, Cole saw Earl Moore gesturing to a rider fast approaching; one of his operatives rode up and dismounted, strode past the rest of Calhoun's posse cleaning and oiling their guns, and marched right up to Starborough, where he stood and delivered. "Scout reporting, sir. The Bar H herd is up the trail three and a half miles, heading this way. They're down to six men. Sir."

"That makes them due to arrive here in an hour and a half," Cole calculated, consulting his pocket watch, smile widening. "High noon."

Perfect. Casting a look up to the cold blinding sun, he saw it was at eleven o'clock; in an hour and a half it would be directly overhead, in the eyes of the helpless men and woman of the outfit when they looked up at Cole's gunmen firing down at them with the sun at their backs. Laura Holdridge's rovers would be too blinded to aim into direct sunlight. It would be over before it began.

It was a perfect ambush. Cole Starborough grinned savagely with pointed teeth.

Let's see you get out of this one, Joe Noose.

Even the Spartans didn't have it so good.

"I don't like it." Joe Noose lowered the field glasses he had trained on the opening to the gorge beneath the cliffs. He was standing with Laura Holdridge a quarter of a mile away, beside the string of cattle now at a standstill after the bounty hunter spotted the chasm they had to pass through. "This place is wrong."

Laura took the field glasses and scanned the inside of the distant gorge and the roof of the cliffs, seeing no movement, adjusting the focus, looking again to see nothing but rocks. "I don't see anything, Joe."

"You wouldn't until it's too late. Any fool can see that spot is ideal for an ambush."

"You really think so?"

"We know what's left of that posse rode on ahead of us. I don't make Cole Starborough or his boss Crispin Calhoun the types to give up. That fancy son of a bitch could be laying in wait ahead, could have rifles positioned anywhere. It's what I'd do if I was him. That passage is too narrow. We'll have to march the stock and our horses and us, single file. Once we're in the chasm we can't turn back, there's no place to go but forward. If they're waiting for us, once we get inside, we'll be sitting ducks." Joe made the finger gesture of a rifle picking off shots, one after the other. "I say no way."

Laura believed Joe and shared his worry, but she looked distraught. "Then *what do we do*, Joe?"

He shrugged. "Find another route. Take the cattle across the Big Empty another way."

"There is no other way! Look around. Nothing but canyons as far as you can see between us and Cheyenne."

"We'll have to find another way around."

"You show me, Joe!" In frustration, the cattlewoman reached into her jacket and yanked out the map, spreading it with a punch of her fist against the saddle, punching her forefinger against the section of the trail on the map. She did it so hard it sounded like a hammer hitting a nail. "Go ahead. You tell me. Where do we drive the herd? You show me. This way? All canyon. Over here, same, all canyon."

Leaning over the map with her, Noose heaved a sigh. Couldn't argue with her, going through the gorge was the only way to get the cows to Cheyenne.

She locked her piercing blue eyes on the map and brushed her blond hair from her face, tracing her finger on the topographical demarcations. "The only other way is to turn the whole damn herd around and backtrack two hundred miles north then turn south again along the Snake River. It will set us back a week. Days we don't have."

He nodded grimly.

The cattlewoman stood up straight and met his gaze with fierce authority. "It's my outfit. It's my decision. We're going through."

The bounty hunter didn't even blink. "Let me go on ahead then. I'll do a patrol of the gorge. Look around.

Report back here directly. If it's safe, we can pass the herd through. OK with you?"

"Fair enough."

"Better safe then sorry."

"Be careful."

"Always."

Noose grabbed his Winchester off the saddle scabbard of his bronze horse and proceeded down the trail on foot to the yawning opening of the gorge. Laura's mouth was dry, so she sipped from her canteen as she watched Joe's huge, strapping figure shrink smaller and smaller down the trail as he approached the gorge, until, when he set foot through the opening, Noose disappeared in the shadows. He was there then suddenly he was gone was how it seemed to Laura, who forgot to breathe.

The rock walls of the canyon were closing in on him, the bounty hunter felt as he entered and stood inside the gorge, as if the tall cliffs were actually physically pressing together to crush him flat; the passage was so narrow it made him claustrophobic, even though he usually had no fear of tight spaces. Reaching out on either side of him, Joe could almost touch each opposite wall at the same time; he had an admittedly long reach, but the space was so tight the idea of pushing five hundred cattle, horses, and wagons through made his sphincter tighten. The gorge had an unpleasant dusty, dank smell with a tincture of dead animal that tickled his nostrils.

Clenching his rifle, Noose was on high alert, his keen eyes scanning the walls, floor, and entrance to the gorge, looking for any sign of Cole Starborough's men.

Nothing.

He tilted his head back and his eyes traveled up the

cliff walls, first one side, then the other, past where the shadowy lower canyon rose into too-bright sunlight that gave him momentary blindness before his eyes adjusted. And then he was looking straight into the sun directly overhead and had to shut his eyes and look away, getting spots in front of his eyes. He rubbed them. Joe didn't like that he couldn't see what was above him on the cliff overlooking the gorge passageway—if Starborough had riflemen positioned up there, the outfit would not be able to see them or return fire with the sun in their eyes.

Noose had a bad feeling about this place, a feeling of mortality about the ground beneath his feet that grew worse with every step of his boots.

It felt like the place he was going to die.

He couldn't explain it.

But he felt it.

Looking up, the sun exploded in his eyes, so he averted his gaze.

And took another step.

Cole Starborough kept Joe Noose in the gunsights of his Sharps rifle, his eye focusing past the circular flip-up sight to the notch on the barrel to the head of the big cowboy, the muzzle inching a fraction left to right with each step the cowboy below took.

Noose was a professional like he was, Starborough was loath to admit, capable and experienced enough to recognize the gorge was the perfect spot for an ambush, and smart enough to go on ahead of the outfit to scout. The smart, tough son of a bitch wouldn't see anything with the sun right above him. Cole was smarter than he was, doubting Noose even knew what a Spartan was, but boy, did Cole want to blow those smart brains right out of the back of the man's skull—he could if he wanted to, right this very second.

The gentleman henchman relished the thrill of knowing he could kill his enemy here, now, any moment he chose.

His gloved finger itched on the cocked trigger.

The slightest pressure and Noose's head would disappear, blown clean off his shoulders.

God, how Cole wanted to do it.

It was animal urge—the beast in him wanted meat, craved blood, this man's blood; the murderous compulsion that grew harder for Starborough to resist with each step the man in his gunsights took as below he walked through the gorge, closing in on the exit. In these terrible seconds, Cole wanted to kill Noose more than he had ever wanted anything in his life, more than money, more than women, more than power. His enemy's hide right now meant more than any of that. He simply had to kill Joe Noose.

His finger tightened pressure on the trigger.

The first *click* of the hammer sounded, about to release and slam down on the cartridge and fire the round that would erase his nemesis from earthly existence.

Only when his other eye saw the moist trickle of perspiration seeping down the canted steel barrel of his rifle did the enforcer realize he was sweating like a pig, his face sopping with it, and saw how close he had come to missing his opportunity to end this whole thing.

If he took Noose now, the outfit would hear the gunshot, know it was an ambush and stay out of the gorge. Cole and his men could, would, still shoot it out with them directly, but outside the gorge were plenty of places for the rovers to take cover, evening the odds even though he had more men and guns. The chance of casualties of his own men wasn't what bothered Cole about an open skirmish.

They'd lose cows.

Cattle would get caught in the crossfire.

Bringing the full force of Crispin Calhoun's wrath.

No, too risky.

Stick to the plan.

It's a perfect one.

Just have to wait.

Just

A

Few

More

Seconds

Down below in the gorge, Joe Noose had reached the other side, a few steps from the opposite entrance. He kept his Winchester rifle at the ready, looking left and right, front and behind, everywhere but up into the blinding sun. He had patrolled the entire gorge.

So far seen nothing.

Heard nothing.

Death he felt was here, Noose was so certain of it, every nerve ending in his body twitching like antennae from danger, a sense of mortal doom weighing in his guts like a rock in his belly, or so it felt, but still he saw nothing, heard nothing, and as he took his final steps toward the opening, Joe figured he was on edge because he was too damn exhausted.

Through the exit of the gorge, he saw a cavernous

ravine, just more of the Big Empty, and as he was about to emerge from the shadowy chasm Joe stepped into a wall of dazzling sunlight that stung his eyes and made him blink, blinding him for a few seconds.

Not ten feet away around the corner, three of Cole Starborough's thugs had their rifles trained on the edge of the opening Joe was just about to step through, itching to pull the trigger the instant a piece of the man appeared, but under orders not to fire until the men and cattle entered the gorge. Noose didn't see them because they were positioned on the other side of the opening. He didn't hear them because the men were very good.

Inside the gorge, the bounty hunter sighed and lowered his rifle.

There was nothing here.

Daylight was wasting.

Turning around, he strode briskly back the way he came to report back to Laura to bring the herd on through.

CHAPTER 25

It was high noon.

The cattle drive entered the gorge.

Proceeding one cow at a time because the narrow space was so limited, the herd progressed very slowly. Laura rode in the lead, ahead of the first steer. She led the livestock in single-file succession and Joe rode five steers behind her and the lead cow, on Copper. Only a few yards into the path between the tight walls of the cliff Noose realized a fresh danger he had not considered: the deadly sharp curved horns of the steer behind his horse were only a few feet behind Copper's haunches. If these cattle spooked for any reason, and cows spooked for lots of reasons, and then took off and stampeded, the bounty hunter and his golden steed would be impaled on those very horns, trampled, and crushed under thousands of hooves. His horse was jittery, realizing the same thing.

Joe's face was sweating not just from the heat as he looked over his shoulder and saw, twenty cows back, Curly Brubaker, just as nervous as he was, casting looks back at the horns of the steer behind him. Beyond the foreman, Joe could make out the figures of Billy Barlow, Frank

Leadbetter, Joe Idaho, and Rowdy Maddox on their horses in the procession of cattle. Looking ahead, Noose saw they still had a quarter mile of the gorge to pass through.

Looking up, the blasting sun directly overhead blinded the bounty hunter so he couldn't even see the top of the cliffs above, and even shielding his eyes with his hand and tilting his hat brim didn't block the blazing white orb of the noonday sun that made him see spots in his field of vision, so he needed to look away.

Every nerve in Noose's body sensed imminent danger. His left hand held the reins, keeping Copper at a patient trot with the pace and rhythm of the cattle. His right hand drew his loaded Colt Peacemaker and his thumb cocked back the hammer.

Seconds later came the first shot. It was aimed at Joe and barely missed, slamming into the leather of his saddle an inch from his ass. Noose instantly fired upwards.

Then the real shooting started.

"Ammmmm-buuuuuu-ssssshhhh!" Joe roared, swinging his head back around to the men.

The sky rained lead down on the cattle drive. A torrential downpour of screaming bullets bringing death from above exploded around the gorge.

Brubaker was hit in the leg as he drew his Henry rifle out of his saddle scabbard now soaked in his blood, crying out in pain as he dropped the reins and used both arms to shoulder his weapon and return fire into the sun-blasted sky.

Leadbetter's horse took a bullet in the shoulder and threw its head back and bellowed, prancing in a death dance on unsteady legs between the moving cattle. Frank tried to control his falling horse even as he fired his pistol at the top of the canyon, hoping to hit something, anything.

Joe took the reins in his teeth, freeing his left hand to draw his second pistol and straightened his arms above his head, triggering his Colts.

A body fell shrieking from top of the cliff, duster flapping, a fountain of blood spurting from his chest, dropping in the midst of the cattle, the sounds of bones being crushed beneath hooves satisfying to the enraged Noose.

The gorge was a sonic echo chamber that amplified the gunfire into cacophonic din reverberating deafeningly. The bawling of the alarmed cattle added to the ear-splitting din.

Many of the rounds struck the canyon walls in loud ricks and flashes of sparks, the slugs caroming back and forth off each side in buzzing zigzags of deadly ricochets. The cowpunchers tried to duck them as they returned fire but couldn't see anything above aiming up into the blinding sun directly overhead. Clouds of dust and gun smoke combined with the haze of dirt kicked up by the cows to create a cloaking fog of detritus, immediately reducing visibility in the chasm.

Laura!

In a panic, Joe looked ahead to see the cattlewoman turned in her saddle ahead, her face a mask of fear, yelling back at him words he couldn't hear amidst all the gunfire and melee, gesturing stubbornly at the cattle with her hands, trying to tell Noose something, and he could just read her lips.

Laura was screaming back at Noose. *"He won't shoot the cattle!"*

"Like hell he won't!" Joe shouted back.

She bellowed at him, her blazing eyes ferocious.

"Starborough won't kill a cow! Calhoun's orders! That's how we get out of this! Tell the boys to use the cattle for cover! Ride the cattle!"

Now Joe understood.

Swiveling in the saddle as he fired his guns upwards, Noose yelled at the top of his lungs back at the men, *"Get on the cattle! Ride the steers!"*

It wasn't like the rovers had much choice—the steers had been panicked by the loud reverberating gunfire and flying bullets and wanted to get out of the boxed-in enclosure as fast as possible, accelerating with dreadful force. Lowering their horns, the lowing cattle bulldozed through the horses ahead of their skulls, impaling the mares and geldings on their horns, causing the whinnying bleeding steeds to collapse in gushes of gore, getting trampled beneath the pounding hooves of the quickening herd.

The wranglers saw it coming and owning quick reflexes, did the only thing they could, jumping off of the saddles of their dying horses and grabbing on to the backs or horns of the nearest cow, holding on for dear life.

A bloody flower of blood bloomed on Billy Barlow's chest as he was shot in the heart. The next round blew his jaw clean off his face in a gory shower of bone and teeth. His eyes rolled up in their sockets in what was left of his head and he fell over in his saddle and off his horse. Joe winced as he heard the man's body squashed under the hooves of the charging steers, a huge wall of blood spraying like an erupting geyser against the sides of the cliff.

Noose saw Curly Brubaker, Frank Leadbetter, Joe Idaho, and Rowdy Maddox were now riding the cattle. A few managed to hang on to the big thundering herd and get shots off with their pistols at the riflemen above. But their horses were done for, the awful death screams of the horses as they got impaled and sucked under the surging cattle was tough for Joe to listen to.

"Jump off your horse, Joe!" Laura screamed back at him. *Like hell he would.*

Joe Noose stayed in the saddle of Copper, his best friend, having long ago decided if his stallion went, so would he. Throwing glances over his shoulder at the huge steer with its three-foot pointed horns charging after them, the bounty hunter jabbed his spurs in his horse and rode him with precision, right behind the running longhorn in front of him, guiding Copper with his legs and reins, keeping a few feet safe distance from the steer to their rear.

Then all at once, he was out of the gorge into the open ravine surrounded by huge boulders, seeing the deep draw gouged in the rocks on the left. It would provide cover. Laura Holdridge had already leaped out of her saddle and ducked into the draw, gesturing to Noose to follow her lead.

Knowing Copper was safe, Joe swung out of the saddle, hit the ground on his boots, and rolled into the draw, letting his horse ride on.

The cattle thundered past in a fearsome train of hooves and cow flesh, the horns and faces of some covered with the blood of the trampled, gored horses left behind in the gorge. The sledgehammer pounding of thousands of hooves shook the ground.

On top of the cliff, Cole Starborough saw the wranglers on top of the charging cows, clinging on to the animals, and lowered his rifle, knowing he no longer had a clear shot at any of them without risking killing a steer while they were down in the gun-smoke-filled narrow gorge.

He waved his arms to his men to stop shooting. "Cease fire! Don't shoot the cows!"

Beside Starborough, one of his posse men took a bullet in the eye, splattering Cole with blood, and fell forward off the cliff, dropping head over heels a hundred feet down and disappearing from view beneath the rushing herd of cows. Wrinkling his nose in distaste, the gentleman hench-man used his handkerchief to wipe the blood from his tailored shirt and he gestured to his line of riflemen to follow his lead.

"Change positions! Shoot 'em when they come out of the gorge and you have clear shots!"

The posse men mustered across the roof of the canyon to where it opened below into the deep crevice of the rock-strewn ravine.

"You two with me!" Cole gestured to two gunmen who followed Starborough as he ran over to the war wagon parked on the trailhead that led to the top of the cliff. There, the henchman tore open the steel-plated doors and threw open the lid of the custom case containing the Gatling gun. "Get this set up!" He grinned viciously, grabbing an armful of .50 caliber ammo belts as his men lifted the hundred-pound machine gun and tripod from the case. Struggling under the weight, the operatives carried it to the end of the cliff overlooking the ravine where their boss directed them to place it and quickly set it up, moving like a well-oiled machine as they had been trained.

A few minor repairs on the previous day had restored the Gatling gun to pristine working order, as Cole had demonstrated by shooting buzzards and obliterating them out of the sky. Now he was going to get a chance to use it on something without feathers.

Down in the draw, peering over the edge of the rocks, Joe and Laura saw Brubaker clinging for his life riding an approaching steer. "Curly!" they yelled, gesturing madly with their arms. He saw them just in time and rolled off the back of the cow in a none-too-graceful dismount, landing in a messy heap inside the draw and letting out a scream of pain. His wounded leg was bleeding like hell.

And the others came, Leadbetter, Idaho, and Maddox, riding the cattle. When Noose and Laura saw them, they got their attention with whistles and cries and hand gestures, and each of the surviving wranglers dove off the cows into the draw. The outfit, what was left of them, huddled together, reloading their guns as Laura used her kerchief to tie a tourniquet around Curly's leg.

Joe, pistols at the ready, chanced a peek over the edge of the draw up at the top of the cliffs a hundred feet across the ravine. There was a lot of movement. He could see the figures of Cole Starborough's posse repositioning themselves, which explained the brief cessation in gunfire, but now they had commenced shooting again. The bullets were slamming against the boulders shielding the draw, making it grimly clear the riflemen saw where the outfit had taken cover down below. The cattle had moved on with the rest of the horses deeper into the ravine where it opened up, so this time there were no cows getting in the way of the posse's shots and making them hold their fire. It was just the six people hiding in the draw, protected by a few rocks and boulders.

Joe figured given their bunkered position, the outfit might be able to hold out, maybe, if they used their limited ammo prudently, just maybe . . .

And then above, the gargantuan Gatling gun suddenly

erupted, raining hellfire on the draw as hundreds of heavy caliber rounds bombarded the rocks the outfit hid behind, and all hope was lost. Noose knew they wouldn't be able to hold out. Not for very long being pounded by a weapon of that magnitude. It kept firing and firing a relentless, ceaseless onslaught of bullets that exploded and ricocheted all around the boulders and rocks, and if the slugs didn't kill them, sooner or later the ricks would.

Noose knew he and the outfit were cornered, wounded, exhausted, and overwhelmed, and there was only one way out of this.

He had to take out that gun.

"Cover me!"

A fusillade of bullets from above exploded against the draw they were hiding inside, showering them with stinging shrapnel of splintered granite chips. Joe shot Curly and Laura and the others whose eyes were locked on him a *wait for it* glance, his body coiled to leap into action, clenching his six-guns.

After the latest volley of rounds ended, there was a break in the shooting from atop the cliff as the posse reloaded, and in that brief ringing silence Noose snapped, *"Now!"*

The entire six surviving members of the outfit leaped up and aimed their rifles and pistols over the edge of the rocks and opened fire, unleashing a barrage of gunfire with every weapon they had, and the bounty hunter leaped up out of the draw on to the floor of the canyon. Firing a pistol in each hand one after the other, aiming blind up at the top of the cliffs, he used the wall of rounds he and his friends were unloading to make a dead run for the edge of the cliff wall and the mountainous boulders that would give him cover. It was a fifty-yard dash out in the open in the clear gunsights of the posse above, and he ran as fast as his boots would carry him, pointing his pistols upward, squeezing the triggers and blasting away. The ravine rang with deafening reports of staccato rifle and pistol shots, almost without pause coming from the guns of the outfit.

Atop the cliff a hundred feet above, Cole Starborough caught a glimpse of Joe Noose scrambling the last few yards to the boulders and swung the barrel of the Gatling gun downward, triggering the handgrips he clenched in both fists, gritting his teeth and opening fire. Far below, the view of his enemy was instantly erased by clouds of dirt and rock and flashing ricochets kicked up by the hordes of bullets slamming into the canyon floor in fire-cracker flashes of sparks.

As he ran for his life, Joe felt the ground explode all around him with the huge machine gun opening up above, splitting the air with nonstop rapid-fire discharges that rattled the walls of the canyon. Geysers of .50 caliber rounds shot up like gophers as the Gatling gun stitched a line of lead across the canyon floor. With each impact of his boots on the dirt, he felt the collision of bullets on the ground narrowly missing him by inches.

The edge of the boulders lay ten yards away, and knowing he might not make it, Noose took a Hail Mary and dived for cover. He hit the ground hard, clenching both empty pistols in his hands, and rolled to his knees behind the shelter of the huge rock formation, slamming his back flat against it. The muffled sledgehammer pounding of machine gun fire sang out on the other side of the huge rock, and the bounty hunter exhaled mightily, knowing he had achieved momentary safety out of range of the deadly armament.

Behind him, across the ravine, Joe saw the desperate figures of the outfit huddling inside the draw actively reloading while the rocks they hid behind were being pummeled by bullets from the posse above them. Making eye contact with the cattlewoman who was relieved to see him still breathing, the bounty hunter gave her a thumbs-up, then pointed upward. *That's where I'm going.* She nodded.

Then Joe looked up the sheer rock incline toward the top of the ravine. A hundred feet up, past ledges and outcroppings of big rocks and boulders, he could see the top of the cliff; that's where the posse was positioned and the only way to neutralize their threat was to climb up there and shoot it out with them. *And he was out of bullets, so he would need to disarm one of the posse to get something to shoot with.* Noose chanced his odds and realized he had no other choice, so he made up his mind and squinted at the way up he was going to have to take—it was a long steep climb to the roof of the canyon, but the stones afforded purchase and Noose figured he could scale it if the posse didn't blow him off the cliff first.

The rocks provided some cover, but part of the way up he was going to be out in the open, and the gunmen would have a clear shot. The good news was the beating sun was behind the edge of the cliff now, so he wouldn't be blinded staring straight into it.

On his right, a hundred feet above and thirty yards to the west, Noose could just see where the Gatling gun was positioned, occupying the high ground. He recognized the duster and bowler hat of the gunner, Cole Starborough, but Joe didn't have a clean shot.

He was going to have to get closer—a lot closer . . .

So Joe Noose began his ascent.

Holstering his pistols to free up his hands, he reached up and pulled himself onto the first ledge. Scrambling over some heavy rocks, Noose jammed his boots into the nooks between the boulders and scaled hands and feet another fifteen feet almost straight up. Looking back behind him over his shoulder, Joe saw he was looking down on the bullet-riddled draw now, the outfit already out of sight. He returned his gaze upward and crawled like a lizard up the side of the cliff.

On top of the canyon, Cole stopped firing and squinted through the smoke drifting in a fog from the twelve-barrel rotating cylinder of the barrel of the Gatling gun. He couldn't see squat. Did he grease that big son of a bitch? He didn't think so; if Starborough had nailed Noose with even a few .50 caliber rounds, there wouldn't be much left of him down there. Trying to spot the shredded remains of the bounty hunter splattered all over the floor of the canyon, all the henchman could see was gun smoke. Soon it cleared.

And Calhoun's enforcer spat a string of profanity, knowing he had missed.

Forty yards away, below, shielded by the mountainous boulders on the steep slope, Noose was halfway up the cliff. He climbed hand over hand, his steely eyes fixed on the next outcropping directly above him that now blocked his view of the top of the ravine.

Gravel crumbled above and showered him with granules and he froze. A few feet over his head, Noose could hear the boots of a posse man clambering down onto the outcropping, hearing the *clink* of his rifle as he got into a better shooting position on the draw the outfit below took refuge in. Tossing a quick glance over his shoulder down to the bottom of the ravine, the bounty hunter could clearly see Laura was partially in view at this height and the gunman would have a clear shot at her. Above, he heard the bolt of the rifle engage.

Noose decided to kill him and take his rifle to rearm himself.

Joe didn't hesitate; if he didn't kill this man quiet and quick, the posse at the roof of the canyon would hear and pinpoint his position, not only robbing Noose of the element of surprise he needed to successfully bushwhack them, but costing his life when they opened fire and blew him clean off the side of the cliff into oblivion.

So Noose leaped up like a pouncing tiger and made a blind grab, his fingers closing on the posse man's boot, and pulled with all his might. The boot jerked off the outcropping and a quick shadow passed over Joe as the gunman lost his balance and plummeted headlong off the side of the canyon, his surprised cry cut short as his skull hit a boulder twenty feet below and cracked like an eggshell, his brains splattering the rocks in messy scarlet splotches as his loose-limbed body bounced off the rocks and landed in a broken heap at the base of the ravine.

No shots came his way. The posse hadn't heard the man's death. Noose had to move. Hauling himself up over the edge of the outcrop, legs dangling, he crawled on top of the ledge. The dead man's carbine rifle lay where the man had dropped it when he took his fatal plunge. Joe scooped the weapon up and slung the strap up over his shoulder, rising to a crouch behind a wall of rock that shielded him from view of the riflemen and the machine gunner on the opposite side of the cliff.

Looking up again, Noose saw he was twenty-five feet from the lip of the cliff and the rocks above would make for an easy climb. But the rest of the way would be out in the open and he'd be visible to the posse, an easy target for all their guns. Glancing behind him he saw it was a long way down to certain death unless he took out those men. Taking a deep breath, Joe began climbing and hadn't gotten three feet before the bullets started flying. He'd been spotted. Across the canyon, he saw the popping flashes of multiple gunmen shooting in his direction.

No time to think. On sheer adrenaline, Noose unslung the carbine and charged up the rest of the steep rocky slope using the power of his legs and sense of balance as he aimed the rifle at the posse and opened fire, loosing a string of shots, his feet clambering upward, shooting at the men shooting at him, bullets exploding everywhere, one round taking a chunk of skin off his shoulder, the other nicking his ear, as still he climbed higher and higher, almost to the top, his rifle clicking empty, tossing it away and scrambling, scrabbling, pulling himself the last few feet up over the edge of the cliff and falling flat on his belly on the roof of the ravine, gasping for breath. Joe had reached the top. He'd come too far to die now.

Noose heard resounding relentless volleys of gunfire from above and below, the posse men shooting down into the draw at the outfit firing back, and just then the bounty hunter understood that his friends must have seen him making the last leg of the climb, providing him covering fire that saved his life.

He was alive.

He was on top of the cliff where the posse were.

But he was completely out of bullets. Both revolvers were empty. Nothing to reload.

Peering over a boulder, all six of the posse came into view, thirty yards away, not looking in his direction, all of them firing madly down at the outfit below. Behind the great Gatling gun on the tripod was Cole Starborough, his body jerking with the vibration of the machine gun as he furiously clenched the triggers, bombarding the wranglers and cattlewoman with rounds and mercilessly pounding their position.

Edging forward in a low crouch along the rocks, Joe Noose slowly made his way closer, nearing his enemies step by step. He approached with Indian stealth. They didn't see him and certainly couldn't hear him in all the din.

When Noose was thirty feet directly behind the henchman, he spotted a fist-sized stone that would serve his purpose. Joe picked up the rock and threw it with all his strength at the back of Cole's head. It flew through the air. Starborough shifted position the instant before the stone hit him, so it smashed into his shoulder instead of busting his head open. The stunned henchman cried out in pain and the bounty hunter charged the gun emplacement.

Hearing Noose's boots pounding against the ground, Starborough lumbered sideways, swinging the Gatling gun around to shoot his attacker and as Joe dived at him, the three-foot barrel swung and clubbed him in the face, the searing hot metal of the muzzle burning his flesh. The force of the impact knocked Noose head over heels and he hit the ground hard, rolling on his back with a grunt.

His eyes blazing with savagery, emitting a bloodthirsty roar, Cole gripped the trigger handles and swung the barrel down to point the twelve muzzles right between Noose's eyes. Joe kicked the cannon upward with his boots just as Starborough pulled the triggers, the muzzle swung up, and a blazing volley of rounds shot into the sky. Jumping up on his feet, the bounty hunter dived over the top of the machine gun and got both hands around the henchman's throat, dragging his hands off the triggers and throwing him to the ground. The two men brutally punched and rolled and kicked each other in clouds of dust, both crawling and reaching for the unmanned Gatling gun. Cole's fingers touched the trigger handle first. Clenching both fists together on the ground, Noose clubbed Starborough in the spine using the muscles of both arms, and when his enemy dropped, Joe hauled him off the machine gun and lunged behind the triggers himself, grabbing them with both hands.

Joe Noose now manned the Gatling gun!

Cole Starborough was already up on his feet running for dear life in the other direction a split second later when Noose swiveled the machine gun on the tripod and got his fleeing enemy in his gunsights, centering the aim on his back and letting loose a barrage of .50 caliber rounds. Seeing the enforcer's flapping duster diving behind the rocks before the clouds of dust and rocks from the bullets obscured his view, Joe knew he barely missed.

Hearing running boots behind him, the bounty hunter hauled the weapon sideways on the rotating axis of the tripod, swinging the smoking barrel of the Gatling gun fast around 180 degrees to point it directly at the two posse men rushing him. And Noose pulled the triggers and let them have it. The twelve-barrel cylinder rotated with a clanking clamor, spitting fire as the ammo belts rattled through the breech, ejecting rivers of casings.

RATATATATATATATATATATATATATATAT!

The hundred .50 caliber rounds instantly blew both posse men to bits in grisly explosions of blood, bone, and guts, flying arms and legs and pieces of their torsos went in all directions, gory chunks of butchered meat splattering the ground in a splashing rain of bright oxygenated blood.

Joe Noose grinned savagely.

He *liked* this weapon.

It was his kind of gun.

Standing up, Noose wrapped his kerchief around his left hand. He lifted the weapon off its chassis, kicking away the tripod, so he held the Gatling gun free in his arms; it was cumbersome and heavy, a hundred pounds, but Joe was very strong. And now his blood was up, the weight felt good because he was going to kill every last man with it. The ammo belts flopped out of the breech of the machine gun, and he let them drape over one arm, getting his grip on the hot barrel with his left hand and holding the trigger with his right, getting the machine gun wrangled just as bullets whizzed past his face from rifle shots fired by three posse men occupying the lower gradation of the cliff roof.

Swiveling his hips, Noose swung the Gatling gun around to his right and trained the barrel on the operatives with rifles socked to their shoulders shooting at him fifty feet away. Joe clenched the trigger and the gigantic machine gun bucked in his arms, staggering him as he sprayed slews of rounds at the gunmen. It was like they'd been caught in a dynamite blast—the fearsome fusillade blew the four men to smithereens, liquefying them in gruesome eruptions of blood, flying limbs, shattering bones and entrails, and when he released the trigger, mounds of bloody, shredded meat on the ground were all that remained; the gunmen had been vaporized. Empty shell casings clattered to the rocks as Joe Noose marched forward with the Gatling gun in his bulging muscled arms, on a search and destroy extermination mission for the last men of the posse and the man they worked for, one Cole Starborough.

"Nobody gets out of here alive!" Joe roared at the top of his lungs. *"You hear me, Starborough! I'm coming for ya! I'm gonna kill all you sons of bitches!"*

His ears were ringing from the eardrum-bursting sounds of the machine gun, and Noose couldn't hear much, so he kept his eyes peeled for any movement in the ridges and contours of the roof of the cliffs as he patrolled the area with the Gatling gun, ready to shoot at the first sign of any movement. A foggy wreath of gun smoke hung like noxious miasma over the area and visibility was limited.

He had killed four of the posse by his count. There were four more, including Starborough, who he knew was still out there.

Three shots rang out to Joe's right. A bullet ricocheted off the steel against the side of the machine gun, the impact nearly knocking the unwieldy weapon out of his grip, but he got the barrel around and delivered a staccato string of .50 caliber fire in the direction of the shots. Over the sound of the gun, Noose heard hideous high-pitched agonized screams and wet sounds of splattered meat. No more shots came his way.

Two more down.

Two left.

Seeing a flash of movement, Joe swung at the pelvis, carrying the weight of the weapon, heaving the barrel of the Gatling gun around on a last posse man standing by the edge of the cliff above the chasm, not ten feet away. As the gunman raised his pistol, Noose squeezed the trigger.

Clickclickclickclickclick . . .

The Gatling gun was out of ammo. The empty bullet belts clattered around, in and out of the breech. Looking up, Noose saw the posse man flinch, then when he realized Joe was out of bullets, crack a nasty grin and laugh before he pulled his trigger.

That split second of hesitation was all the time Noose needed. Joe hurled the Gatling gun at him, tossing all hundred pounds of solid steel of the empty weapon into the gunman's chest standing a few feet from the brink of the cliff, so when the massive machine gun struck him it carried him right over the edge, knocking him off the cliff. The falling man's fading screams were sweet music to the bounty hunter's ears until a distant wet thud abruptly silenced them.

Slowly, Joe Noose turned, eyes full of hell as they scanned the area.

One left.

He went after him.

Joe Noose stepped onto the ledge where Cole Starborough was waiting for him, like Noose knew he would be. The henchman's guns were holstered. Somehow Noose knew that, too. That's why both his own revolvers were in his holsters.

It was time for their long-awaited showdown. The contest needed to be clean not messy. They were professionals.

It had to be a good kill. The bounty hunter took another few steps out of the canyon into the bright sunlight so his whole body was exposed to his enemy, like his enemy's was to him. No tricks. Just the fearsome tradecraft of the gunfighter practiced by two experts.

They took position and stood five feet from one another.

Cole Starborough faced Joe Noose and both men understood at last the moment they had been waiting for to kill one another had arrived and they were ready for it. Their hands hovered over their guns. The bounty hunter's were empty, but he figured it didn't matter because a gunfight was not what the henchman had in mind.

"Any last words?" Noose said.

The gentleman fixer grinned with a truly nasty and vicious camaraderie, his voice betraying actual feeling. "I know you, Joe Noose, we're the same, you and I. Smelled it on each other the first time we both traded glances."

"I ain't nothing like you, asshole." Noose never drew first. Standing braced, ready to pull, Joe held his enemy's gaze because a man's eyes always told you when he was about to draw, but before he drew his gun, Starborough had some talking to do, for Cole's bright eyes gleamed with grandiosity. "Oh yes, but you are, Noose. We share the beast. We both have the beast inside. The beast in us *is* us, our true savage nature, because we're killers and we love the taste of blood. So we keep the beast caged because we desire to be civilized and live in civilized society."

"That's a whole lot of rhetoric."

"Oh, I know we both have different reasons for wanting to be civilized: you want honor and I want the money. But we both let the beast loose, don't we? Yes, you know what

I mean. Because on those rare occasions when we *need* the beast, we let him out of his cage, *unleash* the beast and get *savage*. Get *uncivilized*. I'll show you my beast if you show me yours. Now is as good a time as any, I think, don't you?" Starborough unbuckled his guns, let the belt drop, kicked it over the cliff, showed his empty hands, curled them into fists, then extended his arms pugilist style. "What do you say, Joe? Let's get uncivilized."

"First thing you've said makes any sense." Noose tossed away his guns and raised his fists, ready to go. "Uncivilized it is."

The gentleman villain smacked his lips below his waxed curled mustache as he declared, "I want to feel your spine crack in my fingers when I kill you with my bare hands." With a bloodthirsty cry, Starborough charged.

"You got to hit me first." Noose ducked a roundhouse punch and, clenching both fists together, sledgehammered Starborough in the back of the neck as his center of gravity shifted with the missed thrown punch. The gentleman henchman slammed facedown into the dirt, but before the bounty hunter could hit him again, his enemy was up on his feet, fists up, his grinning mouth full of sharp teeth red with his own blood.

"That's the spirit." He spat blood. "Now it's my turn." Starborough moved in on Noose with lightning speed, bombarding him with blinding fast combination punches, his big fists pummeling Joe's head and face with hammering blows that staggered the bounty hunter, who couldn't get a punch in. Then Cole's fisted combination punches beat Joe's stomach, buckling him over, and a knee to the face knocked Noose clean off his feet. He hit the ground hard, dazed and punch-drunk. Joe shook his head to clear it and saw Starborough standing a few feet away, chest heaving and fists tightly clenched, bristling with violence like a wild animal. No trace of gentleman remained. Noose saw the beast. "You promised me a fight, Noose. On your feet."

The bounty hunter jumped up on his boots, and the two men circled with fists raised. Joe Noose saw he had size and muscle on Starborough but Cole had speed on him; the man was dangerously quick with his fists and threw punches the way his Gatling gun fired bullets. Noose didn't want to get caught in that blizzard of blows again.

Baring his teeth in a mustached snarl, Starborough launched an attack, stepping in swinging his fists, and Noose was ready for him. Leaping on the gentleman henchman, Joe wrapped his arms around Cole's torso, pinning those arms and fists in a crusher vise of his own muscular biceps and forearms. Starborough was not expecting that. The two seconds it took for Cole to react was all the time Joe needed, driving his whole body against Starborough with the force of a locomotive, knocking him off balance, using all his weight to keep his arms pinned as Noose smashed Cole back into the canyon wall with a bone-crunching impact when Starborough's spine struck the stone.

Roaring in rage and frustration, Cole struggled to free his arms to no avail, trapped in Joe's muscular grip as Noose heaved himself against Starborough again and again, pounding Cole's body against the granite canyon wall over and over with punishing force, throwing him a serious beating, until Cole's eyes suddenly bulged like a berserker.

Cole Starborough bit Joe Noose's ear.

Baring his sharp teeth, stretching his mouth wide, his face lunged against the side of the bounty hunter's head, took his left ear in his mouth and bit down hard.

Blood flew. Joe saw it was his, the left side of his head exploding in searing agony; his shocked disbelief a man was biting his ear off made Noose react fast before he lost the ear.

Brutally head-butting Starborough in the face with his forehead gave Cole's skull a nasty crack against the stone wall and the mouth and teeth let go of Noose's ear.

Joe staggered back, releasing his grip on Cole, his hand flying to his left ear. It was still attached, but he was bleeding like a steer. Now he had to finish this business with Cole, because when Starborough attacked this time, he wasn't trying to fight Noose anymore, he was trying to eat him.

Joe backed away as Cole tried to rip his throat out with his teeth, eyes glazed over with blood sport, lunging again and again mouth first, no longer using his fists, regressing into animal savagery,

"Fight like a man!" Noose snarled, but it was a beast that growled back. Revolted, Noose kept his distance, repulsed by Starborough's shocking visage struggling to bite him with a bloody mouth filled with sharpened incisors, and worse, the noisy clatter of his upper and lower molars that collided inside his palate with every snap of the jaws trying to chew a piece off him.

Knowing he had to keep his hands away from Cole's mouth, Noose locked eyes with him but the gaze had gone feral.

Lunging his head, Starborough's jaws snapped at him like a wolf.

He was an animal.

Enough, Noose thought in disgust.

This time when Cole Starborough lunged forward at him, Joe Noose feinted and stepped in with a left upper-cut, putting his whole shoulder into it, aiming his fist at the point under the jaw it would do the most damage and drove a piledriver blow up into Cole's chin with such force it broke his neck. An ugly muffled *crack*, and Starborough's head flopped loose on his neck and his limbs turned to rubber as he collapsed like a marionette with the strings cut, slumped on the ground sprawled on his back, paralyzed from the neck down. His face faced the sky and bore an expression of utter surprise and dismay.

The bounty hunter stood over his fallen enemy, watching the gentleman henchman's eyes come to grips with his condition; a plethora of emotions passed across the paralyzed man's pathetic gaze until a single tear rolled down his cheek. Unable to move his head, Cole was immobilized looking straight up into sky at the vultures circling above, knowing they were coming for him.

Noose crouched over Starborough, looking him square in the eye, the only parts of himself besides his lips he could still move. The mouth moved. "You killed me, Noose. With your bare hands."

"Looks that way."

"Impressive."

"Not really."

"Pity of it is, old boy, in another life we could have been friends."

"No, I'd have killed you in that life, too. Some men need killing, Cole. You're one of 'em."

"Then finish the job." Starborough grimaced; after a

few seconds passed and Noose did nothing, his enemy coughed blood, his eyes narrowing. "Kill me, Noose. Do it. You taste my death. The beast in you must be served."

Flapping winged shadows fell across the two men below on the ground, shadows that circled in a dread rotation. The crouching bounty hunter threw a laconic glance back up over his shoulder, squinting up at the kettle of hungry vultures flying above them. More buzzards joined the congregation. Noose returned his hard gaze to the paralyzed man lying on the ground with eyes forced to look at a sky full of carrion birds blocking out the sun. "Nah. Those buzzards circling will finish you off," Noose said. "While you can still move your eyes, Starborough, you might want to close 'em."

Fear filling his trapped gaze looking up at the vultures coming for him, Cole broke down and begged. "Mercy."

"Fresh out."

"Please, you can't leave a man to get eaten by vultures like a-a . . ."

"Beast?" Joe Noose smiled with cold irony.

Cole Starborough's gaze registered self-awareness devoid of pride or shame and without apology. "True, I am a beast. But even a wounded beast deserves to be put out of his misery. You are an honorable man, sir. Do the right thing."

The bounty hunter returned a pitiless gaze and shook his head slowly. "Not this time. I'm leaving you for the vultures."

"Why?" Starborough croaked.

"Because you remind me of me," Joe Noose replied gravely, his eyes shuttered.

Rising to his feet, the bounty hunter picked up his gun

belt and strapping it on, turned his back on his enemy, walking away never to lay eyes on him again.

Behind, Noose heard Starborough's dying words, "*Ave tenebris Dominus*," before there came a great flurry of wings and the terrible screams began.

The bounty hunter found the leather satchel with the money in it that Calhoun's gang tried to buy Laura Holdridge's cattle with a few weeks ago by the war wagon after a brief search. He took it with him.

When the exhausted Joe Noose climbed down the cliff, it was so quiet after the ceaseless gunfire filling the ravine the last hour, amplified off the canyon walls to deafening decibels, that its sudden cessation was disorienting. His ears were ringing. The bounty hunter was hurt and bleeding but still on his feet. Making a slow descent to the base of the ravine carrying the satchel, Joe saw no movement in the draw ahead where the outfit had taken cover and as he approached, feared the worst. The cattle and surviving horses were milling peacefully outside the opening of the chasm. A haze of hanging gun smoke and dust hung in the air, making him cough. As Noose reached the lip of the draw, he saw down in the murky miasma the outlines of six figures and they weren't moving. His heart sank.

"Hope that's you, Joe, because we're all out of ammo." It was Laura's weary voice.

"It's me."

"Did you get 'em?"

"I got 'em. Every last one."

"Good for you."

"You all OK?" Hers was the only voice he had heard so far. In the hanging gun smoke wreathing the draw he could see Laura getting weakly to her hands and knees, but the other figures sprawled around the pit didn't look injured.

"Inventory. Roll call, boys," the cattlewoman said. "Brubaker."

"Here."

"Leadbetter."

"Here."

"Maddox."

"Here."

"Idaho."

"Here."

"Barlow."

No answer.

"Barlow."

"He didn't make it, Laura," said Joe quietly, reaching down his hand to help the outfit out of the draw.

Over the next hour the last wranglers and their trail boss gathered the cattle and horses, and the bounty hunter lent a helping hand after he had reunited with Copper, who had come through without a scratch. Noose watched with admiration the care and stoicism the rovers of the Bar H displayed in calming the shaken animals under the weight of the loss of Billy Barlow and their own injuries. Laura had proved herself a pretty fair battlefield medic by removing the bullet from Brubaker's leg, which was now bandaged. By early afternoon the outfit was saddled up aboard the horses they had confiscated from Cole Starborough's posse who had no use for them anymore. Twirling their lariats, the wranglers got busy moving the cattle into formation and getting ready to pull out.

Laura caught the leather satchel Joe tossed her. She didn't need to open it, she felt the heft of four thousand dollars inside.

"You earned it," he said.

"This money is Calhoun's."

"He owes it to you."

"He's going to want it back."

"Calhoun can't claim the money is his. If he does he'll have to explain what the money was doing here and he doesn't want the law knowing that. All these dead men work for him, so let him go to the law and explain what his men were doing here with his cash."

"Wipe that grin off your face, Joe."

"It ain't the money that's gonna piss off Crispin Calhoun, it's that *you* have it, and there ain't a damn thing he can do about it and that, lady, is gonna burn his ass for all the rest of his days."

"Now you put it like that, I will keep the money."

"Good. With the sale of the cattle, that cash will get your ranch on its feet."

"Drivers present and accounted for. You boys still in one piece?"

"Yes, ma'am."

"Yeah."

"Yup."

"Then what the hell you waiting for? Let's move this damn herd!"

CHAPTER 26

You forgot a killer walks among you but I have not forgotten about killing the rest of you. You ride with the devil, you fools, and you have lowered your guard. Even Noose. You're next, Joe. Then it's your turn, Laura. You never knew the man you married, who Sam Holdridge really was, you only thought you did. You didn't want to know where the meat came from, you just wanted to eat it. Face the truth. Everything you have, you got from Sam. Everything he had he took from me. He took from me everything I have or ever will have. And now, Laura, I am taking everything from you. I already took your husband. That was just the beginning. Then I took the lives of your men. Once I've stopped you getting the cattle to auction. your precious herd will be lost, too. Then and only then, when you see you have lost everything you love, will I take the very last thing you have, your life. But before I do, you will know how it feels to have it all taken away from you, and feel my pain. Then

you will wish, like I, you had never been born.
When you have everything, you have everything to
lose, Laura. I have nothing and have nothing to
lose. Sam Holdridge got his. Now you get yours.
Will you be surprised to learn your murderer
rescued you yesterday? It makes perfect sense.
If I hadn't saved your life I would never have been
able to kill you. Get ready. Today you die.
Goodbye Laura.

The killer crumpled the letter, balled the paper in his fist, stuffed it in his mouth and chewed. Washing it down with a swig of whiskey, he belched. Like the other letters, nobody was meant to read them; it was written for himself, so he could understand what was inside him that drove him to do what he did. *The journal of a murderer.* The killer swallowed his final entry.

He lay on his bedroll and looked up at the lightening sky on the dawn of the day he would finish it.

CHAPTER 27

A thunderhead of black storm clouds hung over the horizon as the five hundred head of steers were driven across a vast desolate plain that was nothingness twenty miles in every direction. Far off lightning jags behind the black haze of distant storm weather. The sky was about to drop on them. Laura Holdridge knew from years of experience that her crew and livestock were going to get caught in the storm coming their way, and the best thing to do was rest the herd while she and her hands took cover in any refuge they could find from the lightning.

Snapping the reins of her horse, she galloped by the steers, glancing behind her at the bounty hunter driving the cattle, back down the herd. Knowing he was there made her feel secure, but even this man could do nothing to avert a storm.

Joe Noose cast a grim look up at the unrelieved sky.

Black clouds formed overhead in moving mountains of black obsidian, pressing down on the landscape as the increasing pressure system in the atmosphere built like steam in a kettle, filling the Big Empty with foreboding.

A storm was coming.

It was going to be a big one.

The air in Joe's nostrils smelled of the ozone-charged atmosphere.

The herd smelled it, too.

The cattle were restless.

Riding in the midst of the processions of livestock, the bounty hunter could feel the antsy nerves of the steers like a volatile electrical charge coursing through their muscles. This wasn't good. Nothing was as terrifying, unpredictable, or dangerous for a wrangler as a stampede of cattle. There was nothing a rover feared more: hundreds of unstoppable tons of cow flesh, thousands of heavy hoofs and razor-sharp horns out of control, goring, trampling, and crushing anything in their path; right now, the cattle were contained, but storm weather was when stampedes often happened, and although the thunder and lightning hadn't hit yet, it would very soon.

It was headed their direction from the northwest. Looking back to where the black thunderclouds originated, Noose could see the wall of rain and darkness like a towering curtain of doom reaching from the sky to the earth. It was relentlessly coming their way.

The first lightning bolt crashed to earth a mile in the distance.

It was followed by a low frequency sonic rumble of thunder that lasted almost a minute, and the cowboy could feel the ground tremble beneath the hooves of his horse.

Another lightning bolt strobed the world, an electrical zigzag, closer than the first.

In the desolate wastes of the Big Empty, the cattle drive looked as small as a trail of ants across the tundra below the vast lowering sky. The horizon was a flat unbroken line. There was no escape from the storm about to hit.

Nowhere to take shelter.

They had to just keep riding.

And pray there wasn't a stampede.

Feeling the volatile tension in the longhorns all round him, Joe Noose figured it was safer not to be riding in the midst of the herd but outside them. Tugging his reins, he eased Copper through the slow-moving cows toward open country.

Switching his gaze to spot the other wranglers, he got a visual fix on Idaho and Brubaker. The first two met his eyes and even across the herd he recognized the apprehensive look in their gaze spelled stampede.

He couldn't see Laura. *Where was she?*

The rain arrived in a sudden torrential downpour, turning the dirt to mud and Joe's clothes to soaking rags in what seemed like seconds.

Another flash of lightning.

The following thunderclap was deafening as an explosion.

So loud it muffled the gun shot.

The bullet felt like a horse kicked him in the side.

The bounty hunter was blown out of his saddle and airborne by the time he registered the assassin timed his shot just after the lightning flash so the thunder would cover it, and then it was too late—he'd been hit.

Then the bounty hunter crashed to the ground, hard. Everywhere he looked were stomping hooves of the marching longhorns above him on all sides. His reflexes were quick. Rolling out of the way to avoid being trampled, Noose jumped to his feet. Copper reared up on his hind legs and Noose's sudden fear was his beloved horse was going to get shot by the gunman's next bullet—his only thought was for his best friend's safety.

Luckily the bullet had passed clean through and he'd received only a flesh wound.

Whoever shot him had missed. This time.

Spooked by the violent gathering storm and picking up their stride, the steers were visibly alarmed by the rearing stallion, and their massive skulls and jutting horns were milling in an ominous way. Grabbing Copper's reins, Noose patted his horse to calm him and led the stallion calmly as he could through the cattle—at any second the longhorns could charge and gore them or at worst start an entire stampede, trampling man and horse to death in the mud. Hoof step by hoof step, Noose led Copper through the passing rows of cows until the horse was out of peril, safely clear of the cattle on the open plain. Then, guns drawn, Joe got back on his horse.

Turning his head, Noose swung his gaze back in the direction the shot came from, but saw nothing but endless heads of cattle in the dimness of gray overcast light from the gathering storm. Rain was falling in heavy, cold, punishing drops. Giving his reliable stallion a tap of spur, Joe rode alongside the herd.

Whoever shot him was the killer, the man he was after.

It wasn't Idaho.

Not Brubaker—he already knew that.

He'd had eyes on both when someone had taken a shot at him.

Scanning his eyes cross the sea of rising and falling backs and heads and horns of the horde of cows on the march, Joe searched for the hats and heads and horses of the other four wranglers, but it was getting dark fast. Gripping his Colt Peacemaker in his fist, Noose kept a sharp lookout.

There.

The silhouette of a rover on the side of the herd. The muzzle flash of the wrangler's gun lit up his hands and weapon but not his face, but the outline of the figure was enough for Noose to take a shot at. They exchanged gunfire. The two gun blasts were drowned out by a peal of thunder that boomed across the terrain. As he rode alongside the herd, Joe fired again over the heads of the cattle at where the figure had shot from an instant before. For a few seconds, he thought he must have hit him because there was no return fire.

When it came it was bigger and louder. Twin flashes. Two loads of a double-barreled 12-gauge shotgun blew a horn off one of the cows but missed Joe. Driving his heels into his stirrups, Noose yanked on the reins with one hand, steering Copper directly into the middle of the cattle in the direction of the gunman. He tightened up in the saddle, making a smaller target as the stallion plowed fearlessly into the parting ocean of steers, riding straight for the killer with the shotgun. The man was partially glimpsed past the shadows of the livestock.

Noose emptied his revolver at the figure, then in a swift fluid motion holstered it and drew his Winchester from his saddle sheath, spinning the rifle around his hand, cocking the lever and shooting across the herd at his assailant while he was reloading. Another two shotgun blasts exploded and one of the barrels took the top of one of the steers' head off in an explosion of skull, brain, blood, and shattered horn as Noose was hit in the cheek with pellets from the other barrel. Ten feet away the felled cow dropped dead in its tracks, collapsing in the middle of the running herd so the steers following it tripped over the body and tumbled to the ground, causing a pileup of falling long-horns. Joe recoiled from the sting of the pellets in his face and blinked blood out of his eyes, hauling on Copper's reins to get his horse out of the path of the crashing, falling, lowing cattle.

The one cow getting shot was all it took.

Panic sizzled like a lit fuse through the herd and set them off like a thousand tons of dynamite.

The cattle stampeded!

Five hundred bawling steers took off all at once. The cows broke formation and scattered, blindly charging in a mindless flight into the storm. A raging river of longhorns like a runaway train with the power of twenty steam loco-motives, row after row of horns and hooves an unstop-pable juggernaut of sheer animal mass, flattening anything in its path. The ground shook with pounding hooves and mighty force of the runaway herd. Lightning cracked the sky and thunder bellowed and hell came to earth.

Nearby, suddenly Laura Holdridge was living her worst nightmare. Runaway livestock hurtled on all sides of her in a deafening thunder of hooves, She had a cattle stam-pede on her hands. Her first thought instantly was only of her men and getting them out of harm's way from the charging steers. Digging her spurs into her mare, she rode straight for the stampede, waving her hat over her head for her rovers to clear, and hollering at the top of her lungs over the cacophony of hooves. Steering her horse along-side the string of livestock on a rampage.

Maddox, Leadbetter, and Idaho were safe. She saw them as the wranglers rode out of the deadly path of the stampede. They rode alongside it and drew their guns, firing them into the air, to scare the dumb cows back into some semblance of formation.

A few hundred yards back, Joe Noose heard gunshots on all sides now, losing his sonic bead on the killer. He swore under his breath, looking left and right. Hearing the gunfire in every direction, for all he knew the shots could be coming from anywhere. Cocking his Winchester, he brought the rifle up, his eyeballs going one way, his head the other, looking around him as on all sides three hundred and fifty tons of cattle stampeded.

Laura saw that Brubaker was caught in the middle of the runaway herd, and Curly was trapped in the saddle trying to control his terrified rearing horse. It was twenty yards from her. The stallion suddenly froze and came to a complete halt as the rushing cows poured past it, the closer longhorns barreling their way past, battering the horse and rider and knocking the stallion off balance. The horse's front legs went out from under it *"Curly!"* Laura screamed. The ramrod caught her eye from his precarious perch in the saddle as the reins were ripped out of his hands as his horse went down and him with it. The look Brubaker gave Laura said he knew he was dead. Spurring her mare brutally didn't make her mare go where she wanted, so the cattlewoman fired her pistol next to her horse's ear, forcing it to ride straight into the stampede, getting her a few yards closer to Curly on the falling stallion, which was just close enough. *"Jump!"* she screamed to Curly Brubaker and he leaped out of his stirrups onto the back of her saddle right as his fallen horse was trampled under the stampeding cattle, and Laura rode them the hell out of there.

Once safely outside the stampede, Laura and Curly looked back and saw a riderless horse smashed to bits from the blunt-force impacts of hundreds of longhorns, the mangled mare crushed beneath them as the steers charged past.

"Where's Noose?" Laura yelled to Brubaker.

Before he could answer, there were two shotgun blasts.

The first barrel hit Brubaker square in the shoulder and blew him off the back of Laura's saddle.

The second barrel shot the cattlewoman's horse out from under her.

A sudden explosion of lightning lit up the world like a stick of detonated dynamite for just a split second but in that brief instant, Joe Noose saw two things:

A desert rock formation of rocks and boulders about fifty feet high diverting the runaway herd and above the stampeding cattle below was Laura climbing up the rocks to safety.

And the back of the killer stepping out from behind a boulder beside the cattlewoman carrying a very big double-barreled shotgun.

Even at this distance, there was no mistaking his true identity . . .

Drawing both loaded Colt Peacemaker revolvers, Joe Noose tried to pick him off but the mighty wall of stampeding cattle blocked his shot. The barrier of horns and bodies of the steers obscured his view of the two figures on the boulders on the other side of the stampede. He couldn't line up a shot with those longhorns in the way. Joe swung his fierce gaze down the herd and the cows kept coming. Gritting his teeth in frustration, the bounty hunter holstered one pistol to hold the other Colt in a two-hand marksman grip for bullseye aim, squinting down the notch sight to target the killer across the herd, cocking back the hammer so his finger rested on a hair trigger. Noose only needed one shot. One clear shot. But he had to have a target. If he could just see the killer for one split-second past all those damn horns . . .

The shadow of a man on the rocks made Laura suddenly look behind her . . . *when she turned she was looking up both muzzles of a 12-gauge double-barreled shotgun aimed at her face by Frank Leadbetter, licking his lips in anticipation of pulling the trigger!*

"You." She gasped.

"I'm the last face you're ever gonna see," Frank Leadbetter's voice was drowned out by the tremendous noise of the stampede, but Laura Holdridge could read his lips.

Thunder cracked and lightning shimmered in the overcast sky. The lowing cattle were maddened. Joe Noose was caught behind the barrier of rampaging longhorns he couldn't get past or shoot through. The hooves of the herd would crush him to mush if he got in their way. The cows were panic-stricken by the noise of the thunder and flashes of lightning and their hooves were everywhere. The bounty hunter dodged being trampled struggling to line up a shot with his pistol by dead reckoning and whatever glimpses he could get over the livestock of Laura Holdridge and Frank Leadbetter fifty yards away—already he could see the fear in the cattlewoman's posture from the loaded scatter-gun the wrangler had aimed point blank on her. Over the vociferations of the cows Noose could not make out what the killer with the shotgun was saying.

Pressed against rocks engulfed by hundreds of surging cattle below on all sides, Laura Holdridge saw she had nowhere to run, no way to escape the cattle drive killer, Frank Leadbetter.

"Why?" Was all she could think to ask him, her face soaked with rain.

"I'll tell you why!" Frank had her under the gun, right where he wanted her, and as Leadbetter leveled the scatter-gun, he told a tale of revenge. He shouted to be heard above the pandemonium of the stampede. *"My father owned the land your ranch is built on! Thirty years ago he had a little spread on the exact same spot the Bar H Ranch sits on now! Your husband, Sam Holdridge, stole it, stole my father's cattle and stole his life . . . now I'm here to steal yours because you're his wife, the last Holdridge! You Holdridges took my life and I want revenge!"*

Laura listened in disbelief. *"You're wrong, Frank! Sam earned every dollar he ever made! He built our ranch with his bare hands!"*

Frank shook his head in disbelief, just realizing it now. *"You never knew who you married, did you? You really don't know! Reckon it was years before you two met, so he never told you his past! But it's time you knew the truth who Sam Holdridge really was and I'm gonna tell ya now right before I kill ya!"* Leadbetter screamed over the din of the stampede. *"Your dead husband ran the worst gang of cattle rustlers in Teton County 'til one day he decided he could make more money owning steers than stealing them and started your ranch! One night Sam Holdridge led his gang of mad-dog marauders in an armed ambush on my father's ranch and they gunned down my entire family while we were eating dinner! He dragged them out of the house and executed them! Your husband Sam! In front of my face! I was six years old!"* Frank Leadbetter shrieked psychopathically in Laura Holdridge's face, as she cringed from the smoking shotgun barrel he brandished in her face. *"Six!"*

"It's a lie. You're lying!"

"You know I ain't!" The cattlewoman raised her emotional eyes to meet her murderer's and he nodded, almost sympathetic. *"Time to find out what you really are, Mrs. Laura Holdridge, and where you got what you have, and what your name stands for, because your husband's sins were passed down to you when you inherited the Bar H Ranch, and the blood on his hands is now on yours! You gonna pay for his crimes!"*

"If my husband shot your family like you say he did, how did you survive?"

"I was in the outhouse! I hid there! Looked through the crack in the door and saw my whole family slaughtered! I escaped but Sam Holdridge took possession of our ranch and our cattle by forging a bill of sale and in them days, nobody bothered to investigate why the Leadbetter family up and disappeared because we was poor white trash and Sam Holdridge was rich! You call yourself a cattlewoman and say this is your herd! Your husband started his herd with my father's stock he murdered him to get! How can you live with yourself? Well, you don't have to!"

Laura saw the naked anguish beneath the feral gaze

and twisted face of Frank Leadbetter and she felt shame and pity even as his finger was closing on the trigger. *Maybe she did have it coming and deserved to pay for her husband's sins.*

But the young wrangler needed to keep talking; having kept so much bottled up inside, waiting a lifetime for revenge against the Holdridges, he wanted to squeeze all the juice he could out of it. *"It was all part of my plan! Me joining your ranch and working for you all these years was the beginning of my big revenge, and it all ends right now, here on this cattle drive with me killing you because your husband murdered my daddy for his cows!"*

She believed him.

Filled with shame and remorse for her husband's crimes, a tearful Laura Holdridge looked Frank Leadbetter honestly in the eye. *"I'm sorry!"*

"You are now! Know this!" He grinned savagely. *"It was me who killed your husband, took him from you, made you a widow."*

She choked. With a look of pure hatred, Laura glared through her tears into Frank's vicious, crazy face and her flashing eyes didn't blink.

His cruel grin grew meaner still. *"I killed Sam Holdridge a year ago in the same outhouse I had to hide in as a boy listening to my dad and mom and sister's dying screams! I want you to know it and take it to the grave, Laura Holdridge, and tell your husband while you're fucking him in Hell!"*

Laura Holdridge spat in Frank Leadbetter's face.

Dripping saliva, Leadbetter socked his scatter-gun to

his shoulder, looking murderously down both barrels, ready to blow Laura's head clean off.

Fifty yards away, Joe Noose crouched with his pistol on the ground and took aim at Frank's exposed legs between the passing cow hooves, ready to blow his kneecaps off. Noose squinted to aim but couldn't get a clean shot—first Laura was in the line of fire, then more steers surged past and their hooves blocked his view.

Frank pressed the twin muzzles of his shotgun against Laura's bosom and tightened his finger on the dual triggers and there came a loud gun blast.

Noose got a clean shot and took it, blowing Leadbetter's left kneecap apart in a bloody shrapnel of bone and cartilage, collapsing the killer's leg, but as the screaming gunman fell he pivoted, unloading both shotgun barrels at Joe Noose under the cattle. The legs of a huge steer took the blast, shielding the bounty hunter. As the cow fell, he jumped back before nearly a ton of dead longhorn landed right on top of him.

Hearing the louder thunder of hooves over the thunder in the sky, Laura Holdridge blinked against the fusillades of blinding lightning and the rain in her eyes. Hordes of rampaging steers surged around the rock formation as she climbed to safety up onto a high boulder. The stone was wet and slick from the rain and Laura's fingers scrabbled for purchase on the slippery surface. The cattle stampede was danger in its purest elemental form; a primal force of physical animal aggression and violence. A few feet below her perch, row after row of sharp horns meant impalement if she fell. Torrential rain poured, lightning exploded, and the earth quaked under the driving impacts of thousands of pounding hooves and anvil detonations of deafening thunder. Amid the apocalyptic chaos, the cattlewoman struggled to get a glimpse of Noose or Leadbetter, but there was no sign of either of them in the relentless stampede. She closed her eyes, assuming Noose had to be dead.

Suddenly, a bloody figure leaped onto the rocks below. Frank Leadbetter, mad white eyes in a mask of gore, pulled his wounded body up the boulders out of the path of the stampede. His psychotic gaze was fixed on Laura, the object of his demented fury above him, and the deranged wrangler clawed his way up the rocks toward her like a grisly panther. He had a bowie knife clenched in his bloody teeth. She kicked him with her boots but he held fast to the stones and kept coming for her to kill her.

Noose could just see the top of Laura's face above the hurtling heads of the passing cows, higher on the rocks than Frank, who his bullets hadn't stopped, hidden from view behind the stampede—the imperiled cattlewoman's expression of raw terror told the bounty hunter she knew she was about to die, the murderous wrangler about to kill her, and Joe had run out of time to rescue her.

The only chance he had to save her life was get on the other side of that herd, and there was only one way to do that . . .

He'd have to run through the stampede on foot.

The rear of the herd was going past him now, the procession of steers thinning, so there were breaks in the cows . . . *Joe figured if he timed it right and ran very fast, he could run through the spaces between the cattle, narrowly dodging the horns no doubt—it was about fifteen paces to clear the herd and once Noose was on the other side he'd put a bullet in Frank Leadbetter directly—but once he was running inside the stampede, if Joe's boots slipped in the mud and he fell he'd be trampled, or if the steers were wrongly spaced during his crossing he'd end up on the horns, a hard death either way.*

A gun in each hand again—*firing both the instant he emerged on the other side of the herd*—Joe Noose placed his feet squarely beneath him on the ground quaked by pounding cattle hooves to make his suicide run through the stampeding cattle, every fiber of his body charged with fear and adrenaline as his keen eyes swung up and down the oncoming herd looking for a big enough space between the running steers, until he saw an opening and dove into the center of the stampede.

Leadbetter grabbed Laura's leg to pull her off the boulder.

Then someone grabbed him.

The massive figure of Joe Noose landed on top of Frank Leadbetter and pounded the killer with his huge fists, breaking bones with each blow. The wrangler spat his knife into his right hand, stabbing at the bounty hunter. The two were locked in mortal hand-to-hand combat on the rocks as the cattlewoman watched them from above. Noose knocked away the knife, seizing Leadbetter by the face, digging his fingers into the man's eyes and heaving him headlong off the boulders down into the herd below.

Frank Leadbetter fell onto the horns of a steer that impaled him clean through, bloody tips bursting out of his chest. The killer was carried away with the stampede on the horns of the cow. Joe Noose and Laura Holdridge huddled safely together in the rocks above the massed charging cattle, watching Frank Leadbetter gored on the longhorns swept off in oceans of cattle, his screams fading, dying slow and hard until the steer shook him loose and the broken rag doll of a man vanished beneath the hooves of the herd.

Noose and Laura embraced.

The stampede passed as the runaway steers vanished in the distance.

"It's over."

"Like hell it is," she replied. "Now we got to get 'em back."

"Here."

Noose looked at the leather satchel Laura dropped in his saddlebag. He cocked an eyebrow at her. "What's this for?"

"Partial payment on the bounty. Four thousand dollars cash. It's yours. You earned it. You found the man who was killing my men. Still owe you a thousand. I'll pay it to you in Cheyenne after we sell off the cattle."

"Much obliged."

They rode side by side across the Big Empty. The string of weary steers marched in a long procession in front and behind, now back under the control of the three dead-in-their-saddles exhausted rovers Joe Idaho, Rowdy Maddox, and Curly Brubaker. The tough foreman had survived the shotgun blast as well as the bullet in the leg and was bandaged like a mummy, but still he rode on, the living embodiment of the Bar H motto, *Ride or Die*.

"Congratulations, by the way." Noose smiled.

"Congratulations?" Laura squinted. "What the hell for?"

"Cheyenne's just two day's ride across yonder mountains." Joe pointed. "Tomorrow's Tuesday. You got until Thursday. You made it."

Laura nodded absently, lost in herself.

"That should make you happy, Laura." Then he saw how upset she was. "What's eating you?"

"I'm just as bad as they are, Joe."

"Nothing could be further from the truth."

"Frank Leadbetter was right. My Bar H Ranch was built on the blood of honest folks my husband murdered to steal their stock and build our herd. This herd. My herd. That makes me no better than Calhoun. I ain't no better than any other of those dirty rotten cattleman sons of bitches, Joe. Don't you see? My hands are as dirty as theirs. If they're going to hell, then I am, too." Laura's shoulders shook as she broke down and sobbed, just wept and wept. He let her cry it out until he didn't.

"Want a piece of advice, Laura?"

"Sure."

"You want to get philosophical, fine, but do it on your own time because now you got business. It's like your outfit always says, Ride or Die. Remember what it took you to get this far, the men who worked for you who gave their lives getting these cows here, and it's up to you to finish the job. Right now, you got five hundred head of livestock you got to get to Cheyenne in two days. You got three tired crew need to get paid, see a doctor, fed a decent meal, a hot bath, and a proper bed. You're a cattlewoman and you got a job to do."

It made Joe Noose feel fine to see Laura Holdridge smile.

That was what she needed to hear.

CHAPTER 28

Laura Holdridge's cattle drive hit town like a ton of bricks, the herd pouring into the streets of Cheyenne at exactly five past seven on Thursday evening the sixteenth of February.

Flyers for the cattlemen's auction were everywhere, advertising it for today. The Bar H outfit had gotten their livestock to market in time.

Like she vowed she would.

Like often it had looked like they never could.

Like Noose always knew she would.

Joe was damn proud of her.

Laura jumped up in the stirrups, swept off her Stetson and flagged it over her head at her weary wranglers driving the long procession of cows. "Five minutes past the hour of seven p.m., boys! We did it! Yee-ahh!"

The outfit tossed their hats in the air and let out a cheer that turned all the heads of the cowboys on the streets.

So did the spirited beautiful blond lady atop her dusty horse, covered head to foot in dirt but whose bold grin was wide and white, hooting and hollering like a madwoman.

Beside her, the bounty hunter flicked Copper's reins and steered the herd, leading the longhorns toward the huge circus-tent arena at the end of the street. He didn't need directions, he could already smell the cow shit, so he just followed his nose.

Joe Noose just grinned.

It was the end of the Crimson Trail.

"Want me to come?"

"If it's all the same to you, Joe, I'd like to go alone."

Taking a deep breath, Laura Holdridge gathered her courage and stepped through the open tent of the Cattlemen's Association amphitheater where the cattle auction was underway. The smell of sawdust, peanuts, whiskey, cigar smoke, cow dung, and male sweat was pungent as she walked inside and stood by the entrance. She was finally here. Her stomach felt like it was clenched in a fist.

Inside, the tent was as big as a circus big top and the atmosphere had a carnival ambience. It was standing room only. The place was packed wall-to-wall with expensively dressed, well-fed cattlemen in suits and cowboy hats and boots, the uniform of the profession. Hundreds were seated in the circular seating around the arena where the auction was being held. The men had come from all across the forty-nine continental United States to buy and sell and fraternize.

Behind her, through the tent opening, the thundering hooves of her longhorn cattle passed in a lengthy procession on the street. The cattlewoman had arrived. This was what Laura had traveled so far and fought so hard against overwhelming odds to achieve: getting her cows to market. They said she'd never make it and she and her rovers proved them wrong, with more than a little help from Joe Noose—she had to admit she couldn't have done it without him—but her appearance at the auction was *her* moment, she deserved it and she savored it. Her bosom swelled with pride of accomplishment and defiance. "I showed all of you sons of bitches," she muttered to herself.

The cattlewoman was the only female present in this stag convention, and Laura Holdridge saw her arrival had gotten noticed. The eyes of the crowd of cattlemen were on her, and she experienced the exciting charge of all that attention as now most of the audience of her male counterparts were staring at her, a few mouths agape. The rumble of conversation in the tent quieted to a murmur, as the cattlemen stopped talking amongst each other and focused their attention on the dramatic arrival of the woman standing by the mouth of the tent.

Laura knew how to make an entrance. What a bigger-than-life epic figure she struck, backlit by the sunset, framed by the procession of her longhorns outside the tent. Her chaps, jacket, hat covered with three hundred miles of dust and sweat and blood, and she hadn't washed her face or brushed her tangled blond hair, but the swagger in her posture with her chin out and hands on her hips was full of piss and vinegar, as with a bold grin she yelled in her loudest bugle voice, "I made it, boys. Don't start without me. I got me some cows to sell!"

The entire tent fell silent. You could hear a pin drop. Nobody moved.

Down in the arena, somebody stood beside the auctioneer and as she felt the acid of his stare, Laura swung her fearless gaze to meet his.

Laying eyes now on Crispin Calhoun, Laura Holdridge was not impressed. The infamous cattle baron was much shorter that she imagined he'd be, given his fearsome reputation and all the trouble he'd caused her. He was in fact a diminutive man, whose huge mustache and sideburns on his tiny head made him look smaller. His persnickety grooming and too-tailored suit bespoke vanity born of inadequacy. But if his stature was small, Calhoun's hate was big enough to fill the tent, and every ounce of malevolence in his beady eyes was directed at her.

Today, the cattlewoman's hatred trumped his.

Laura Holdridge strode down the ramp looking Calhoun straight in the eye the whole time, entered the arena, and walked right up to Crispin Calhoun and stood toe to toe. There they faced each other like prizefighters in front of the entire hushed audience of every prominent cattleman in the whole United States. Laura was a head taller than Calhoun, even with the lifts in his boots, so he was forced to look up to hold her blue-eyed stare-down. Laura met the cold fury in Calhoun's evil eyes and thought she had never met an individual so unspeakably foul.

He blinked first.

Clenching her fist, Laura Holdridge punched Crispin Calhoun in the face just as hard as she could, hitting him with a haymaker that knocked the son of a bitch clean off his feet, those fancy boots of his leaving the ground as the cattle baron landed with a big splat in a huge steaming pile of fresh cow shit. He was a little man and it was a big pile. Calhoun sunk into it like quicksand, until excrement covered him completely. His hysterical shrieks sounded like a squalling infant and his flailing arms and legs looked like a baby throwing a tantrum.

Gasps of shock went up around the arena as the cattlemen rose to their feet, and Laura figured there was every chance she was about to get shot, but hell, it was worth it.

The cattlewoman stepped over and stood above the cattle baron as he emerged from the stinking pile of dung, spitting it out, unable to talk with a mouth full of crap. She couldn't resist. "Like I always said, Calhoun"—Laura chuckled—"you're full of shit."

That's when she heard the claps. A few of the cattlemen were actually clapping, others started laughing, and to Laura Holdridge's stunned astonishment, the entire audience of the Cattlemen's Association, seven hundred strong, were applauding and cheering, whistling and shouting cries of "Hear hear!"

It looked like she wasn't the only one who hated Crispin Calhoun; everybody did.

Well, not everybody.

One group of thirteen sour, bitter old cattlemen dressed in funereal black sat with their arms crossed, giving her the same evil look Calhoun gave her, and they were very displeased. She figured these were probably his supporters. But majority ruled, and the rest of the cattlemen on all sides of the arena were giving her a thundering standing ovation that shook the rafters. Apparently realizing they were the minority, the malignant Calhoun contingent rose and walked out under a black cloud.

Can't please everybody, she figured.

The cheers and applause still booming inside the tent was what greeted Crispin Calhoun as he stumbled to his feet and wiped the cow shit out of his ears and eyes. With his sight and hearing back, he could now see and hear why everybody in the Cattlemen's Association was laughing at him, applauding the sight of him covered with shit. Calhoun crumbled, his priceless expression of unimaginable humiliation was for Laura reward in itself. It was a biblical punishment. Calhoun's disgrace was complete. His dignity forever lost. His reputation permanently soiled, pun intended. The man was finished. His rancher peers, if he was still a peer after this debacle, would never let him live it down, laughing about it long after he was in the grave; it would never end. Up until a few moments ago he was the most powerful and feared cattle baron in the American West, and now Crispin Calhoun was a joke.

She didn't feel sorry for him. He had this coming.

Covering his ears to drown out the deafening applause that mocked him mercilessly, Crispin Calhoun made his retreat. As he slunk from the arena covered in dung, he threw Laura a parting glance. His eyes were horror holes, and when she saw the bottomless pain in his gaze, she understood what hurt him the very most.

She smiled. "That's right, Calhoun, you got your ass kicked by a woman, and everybody saw it."

Her words made him hiss like a demon hit by holy water, and the foul little troll of a man scuttled out of the tent and withdrew.

But before Crispin Calhoun could make his exit from the tent, five men stepped out and blocked his way; the cattle barons in the Cattlemen's Association he'd ridden

the train with were happy men indeed. They had won the
bet. Calhoun had lost—not just lost the five hundred steers
he'd tried to steal from Laura, but *twenty times* that
number of his own cattle, a debt now due and payable; in
his own terms, *a million and a half pounds of flesh* that
this time *he* had to pay. The disgraced cattleman, completely covered in shit, stood before his well-dressed colleagues, and could do nothing but endure their mocking
attentions. Sherman Rutledge reached into his jacket and
with a flourish produced the promissory note and crowed,
"You owe us ten thousand cattle, Calhoun!"

Across the tent, Laura saw the comical wretch of an evil
cattle baron in conference with five other cattle barons who
strutted like roosters and looked mighty pleased with themselves. She couldn't hear what they were saying, but judging by Calhoun's aspect of misery, the conversation was to
his considerable disadvantage. The cattleman squirmed
like a cockroach covered in filth, waving his arms like a
bug pinned to the wall, but the more he made gestures of
protest the more the men laughed, until legal papers and a
pen were pressed into his grubby little hands and, defeated,
he scribbled signatures.

The cattle barons pocketed the signed papers in their
elegant coats and rejoined the cheering crowd, and these
tycoons applauded the cattlewoman on stage louder than
anyone.

Suddenly feeling the weight of Crispin Calhoun's baleful stare, Laura Holdridge turned her gaze to pick him out
of the back of the crowd, and even at this distance, as
small as he was, she met the full force of his hellish glare,
his foul eyes fixed on her and then he was gone.

A little voice inside Laura's brain told her to expect this wasn't over . . . that perhaps it wasn't the best idea to lay a hand on a man as powerful and dangerous as Crispin Calhoun, let alone knock him in a big pile of shit. But feeling so good she figured she'd worry about it tomorrow, Laura ignored the voice inside her.

She was too busy listening to the roar of applause as the cattlemen were still cheering her. Bewildered, Laura Holdridge stood in the middle of the arena where she was the center of attention, looking around her in confusion at all the cattlemen on their feet clapping. Why were they still applauding? Calhoun had left, so it didn't make sense to keep ridiculing him. Then Laura realized. Her hands went to her mouth. "Oh my God." They weren't clapping at Calhoun.

The applause was for her!

These men all must know about her ordeal driving her herd of cattle down a crimson trail, the insurmountable obstacles she overcame getting them to Cheyenne, the guts and sheer toughness that got the livestock to auction here today. They were cattlemen, of course they knew. Her husband, Sam Holdridge, had been a member. His counterparts were probably laying bets and giving odds on the chances of his wife's success or failure.

The Cattlemen's Association was cheering her.

She had been accepted.

It meant she was one of them now.

Laura stood basking in the clapping, foot-stomping roar of approval of the cattlemen. It was the proudest, happiest moment of her life. Choked up with emotion, it was all she could do not to cry; as her eyes filled with moisture, it took every ounce of willpower and self-control to hold back the tears. *No tears, not today of all days*, she told herself. *You're a cattleman. Stand tall in your boots and show them who you are.* Instead, Laura Holdridge raised her arms high above her head and waved to the crowd with the biggest smile that showed all her teeth, blowing kisses, curtseying and bowing, spinning deftly on her boots in a graceful rotation to face cattlemen on all sides and the showering of glory she wanted never to end, and as she pirouetted once again she saw Noose.

Joe was standing at the mouth of the tent leaning laconically against the support with his arms crossed, watching her big moment. Noose was happy for her; she could read it on his face. Breathless from all the adulation, Laura gave him a wave. He gave her a wink. She made another full revolution in the arena to uninterrupted applause. The next time Laura Holdridge looked over at the tent entrance, Joe Noose was gone.

CHAPTER 29

When he saw the Tetons, Noose knew he was home. It was early March. Those titanic mountain crags towered so high into the clouds it looked like they held up the sky. He had been gone for almost a year from Jackson Hole, by his reckoning. It had been fall then. Now spring was in the air. Everything was very green. The familiar smells of the Snake River and the whispering pines gave him succor. He had almost reached his destination.

His vision was blurry and his center of gravity kept shifting so he had to grab the saddle horn to hold on. Joe needed nobody to tell him he was so tired he was delirious. He was ready to fall off his horse. The bounty hunter had ridden a long hard trail and he was tired through and through. The first thing Noose intended to do when he got back to Jackson was sleep for a week. Then he needed some time off. Sometimes, a man had to hang up his guns and spurs and put his feet up for a while. After the Butler Gang, Bonny Kate Valance, The Brander, and taking a ride with Laura Holdridge down the crimson trail, all in a row, Joe Noose needed a break.

It was hard to keep his eyes open, so he didn't try. Copper knew the rest of the way.

Joe Noose never collected the thousand dollars Laura Holdridge still owed him on the bounty before he rode out of Cheyenne. The satchel with the four thousand dollars was stashed in his saddlebags. The cash was enough. It was never about the money. Not for him.

It was enough to know he'd helped Laura.

He hoped he'd see the cattlewoman again. She had the heart of a lion, true spirit, and a real piece of woman she was, a rare breed. Joe Noose and Laura Holdridge's paths would cross again sooner than he imagined, but there was no way he could know that as he rode through the bright sunshine and fresh crisp air down into the valley.

A few hours later he was back in Jackson. Copper rode through town. Taking a look around, the bounty hunter got his first look of Jackson in a long time. The town lay at the base of the big valley in the shadow of the Tetons. There were a lot of people out on the street. Now he could fall off his horse if he had to. The place looked just like he remembered it. A few new buildings had gone up, but not much had changed. Copper trotted at a comfortable clip, and Noose saw the stallion was happy to be back in familiar surroundings. The horse went straight to the U.S. Marshal's office as his owner knew he would.

The first glimpse he got of Marshal Bess Sugarland was her with an axe. She was chopping firewood by herself in back of the U.S. Marshal's building. Her attention on splitting logs, she didn't see Joe Noose sitting on Copper but a hundred feet away.

Noose was so dog-tired he was seeing double, but two Bess Sugarlands was even better than one. A sight for sore eyes. Right at this very moment, Joe was so happy to see Bess again all he wanted to do was look at her, so he sat on his horse and made the moment last.

Bess grabbed an armload of chopped firewood and came his way, eyes downcast. Copper whinnied, clearing its throat to get the marshal's attention. She looked up. Bess stopped dead in her tracks, arms full of firewood. At the sight of Joe, she lost control of her emotions and Noose saw the love flood her face like the sun breaking through the clouds a quick instant before she recovered her composure, then Bess Sugarland was back to her usual self, giving Noose a look of friendly disregard.

"What took you so long, Joe?" She turned with the firewood and walked back into the U.S. Marshal's office.

Acted like she seen him only yesterday. Just like her.

Joe Noose just smiled.

It felt damn good to be home.

Keep reading for a special excerpt. . . .

**Joe Noose hunts down the first known serial killer
on the American frontier—in this trailblazing
thriller from acclaimed author Eric Red . . .**

SCARRED FOR LIFE

A new kind of evil has come to the Old West.
A killer as cold and hard as the Wyoming winter.
He wanders from town to town.
Slaughters entire families along the way.
With grotesque glee, he brands the letter Q
upside down in his victims' flesh.
Joe Noose knows the killer's identity.
He recognizes the killer's brand. He bears the
same scar from his childhood—and he's determined
to stop this madman once and for all.
Two U.S. Marshals have agreed to help Joe.
But they've never hunted a killer like this before.
A sadist who kills for pleasure—and scars you for life . . .

Look for **BRANDED,** *on sale now.*

PROLOGUE

The kid was thirteen, younger than the others, but the only one who had killed a man. His outlaw pals Clay, Jack, and Billy Joe were all between eighteen and twenty-one years old; only one of them, Clay, knew his exact age. The others were runaways but the kid was an orphan who had never known his own parents. Even though he was the youngest, he had size on his friends, and at already six feet stood a head taller than any of the other three. If the boy had a name, he didn't know it, so Billy Joe, Clay, and Jack just called him Kid. The others knew he had been on his own since he could walk and like them, could handle himself. And the kid was a lot meaner. He hit harder in a fight. The Colt Peacemaker in the thirteen-year-old's fist was, of all of them, the only hand the gun looked like it fit.

The four youths were robbers, horse thieves, and petty criminals. Over the last year, the motley gang prowled like a scruffy wolf pack across the Wyoming, Montana, and Idaho territories, pulling random crimes and taking down small-time scores. Nothing heavy, kid stuff. Holdups of unarmed civilians the ruffians happened to encounter were their stock-in-trade. For the three years since they joined so-called forces, the young delinquents had stayed a step ahead of the law, avoiding arrest because their crimes were nickel-and-dime in nature, and law enforcement manpower was stretched too thin over the frontier to bother with penny-ante crimes. Plus most folks made them for kids. Kids with dumb luck. But their luck was about to run out.

Living hand to mouth, sleeping outdoors, roving aimlessly, by spring of 1865 the hooligans drifted to western Wyoming and had the poor judgment to try their hand at something bigger.

Tonight, the gang was moving up to rustling. The four young outlaws had spotted the small Wyoming ranch with the hefty herd of steer quite by chance when they had ridden off a washed-out trail and cut across a plain, trying to make their way south. It had been noon when the thirteen-year-old kid had spotted the stockade full of longhorns through a thicket of trees and whistled quietly for his friends. Clay had the idea first. Jack and Billy Joe said what the hell. The kid just shrugged.

None of the greenhorn outlaws had ever rustled cattle before or given thought to how such a crime might be managed or the stolen cattle sold even if it was managed; *rustler* just sounded good as a word and the young fools figured they could add it to their list of crimes that would be on their wanted poster one day. When they had one. It was a constant source of irritation to Clay that the gang didn't have a wanted poster. Nobody knew who they were and Clay wanted the gang to make a name for themselves. Trouble was, they couldn't think of one. Gangs usually had places or last names as the name of their gang and since the four weren't from anywhere and none of the boys knew their last names, coming up with a name for the gang was proving to be a challenge.

The youngest didn't care about making a name for himself for he was amoral and didn't care about anything.

The kid thought nothing of their crimes. The thirteen-year-old had no concept of right or wrong. Such notions never entered his thinking, or whatever passed for it inside his thick skull. He just did what he did to survive like he'd always done. The boy couldn't read. Had not had a day of schooling. Had never been in a church. He trusted in his own speed, strength, and violence. At twelve, he had killed a man and felt neither good nor bad about it other than glad it was the other guy who was dead, not him. The kid rode with the other boys because he just kind of fell in with them; he had no feelings about his friends to speak of; in fact, preferred to be alone. The thirteen-year-old was a brute, a rough figure of a human being God had sculpted out of clay but forgotten to fill in the features.

They waited until sundown.

When it was good and dark, the four young outlaws gave their horses a nudge with their spurs. Broke cover as they rode out from where they had waited out of sight in the woods. Drawing their guns, the gang kept low in their saddles and trotted out onto the grounds of the ranch, sticking to the shadows. The place was pretty big. A large buck-and-rail stockade filled with cows. A two-door barn adjacent. A farmhouse on the far side of the corral on the hill. Everything was quiet. The kid looked over the spread in the hazy moonlight and didn't see any people in the area. Just lots of steers in rows of shoulders and hindquarters and longhorns stretching off into the darkness.

One of his friends said something about them having so many cows they weren't going to miss a few but the kid couldn't hear or see who said it because he was riding in the rear and saw only the backs of the others' heads in the dim. They were riding around the stockade to find the gate and a way to get in, the thirteen-year-old guessed. He just followed the others' lead, not caring one way or the other.

The hooves of their horses squelched in the mud. The smell of cow shit was strong.

A slap of a hand on a mosquito made the kid's gaze snap front as Billy Joe wiped the bug off the flesh of his neck.

The kid grabbed the coil of rope in his saddle, not knowing how to rustle a cow but figuring a lasso was probably part of it.

It was almost too dark to see, but not quite. Resuming his inspection of their surroundings, the kid looked for any sign of people. A quarter of a mile off, the large timber ranch house sat atop the hill overlooking the buck-and-rail cattle stalls. A light burned in a kerosene lamp in a window but there was no movement. He couldn't see a living soul. The smell of cow dung and dirty cattle hides filled his nostrils. The lowing of the steers was intermittent; sounds of their penned movement covered any noise their horses' hooves made in the mud.

His friends' horses slowed.

The would-be rustlers rode up to a gate made of hewn wooden posts with a sign atop the youths would have read as Q-RANCH had any of them been able to read.

Fatefully, the kid regarded the *Q* letter's circle and squiggle and thought it reminded him of an upside-down hangman's noose.

Seeing the flash before he heard the gunshot, his saddle

jerked downward as his horse dropped dead beneath him, tossing the kid headlong to the ground.

The thirteen-year-old hit hard but his skull was hard. Busy dodging rearing horses, the kid rolled out of the way to avoid getting trampled as hooves of the panicked animals came down and pounded the earth near his head. Then the boy was dodging the falling bodies of Clay, Jack, and Billy Joe as they got thrown from their saddles. The three good-for-nothing nags galloped off into the darkness in fear.

Before he could get up the kid heard the *click*s of the hammers being pulled back on three rifles, very close by. He froze. It was a bad sound to hear from a gun when you were on the wrong end of it. They were all surrounded.

The other boys heard the guns cocking, too, and knew when they were beat, so the four did the smart thing.

They all put up their hands.

Crunching of boots on dirt sounded on three sides opposite the cattle stockade. The steps were menacingly slow and deliberate. The people making them were cloaked in darkness, that deep country dark you can't see anything a foot from your face.

Exchanging glances, Clay, Billy Joe, and Jack looked very afraid of what would happen next. The kid, acting calm, figuring he would find out soon enough. None of them dared reach for their pistols.

Out of the darkness, the rancher appeared first. A tall and skeletal figure in a weathered leather duster, with long white hair. Hatred and meanness radiated off him. The old man's right hand was a mangled stump missing three fingers. It looked like an ax had been taken to it once. One of those digits was on the trigger of an immense double-barreled scatter-gun the left hand braced to his shoulder.

"Get their weapons." He spat. "Disarm 'em."

The rancher's sons, two boys the same age as the gang, appeared out of the shadows, holding revolvers. One was older than the other by a few years, it looked. Both boys were young and raw, but meant business. The older of them reached in and yanked the six pistols one by one from the hooligans' side holsters, handing them off in turn to his young brother. Neither of the rancher's sons said a word.

Walking ominously over to a fence post that had coils of rope hung on it, the father unslung four lariats and tossed them on the ground.

"Tie 'em up," the old man barked.

His two boys seemed reluctant to relinquish the grip on the revolvers they held on their captives by picking up the ropes, but their father raised his shotgun to his shoulder and stepped into position over the hooligans, sighting them down the barrel he moved back and forth aiming at their heads. "My boys is gonna tie you up now and any of you punks move a finger, I'll blow his head off and the head of the punk next to him. Savvy?" The boys on the ground nodded they understood. Finally, the rancher's sons put their captured revolvers on the ground, snatched up the ropes, and got to work.

His two sons clearly had experience roping steers and had the four young outlaws bound in just a few minutes. The kid and his friends were hog-tied by their wrists and ankles with their arms and legs behind their backs. The old man's boys were strong and rough and got their prisoners tied up with ropes quickly. The kid and his three would-be rustler buddies were soon facedown in the dirt, breathing soil. The rancher's sons had now retrieved the guns they had taken and were pointing them down at the prior owners, fingers on the triggers, looking like they knew how to use them. The boys followed their father's orders without argument as if he had them trained like animals. The kid thought they looked more scared of the skeletal old man than his friends were of having their own guns pointed at them.

"Get 'em over to the tree," the rancher said.

The kid had never seen anybody hanged before.

Tonight that changed.

Everything did.

The tree was big and dead, but it had a long, thick overhanging branch that made for a sturdy gibbet when the old man threw the first coil of rope up around the branch. Then he tied off the rope with a mean yank; one end of the rope was already secured to the saddle of the first horse—all four horses were stupid and easily retrieved from the neighboring creek they stopped to drink at by the two young sons of the rancher—the other end he knotted into a noose. The kid wondered how the old man could knot a rope with the few fingers of his chicken claw of a mangled hand, but he did. The noose dangled directly above the saddle of the first Appaloosa, who stood chewing a carrot.

The elderly rancher finished with the first noose and let it hang, approaching the tied-up boys with a Grim Reaper countenance.

Somebody was about to get hanged.

The kid preferred it wasn't him.

His friends all exchanged terrified glances.

The rancher's two sons just looked at their father, keeping the pistols trained on the prisoners.

Instead of selecting one victim to be hanged, the old man threw some coal oil on a pile of coals in a metal brazier with iron cattle brands resting in it. Tossed a match. A *hiss* and *whomph*. The roaring uprush of flames splashed a hellish firelight over the scene. Flame and shadows bloomed on the menacing oak tree with the ropes dangling from the branch, empty nooses swinging over it.

The old man turned from the captured boys and didn't take one to be lynched. Not yet.

Instead, the old man grabbed a second rope. Tied a second noose. Threw the rope over the branch. Then knotted the other end to the saddle of another horse.

Then he made a third noose and tossed the rope over the branch. He tied that to the saddle of the last horse.

The kid's horse was dead, shot out from under him, and he didn't know if that was a good or a bad thing.

The minutes dragged on into an hour, the aroma of burning charcoal mixing with the rank stench of urine. The kid could see two of his friends had pissed themselves in terror. One of them was crying, snot smeared all over his screwed-up face.

The thirteen-year-old kid had nothing to say.

But his friends sure did. They were talking plenty.

"—Just let us go! Please! You'll never see us again!"

"—Take us to jail! Don't lynch us!"

"—Please don't hurt us, mister! We're sorry."

Sorry for what? The kid thinking the only thing he was sorry about was getting caught.

He knew the rest were wasting their breath anyway. Nothing his friends were going to say was going to get them out of this fix. The kid didn't care one way or the other. It was what it was. It was going to be over soon—he just wanted to get it over with. The thirteen-year-old felt the heat on his face from the coal brazier, felt the cold night wind on his back facing the dark stockade, but those sensations were all the kid felt.

"Get 'em up," growled the old man. He had returned and stood. "That one. That one. And that one."

The gaunt skeleton of a man lifted a crooked finger on his mangled hand to point out Clay, Jack, and Billy Joe. "Put 'em in their saddles. Throw ropes around their necks." The two strong rancher boys took the captives one at a time, both sons hauling the trammeled young outlaws to their feet. In turn, they dragged them to the tree and pulled a noose over each of their necks before pushing them by the ass up into the saddles of a horse. The old man had the huge scatter-gun in the faces of the kid's friends when the ropes were put around their necks. All the kicking and screaming didn't save the boys. Two were pistol-whipped to make them compliant and shoved onto their steeds. Moments later, Billy Joe, Jack, and Clay were perched in their saddles with nooses around their necks and all stopped resisting—if they fell off their mounts or their horse bolted, those nooses would break their necks, so none of the boys moved a muscle.

The two nameless sons turned and walked back to the kid, who could now see they were more scared then he was, especially the smaller of the two. Both lads were shaking with fear and close to tears and the kid wondered why, since it wasn't them being hanged. Four hands took his arms to pull him up.

"Not him." At their father's sharp barked command the

two sons let go of the last boy lying hog-tied on the ground. The kid looked up at the rancher's towering silhouette framed against the leaping fire and black night sky, the old man's face one big shadow, a hole in the darkness looking down on the kid, who couldn't see the eyes he felt drilling into his skull.

"How old are you, son?" the old man asked.

"Thirteen," replied the kid.

"Just a boy. Too young to hang."

With that, the old man turned his back on the kid and walked over to the tree where the wretched three condemned youths sat like bags of shit on three horses with three ropes around the neck awaiting cruel vigilante execution. His two sons walked with him, one on each side, heads hung and shoulders slumped, like it was a march to their own gallows.

The kid couldn't believe his luck.

He'd slipped the noose.

His friends were about to swing but all the kid felt was glad it was them, not him.

The rancher asked the three young outlaws if they had last words.

All three cried for their mother.

Seeing his two sons were looking away, the old man struck them both hard on the heads with his fists, forcing their full attention to the hanging. "This is what happens to those who do wrong. Time you boys became men and knew what delivering hard justice means."

Pointing the ugly scatter-gun into the sky near the heads of the horses, the old man triggered both barrels, unleashing twin *kaboom* blasts into the heavens.

The three startled horses bolted.

Clay, Jack, and Billy Joe were jerked out of their saddles as the ropes snapped taut on the branch. Their bodies swung suspended in midair, boots kicking off the ground, bumping into each other like sacks of grain, necks stretching grotesquely elongated until they cracked. The fat one, Jack's head popped clean off and his decapitated body hit the ground with more blood than the kid had ever seen. Billy Joe and Clay got covered with it, eyes bulging and tongues lolling, spinning around and around on the ropes in convulsions until they hung limp on the nooses. The ground below them was stained with their waste as they evacuated. It was ugly. An ugly way to die.

The old man wasted no time, drawing his knife and slashing the ropes, cutting the bodies down where they landed in a pile.

His two sons were traumatized. The smaller one buckled over and puked in the dirt, shaking like a leaf. The taller one just stood and wept. His body was heaving in sobs.

The kid just watched from the ground.

Walking to his boys, the father put a hand on each of their shoulders. "You're men now. I'm proud of you."

"Can we go home now, Pa?" the older son asked.

"Once we deal with the other one," the old man replied, swinging his gaze to the kid. The thirteen-year-old, all brawn and no brains, locked eyes with him defiantly. As the rancher family walked in his direction, he knew he was not going to get off that easy.

"Hold him down, boys." Faces smeared with dirt and tears, his two sons grabbed the hog-tied kid by each shoulder and pinned him to the dirt so he couldn't move. The kid looked up at the old man looming over him glowering down in judgment, his fearsome countenance inflamed by the angry blaze of firelight from the nearby coal brazier. Yet the old man spoke quietly with something like pity in his eyes as he gave the kid a considering look.

"Where are your parents, boy?"

"Don't got none. Never knew 'em if I did."

"Poor soul. Nobody ever taught you right from wrong. You're just a boy but you ain't ever going to grow up to be a man unless you learn good from bad. A man that doesn't know right from wrong ain't nothing but an animal, no better than cattle. And cattle get branded."

The old man lifted the fiery *Q* brand from the brazier. It glowed red-hot. Firelight reflected in his sunken mean eyes made them shine with hellfire. To the kid, he looked to be devil, not man.

"Open his shirt," the old man commanded.

The sons ripped open the kid's shirt, tearing cloth and popping buttons, exposing his muscular hairless unmarked chest.

The kid knew what was coming. Now he felt something.

Fear.

The fear grew to raw panic and terror with every inch closer the blazing cattle brand came toward his chest, the heat against his bare flesh growing unbearably hotter, until the old man pressed the red-hot brand into his skin. The sizzling *hiss* of his own roasting flesh filled the kid's nostrils as the smoke from his cooked skin billowed over his face and choked him. The searing blazing *Q* brand burned deep into the center of his chest, the old man leaning against the brand with both hands applying pressure.

As the kid screamed and cried and begged for it to stop, he thought he heard the two sons screaming, too.

It didn't stop. The kid felt the red-hot brand burn all the way through the bones of his chest to his heart and brand him to his soul. Then he went into shock.

Finally the old man lifted the brand off and tossed it on the ground. "Throw water on him." His two sons were hysterical with tears as they bum-rushed a water keg, lifted it, and poured the frigid liquid contents all over the kid, soaking him from head to foot.

The kid didn't move, splayed akimbo in the dirt, a charred and bloody *Q* scorched into the center of his chest. He was in shock and his lips were frothed and eyes rolled up in their sockets, revealing the whites.

But somehow the kid heard the old man's parting words:

"Every day of your life you will look at that brand and remember a man has a choice to make between right and wrong."

Words he would never forget.

When the kid's vision began to focus, his gaze had congealed with a cognition birthed in his eyes that was new, like a star born in the swirling cosmos.

"Put him on a horse."

The kid didn't know where the rancher and his sons found the horse, but somehow they put him on it and sent the mare off into the night with him slumped in the saddle. Then all he knew was pain and darkness until the sun came up and then all he knew was agony.

Long the pain lasted.

But that was a very long time ago.

Now, twenty-one years, three days, and five hours later, Joe Noose, the man the boy had become, was going to get his revenge for what they did to him . . .

CHAPTER 1

His retribution came one fateful winter morning in the unlikely guise of a little boy Joe Noose had never laid eyes on before.

It was December of 1886. The bounty hunter was presently employed as sheriff of Victor, Idaho. A group of badmen led by a very bad woman had killed all the lawmen in Victor. Noose had killed all the villains in turn. The town made him sheriff. Noose took the job only because of his horse. It was a long story.

Physically, Noose looked intimidating enough for law enforcement. Now thirty-four years old, he had grown to be a very big man who stood six foot three without his boots. He was built of solid muscle. The man's pale blue eyes had a steely gaze in a hard face with chipped ruggedly handsome features carved on a boulder of a head covered with thick brown hair. His hands were as large as cattle hooves and the biggest pistol seemed puny in his grip. He would have towered over his former self, the helpless youth who had been tortured, but that boy remained locked forever inside Joe Noose within his mighty frame, for his life began that terrible night long ago . . . the branding had burned a moral code into Joe Noose's soul—a code he'd come to live by.

Over the twenty-one intervening years, the man of action became a bounty hunter whose reputation across the western territories was bringing his dead-or-alive bounties in alive. Joe Noose had a brute instinctual sense of justice and always tried to do the right thing; his credo was never kill a man he didn't have to, but that hadn't stopped him from killing quite a few. He did what he had to do enforcing his own personal code of justice. Sometimes that was complicated. The bounty hunter dabbled in legitimate law enforcement and of late had worked as a Deputy U.S. Marshal and now a sheriff although the badge with the star on his chest was temporary.

The sheriff job ended the day his best friend, Marshal Bess Sugarland, walked into the Victor sheriff's office with the little boy and had him open his shirt. Bess had come with another young U.S. Marshal and together she and he had ridden over the Teton Pass with the child in tow. It was a frozen winter morning as the four of them stood in the warmth of the room.

Shutting the door to the sheriff's office behind them, Joe Noose showed Bess and her two companions to three chairs set in front of the wood-burning stove. The small room was cold and their breath condensed on the air.

She had still not introduced her fellow travelers to Noose. One, the rugged, brooding U.S. Marshal, the other the quiet, reserved little boy of perhaps nine or ten. Noose guessed Bess would make introductions in her own good time, knowing that they were here for a reason. The child seemed nervous and fearful and stayed close to the woman as she showed him a seat then took one herself and smiled at Joe. "The badge looks good on you."

"I'm just the interim sheriff while they find a replacement," Noose explained. "Bonny Kate's gang killed the last sheriff and his deputies before I did for them and the town needed someone to wear the badge. Seemed like the right thing to do when they asked me. You heard about all that fuss." A nod from Bess. "I have a deputy when I need him, which ain't often because the town's pretty quiet these days now that hanging business is done with. Best believe I got the situation in hand. But I'll be moving on soon, I reckon."

"Bounty hunter, then marshal, now sheriff. A body has a hard time keeping track of your movements, Joe," Bess joked.

Noose was glad to see she hadn't lost her ornery sense of humor, but was worried about the huge wooden leg brace she wore on the wounded leg—it was bigger than the one he last saw her wear, and he hoped that the bullet Frank Butler had given her to remember him by wasn't going to mean she would lose that leg. Bess saw him looking at her brace and looked crossly at him. "It ain't gangrene. I'm not losing the damn leg. Just got it jacked up again thanks to you when my horse fell on me while I was riding up the pass with my deputy, looking for you during the fires."

With a sigh of relief, Noose looked over at the lawman who had just sat beside her by the stove. The young man had a hard, angular face, an intense, dark gaze, and was watching Noose closely. "This him, your new deputy?" Noose inquired.

Bess shook her head. "No, my deputy is a greenhorn named Nate Sweet I left back in Jackson to man the U.S.

Marshal's office while I came here. Somebody had to mind the store while I was away. Good man, Sweet is, lots of promise." She looked over to the officer with her. "This here is Marshal Emmett Ford."

Joe Noose gave Marshal Ford a long, hard stare—something was familiar about his face, but he couldn't quite place it. "We met before, Marshal?" Noose asked. "I seem to recall your face."

Ford held his gaze respectfully and shook his head, demurring. "No, sir. I don't rightly recollect so."

Noose shrugged. Maybe he was mistaken. He looked a question at Bess. Drew her gaze with him to the silent little boy bundled in coats, sitting staring into the fire. She spoke up. "The boy, we don't know his name because he won't talk. Marshal Ford brought the boy to me a few days ago. So I brought him to you. He's why I come, Joe."

His brows furrowing, not following her conversation, Noose went to the stove, where the pot of coffee brewed, filling the room with a warm, toasty aroma. Without asking if they wanted any, Noose poured two cups and handed them to Bess and Ford, both of whom accepted the hot beverages gratefully and sipped. The boy just watched the fire.

"Sit down, Joe," Bess asked politely. He did. He was about to hear the story and the reason for her visit. "I'll let Marshal Ford tell it. Go on, Emmett."

The young lawman cleared his throat and spoke plainly. "This boy was the only survivor of the massacre of his entire family near Pinedale. Father, mother, two sisters all cut to pieces and strewn about."

"Go on."

"They weren't the first victims of this individual. We think it is one man. Twenty-five people, families, men,

women, children, have been butchered by this killer. The
ones we know about, anyhow. He has been leaving a trail
of bodies from the southern border of Idaho across up
into Wyoming and I've been hunting him ever since the
spring." The marshal spoke gravely. An intense, personal
dedication to catching this killer was plain in his eyes.
This was more than a job for Emmett Ford. It was a
mission.

"Good hunting," Noose said.

Bess interrupted. "I came to you for a reason, Joe. So
did Marshal Ford."

"What reason?"

Ford answered, "You're the best bounty hunter in the
western states, Noose. Everybody knows that. There ain't
a man in the world you can't track down and apprehend.
I haven't been able to catch this killer on my own. I need
your help. And there is a five-thousand-dollar dead-or-
alive bounty on this individual."

"That's serious money," Noose replied, warming his
hands by rubbing them together by the fire. "Very serious
money. But the thing is, Marshals, I took a job as sheriff
here in this town and gave my word I would perform those
duties until a replacement is found. Nobody's arrived to
relieve me yet, don't rightly know when they will. I'd
surely like to chase down that bounty, but I have a job."

Rising to her feet, Bess's spurs jingled as she walked
to the wall and leaned against it by the stove, fixing Noose
in her persuasive gaze from an elevated vantage. "Only
you can catch this man, Joe."

Noose raised an eyebrow in question, letting her continue. "You don't know the rest. This killer, he always

leaves his signature. One you'll understand, Joe." Gesturing
to the boy, Bess made the motions with her hands of opening her shirt. "Show him," she gently but firmly bid the
child.

Swallowing hard, his eyes vacant, the little boy obediently unbuttoned his coat, then opened his ragged cloth
shirt to expose his chest.

When Noose saw what was there, his eyes widened in
raw emotion and he rose from his chair to his towering
full height, staring unblinkingly at what was on the kid's
naked, chicken-bone chest: *The brutal mark of a red-hot
branding iron was savagely burned into the child's very
flesh—half-healed and raw was seared a single upside-
down letter . . .*

$$\partial$$

It was the same brand that Joe Noose bore forever on
his own chest, a mark burned into him when he was little
older than this boy, by the same brand, by the same man.
He felt his own long-healed scar burn freshly under his
shirt like a phantom pain, feeling again the white-hot
agony of long ago. Noose was speechless as he just stared
at the poor child looking up at him with hangdog eyes,
displaying his disfigurement with shame.

His knuckles whitening, Noose's fists clenched at his
sides in a murderous cold fury that made the cartilage
crackle.

When his gaze swung back to Bess Sugarland, she held
it confidently. "This is a job for you, Joe. Only you can
stop this man."

Nodding, Joe Noose pulled the sheriff's badge off his coat and laid it on the desk.

Noose knew what he had to do. And he wasn't going to be able to wear the sheriff's star doing what he was about to do; no proper lawman could. The big bounty hunter currently employed as interim sheriff of Victor, Idaho, said good-bye to the badge. He was not going to be upholding the law when he caught up with the son of a bitch who branded him, because this was personal and when it was personal the only law was the Law of the Gun.

Lawdog never suited Noose much anyhow.

He just took the job for his horse but his horse was fine now.

Noose stretched his muscular six-foot-three frame to his full height and walked to the window, his leather boots and spurs creaking the floorboards until he stopped, looking out with his pale blue eyes distant and lost in thought. The wintery Idaho sunlight filtering into the Victor sheriff's office showed all the faded bruises and old scars on his handsome granite-block face. His breath condensed in the cold hair in a haze around his face, fogging the glass and clouding and obscuring the view of the town street—a wall that shut off his view as if to tell him his fate was inside the room, which he already knew.

Joe Noose felt Marshal Bess Sugarland's eyes on his back. His friend knew to patiently give him his time to think.

A branding mark the same as his.

Made by the same man, twenty-one years apart.

He had a lot of questions.

"Tell me everything." Joe Noose turned from the window to face Marshal Emmett Ford, fixing him in a hard unwavering gaze that demanded answers, all the facts.

Across the room, Ford stood by the small coal stove, having just poured himself a fresh cup of coffee. He met Noose's gaze without blinking. Despite Noose standing a head taller than Ford and having a hundred pounds of muscle on him, the marshal looked iron fit and was not intimidated. Ford was about Noose's age, rangy and lanky, a lupine cowboy face weathered by the elements. His intense brown eyes bored back into Noose's own as he took a sip of coffee and began his tale.

"I first heard about the branding murders three years ago, where I was posted at the marshal's office in Laramie," Ford said in his soft, even voice. "People passing through from the far north states brought talk with them about folks hacked to pieces who always had the mark of a brand in their chest, men and women. No survivors of any of these attacks, just branded bodies. Like somebody was leaving a message. Of course, the marshal's office got called in to investigate. The assumption was Indians. But that didn't make sense to me because there were no scalpings. It was the brand that made me know this was the work of a white man. Indians don't use cattle brands to mark their cows. Nobody at the U.S. Marshal's office listened to me, though, so I requested special assignment, set out alone, and went to track this murdering SOB down. Been on the bastard's trail ever since. But I come up short. So I'm coming to you."

Noose looked and listened as the wiry male marshal took another sip of coffee. Ford's face looked familiar somehow. But the man looked like a lot of people, not good- or bad-looking, face and hands suntanned from the outdoors; an honest, plain face. It was his eyes that made him different, the deep wells of a man who had seen things no man should see and live to tell. Noose liked that about him and felt an instant kinship with the marshal for unknown reasons he didn't quite understand that made no sense. Snapping his pale-eyed gaze back to Emmett Ford, he saw the Texas marshal was watching him intensely. Noose said: "Go on."

Ford reached up to adjust his weathered Stetson and shrugged in a rangy cowboy way. "Through '85 and '86 I tracked him through Idaho and Utah, then up into Wyoming. Came across bodies in every state. All of them butchered like steers. All of them branded. This villain he moved like a ghost. Nobody saw him." The marshal spoke in a lazy twang, but Noose noticed that the drawl seemed to come and go as it did with some men.

"Where did you find this boy?"

"Wyoming. In Pinedale. South of Jackson. His entire family was . . . father, mother, sisters. Two sisters, girls, at least I think. Honest, it was hard to tell who was who the condition I found them in. All branded. The boy must have got away during the attack, because I found him hiding in the food cellar, got away during the fight maybe because it was . . . well . . . a mess. He had the brand, but he was alive. I took him with me, had him riding with me, hoping he would start talking, give me some clues about the killer, but fact is, the boy ain't said a word since the day I found him. I had him on back of my saddle the last month but The Brander's trail, it went cold. I know he's out there, still killing, still using a red-hot iron to defile the human remains, but truth was I'd just about given up."

Ford's eyes lit up. "Then I hear about a bounty hunter who could find anyone, anywhere, who could track any man that walked on two legs." Ford nodded respectfully in Noose's direction. "I heard about you, sir."

Noose just regarded him evenly. Out the corner of his eye, he could see Bess smiling proudly at him. Ford went on.

"People say Joe Noose is the best bounty hunter in the western territories. Figured I needed help, and if anybody can track the branding killer down it would be you. So I come to find you."

"You did."

Bess piped up. "Marshal Ford came to the U.S. Marshal's office in Jackson and found me first, asked about you. Showed me this boy. Showed me, well . . . I knew this was a job for you, Joe."

While he had been talking, Emmett had also been watching Noose and Bess exchange cryptic glances, unspoken guarded exchanges about the man they were after during the ride. Finally, Emmett spoke up.

"You two know something you're not telling me." When they didn't respond, he added, "With due respect, we're all supposed to be partners on this."

The bounty hunter looked a question at the lady marshal and she nodded, so he shrugged. "Bess didn't tell you, Marshal, because she didn't feel it was her place to. Not until she spoke to me first. Reason is, me taking this job, it's personal. You see, it ain't just because I'm a good manhunter she come to me to track down this killer you're after. I've had dealings with him, a long time ago."

Emmett looked like he'd been slapped. "What the hell are you talking about?" he said.

Noose eyed Emmett evenly with a pale-eyed gaze. "I know who he is."

"So who is he?"

"Same man who did this to me." Noose bit the fingers

of his gloves and tugged them off his hands. Then he unbuttoned his coat, then his shirt, exposing his bare torso. Displaying the old scar of the upside-down Q burned into his chest.

Turning pale, the young marshal gaped at the wound, getting his mental bearings until he put it all together.

"Get the picture now?" Noose said.

Emmett nodded. He seemed dazed putting it all together, going through a struggle to maintain his composure.

The bounty hunter closed his shirt and coat and pulled on his gloves.

"But . . . when?"

"Long time ago. Twenty years thereabouts. He was fifty, sixty, mebbe then, puts him seventy to eighty now. Old, but he's the one we're after."

"Who the hell is he? Who *are* we looking for?"

"An old rancher is the one who branded me. He had a mean and twisted sense of justice back then. Reckon he's gotten a lot crazier in twenty years. But it's him. Can't be but one man going around branding people with a Q brand iron. I know who we're looking for."

Emmett nodded. "He has a name of sorts, this killer. Some are calling him The Brander."

"It ain't his real name, but it'll do until we learn his true one."

"It's your turn. Tell me everything *you* know," Emmett said.

Noose had already told his story to Bess.

Now he told it to Emmett Ford.

Ten minutes later, the horrific account of his branding as a thirteen-year-old was finished. The young marshal was a level-headed, reserved man not given to displays of emotions. But Noose thought he saw moisture in his listener's eyes when he got to the part about the rancher's sons participating in the hanging and the branding.

"The old son of a bitch lost whatever wits he had, it looks like. Back then, he hanged my friends but just branded me because to him I was too young to hang. Now he's murderin' and brandin' everybody. What I'm saying is he used to have his own kind of moral code, but now he ain't playing favorites. From what you're telling me, his only code is *kill 'em all*."

"You really sure it's him?" Emmett asked. "The Brander."

"Sounds like it, but it's been a long time and we don't know nothing for sure."

The only thing Noose knew for sure was the fiend was escalating his predations. He slaughtered families of men, women, and children and the corpses were piling up. Only this little boy had survived, and he wasn't talking. He didn't have to. All Joe Noose needed to see was the sister branding weal to the one he bore to know who the killer was, who he had to be.

Marshal Bess was sitting with the little boy on her lap near the warmth of the stove, her eyes moving back and forth between Noose and Ford as they talked. Noose gave her a glance, touched by the tender protective way his friend was holding the child, a warm touch that promised no one would ever harm him again the way he had been harmed. That was Bess to the ground.

Switching his gaze to the silent little boy, Noose could not tell if Bess's ministrations had any effect on him, since the kid just stared into the crackling stove fire with a forty-yard stare. The flames danced in his blank eyes, and the pulsing glow of the small fire inside the grate played off his empty features. Noose knew that the little boy was intact on the outside, but inside was gone and not coming back.

His own branding scar began to itch and burn the way it did when it was telling him something. *There but for fortune.* This nameless boy could have been Joe, his scar was telling him—he'd just been stronger, or luckier, but for whatever reason was in a position to put down the fiend like a dog and be sure that the man they called The Brander never branded another living human soul.

So Noose stood across from the small boy, both with the *Q* brand seared on their flesh beneath their shirts, the adult and child version of the same victim.

Emmett Ford set down his coffee and walked up to Joe Noose and with his back straight looked him respectfully square in the eye. "Will you help us catch this killer, sir?"

Noose held Ford's gaze and shook his hand. "Yes, I will."

Jumping out of her chair, Bess swaggered over to the two men, screwing on her hat. "I'm going, too, Joe. Don't you think I ain't. This is the three of us."

No point in arguing with her.

Giving her a big cracked grin, Noose just nodded.

It was decided.

"Let's ride."